MW00575347

Dancing on Seaside – Julius James DeAngelus
A Novel

BookBaby
7905 North Crescent Boulevard, Pennsauken, NJ 08110
877-961-6878
info@bookbaby.com

www.juliusjamesdeangelus.com

Creative Direction and Graphic Design by Susan Hutton DeAngelus, shd graphics :: shdgraphics.com

Notice of Liability
This is a work of fiction. Names, characters, businesses, places, events, locales, and incidents are either the products of the author's imagination or used in a fictitious manner. Any resemblance to actual persons, living or dead, or actual events is purely coincidental.

Disclaimer
This book is an independent publication and is not affiliated with, nor has it been authorized, sponsored, or otherwise approved by any other third party.

ISBN (Print Edition): 978-1-54398-176-6
ISBN (eBook Edition): 978-1-54398-177-3

Printed in the United States of America

Dancing on Seaside

A NOVEL

Julius James DeAngelus

For Susan, Frannie and Chris

You are all in this book because you are always in my heart.

For my mother (my Queen of Atlantic City) and for all of the

Inlet rats, wherever you may be right now.

CHAPTER

I

Jamie

Where the hell was Nicky?

I hopped down the front steps two at a time until I hit the cracked sidewalk.

"Shoes!" Mom shouted from the house but I was already racing down Seaside Avenue, my converses still empty and laying under my bed. I never wore shoes down the shore unless I was walking the boards and that was only out of fear of splinters. The sun was lighting the dark alleys between the houses and already the warmth was coming through the cement under my feet. Stubborn weeds sprouted through cracks in the pavement and bits of brown and green glass sparkled like tiny jewels. I passed three black girls double-dutching in the street, their brown and pink feet skipping to the slap of the rope while they sang.

Atlantic City was waking up.

The faint flavor of ocean air rested on the back of my tongue as I breathed. It mixed sweetly with the scent of fresh paint somewhere not far away. Summer had finally begun, thank God.

I flashed past a man with a head of messy white hair who was checking the blue and white striped awning over his small porch, his hands on his hips and nodding like he was inspecting the sails of his ship before heading out to sea. The veins in his legs climbed up to his knees like ivy creeping up two old fence posts. More houses, their porches like familiar faces, blurred past as I made my way to the end of the block.

Nicky Marte's house was at the end of the block: squat, plain-looking and made of painted red brick. The large window on the first floor facing the street was covered with a piece of fresh plywood. A dull black roof slumped at the corners, supported by two thick white columns with paint flaking off in large, puzzle-like pieces.

Nicky's room was on the third floor and I could see that the single window that looked out over the street was closed. Unpainted wooden stairs climbed the side of the house and I took the steps two at a time. Before knocking I leaned over the railing and looked into the rough, overgrown yard behind the house. Plate-sized leaves sprouted from weeds that had grown into small trees, giving the whole place a look like something from The Land of the Lost.

I knocked and waited. Nothing from the other side of the door.

I saw my face looking back at me in the small window of the door. The smudged glass hid the parts of my face that were nothing to get excited about. I preferred this face to the one that stared back from the clean mirror in the bathroom at home: the face with the pimples, the pale green eyes that were too far apart and the blonde hair that just sat on my head like a nest.

I knocked again, harder this time, but no one answered so I rubbed a tiny circle in the glass with one finger and peeked in. The kitchen was empty and the lights were out. Shit.

I headed home.

Day one chores (the *other* sure sign that summer had begun) would be the first thing when I hit the door and I wasn't looking forward to them. The slower I walked home now the better.

The house on Seaside Avenue was really my grandparent's house. Like mom, I was born in Atlantic City, but the difference was she grew up here with her brother and sisters while I went to school with a whole different set of friends in Philly. My family came down every summer and to me there was something special about this place. My best friend lived right down the street (even though he wasn't there right now) and the beach was only a half block away. I squinted and watched gulls frantically circling and dipping like flecks of pepper in the sky over the beach.

Behind me Nicky's house sat empty. He would *always* be the first one to meet us and even though we didn't show up until last night I still expected to see him run out when we got here. That was truly the best sign that summer had begun.

So where the hell was Nicky?

* * *

I walked into the living room, through the early rays of light. Along one wall was a sofa with cushions that had a colorful jungle pattern on them. Two old recliners, their green vinyl cracked with age, faced a quiet TV in the corner. Small clay sculptures sat on a dark wood mantle above the fireplace on the opposite wall. Mom had made them a long time ago. Painted scenes of the beach, boardwalk and ocean hung from the walls. Those were hers, too. They were actually pretty good.

I followed the smell of bacon and coffee into the kitchen.

Mom was standing by the stove, her back to me, wearing a blue cotton robe that tied at the waist. Her blonde hair, which normally reached down to touch her shoulders, was pulled into a small ponytail. She had cheap flip flops on, the ones you get at any souvenir shop on the boardwalk. They were her favorite kind. She also had her gold and silver toe rings on, the same two that she always wore in the summer. Next to her, a cigarette was burning in a gray and white clam shell sending a string of smoke up to the ceiling.

The small radio in the kitchen window was playing jazz, which I didn't get at all…and was that actually a *xylophone* I was hearing? Mom and dad loved it for some reason.

"Morning sweetie," she asked without turning. "Hungry?"

I nodded then realized she couldn't see me. "Um, sure."

I smelled Pine-Sol beneath the scent of breakfast so she must have already been cleaning.

"Can you bring grandma her coffee?" I wondered why, lately, grandma got up so much later than she used to. Maybe it had something to do with grandpa dying. Maybe she didn't feel like facing the morning without him. She'd been living with us for almost half a year now and seemed to have aged a lot in that time. I pulled a mug and poured.

"Is Liz up yet?"

I shrugged. The later the Lizard got up the better it was for the rest of the world. My older sister was not one to be tangled with in the morning, though, to be honest, her attitude didn't improve much over the rest of the day, either. I added a spoon of sugar to the coffee and stirred.

"Could you please get her up?" she asked.

I let my breath out, probably louder than I should have.

"Honey, this is only the first day and we have work to do so don't start sighing already, okay?" She moved to the table and spread a table-cloth across. "The house isn't going to get ready all by itself."

God, do they all have to say things like that?

I turned and left.

The second floor of the house had four bedrooms and the rooms pretty much looked the same: two windows, a bed, dresser and a closet in the corner. Nothing fancy. The only difference was the color of the wallpaper in each.

I knocked softly on grandma's door and went in.

She already had a Benson and Hedges in her lips and the tip was glowing. My eyes adjusted to the cool shade of the room and I saw that she had propped herself up on a long colorful pillow. Thin curtains were drawn over the windows. The Blue Room (we called it that for as long as I could remember because of the thousands of tiny blue flowers on the wallpaper) was my mom's when she was growing up. Blue is still her favorite color.

"I just don't think I could go back in that room," I heard her say last night and guessed that she meant the third floor room that she had shared with Grandpa Jerry for so many years. "At least not yet. It's too soon." I hadn't seen grandma even go to the third floor since Grandpa died, not even last year when we came to help pack her things and take her to back to Philly with us. Mom went up and got everything.

I pulled one of the curtains aside and let in a bit of sun. Grandma still had some color in her hair but mostly it was snowy white. The weak light in the room made her look older. She was sixty-four years old (I'm told that that's not old but don't believe it) and the creases in her skin looked more permanent, but her eyes were as alert as ever. She thanked me and lifted the coffee to her small mouth and took three small sips before turning on her bedside lamp and reaching for the *TV Guide*.

I gave her a hug and she asked me about my chores. I jokingly rolled my eyes and she laughed which turned into a familiar cough. The sharp scent of cigarette smoke was in the air around her and I still wasn't sure if I wanted to try smoking someday even though Nicky said he had tried it and that I should.

"I'll be down in a few," she said as I closed her door.

Directly across the landing was the orange room (covered from floor to ceiling in soft tangerine-colored flowers, of course). This was Aunt Brenda's old room. It was in the front of the house so was usually filled with morning sunlight.

Next to that was the Yellow Room which used to be Aunt Abby's room. I saw that the Lizard had already taped up her cherished poster of Frampton on the outside of the closed door. The door would remain closed for pretty much the rest of the summer which was fine with me. I put my hands on my hips and looked at the poster with its tiny tears on the edge and the multiple staple holes from being moved so many times. Frampton was leaning back on one arm and dressed in pink shiny pants with a weird shirt that showed his chest hair. He had a lot of it. According to all the girls in school he was a fox. I thought he looked like a girl with a hairy chest.

It was crazy that the room on the other side of this door, the one with walls blooming with sunshine and lemon-colored flowers, would be the one that my miserable sister always claimed. If I had to pick a wallpaper for her it would be crawling with thorny vines that ended in dead roses. By now the walls would be covered with pictures cut from Tiger Beat or another one of those stupid magazines. Her dresser would be a shrine to Tommy Shaw and the floor would already be a jumble of record sleeves and little yellow 45 inserts.

She hadn't always been such a bitch. There was actually a time when we used to get along, but that seemed like forever ago. Now when she looked at me, I felt like I had a disease or something. Fifteen must be the required age for sisters to act like total shits.

The room I always chose was the Red Room. It was across the landing and used to be Uncle Max's. He was mom's brother, but he died a long time ago, before I was born so I never met him. I don't know if I chose that room or it was chosen for me, it was too far back to remember. Maybe red had been my favorite color once, but I don't think thirteen-year-old boys are even supposed to have favorite colors anymore.

I held my hand up, ready to knock on the Lizard's door. Rap my knuckles right on Frampton's pretty face.

Not yet.

I cupped an ear to the door and heard nothing except her snoring like a lumberjack. I pounded Peter right between his pretty little eyes.

"Hey! Get up and get to work!"

A squeak came from the other side and something hit the floor. Footsteps raced to the door and I leaped down the stairs three steps at a time, laughing.

"You ass! Knock it off!" she growled.

I was still wearing the grin when I skidded to a stop at the bottom of the stairs.

"Not exactly what I meant," my mother said, her arms folded over her chest. She waved in the direction of the front door with a spatula. "Go tell your father that breakfast is ready."

I made my way between the houses, running my fingers along the rough stucco wall of the house next door. Dad was in the back-yard, pulling open the basement door and then closing it again. His dark green tank top and rumpled gray shorts were flecked with paint and the black hair on his shoulders was pasted against his pale skin. He removed his glasses and wiped the bridge of his nose with his shirt before pulling a small square can from his pocket and squirted some oil on the hinges. He slowly closed the door and opened it again and nodded.

"Hey, Dad."

"Oh, hey," he said, tapping the door and turning the knob a few times, "Well, that's at least one thing done, eh?"

"Mom said to tell you breakfast is ready."

"Ok," he said and walked over. "Ready for some work after we eat?"

"Guess so," I mumbled.

The first day of the summer, at least the morning, was dedicated to the house: rooms swept, porch cleaned, the screens brought up from the basement and switched out with the storm windows, the alleys swept free of sand and trash. It was amazing how much work had to be done just to get the house ready for the next three months.

"The salt in the air plays hell with everything," Grandpa Jerry once said to me while the two of us circled the house, adding fresh spots of steel blue paint where needed. I liked watching Grandpa paint because he made it seem so important, like taking care of a pet or something. He was gentle with the brush and would stop every few minutes and step back. He checked from the basement windows up to the roof to see where things needed "touching up." It made everything take twice as long but I didn't mind - I liked the look he got in his eyes, sort of like a little kid. He would smile and go back to work, sliding next to me, smelling like cherry tobacco and whisper, "but it's good for the soul, hmm?"

Dad and I joined everyone at the kitchen table. I helped myself to scrambled eggs and sausage while the Lizard grumbled something about passing the toast. Grandma Ruth spooned apple butter onto a slice of toast and smiled, saying how nice it was to be back near the ocean. She paused as if listening and I wondered if she could actually hear the waves from the kitchen.

Mom finally sat down and blew a strand of hair from her fore-head. She looked pretty with her cheeks flushed with color and a satisfied grin on her face.

"To a wonderful beginning of another summer," dad announced and held up his glass of orange juice. Behind her messy morning dark curls Liz made her glass seem like it weighed a hundred pounds while aiming her brown eyes on me with deadly accuracy. I didn't care and only thought was that they were the same color as Dads. She got his eyes and I got mom's.

We all touched our glasses, making a delicate, fragile sound.

* * *

I climbed to the third floor, holding the broom over my shoulder like a rifle and a dustpan in my other hand. My list of jobs was long, but I got first choice since I was up before the Lizard. She ended up with the bathrooms and the basement and shot me one last stabbing look before leaving the kitchen.

I went to my grandparent's bedroom. None of my chores required me to be on the third floor but I crept up anyway. There was no new rule about going up there or anything but I still made as little noise as possible and wasn't sure why.

The sheets on grandpa and grandma's old four-poster bed were so smooth it looked as if no one had ever slept in it, much less died in it. A padded gray chair sat under the floor lamp that he would read by and a worn green and blue carpet lay partly hid under the bed. Dark wood end tables stood on either side.

I waited for any lingering scent of grandpa's tobacco, the kind he smoked with his thin black and brown pipe, but there was nothing. The air smelled stale and unused.

Light cut through the blinds, falling across the bed in thin slices. I moved to the window in small steps and pulled the cord. Specks of dust whirled and glowed as they floated into the beams, making them look alive. The sky was cloudless and just beyond the tops of the houses was the foaming ocean, churning and waiting for me.

I imagined Grandma Ruth, asleep and not even knowing that she was next to a dead person. *What the hell was that like?* A chill slipped down my back.

What do you do with a room where someone died? It seemed wrong to just use it like you used to, as if nothing had happened in here. Maybe things should be covered with those sheets that makes everything look like ghosts (something I never understood) and what's not covered could gather dust. Maybe no one should ever come in here again. Maybe they could make it a museum.

I walked along the walls, looking at framed pictures. There was an old photo of grandpa and grandma when they were younger. They had their arms around each other and were smiling (although I know their real smiles and could tell it was just for the picture). Grandma's blue eyes looked gray and Grandpa was already losing his hair. There was a picture of mom and dad on their wedding day. Unlike the other one, which was black and white, the colors in this were almost too bright, like someone tried to paint it after it had been taken. They were in the living room. Dad was skinnier and kind of goofy-looking in the tight gray suit and tie. His dark hair was slicked back against his scalp, not curly like it is now and mom was wearing a cream-colored dress and held a bouquet of purple flowers. She looked beautiful with her blonde hair pulled up.

On another wall was a picture of Aunt Brenda in a striped bathing suit on the beach, winking and posing like a movie star. She was young in the photo, maybe younger than I was now. Someone's fingers were behind her head, making her look like a rabbit.

The next picture showed mom buried in sand up to her neck. She looked like she could have been old enough for high school and was laughing. Aunt Abby had written "No Hope" in the sand and was pointing to her, smiling. In another, one that I couldn't recall seeing before, mom was standing in front of a pile of black rocks. She was sticking her tongue out and stood on one foot. I could tell that she was about to laugh, I could see it in her eyes. Her hair was long and a curl fell over one eye. Next to her was a handsome man with short blonde hair: Uncle Max. He was looking at the camera with one eye closed like Popeye and flexing his arms. His smile was nice and a lot like mom's. I stared at his face in the picture. It's weird calling some guy uncle when you've never even met him.

I didn't know much about Uncle Max, just that he died before mom and dad had met. I think he had just graduated high school. Mom didn't talk much about him and the few times she did she fumbled with her hands a lot and her voice would get very low.

There was a picture with grandpa and Liz on a fishing trip a few years ago. She looks a lot different because she's smiling. Lizard couldn't be bothered with fishing these days. It was all boys and clothes and music now.

There was a painting that mom had done of Grandma Ruth. She was leaning against the silver railing of the boardwalk and looking out at the ocean. A bright red shawl was lying across her shoulders.

"Jamie!" mom called and for a second I felt guilty, like I was invading a private space. It had been so quiet and I tried to listen to the silence once more but could hear faint voices down in the street. I couldn't make out any words but the voices sounded happy. Children playing.

I walked to the window, listening as each step touched the floor, trying to remember if I had even heard the squeak of my own sneakers when I first came in.

Grandpa Jerry would prefer to look out at the ocean so I left the blinds up before walking out.

CHAPTER
2

Hope

When we arrived last night a pile of mail greeted us and now it sat on the dining room table before mom and I, demanding attention.

I put a trash can between us and we dove in. While mom sorted and commented on each piece of mail my mind roamed the rooms of the house and how much still had to be done. The dining room (like the rest of the house) already felt a bit too big, like every wall had taken a step back.

I looked at dad's library of books sitting lonely on the shelves in the cabinet that he built so long ago. Max and I had helped while Abby and Brenda looked on and asked endless questions.

"What's that for?"

"What are you doing now?"

"Can I put my toys on it when it's done?"

Thinking about dad's books or the living room and dining room furniture was too much right now - even the pile of mail was menacing. The plan for now was to hang on to the house for as long as we could, even if just for the summers. It would be heartbreaking to sell this place: the memories were soaked into the walls like wood stain.

But what was ahead? The city was practically broke and finally voted to allow casino gambling - the first one would be ready by next summer and everything would be different from then on. The original idea was to save Atlantic City if it could be saved. I had a hard time believing that the casinos gave a shit about my home.

I looked at the letters and junk mail and knew that we could throw most of it away. I wanted to take the whole mess and toss it but could see that mom was taking some sort of comfort in looking at each piece with her or dad's name on it. There were a couple letters that offered condolences along with some sympathy cards that I assumed had been dropped off personally because they had no stamps. Some were from folks in the neighborhood or people who had worked with dad over the years. Mom's lips moved silently as she read each one.

I heard Liz rummaging loudly through the kitchen closet, probably trying to find the cleaning supplies she needed. Best to stay away from her until lunch time.

And then we could go to the beach. It seemed too long this time.

For the past month my classes had been hard, like teaching a can of jumping beans. I can't blame the kids though - I remember the excitement of those last empty days of school with the sunlight cutting into the windows at new angles. The promises were so much bigger when you were young. Summer. What a wonderful word.

It had taken time to get used to this school and my new room, which had been a storage room before they transformed it into room

115 (Art with Mrs. Shepherd). The fluorescent lights glared down in two long tracks and drained the color from the bright pictures that covered the walls like it was a personal vendetta. What little natural light did come into this half-basement room found its way through horizontal slits that would have been wonderful for defense if the school were ever under siege.

I fought the harsh fluorescent by bringing in my own lamps from home: tall, shaded ones and squat ones without shades where I'd place colored bulbs. I'd turn off the overheads and turn on the lamps and the softness of the light threw wonderful shadows around the room where all kinds of creativity was born.

One of my fellow teachers asked what I was doing over the summer and my answer got this curious (maybe even sympathetic) look from her. Apparently, the Shepherds had become part of a rare breed that spent the whole summer down the shore just *being*...and in Atlantic City no less.

Other families were busy packing for a week of camping in the mountains or flying to Disney World and I was wondering how long it would be before Jamie or Liz would ask to join them. There was no getting around the fact that fewer folks were going to Atlantic City anymore. Maybe the love affair between her and the rest of the world was really over.

Thankfully, Jamie was still excited. Nicky and he would be inseparable for the entire summer. Liz, however, rolled her eyes whenever the topic was brought up. She had only one real friend here, Crystal McAffery, who also visited with her family, but soon that wouldn't be enough to lure her.

Randy would do his normal back and forth from here to Philly for work. We'd see each other only on weekends.

Mom placed a few open letters and cards on my pile so I could see "what kind things" people had to say about dad. I read through them and then faced the rest of the mail: a few bills, a TV Guide subscription renewal and fliers from the supermarket with coupons.

The corner of an envelope caught my attention as it poked out from the bottom of the pile. The color was a lovely robin's egg and I plucked it from the bottom and saw my name in elegant lettering across the front.

I held the envelope closer to my face, pinching it between the index finger and thumb. I could feel folded paper inside and read the address again. The return address was Tampa and had a last name I immediately recognized: Patchick. A shiver ran through my belly. Did he think I still lived here? Was this letter some sort of endlessly ringing phone, one that had been waiting for weeks in this house to be answered? The thought put a sour taste in my mouth and I felt as if I was standing in front of a dark cave but was too scared to push the weeds aside and venture in.

Mom handed me another short stack of mail and I slipped the envelope into my pocket, happy to have it away from my eyes. Why did Stuart send me a letter after all these years?

We got through the mail and mom started working a crossword puzzle. She held a cigarette between two fingers. The ash had grown long and was about to tumble off so I plucked it from her fingers, tapped it into the clam shell and took a puff. Heaven.

"How are you doing, mom?"

It took a moment for her eyes to focus from the page to me. "I'm okay," she said, smoothing the tablecloth with her thin fingers. It was the one nervous habit she had. "I don't know if I ever thanked you and

Randy for letting me stay with you through all this. I know it can't be easy with both of you being so busy."

This was going be a tough summer for all of us. With dad gone the house seemed enormously hollow. It was only after the funeral that I suggested she come live with us and I half expected an argument but got none.

"We'll never be *that* busy," I said. "School is pretty flexible with my time, you know, and the substitutes love getting their hours. Besides, Brenda and Mike didn't have the room and we did, simple as that."

"I love your sister dearly, you know that," mom nodded, "but between you and me Brenda has always been about Brenda."

"Well, we're also closer than Richmond," I said. I didn't know why I was making excuses for my sister. Mom was right, Brenda couldn't wait to get married and get away from here. "And you're not *staying* with us - you're living with us, okay?" I added softly and took her hand. "Philly is your home now, too."

"I suppose Abbey is off again to God knows where," mom said and looked down at the table. She smiled helplessly and then shook her head. "Probably off climbing another mountain somewhere."

I shrugged and grinned. "Brenda told me she's somewhere on the west coast with her professor or ex-professor-now-boyfriend. I don't know, I can't keep track of them but I'm sure she's fine. Maybe we'll see her this summer."

I didn't really believe that and felt guilty. Like the rest of the world, both of my sisters had given up on Atlantic City a long time ago; Brenda and her family, if they came, never stayed for more than a few days and Abbey was just one of those nails that wouldn't go in straight. She could be in Europe with boyfriend A one month and taking archery lessons in Texas with a boyfriend B the next. If we heard from her twice a year it was considered along the lines of a miracle.

Over the years I swallowed most of the resentment about having to be the responsible daughter, the one who checked in on the parents with a phone call every couple of days and came to see them for more than just a long weekend (like Brenda) or because she needed a place to crash between lovers (like Abbey). I knew that when the time came to switch roles and the children start taking care of the parents the task always fell on one of the children and that it was always going to be me.

Having Jamie and Liz around for a couple months helped keep mom and dad young; dad would take them fishing and mom and I would work a jigsaw puzzle or sit and watch the game shows. Sometimes we would sit by the porch window and make up elaborate stories about the folks we watched, creating our own neighborhood soap operas. The days didn't need to have a purpose.

"Max has been on my mind a lot lately," mom said. Her eyes were holding onto a picture next to the kitchen door - a small photo that had been taken soon after Abbey was born. Max was bleach blonde and smiling proudly at the camera as he held her.

It was hard to believe that it had twenty years since that horrible summer, but what disturbed me most was the quietness we all seemed to retreat to after. As a family we rarely talked about him. Maybe it was the pain or because we were all too tied up in living our own lives but before any of us realized it Max had been relegated to some old photos on the walls.

When I looked for a reason why Max's memory was kept in a glass case and everyone tiptoed around it so cautiously, my thoughts always circled back to dad.

In the days that followed Max's death dad fell into a frightening tailspin. He became distant and would drink until his face had taken on a wooden quality. It made meals awkward, silent affairs during those times. While the rest of us made strained attempts at conversation he would eat quietly, a beer nearby and his eyes fixed on the pushed in chair where Max used to sit. He would kiss each of us on the top of the head before climbing the stairs and closing the door to Max's room. Sometimes he would walk out the front door and I would watch him walk up the boardwalk ramp and then disappear down to the beach.

One night I found him in the backyard with a small green balloon in his hand. It was from the graduation party we threw the week before. We had all taken turns blowing up the balloons that morning, even Max. Dad had untied it and was slowly letting the air blow over his face. Streaks ran down to his chin and he looked at me, "Do you think he might have blown this one up?"

I didn't know what to say. I nodded and closed the back door.

When these bouts came I wanted to grab him and scream into his face that he wasn't the only one who lost Max. The rest of us weren't allowed the luxury of folding up the tent and climbing into a bottle. Dad never left for good, though, always coming back and apologizing and things would get somewhat more normal or as normal as it can be with so many beautiful and horrifying memories floating through the house.

Eventually it became an unspoken rule between mom and us to not talk about Max. Watching dad destroy himself that summer was too terrifying. It felt like betrayal, but under the pain and sadness of losing Max I still had reserves of anger. He broke my heart that night and he probably didn't even know it. That anger was keeping me in check and wouldn't let me slide completely into the dark where dad went when he thought of his dead son.

Over the years, as we grew our own families, it took more effort to bring Max to the surface of my mind, like trying to tune in a distant station on the radio.

"I've been thinking about him, too," I said. "This place has got a lot of memories in it."

"You know, I always thought I would feel safe here," mom said, "but with your father gone, I...I just don't think I could stay here all alone."

Mom was right. As much as we loved the old neighborhood, it had changed a lot over the years. Crime was rampant. More and more houses were just empty shells. There was even a curfew siren that echoed ominously throughout the city at nine o'clock. Children were to be indoors or with an adult by that time.

After I convinced mom to move in with us, I leaned in and rested my chin on her shoulder. "We can still have our summers here. When we have to get back to Philly - " I said and took her hand, not sure of how to finish the sentence. "Well look, if it gets really tight we can always rent the room you're in and you could move in with Jamie. I already talked with him about it and he said he'd even let you have the top bunk."

She turned to me and smirked. "You're sweet... not, *funny...*" she added, squeezing my hand, "but you *are* sweet."

* * *

I sat on the lid of the toilet, waiting for my hands to move. The envelope was still in my pocket, but it felt like it weighed pounds, not ounces and an uneasy feeling had settled into my bones, flowing through like marrow. The color of the envelope was inviting, gentle and calming, but something was telling me that the words inside were going to throw everything off kilter, make me feel like I was on a boat in a storm. I had to force my fingers to pull out the letter and put it before my eyes again.

It looked harmless enough.

I pushed aside the fear with a quick shake of my head and slid open the flap. A folded piece of paper inside and a small square...a photograph. The photo gave me pause and I pulled out the letter first. Elegant handwriting, gently sloping from left to right. Blue ink on cream paper. Good quality paper.

Dear Hope,

I am so sorry to hear about the passing of your father. For the short time I knew him he always seemed to be a very kind and thoughtful man - please pass on my condolences to the rest of the family. I actually came to the funeral but stayed near the back and thought about saying hello afterwards. I thought it better to leave because I knew it was a tough day for all of you and, well, I didn't want to add any stress you might already be feeling. I'm not sure how you or your family would have reacted after all this time. It was a beautiful ceremony and to be back in the old neighborhood was both wonderful and sad. As I hear it, you and your family have been coming back every summer and that makes me feel good - it sort of makes it all still connect if that makes any sense.

I have been living in Tampa Bay for the past 10 years, working mostly as a wedding consultant, if you can believe that people actually pay for someone to do that. They do! It's nice here but the beaches are so different from the ones back home and, yes, I still call it "home". I guess we all still do, right?

My family is selling our house in Brigantine and I was there in the winter to see if there was anything that I needed to get while I still had the chance. I went through some old boxes and found mostly stuff that I just couldn't get rid of over the years. I did, however, find a book that belonged to Max (I remember he was going to let me borrow it after he was finished) and when I flipped through it I found a letter inside that was addressed to you. I'm not sure if it was supposed to be mailed but I've enclosed it here.

I know that there was a lot of anger and sadness after Max died and that some of that was directed at me. It was because of that I have chosen not to contact you all these years...hard to believe it's been so long! I understand if you don't wish to see me or hear from me but I feel like I had to try. I can only imagine that he wrote this letter after you and he had stopped talking and, though I haven't opened it (I would never do that), I have to admit that I'm beyond curious to hear what he had to say.

I will be in town in August and would love to hear from you but If I don't I understand. Again, I hope that you are all well and please accept my sincere condolences.

Sincerely,

Stuart

P.S. I enclosed a photo I found in one of my "need to deal with this now" boxes as well.

He had written his phone number in the bottom corner of the letter. The area code must for be for Tampa. Where he was now a *wedding consultant*? Not what I ever pictured him doing (I thought back then that his looks would have sent him to Hollywood), but then again that summer changed most of what I assumed for the rest of my life.

I thought about the photo he tucked inside and hesitated. I knew it would be Max, one I had probably never seen before and for me to remove it, to look at it and make it part of my reality would be to accept an invitation. I wasn't so sure that I was ready to accept any invitation from twenty years ago.

I slid my fingers in and removed the photo as delicately as if it were a splinter.

Max looked at me with eyes that were the same shape and ocean blue as mine. His blonde hair looked a bit messier than he usually kept it and a few strands had fallen across his forehead making him look lazily handsome. He was smiling as if someone had just said something funny and then surprised him by taking the picture. He wore striped swim trunks that I had forgotten about over the years and his hand casually rested on his hip. He was leaning on a white painted railing in a yard that I couldn't place. What I noticed most was his smile – I hadn't seen it in such a long time and before I knew it I was smiling with him, forgetting how infectious it had always been. But I didn't deserve to smile and it felt suddenly wooden, like invisible strings were pulling my muscles into shape.

I had treated him so badly that night, but what could he expect of me?

I cut the threads of my smile and slid the picture back. I pulled out a folded envelope that was dulled a pale yellow with age. My name was written in pencil in Max's blocky letters and nothing more – no return address and no postage. Maybe he was going to slip it into my pocket when I wasn't looking or maybe he was going to wave it in my face while he screamed at me for being such a bitch that night.

Time had softened the handwriting like it was slowly blowing it away. I wasn't ready to open the seal of the envelope yet – not ready to roll back the rock that kept that cave closed for so long.

Outside, the sound of joyous, anticipating screams of children reached me through the bathroom window. I could picture them playing and laughing, sprinting towards some unknown adventure that awaited them. Summer did that - it whispered to you that anything was possible because the next three months were yours. Even in a place like this.

Absolutely yours.

CHAPTER
3

Jamie

I finished sweeping through each room (except the Lizard's of course, that would be suicidal and God forbid I accidentally knock over her cauldron). She was swearing under her breath as she scrubbed away in the bathroom and I grinned, waiting for her to find the spider above the tub that I saw earlier but decided to leave for her.

The doorbell rang and I threw the broom to the floor and raced for the stairs. Liz flew out of the bathroom and shoved into me and I went tumbling into the open door of the blue room, landing on my ass.

"Hey!" I yelled but she was already halfway down. By the time I reached the living room I could see Crystal McAffery at the front door with an armful of albums and the two of them jumping and squealing like idiots to each other. Girls are good at that.

Crystal had a plain, freckled face and pencil-straight strawberry blonde hair which looked better now that she was letting it grow long.

She tucked it behind one ear and it reached down to the middle of her back. She was wearing bright green shorts and a tight t-shirt with a picture of Hall and Oates on it. I stood there wishing it was Nicky at the door as she walked through the porch and into the house, but I couldn't help but notice that her chest had gotten bigger and tried not to stare. She could be just as much of a jerk as the Lizard but she wasn't bad looking, actually. Nicky once said, "Well, I wouldn't kick her out of bed for eating crackers." I laughed but didn't really get it.

Crystal's family rented the same house every summer; a two-story gray and white one with a small exposed porch that was just down the street. The only good news now was that Lizard would likely spend half of her miserable time over at the McAffery's house and not here. If I was lucky she would sleep over there and Nicky and I would have the house and TV to ourselves...if he ever showed up.

Liz pushed past me and climbed the stairs.

"Hey, Jame," Crystal said, smiling as she passed.

"Oh, hey." I tried to sound uninterested but my hands felt useless so I put them in my pockets and let my eyes wander after her.

The bedroom door closed and that high pitched sound of giggling was followed by the scrape of a needle as they put a record on. I thought about telling mom that she wasn't doing her chores and starting another war so early in the day. Better not and besides, now it would be two against one. Not good numbers.

I went upstairs and out to the deck that overlooked the street. I could hear the girls through the bedroom window singing along as Shaun Cassidy blabbered "Da Doo Ron Ron." I slid my hands over the railing and felt the roughness of the paint that had begun to flake like peeling skin.

I looked from one end of the street to the other: ocean on one end and the maze of streets and houses on the other. With the sun shining down, brightening everything a bit, you might think for a moment that this was a place that couldn't change, a place where every summer was as beautiful as the one before it.

But things *were* changing in the Inlet, in fact all over Atlantic City and I knew it. Hell, everyone knew it.

Seaside Avenue stretched from Pacific Avenue to the boardwalk - a total of two blocks. There weren't any shops, arcades or piers on this part of the boardwalk. The closest thing to entertainment was a miniature golf course a block over that for all I knew was closed by now. The Nevada apartments were at that end of the street. Most of the windows of the sand-colored building were covered with plywood and the ones that weren't looked dead and black.

I looked down to the other end: a shirtless skinny black guy was working under the hood of a car. Sweat shined off his back as he leaned over the engine. Nicky would probably know what kind of car it was because he was good at that sort of stuff, but I usually couldn't tell one from another. Further down a bald man was sitting on his porch reading the newspaper.

The next block was full of small, tightly-packed two story brick row homes like back in Philly. Seaside came to an end at the next street, Pacific Avenue.

In a way this place was a lot like back at home: it was a city of neighborhoods. I'd had heard the names of the different parts of the city, but could never be sure exactly where they began, where they ended or even if they still existed. Mom and dad would talk about places called Ducktown and Northside. I only knew the Inlet, that part that was shaped like the heel of a foot and ran along the bay to the north and the open ocean to the east.

At one time or another I had been to all the towns along the South Jersey shore like Margate, Ocean City, Avalon and Cape May and none of them looked like Atlantic City. They had mostly candy-colored houses with grassy lawns, white fences and driftwood in their front yards. They looked...healthy.

There was a vacant lot on the other side of the street a few doors down from Nicky's house. I was sure it wasn't there last summer and it took me a few minutes to remember that it used to be where Mrs. Elgenhurd's house stood. She lived there with her son after Mr. Elgenhurd died.

The first time I had been inside was two summers ago when Nicky and me broke the bathroom window on the second floor. I threw the pitch and Nicky hit the ball.

Boy, did he hit it! Unfortunately, Ms. Elgenhurd, who was in her eighties, was using the room at that exact moment. All the kids in the street saw it and immediately scattered. I froze and looked at Nicky and he broke out laughing.

Our parents marched us over. The parlor was huge, dark and air-conditioned so it wasn't all bad. I had only seen Mrs. Elgenhurd a few times - she didn't come out much - but I recognized the old woman sitting in front of the television. The TV was one of those old wooden ones with a record player on the side. *Let's Make a Deal* was on and Monty Hall was laughing with a woman who was dressed as a box of crayons.

The room smelled like medicine and dust. A faded dark red and gold carpet covered the floor and Mrs. Elgenhurd sat in a plastic-covered lime-green chair that crumpled loudly whenever she moved.

She listened while Nicky and I mumbled our apologies, her head moving from side to side and I couldn't tell if she was disagreeing with us. Her small hands quivered in her lap and she removed her glasses, letting them hang from a thin chain around her neck. With the glasses gone her eyes looked tiny and I tried not to stare at the loose skin of her throat that wriggled when she talked.

"It's alright," she said in a creaky but comforting voice and took my hand, "Believe it or not, I was young once, too." I could feel every bone under the papery skin. Holding her hand was like cradling a small bird. Christ, we really could have killed this woman while she was just trying to do her business! Nicky shifted nervously behind me, saying nothing until we got back home.

"Well, if she got the shit scared out of her at least she was in the right room!" he snorted and fell to the floor, howling and holding his stomach. I cracked up as well because, well, watching Nicky laugh always made me laugh. Still, for the next three weeks I had to walk over with my allowance to pay off what I owed. Nicky would go with me but he never had any money.

Now there was nothing left but weeds and it felt like a tooth missing from my mouth.

Did she die or just sell the house and move?

Across the street the front door of a mint green two-story home opened and out came Mrs. Falso, dressed in white shorts, white t-shirt and skin already so deeply tanned that she looked like she was made of wood. The hair piled on top of her head was bright gold (not a natural color, even I could tell that). She scurried across the street in her heels, slowing an approaching car with one hand and balancing a drink in the other. She looked up, squinted and waved. I waved back.

Her son, Teddy, was a goofy kid that occasionally hung around with Nicky and me. I didn't really care where Teddy was right now. The first face I wanted to see was Nicky.

The largest house on the street was right next door: a salmon-colored three-story job with a Spanish tile roof. It belonged to the Natone family (or what was left of it) and took up twice the space of any other house on the block. An obnoxious, dazzling white stone fountain sat in the gated front yard which also contained a two car garage. Seth Natone was three years older than me and was the only thing that I didn't like about Atlantic City though I couldn't really blame the city.

Seth's real mom left two years ago. I was one of the only witnesses to what would become a legendary moment in Seaside Avenue history. I watched from the deck as she peeled away from the house in her blue Mustang, smoke pouring from the tires and her arm out the window with middle finger extended while Mr. Natone watched helplessly from the driveway, unaware or simply not caring that someone might have heard her screaming about another woman. This was after she had put two bricks through the windshield of his gold Cadillac. Classic.

You had to love our neighborhood. The tire marks in the driveway lasted the entire summer and Nicky busted out laughing every time he saw them.

Bernie Natone owned some buildings in the neighborhood: mostly small, two-story walk-ups somewhere on Maine and Pacific Avenue, but he also had a couple larger buildings on Baltic and New Hampshire. Other than his house, the only other property on Seaside that he owned was a creaky, four-story yellow brick apartment building near the beach.

At Seth's house a round black woman dressed in a white apron came out onto the second floor balcony to shake out a large blue sheet.

I was only in Seth's house once, about five years ago. My mom had sent me over thinking it would be a nice gesture because they had just finished building the house that summer and were new to the neighborhood. Seth made sure that he showed me all the rooms and there were a lot. The kitchen had shiny white marble counter tops and bright orange Italian (Seth pronounced them EYE-talian) tiles on the floor. The dishwasher and eight-burner stove were new.

The dining room had a large, smooth, black table that reflected the polished chandelier above it. The legs looked like black horns from some animal and that was actually pretty cool. Just as I was about to ask what animal they came from, he started on about the chandelier - how it had been bought from some famous place in New York. I quickly forgot the name. It seemed everything in the house had some story that went along with it. Nothing was just what it was. Even the *refrigerator* had a story: his dad had bought it from a company that supplied the best restaurants in Manhattan. I could just tell it was big.

The white wall-to-wall shag carpeting in the living room was almost blinding. A gray leather L-shaped sofa sat against a wall that was one big mirror. It made the room look enormous. Large, sliding glass doors looked out onto a patio with a bar and a pool that was sur-rounded by brightly colored lawn chairs and big umbrellas. He said he never used the pool.

"Too small," he said.

I could see the beach beyond and the white waves cresting just over the dunes and realized that that was exactly where I wanted to be, not in this house listening to stories anymore.

Seth's mother was lying in a lounge chair out on the patio, wear-ing a black bathing suit and holding an empty glass. She had a large straw hat over her face and Mr. Natone walked into view, waving his arms and yelling something but she didn't move. I couldn't hear what they were saying through the glass and Seth made a sound in his throat before walking away.

She came in and asked me to stay for lunch and I couldn't really say no. I joined them but only wanted to get out of there. Something was wrong here and I didn't like it. Seth and I never really did anything – no Frisbee or swimming, we didn't play ping pong on the new table down in the rec room or watch television. I felt like I had just been on a tour.

While we ate Seth's mom moved unsteadily around the large kitchen. Her smile was too wide to be comfortable and her eyes looked wet and red. Every question she asked Seth was answered sullenly while he kept his eyes on the table as if praying. His lips sometimes moved without making any sound.

"So, Johnny, where are you from?" she asked and leaned on the counter to steady herself.

"His name is *Jamie*, mom," Seth mumbled. He glanced over and then looked down. "He's from Philly."

I nodded and poured out a fake smile. I couldn't tell if there was something funny in the way Seth said Philly like it was an insult, but by then I didn't really care. I finished lunch quickly and made up an excuse about having to go. Seth didn't walk me out. He just nodded and I could see tears had begun tracking down his cheeks.

That was the only time I ever went into the Natone house.

I shaded my eyes and looked down the street at the white-framed windows of the building they owned, searching for signs of life. An image of Benita Canizares took over: jet black hair and a crooked smile with the small space between her front teeth, her dark eyes, almond-shaped and dipping slightly at the corners (which made her look sad sometimes) and the patch of rose-colored skin on her cheek.

Benita had been a friend for years but before the end of last summer I had started getting this weird feeling somewhere down near my belly whenever I saw her. I hated it. I mean I've always liked girls but this was different than the girls in school or the ones I saw on TV. I'd known her almost as long as I've known Nicky! Still, whenever she showed up it felt like I had eaten too much food, or maybe not enough. I couldn't tell. Sometimes it felt like I was about to get on a ride that I'd never been on before. So is that scared? Excitement? When she talked to me or smiled the hair on my neck and arms would tickle and suddenly I didn't know what to say. It felt like I was actually growing *younger* not older. I didn't like that she suddenly had this strange power over me.

I waited for a sign of her in the apartment windows but saw nothing. Both were empty.

Jesus, where the hell is everybody?

Children raced up the street to the ramp of the boardwalk. They disappeared one by one as they leaped off the steps that led to the sand, looking as if they were jumping off the edge of the world.

CHAPTER
4

Hope

By noon everyone was finished their jobs and had changed into bathing suits. I held mom's hand and shouldered a black canvas bag stuffed with towels. The sun glowed directly above and my large sunglasses bathed the world in a cushion of soft amber tones. Jamie carried the beach umbrella while Liz and Crystal, laughing a bit too loud (most likely just to annoy him), handled the beach chairs. Randall followed, wheeling the cooler full of sandwiches and sodas.

The sounds of the beach were growing and I felt something bubble inside. It happened whenever I got close to the ocean, especially the first time of the summer. It was like there was saltwater mixed with my blood and it only came alive when I was near enough to hear the sound of crashing waves and crying gulls.

We crossed the boardwalk and I leaned against the worn silver railing that overlooked the sand as a warm breeze washed by. Sounds lost over the past nine months whispering in my ear: distant radios bleating against each other across the dunes (that special sound a radio makes when it's at the beach - it's different I tell you), the hum of families, the terrific pounding of waves and the piercing whistle of the lifeguards.

Behind us stood the Vermont Apartments, once a colorful building full of life but now a near empty shell standing vigil over a dying neighborhood. I took mom's hand and helped her cross the sand and, for the first time I could remember, sensed the uncertainty in her steps.

* * *

1940

I hold mommy's hand tightly as we cross the beach together. The short brim of my hat keeps some of the sun out, but when I look up I have to close one eye so I just look down at our shadows as they move across the beach.

The hot sand is now toasting the soles of my feet. Max tramps alongside, proudly wearing his new bathing suit and his shoulders covered with a bright blue towel. He hisses through his teeth and hops from one foot to the other before racing down to the water. I giggle and run after him to where the sand is darker and cooler.

"Don't go in the water yet, you two" mommy calls. "Wait for us."

I look back and wait but Max runs to the ocean's edge. Daddy digs a hole for the umbrella as mommy places two small striped beach chairs on either side and then puts out the big green blanket we always bring with us.

I move closer to the water and test it with my toes: it's cold but feels good. Tiny bubbles appear in the wet sand as the water washes back and I bend down to look at them. Just as I'm getting ready to dig into one a wave rushes in and the water is up to my ankles. I let out a squeak and run a few steps back.

Max walks into the water, stomping his feet, but he soon wraps his arms around his chest and laughs. I want to reach Max and hold his hand but he's too far out for me. I'm not old enough yet.

Foam floats past, looking like islands and I slip my hands under the water, scooping up a tiny clump of seaweed. It feels so slimy that I almost drop it right away, but instead pinch it between my fingers and bring it close enough to sniff. It smells alive but kind of stinky so I wrinkle my nose and squeeze one of the smooth green bubbles, popping it. It's so much fun I quickly pop the rest.

Max has gone out up to his hips and daddy splashes out to join him. He laughs, picks him up and drops him into the water. Far behind them I can see the pier with the sign that has the big "57" sign on it. We went there yesterday and all of us got a pin to wear that looked like a pickle. Mommy and daddy put theirs on their hats and I thought that was silly. Max put his pin on his bathing suit before we left the house. I couldn't find mine today and daddy said that they'll get me another one and that stopped me crying. I hope we go again today.

Two hands gently wrap around my shoulders. "Hey sweetie," mommy says softly. Her voice always sounds like she's about to begin singing. She sits down in the shallow water and pulls me into her lap. I feel her warm round belly behind me.

A wave comes at us and my eyes go wide. We both giggle as the chilly water rolls up our legs. Daddy is lifting Max up over the bigger waves and he's laughing and kicking his feet, making white splashes. The sun is sparkling all over the water around us.

I want to go farther out, to the place where the sky and water meet, however far that is. I want to see where the water ends if it ever does. A large boat with a white sail rocks gently in the distance and I wondered where it's going. The sail has a picture of a red lobster on it. Other boats are in the water too, and I want to be on all of them, especially if they're going to where the ocean ends. It must be very beautiful there.

Mommy and I get up and walk along the water. A little boy with curly yellow hair is building a castle where the warm sand meets the cool sand and we sit and help him dig a moat. Mommy mixes water in the sand to make it harder and builds a small tower. A breeze blows off her hat and the three of us chase it.

Later we buy ice cream from a strong-looking man dressed in white shorts and shirt. He is carrying a large silver box on a thick strap and shouts, "Ice cream! Ice cream here!" He must really love ice cream! Max and I both ask for Fudgesicles and the man sets the box down. Cool mist curls out like it's a magic chest. The mist touches my face and arms as he hands us our ice cream.

I try to eat it as quickly as I can, but it melts and a chocolate mess runs down my arm and makes it all sticky. When we finish daddy takes us to the shallow water to wash off.

Other boys and girls from our street come with their mommies and daddies. I know most of them but stay near Max where I feel safer. Some of the them run to the edge of the water and splash each other and laugh. Max wanders down to them and I follow with my thumb in my mouth, something mommy has told me I need to stop doing.

The children find a small crab with a pink, spotted shell in the shallow water near the short jetty. I watch but don't get close. They laugh *and surround it. The crab crawls sideways with its claws out and open, toward a dark-haired boy and he yells and runs away. I start laughing. I wonder why the back legs of the crab are flat but the others are all pointy. A girl tries to come up behind it, but it turns quickly and she backs off.*

The boys and girls keep it from getting to the water and I'm not liking how I'm feeling right now. I stand closer to Max. The largest kid in the group, a boy with straight red hair, quickly picks up a rock and smashes the crab. The children stop laughing and I see that the boy has a weird smile on his face.

"Why'd ya do that?" Max yells but the kid just shrugs. I want to cry but Max takes my hand and we walk away. I turn and see that the children are all leaving and the crab is still there but soon a bird swoops and picks it up.

"That was a crab," Max says as he moves next to me and puts his arm around my shoulder. I just nod, knowing full well what it was but not saying anything. My stomach feels bad. Max likes to think I need to be told everything but that's okay because I love being with him. Some of the children now run down the beach and Max follows. I want to run after them but watch as a large gull cries out and stretches its wings while the waves fall on the sand.

Jamie

I walked to the water and stopped at the edge. The waves were breaking real nice, rolling straight in from one end of the beach to the other. The ocean was dotted with boats and broke the sunlight into a million pieces. I waded in, letting the foam splash around my legs before finally plunging into a wave. The chill of the June ocean was sharp but I stayed under, listening to the rumbling sound of a wave rush overhead and fade somewhere behind me. It felt safe, and I held my breath for as long as I could before coming back up.

I took in a mouthful of water and spit it out, enjoying the tang of the ocean on my lips and the back of my tongue. Other people complained about the taste of salt water but not me...it brought back memories. Fun times with Nicky and Benita...and…

...dammit, there she was again, back in my head.

I couldn't help but wonder if she had changed much since I saw her last. I never took much notice of how she looked before, but last summer I couldn't help but see little things like how there were tiny, soft hairs on her shoulder and her neck. She had dimples when she smiled. Did she always have them? She had this habit of tucking her hair behind one ear and it was so...

Someone was racing across the beach shouting my name.

Nicky! It had to be him!

He was wearing denim cutoffs and his long curly hair was the color of an old penny in the sun. He was throwing huge arcs of sand in the air as he ran. He stopped to quickly hug mom and dad and then rushed to the water, a wide smile splitting his tan face. He leaped easily over the small waves before disappearing with a dive.

Nicky's always been able to stay under longer than me and I scanned the water for him. Suddenly he surfaced next to me and I was grabbed around the shoulders and pulled under. When I came back up Nicky was floating in front of me wearing a stupid grin, his hair hanging in wet rings over his light brown eyes. He looked the same as last year, maybe a little leaner, but he had the same straight nose with a tiny scar under it, the same ears that poked out a bit too much from his head and the same face that many of the girls found cute.

He wrapped his arms around me and shouted above the thunder of an approaching wave. "When the hell did you get here?"

"Last night!" I shouted and began swimming out to where the larger waves were breaking.

"Shit, it's freezing, man! Are you crazy?"

We stopped at the point where I knew the lifeguards wouldn't blow their whistles. I could barely feel the sand with my toes. "So, where the hell were *you*?"

"Visiting my cousins up in Virginia," he said. "We just got back this morning, man. I saw-"

"You mean *down* in Virginia."

"Whatever, Mr. Kotter," he said and pushed me. "Anyway, I saw your car and ran over but no one answered so I knew you had to be here, right? I left mom and Gary with the suitcases. You shoulda heard my mom cussin' after me the whole time I was runnin' here," he cackled.

He looked past me and yelped. Around the jetty came the Miss Atlantic City II, the famous speedboat that raced along the beaches all summer. She bounced and growled across the water packed with about twenty people and Nicky and I knew (as did all the folks who swam on these beaches) that the sight of her always meant big waves would be showing up in a few minutes. I looked to the beach and saw people heading quickly to the water, hoping to get out for the coming waves.

"You with me, Jackson?" Nicky asked, following the boat with his eyes.

"'Course, fool," I said and chuckled.

A big wave soon came. Others saw it and began desperately swimming out to reach it before it formed but they would never make it. This one was mine and Nicky's alone.

"Suckers! You gotta keep your eyes open out here!" he laughed and pointed.

The wave rose higher and towered over us. I turned and stroked the water quickly before straightening my body out. Nicky and I rode the waves differently: I liked to keep my arms at my sides and fly through the water like a bullet. Nicky rode with his arms out in front like Superman. We've had several serious debates about each technique over the years. Every wave was a competition to see who made it closer to the shore.

The crashing in my ears was terrific and I realized I was smiling, maybe for the first time since we got to the shore. I was just fired from a gun. A cool bullet aimed straight for the beach. The pressure against my closed eyes and the rush of water against my face was beautiful. I had been waiting for this longer than I knew, I guess. I wanted to reach out and see if Nicky was next to me.

Eventually the wave faded and my body dragged against the water so I put my arms out and slowed to a stop. I pulled myself up on my knees and wiped my face as Nicky batted me on top of my head and immediately rushed back in. We rode waves until we both got too cold and tramped up the beach to where mom and dad were.

Oh yeah, and the Lizard and Crystal.

Mom got up and gave Nicky another tight hug. "Now give me a proper hug! How're you doing, sweetie?"

"Good," he answered, looking a bit embarrassed. "So glad school's over."

"Amen," I added.

"You *do* both know that you're talking to a teacher, right?" mom asked.

It was sort of a "beginning of summer tradition" to say this and I saw mom's half smirk. I shrugged, feeling good, and reached into the cooler to toss Nicky a can of 7UP.

Lizard and Crystal were lying on their towels, facing the sun with sunglasses on. Why the hell is Crystal even trying? She never got much darker than a white Crayola all summer. These days both of them were more interested in tanning and watching boys than swimming anymore. ABBA was singing *Fernando* on a nearby radio and both girls rocked their heads slightly from side to side. I caught Nicky watching them for a moment too long and elbowed him from behind.

"How's your family?" Dad asked, peeking out from under his straw hat with the colorful band.

"They're good, real good," he answered and grabbed a fist of his hair and began twisting it, squeezing the water out. "Mom's still working at the hospital," he continued, "but they moved her up to a floor lead, so she's in charge of, like, three or four other janitors." He plopped down on the sand. "Gary's got a new job working at a garage on Arctic."

"Living the dream, huh?" Liz muttered loud enough for mom to hear.

"Elizabeth…" she said in her warning voice. Both girls rolled over on their stomachs.

We finished our sodas and grabbed a couple of ham sandwiches before getting up and heading across the beach.

Hope

I watched as Jamie and his first and best friend headed toward the far end of the beach. How long ago was it, eight, nine years? Can they really have already known each other that long?

The day they met was cloudless and boiling hot even with the wind blowing in off the ocean. Randy had just taken Liz to the long jetty to see if the fishermen were having luck. Nicky and his mother Charlotte had been sitting near the water. They were new to the neighborhood and I had only seen them a few times before so I took Jamie by the hand and walked over to sit next to them.

"Hello," I offered in my friendliest voice, "you're new to the neighborhood, aren't you?" Charlotte turned to me with a slightly annoyed expression on her round face, but it softened quickly to an approachable and pleasant smile when she looked at the two of us. I got the impression that this woman (whom I would later consider a friend) was so used to being hassled by life that anyone who approached was first to be considered a threat. I was relieved to see her smile surface on her pretty face and continued, "Um, it's Charlotte, right?"

"Charlotte Martre," she answered in a gravely, grinding voice that I immediately liked. She extended her hand and asked, "You live down the street, don't you?" Charlotte was a solid-looking woman with haunting light green eyes and wiry black hair pulled back into a loose bun. I recognized the pocked skin of a teenage battle with acne on her cheeks.

I nodded and took her hand. "It's actually my parents who own the house," I said and saw Charlotte make a quick funny face to Jamie and he giggled. Nicky was quietly watching Jamie with large, beautiful brown eyes that were the same shape as his mother's. "We live in Philly and I teach so we come every summer with the kids. I grew up here."

"Nice place to grow up," Charlotte said. "So close to the beach."

"Can't beat it, in my opinion. And who is this?" I asked, looking at Nicky.

"Well, this is Nicolas and over there," she said, peering out to the ocean and pointing, "is his big brother Gary." I watched as a young boy with long dark hair rolled around in the waves, horsing around with a group of kids. Jamie and Nicky continued to silently eye each other.

I introduced myself and Jamie. We all moved to the shallows and I dug into the wet sand with both hands while Nicky, Charlotte and Jamie looked on. I scooped out handfuls and let it run between my fingers and made a funny face. Nicky grinned and gazed down into the growing pit in the sand. A small wave came and poured some water into the hole.

The boys watched as tiny creatures – minuscule clams and tiny worm-like animals - spun in the water and then swiftly buried themselves. I plunged my hand into the sandy bottom of the well and gently pulled out my fist with a childlike look on my face. I rinsed my closed hand before holding it out to Nicky.

"Want to see?" I asked in my best mysterious voice and held my fist out toward Nicky. He hesitated, first looking to his mom with a cautious smile then nodded. "You have to pull my fingers open, okay?"

Slowly his hand moved to mine. Nicky peeled back each finger until he saw the gray and silver thing shaped like a bullet scuttling around in my palm. His jaw dropped open. The small thing was frantically pedaling its many legs.

"Cool, huh?" I said proudly and Nicky nodded, staring. "Sometimes they're called sand bugs but my brother always called them sand crabs. They tickle, watch."

I took Nicky's hand and carefully placed the crab in it. It scrabbled on his fingers and he let out a yelp, throwing his hand up. Immediately a passing gull dipped and snatched the crab from the air and Jamie laughed out loud, splashing both of his hands into the hole. Nicky let out a loud cackle. More gulls arrived and beat their wings around us, squawking and crying for food. Laughing and shrieking, the four of us retreated to the safety of our towels.

The next day I invited Charlotte and her boys over for lunch. We ate on the porch and Gary sat next to Charlotte with a bored look on his face. Nicky and Jamie ate quickly and then began playing with toy cars. Charlotte finished her slice of crumb cake with an appreciative nod and dusted powdered sugar off her fingers. "We all moved from Lynchburg to be with the boys' father," she said, lifting her coffee to her lips and taking a slow sip. "He had just got out of the army and needed work real bad. Managed to scare up a job working on a trawler that was out for at least six months every year. That was," she said and looked up as if the answer hovered in the air above her, "God, two years ago. Haven't seen him since."

I watched Nicky as he rolled a tiny car back and forth and thought that he looked so small. Gary asked to be excused and Charlotte hesitated before looking at him and then over at me. He turned to me and mumbled, "Thank you, Mrs. Shepherd," before quickly leaving.

"I'm not even sure how it happened but things changed," she continued and watched Gary walk toward their house on the corner. "Too much time apart, I guess, but things never went back to the way they were. Do they ever, though?" Charlotte asked, looking at me and

I thought she looked tired. The skin below her eyes was discolored and irritated looking. The eyes themselves seemed hollowed out and in some way, empty. I hadn't noticed before but then again I wasn't looking, either. It felt nice that Charlotte felt secure enough to let her guard down in front of me.

By the end of that summer Nicky had become a fixture at our house. Charlotte worked very erratic hours and I would often invite Nicky over to play with Jamie. The boys quickly bonded over matchbox cars, action figures and daily trips to the beach. Nicky joined us for walks down to the piers and had slept over too many times to count and Jamie's face brightened whenever Nicky was with him.

We all should have a friend in our lives like that, I thought as I watched Nicky throw his arm over Jamie's shoulder, both looking like they were about to shed their young bodies any second. Jamie grabbed Nicky and shoved him into the rolling waves and then made a run for the jetty. Nicky ran after him, shouting and waving his arms.

Jamie

We slowed as we passed the lifeguard stand and looked at the four girls with the two handsome men with their muscles and cool sunglasses. One girl was wearing a snow-white tank top over her bright green bikini and it looked ghost-like against her tanned skin. The other girls were giggling back and forth to each other.

"Man, oh man, they have the life, ya know?" Nicky moaned, craning his neck.

I nodded and watched as one of the girls, this one a blonde, playfully tried to snatch the whistle from one of the guards.

"Pretty soon I'm gonna have chicks like that hanging all around me," Nicky said.

"Yeah, right," I snorted, "how the hell are you gonna pull *that* off?"

Nicky looked at me like I just jumped off a spaceship. "I'll be a lifeguard, brainless."

"Knowing you, you'd drown."

"Me? Never, but man," Nicky said, taking another long glance over his shoulder, "it would almost be worth it."

I spotted Seth up the beach and felt my stomach drop. He was sitting on a towel, his arms resting on his knees, skin already deep gold, with a bright blue surfboard sunk into the sand next to him. Around him was his usual group of knuckle draggers: Tony, Fat Ass Chuck, Mark and Brian. They looked over and Tony pointed, grinning. A couple girls were laying out on towels and pulled themselves up on their elbows to watch.

"Ah, shit," Nicky muttered.

"They won't do anything," I said, "not here." The crowd on the beach made me feel a bit safer, but I still made sure not to make eye contact with any of them. Why ask for trouble?

Seth was already tall for his age. He had a muscular, surfer's body and his brown hair, parted in the middle and feathered back, fell just to his shoulders. If you looked at his face - his wide smile and bright blue, honest-looking eyes - you might think that he was a decent guy but he had a real cruel side that both Nicky and I had become very familiar with over the years.

It had become a summer ritual for Seth and his asshole friends to harass us whenever they could. None of them were dumb enough to really hurt us but they loved to threaten and chase. They excelled at things like that. They might lay a smack on the back of one of our heads if they got close enough and last year they caught us and poured a coke over my head and then threw Nicky over the railing of the boardwalk. He landed pretty hard on the sand but it only knocked the wind out of him.

Brian Pogust had a long face full of pimples and brown-like hair that hung like a mop over his eyes, making him look like the sheepdog from the Looney Tunes cartoons. His house was at the other end of the city, closer to Ventnor, but he was always around and it was almost like he had moved into Seth's house. To me, he looked as if he had nothing else to do or no one else to hang around with. He was a year older than Seth and drove a used, shit-brown Monte Carlo whose engine could be heard from blocks away.

Tony Tellori (the best-looking of the bunch and knew it) was from that neighborhood called Ducktown that I mentioned earlier. It was apparently where the Italians lived. He had long shiny black hair that the girls went crazy for. There was always some chick hanging around him and sometimes they even combed that beautiful hair while he went on talking and ignoring them.

Both the Lizard and Crystal thought he was "super fine."

Fat Ass Chuck (did he even have a last name?) had a head of curly white-blonde hair and almost invisible eyebrows that lifted comically whenever he told a joke. I hated his laugh - a sort of squealing explosion that began somewhere deep in his vast guts and vibrated through his body. It always sent the rest of the gang into hysterics, especially when Nicky and I were the targets. I pictured him living somewhere under a pier surrounded by empty Gino's food wrappers like a fat troll.

Mark Sespro was the one that scared me the most. All I knew about him was that his family lived in Margate (two towns over) and that he wasn't going to school anymore. He never said much and to me he looked dangerous. There was something wrong with the eyes. They weren't stupid eyes for a guy who wasn't in school anymore, but that was what frightened me more than anything. I tried telling Nicky about it, but he didn't get it and I let it drop. It was like he was looking at something behind you…or through you. He had sandy hair that fell over the pale skin of his forehead and his cheeks were dotted with freckles. I heard he didn't get along with his family - or anyone else for that matter and stayed at Tony's for days at a time. I don't think that even Mr. Natone wanted him staying in his house. Mark Sespro just gave people that feeling.

All of them spent a lot of time at Seth's. They loved parking their cars in the large driveway, leaning their boards against the house, ordering the help around and drinking beer when Seth's folks weren't home. None of the others had the kind of money that Seth's family had and I wondered where they would be hanging if Seth's family didn't have maids, a pool or a 35 foot sailboat docked down at Gardiner's Basin.

They all watched us and I saw them smirk and nod. Except Mark…he just stared. Shit, another summer…another open season.

"Man, what do your folks do, bury you in the ground in the winter?" Nicky chuckled. "You're paler than pale, my man." He held his tanned arm against mine.

"Oh, shut up," I said and grinned. I looked down as we walked: a couple of broken scallop shells, a small piece of brown glass that was worn smooth and the discarded legs of a crab. The water rushed up and covered our feet, feeling cool and new. When it receded the brown glass was gone.

Nicky scooped up a clam shell with one hand and spun it out over the waves with a flick of his wrist. It arced to the right before cutting towards the water and plunging in with a small splash.

"Not bad," I said casually. I picked one up, placed it into the cup between my thumb and index finger and hurled it. It raced close to the surface before slapping into a small wave. It faded into blue and vanished.

"So what's the big deal in Virginia?" I asked.

He picked up another shell. "Nothing much, cousins and stuff." He spun the shell out over the waves.

Nicky had never mentioned family in Virginia before and an uneasy feeling grew in my stomach. "So why are you visiting them? I never heard you talk about them." He wasn't looking at me so I grabbed his shoulder and turned him. "Hey, you guys aren't thinking of leaving, are you?"

"Leaving? Hell, no. Where would we go?" he said and grinned. "Besides, I got too many chicks here that would miss me, Jackson."

We climbed onto the jetty and wandered to the end, stepping around small pools of warm water green with algae. A handful of people were fishing, their lines thrown to the bay side. The salt scent in the air mixed with the odor of drying pieces of squid and fish dying in plastic buckets.

"Hey," Nicky said and pointed. He climbed down to a rock that was the size of a small car and covered with white and gray barnacles. He knelt and grabbed a thin strand of fishing line, one that was invisible until the sunlight hit it, and slowly pulled it to the left and then the right.

"So," I started, trying to sound casual, "you see Benita around?"

I heard a wet slapping sound behind me and turned. A tall, strong-looking woman with pink skin and a kerchief over her brown hair had brought in a small sand shark. She unhooked it, shook her head with disgust and quickly rapped its head against the rocks before tossing it back onto the rocks. I hated it when they did that.

Nicky was peering into the crack that the line was stuck in. "What?" he asked and reached in, his voice sounding hollow and distant. "Ow!" he yelped and quickly pulled his hand back.

"How is Benita?" I asked. Now I just wanted to believe that she was still here.

"How the hell should I know?" Nicky answered and tugged on the line once more. It gave a bit of slack and he wrapped it around his hand as he pulled. A wave pushed up against the rocks and he scooted back, the white foam just missing him. "I never see her. Her mom keeps her cooped up in that apartment most of the time. She's always working, cleaning or doing homework."

Okay, so she's still here. I could feel a weird pressure in my chest let up, one I didn't realize was there until a moment ago. I had no idea where it came from, this spinning in my stomach, every time I thought about her but it was beginning to piss me off, for sure.

Last summer I noticed things like, when the sunlight touched her, it changed color somehow like she had superpowers or something. I saw how it made her hair look different, how her skin glowed in other special ways and her eyes, which were usually dark as night, let in a hidden, deep blue.

Benita and I had talked a thousand times before, but last summer, just about when I noticed how the light traced her outline so perfectly, I had the problem of not being able to come up with anything to say to her. It was like talking to a brand new person. A brand new person that I had known for years? It was enough to give you a damn headache.

"How is high school?" I asked, standing up. I really wanted to ask if Benita had said anything about me, but thought it was too obvious and Nicky would never let it go. He never really liked her much anyway. I watched him reel in more line and dark clots of seaweed dropped from it to the rocks below.

"No idea," he said flatly. "I got held back."

"Wow, really?"

"Uh, huh. They said I missed too many days of school or some shit like that so they're making me go again," he said. "Mom had such a Goddamn fit I thought she was possessed or something. Guess we'll be starting high school the same time, huh?"

"I guess," I said, "unless they hold *me* back."

"Why the hell would they do that?" Nicky looked up at me and squinted.

"Bad grades, you know, just getting in trouble," I said, not liking the way his lips were curling into a grin.

"Uh, huh," Nicky chuckled, "that'll happen."

"It could," I said but we both knew it wouldn't.

He turned and tugged on the line a few more times and finally dislodged a wiry mass of fishing line.

"How's Liz?" He asked and put on a devilish smile as he pulled apart the knotty clump.

I couldn't help but feel bad for him. Liz practically shuddered whenever Nicky or his family came up in conversation. Crystal was no better. They loved insulting him: the house he lived in, the clothes he wore or the way he talked. Nothing was ever good enough.

What amazed me was that it never seemed to bother him. He would wait until they were done and then smile, slap me on the shoulder and say, "I never would have guessed that *both* of them wanted me." That would send them into fits. If it really did bother him he didn't want to show it. I could see him doing that.

It wasn't the insults thrown directly at him that pissed me off as much as the ones that were said when he wasn't around. Those were the genuine feelings Lizard and Crystal had about my best friend and most times I was left feeling like a traitor because it was too much to defend him against the both of them. I wouldn't think of the perfect thing to say until ten minutes later.

"You saw her."

Nicky continued to wrap the clear line around his hand. "Sure did," he snickered.

I sighed and put my hands out. "She's a pain in the ass, what do-"

"Hey! Check it out!" Nicky said, holding the line up for me to see. Two tear-shaped sinkers were tied to it. He smiled and pulled them off the line, handing one over and pocketing the other.

We walked over to a group of men were near the end of the rocks. They were drinking cans of Miller and making (I guess jokes) in Spanish as they waited by their rods. We looked into each bucket. One had a nice-sized flounder in it. It gasped for breath and looked back up at me with its round, glassy, unblinking eyes.

* * *

Dinner was roasted chicken with the seasoning that mom made that I loved; it cooked right into the skin and made it crispy and a bit salty. A bowl of red potatoes sat next to a plate of fresh asparagus with butter. Nicky had two helpings. The Lizard had to mutter about that, of course.

When dinner ended Crystal came over and the two of them planted themselves in front of the TV and watched a rerun of The Hardy Boys, quietly ignoring any complaints by Nicky and me. A heavy silence hung in the air outside and dulled the voices of the children who had gone back outside to play after dinner while there was still daylight. The air cooled quickly and the drapes in the living room fluttered, letting a rush of salt breeze to flow in.

The sound of rain came and soon large drops were spattering on the screens and the rooftops, sounding like an army approaching. The children outside squealed with excitement and everyone went through the house and lowered each window a bit. The shower was warm and heavy, strumming car hoods and splashing onto the windowpanes. The streetlights came on, first glowing pink and then to gold.

Nicky and I went outside and let the water pour over us, making our shirts stick to our bodies and soaking our hair until it hung down in front of our eyes. We stayed out and threw my football around until the curfew siren went off.

I walked over to him and wiped water from my face. "So, you wanna stay over?"

"Can't" he said.

"Oh." I said, turning the football over a couple times. I didn't want to sound too disappointed.

Nicky grabbed the ball from my hand. "I still have to finish unpacking. Mom's probably still waiting to give me hell for that." He took a few steps backward before laughing and running down the street. "See you in the morning, Jackson!"

"So long!" I yelled and watched Nicky until he disappeared into his house at the end of the block. The rain running into my collar found the curve of my back and made me shiver.

I climbed slowly up the front steps and closed the door while the rain made a million tiny explosions on the street.

CHAPTER
5

Jamie

Nicky and I spent the morning riding our bikes down the boardwalk and then mom sent us off to the store which made the Lizard smile cruelly because she had gotten out of a chore. I didn't care and actually liked going to Walt's. The shelves were lined with all sorts of great stuff: all my favorite cereals, tons of soda, frozen dinners and every kind of Tastykake there was. The radio was always on and played cool tunes.

We came out, each of us carrying a bag and had to step around three men who were leaning against the store's painted brick wall and taking cover from the sun under the store's faded awning.

Nicky stopped on Oriental Avenue to watch a bright orange Nova with two thick black stripes across the hood peel its tires against the asphalt. Neighborhood kids gathered around and cheered as a cloud of blue smoke bloomed like a flower under the roaring machine. The driver threw off the brake and the car screeched down the street, sending sand and gravel into the air. Screams followed from the small crowd.

Nicky had grown quiet since we left Walt's. He kept his eyes on the sidewalk while we talked, a habit of his ever since he found a twenty-dollar bill on the pavement two years ago. Still, I could tell that something was wrong.

"Shit, don't that old guy ever shut up?" Nicky muttered and scratched his cheek with one finger.

"Who, you mean, Walt?"

Walt had owned the store before I was even born. He had known mom since she was a little kid - that's how long he'd been here. He had a friendly, round face and bushy white sideburns that practically hid his large ears. He always asked about my family and even though we weren't little kids anymore, still tucked in a treat or two for me and Lizard when he bagged the groceries.

I knew what Nicky was complaining about and he was probably right. Walt obviously kept his eye on Nicky as we wandered through the store. I could hear it in his voice whenever he had to speak to Nicky. He sounded a bit like my sister when she spoke to me.

Nicky spread his lips into a wide grin. "Oh, boy, look who it is! Hey, James, how is your family?" He batted his long eyelashes. "We *really* miss you guys down here!"

I shrugged. "So? You live here. It's not like he's gonna say that to you."

"Yeah, but he's *never been* like that to me," Nicky said, spitting into the street and then wiping his mouth with the back of his hand, "always giving me funny looks even though I never did nothing. He watches me all the time like I'm going to steal something."

He shifted the bag in his arm and picked up a bottle cap from the warm pavement. He flicked it over a fence with a snap of his fingers and a small brown dog raced up and barked at us from the other side.

Across the street a group of boys were smashing caps on the sidewalk with a brick. At the corner of Vermont Avenue we passed a store with fresh plywood covering the windows.

"What happened to Chick's?" I asked, a sour feeling growing in my belly.

"Oh, yeah, I forgot to tell ya," Nicky said, wincing almost comically. "He finally got tired of getting robbed, I guess. At least that's what my mom said. He closed up a few months ago. Sucks, huh? He was a pretty nice guy. Never gave us a hard time, ya know?"

"Did he move out of the inlet?"

"Yup. Closed up and left."

Chick Dawson: bald, small, shiny dark skin with a raspy voice, bending over his order forms and trying to read the tiny words with his thick glasses. Nicky and I never had to buy anything when we came in. Chick would just talk about old times when the boardwalk was the place to be, when old guys like Frank Sinatra and Sammy Davis Jr. (he always called them Frank and Sammy like he knew them) would sing at a place called the 500 Club and even though we had no idea who he was talking about we would listen and nod while rooting through bins of cheap plastic toys and comic books. He told us it burned down about five years ago. "Goddamned shame," Chick would complain.

"Shit, I wish I could've said goodbye," I moaned.

"Lots of people are leaving," Nicky continued. "Remember Mr. Blake's, on Pacific?"

Good chicken roll sandwiches. Mr. Blake used to call them "sammiches." There was an air pump outside that we could use for our bikes. Nicky crashed his bike into that hydrant that day and tore his knee up and Mrs. Blake ran out and helped me carry him in. That was the only time I saw Nicky cry but who could blame him with all the skin on his knee gone? Mrs. Blake patched him up until Gary came and got us. They even fed the two of us for free.

"Gone?"

Nicky nodded.

We turned onto Seaside and Nicky's face dropped. Gary's faded purple Gremlin was parked in front of his house. "Oh, shit, Gary's home early! Quick, man, split this with me." He reached into his pocket and handed me a package of Yodels. "If he sees us, say you bought it, okay?"

"Wait, why?"

"Because he knows I got no money."

"Where'd you get it?"

"Back there," Nicky said, nodding toward Walt's but keeping his eyes on his house, "where do you think?"

"What the hell did you do *that* for?" I snapped.

Nicky quickly turned to me. "Hey, if he's going to act like I'm stealing I might as well steal, right? Stop being such a goddamn girl."

"I don't know, man. Can't you just return it?" I hated the idea of lying to Gary.

Nicky grabbed the Yodels back and tore open the wrapper. Quickly shoving one into his mouth, he smiled. "Not now."

I shook my head, swore, and jammed the other Yodel in my mouth.

Down the block was a girl sweeping the sidewalk in front of the yellow brick apartment. I recognized the long black hair even from here and it felt like warm water had been poured into my chest. I coughed out a few crumbs of Yodel.

Benita stopped, almost as if she sensed us, and looked up and waved. She was wearing jean shorts with a white stripe down the side and a tube top. I smiled and waved back.

"I mean, how can someone have something against you when you haven't even done anything?" Nicky went on, working his words around the chocolate cake in his mouth. "I'm telling you, it makes you *want* to steal something. He's probably still thinking about Gary and all the shit he got into way back."

Benita smiled and leaned on her broom, waiting in front of her steps. Her hair was tied into a tight ponytail that hung over one tan shoulder. She had a delicate chin that arched away elegantly from her throat and her skin was the color of coffee and cream. I noticed that her body had changed: her legs were longer and she now had a chest that showed off her slim waist.

Nicky looked up and let out a grunt. He sat down and plopped the bag next to him but I kept walking.

"Were you even listening?" he asked.

I held up my hand without turning around. "Yeah, yeah."

Benita's mom and my mom became friends after Benita's dad left. I think she was about three years old or so. Soon she was tagging along with Nicky and me whenever she could. The three of us would sit along the water and build huge castles by scooping out sand with broken oyster and mussel shells and then try to save it when the tide came. Benita was great at digging channels in the sand to stop the waves that came in. Of course, Nicky liked to be in charge. I gathered the sand and would construct the walls.

When we swam together and saw a wave coming we would hold hands and dare the waves to pull us apart. We would let out a shout and jump up and down when the wave had passed by and we were still holding onto each other. No wave had ever beaten us.

As we got older, Benita became almost as much a part of my summer life as Nicky. He would grudgingly put up with her, but he would also tease her and always went after what she was most sensitive about: the rose-colored birthmark on her cheek. It flushed perfectly with her beautiful skin and was nothing more than a discoloration on her lower cheek that ended just below her jaw but it was enough for Nicky when he wanted to use it. He would convince me to go to the beach without her and because I didn't see the point to the whole thing, I would usually shrug and follow.

"See ya, Spot," Nicky would chirp and then laugh as the two of us jogged to the beach and left her standing alone in her bathing suit with a bucket in her hand.

Sometimes, though, she refused to be left behind and would find the two of us on the beach and join without even asking. She was also smart enough to ask my mom where we were if she couldn't find us, knowing that mom had a soft spot for her. The two of them would wait together on the front porch for the us to return. When we finally did show up mom would scold us for leaving her behind and Benita would stand behind her and stick her tongue out. Nicky considered her a tattle who couldn't be trusted.

If Nicky was the closest thing I had to a brother then Benita, well, I would have said she was like a sister to me, but something had changed. There was no way I could ever think of the Lizard like I had been thinking about Benita Canizares.

Last summer, whenever I watched her walk back to her building after the curfew siren sounded, her apartment would grow into a mysterious place and I couldn't stop wondering what she was doing. I found myself always looking to her window to see if he could see her shadow pass and I wondered if that made me a pervert or something.

Lately she seemed to be happy just by herself or with her girl-friends from the neighborhood and there was definitely a different rhythm in her step when she was walking with the other girls. Sometimes she seemed lost in a dream instead of laughing along with the other kids. There were still times when she followed as we raced along the jetty, hopping from one black boulder to the next, Nicky I'm sure hoping that we would lose her, but sometimes she would quit halfway, turn and simply walk back to the beach. I wouldn't even notice she was gone until we reached the end. Then, over my shoulder, as we were gathering our breath, I would spot her tiny figure strolling along the sand alone.

"Aw, she's just getting tits and all. It makes 'em crazy when that happens," Nicky had said one day as he placed his hands on his hips and panted. "At least that's what Gary says."

"Hey Jame."

She had grown bangs and they hung just above her eyes, eyes like two pieces of black glass. She was as beautiful as ever. I caught myself looking at the corners of her mouth and then back to her eyes and felt slightly helpless for a moment. "Hey," I said. "I was wondering if you were still around."

She looked down both sides of the street, put a crooked grin on her lips that amazed me and nodded. "Where am I going to go, right?" She had a candy necklace and it had left a few soft pastel marks at the base of her throat. "I've been busy helping mom."

"Is she's still doing the, you know, the hair stuff?"

"You mean the 'salon'?" she asked and chuckled, showing the tiny gap between her front teeth. I was glad to see that there were things about her that hadn't changed. "Yeah, they're teaching me the business."

"Really? That's cool." Benita's mother worked with other women doing nails and hair for the neighborhood ladies who couldn't afford the pricier places. They always worked out of one of their apartments and charged very little but they had no license. Occasionally they would get visited by official people who checked on things like that and they would receive a notice to "cease and desist" or face "severe penalties," but they would simply move their small operation to another apartment.

"Right now they're working at Ms. Ortiz ' on Maine," she said. "They found them last month in Mrs. Vargas' and the landlord made them clear right out. Usually they don't bother them much as long as they stay under the radar, but they've been pretty tough around here lately. Ms. Ortiz is real good with nails and all so she's been teaching me." She held out her hands and spread her fingers. "See? I did them myself."

"Yeah," I answered and looked at them for as much time as I thought polite. They seemed pretty enough, a light purple color, but I couldn't really tell. The skin on her hands looked rough and a couple of her nails had broken edges.

"Also, mom has me doing stuff like keeping track of the money," she added proudly.

A sharp tapping sound came from the first floor window apartment window behind us and we turned. A woman with cool, dark skin and a cloud of gray hair was frowning and waving us away with her bony hand.

"Alejate di mi ventana!" the woman cried.

Benita rolled her eyes.

"Ahora!" the woman yelled.

Benita shouted back without turning. "Okay, okay!" She sighed heavily and moved away from the window, folding her arms and muttering, "Miserable old woman."

"Well, you were always good with that stuff, right?" I continued, trying to get her attention back on me.

"I guess so," she said, still glaring as the old woman disappeared back into the gloom of her dark apartment. She turned to me and her face brightened. "Well, ready for high school?"

"Nope." I looked back and saw Nicky. He was still sitting on the cracked curb with his arms folded onto his knees, tapping his foot. "You?"

"I don't know. I guess." She glanced at Nicky and waved. He held up one hand silently.

She's enjoying this, I thought. *Hell, I'm enjoying this.* She pulled her necklace to her mouth and bit into one of the small round candies. It made a crunchy sound as she chewed and I watched as her tongue moved behind her teeth. "What's his problem?" she asked and began sweeping again, pushing the sand into small piles and then into the gutter.

"Who?" I was busy watching her body sway back and forth with the broom and the way the muscles moved under her skin.

"Who?" she answered and put her hand out in the direction of Nicky. "Who do you think?"

"Oh, yeah. Well, you know him." I looked at Benita's bare shoulders, so perfect and bronze and suddenly I felt warmer. "He gets in moods."

She looked over her shoulder at me, somehow able to look both amused and annoyed at the same time. "That's one long mood, y'know?"

I nodded and chuckled. A breeze pushed a few scraps of crumpled paper along the pavement and as I watched her sweep the thought came to me that she could sweep forever and never really get rid of all the sand. The tiny grains were always there, as if the entire sidewalk was made from it. It rested on the streets, on the floor of every apartment and house, everywhere.

I was busy trying to come up with something else to say when I noticed that she was looking past me and just over my shoulder.

"Oh, hell, my mom! I should be finished by now. I need to go up and check the clotheslines," she said and vaulted up the front steps and I couldn't help but stare at her slim, golden legs.

She ducked into the doorway, then turned and quickly peeked around the corner, her face half in shadow.

"Hey", she whispered like was about to tell me a great secret and I got a chill that ran up my legs and stopped somewhere near my belly. "You guys having your party tomorrow?"

"Sure." I asked hopefully, "are you coming?"

"Yup. Mom said we're bringing something, but I don't know what it is yet," she said. "See ya then?"

"Okay."

"Bye," she said and stole another look to her mother who had now crossed the street. She looked at me and the shiver raced from my belly up to my scalp. Dammit. I thought maybe it was my imagination that there really was a little blue in her dark eyes, but when the sunlight hit her, well, there it was. I knew right then that I would noticed it every time from now on. "I'm really glad you're back, Jame."

She disappeared into the stairway.

I turned and watched Benita's mom, Evalisse, wave her hand in my direction and smile. She tilted her head, passed Nicky and walked up to wrap her arms around me.

"Hey, sweetie, how are you?" she asked and kissed me hard on the cheek, bringing a spicy scent that I had forgotten about over the winter. Benita's mom always smelled great. "Exotic," my mom would say.

I had never seen a picture of her dad but could see that Benita got much of her looks from her mother; they both had the same smooth, caramel color to their skin (though her Mom's was a bit darker) and the shape of their eyes. Her mother's face was elegant, with high cheekbones and a long, slim neck that almost looked fragile. She usually kept her hair in a colorful wrap and wore loose dresses that had colorful patterns on them: birds, trees or fish.

"Good," I said, "Benita told me you're coming to the party tomorrow."

"Absolutely, honey. Wouldn't miss it," she said and gently pinched my chin between her thumb and finger. "You tell that momma and grandma of yours that I'll come by soon and give them both a big welcome back squeeze. I've been thinkin' about them a lot lately." She shifted the bag in her arms. "How is your grandmother doing?"

"Okay, I guess."

"Well, you keep an eye on her. She's special and I'm sure she misses your granddad a lot. You're lucky to have so many special women in your life."

I nodded, knowing that she could only be talking about mom and grandma, not The Lizard. She smiled, stroked my chin, gave me another hug and then turned and went into the black-windowed building.

I walked slowly, with the last image of Benita in my head - her magic blue-black eyes peeking around the corner of the door and looking like the two of us shared a secret - and plopped down next to Nicky.

"You didn't tell Spot we're going down the boards tonight, didya?" Nicky snorted.

"Nah, but I think she's busy tonight anyway."

"Good," he said, "She's always such drag on the piers anyway, ya know? I bet she's still too chicken to do any of the rides." He lifted his bag into his lap. "So what the hell *were* you guys talking about?"

"Nothing, really, just school and stuff," I said and looked at him. "We agreed that you have prettier hair than she does."

Nicky smirked, got up and handed one of the bags over to me. "Wise ass."

* * *

We gathered in front of the house and a breeze off the ocean cooled the air. I felt the familiar pull in my stomach, the excitement of the first trip down the boards. I couldn't help but wonder what else, if anything, might have changed. Nicky had forgotten to tell me about

Chick's Drug Store and Mr. Blake's Deli, so it was possible that other surprises were coming up. I hoped not.

To the west, the sky was turning the kind of blue you would find on a parrot. Children played on Seaside, pulling wheelies on their bikes and making up their own games. Mom came down the front steps wearing a white dress, a beige net bag over one shoulder and sandals that showed off her painted nails and toe rings. Two strings of beads hung around her neck and glowed against her skin.

Dad was behind her, wearing his wide-brimmed straw hat, a dark blue shirt with a white collar and pockets, loose fitting pants and blue boat shoes. Grandma Ruth had on a thick, ivory knitted sweater that she had gotten while on a trip to Ireland with grandpa.

Liz and Crystal were last to appear, no doubt trying to impress everyone with their outfits and fashionable lateness. Lizard was wearing a pair of denim shorts with the rainbow belt she loved so much and a t-shirt with a faded *Ziggy Stardust* decal on it. Crystal had on orange shorts, a white half top and flip-flops. I didn't think mom would say anything, but she must have noticed that the girl's shorts were so tight you could practically count the number of teeth in the Goody combs in their back pockets.

"It's still early in the summer, you know," she warned. "The night still gets cold." I guess that was her way of saying put on more clothes, but she sounded silly even to me and Liz rolled her eyes before they both turned and began walking.

Hope

Jamie and Nicky were already far ahead, at the ramp of the boardwalk, arms out and balancing on the railings.

A cloud of seagulls rose from the sand and glided over the ocean. Some broke off and turned, soaring above the boards. A woman appeared around the corner of the Vermont Apartments, wearing a white rag over her tangled hair and holding a brown paper shopping bag. She sat down on one of the peeling blue wooden benches and began tossing crumbs of bread as if she were spreading seed. Pigeons and gulls swarmed and fought over them, crying to each other.

Down Vermont Avenue I noticed that a few of the houses, some that had been standing as recently as last summer, were gone. In their place were empty lots sprouting stubborn weeds. The burned out corpse of one building still managed to stand upright near Oriental Avenue. There had been a lot of fires in the Inlet over the past few summers and the tired old buildings usually went up like a box of matches when a blaze started. Some broke out from something as simple as bad wiring that had never been brought up to code by negligent landlords and occasionally a fire started when a family, freezing in the bitter winds off the ocean during the winter, used an unsafe space heater. Some were squatters who got desperate enough to try their own indoor fires. Others were the result of arson, either by gangs or owners looking to cash in on the insurance.

The boardwalk now made another soft bend to the right, curving around the squat brick and steel Golden Days Rest Home. Its wide balcony with black railings looked out toward the rolling ocean. A handful of people sat and stared out, watching the closing day. A few waved at us. One woman dressed in a long bathrobe and balancing herself on a cane, blew a kiss and I waved back, wondering how often, if ever, they had visiting family.

Past that the houses gave way to a quilt-like series of empty lots. It didn't shock me: it had been this way for quite some time. Still, the view always ran cold through me and made my teeth clench. The tide could roll in for a block and a half and not touch a single doorstep. This area used to be hotels, corner stores and hundreds of nice homes. How did it get this bad? How did anyone let it get this bad?

Ahead, as we approached the piers and shops, the sky above the boardwalk was lit with artificial white light. Familiar sounds reached me: the squeal of children on rides, the low rumblings of a hundred conversations mixed with the mechanical beeping of the arcades. We passed by the boarded up Virginia Theater which had been closed for the last three years. Randall and I had gone many times when we were dating and it was where we took Liz to see her first movie. The last theater still open on the boardwalk was farther down, the Strand, but there had been many more of them one time - years ago when going to the movies on the boards was quite a thing.

We looked in the windows at Fralinger's and gazed over rows of saltwater taffy and macaroons. Next door the warm scent of roasting peanuts flowing from the Planter's Peanuts store lured us. Mr. Peanut was out front, shaking folks' hands and waving to everyone who passed by. Customers made their way through aisles of souvenirs and trin-kets, all either in the shape of, or with the picture of, Mr. Peanut on it: salt and pepper shakers, glass jars, toy trucks, brightly colored plastic swizzle sticks, straws, Frisbees, plastic cups and t-shirts.

A conveyor belt ran along the ceiling, delivering a river of freshly roasted peanuts to a bin where they were quickly scooped into paper bags. I bought a small bag from a girl with bright red hair and pimples who blinked a lot when she spoke.

Across the boardwalk, Steel Pier reached into the dark ocean like a skeletal arm. The noisy arcade at the entrance looked like a great gulping mouth and young kids milled and smoked cigarettes inside among the flashing lights and sounds while they pushed quarters into the machines.

Max and I would race here every week to hear the bands or go dancing in the ballroom at the end. God, you could do anything there, see anything: the diving horse, the water circus, movies. If you mattered at all back then you played Steel Pier at one time or another- Krupa, Bobby Rydell, the Lennon Sisters. Abby and her friends went to see Ricky Nelson and everyone was worried that there were too many kids and the back of the pier would collapse into the ocean. It never did, but she swore that it swayed when everyone started jumping and dancing.

In the center of the boardwalk near the front of the pier, a thin, bearded black man wearing a tall red, white and blue hat was singing loudly to a small group of curious onlookers. Sweat gleamed on his hairless and dark, hollow chest. Faded jeans with the knees worn out hung off his bony hips. A radio next to him was playing Barry Manilow singing about how it looked like he and his love had made it and the man joined off-key and smiled at the small circle of onlookers. Occasionally someone approached and dropped some change into a small, plastic pail. Two police officers leaned on the hood of their cruiser, watching and chuckling to each other. The whole scene put a desperate and sour taste down in my stomach.

The girls walked up ahead of us and for a moment I could see Liz again with straight hair colored brightly with ribbons and legs not quite so long. A tiny, long ago laugh whispered in my ear and I caught myself waiting to see if she would turn, just one last time, to check that good ol' mom was still keeping an eye on her, that it was okay if she and Crystal were so far ahead, but she didn't. She leaned into Crystal with some private joke which caused them both to laugh and they vanished into the crowd heading onto Steeplechase Pier. Young girls dressed in tight tops and short-shorts smiled and waved at groups of boys who sat on the railing of the boardwalk and grinned. Whistles and catcalls sounded out.

I reached for Randall's hand as we passed counters lined with people waiting to buy soft ice cream, cotton candy and corn dogs. The rides on the pier were churning and lighting up the sky. The clack of the roller coaster and the insect-like sounds of the spinning wheel games of chance competed with voices crying through cheap microphones.

"Five chances for a dollar, folks!"

"Knock down the milk bottles and win a prize!"

"Shoot out the red star!"

There were walls of colorful stuffed animals of every size and shape, rubber frogs that leaped across plastic lily-covered ponds and water pistols that shot into clowns' mouths. The thud of baseballs hitting loose canvas and bells announcing winners flew from one end of the midway to the other.

Randall and I climbed aboard the Sky Ride while mom rested on a nearby bench. I looked down at the tiny people and giggled nervously each time the swaying cable car bounced over each support pole. We rocked gently, both kicking our legs like children. I leaned back and watched the lights of ships and buoys wink at us from the ocean. I got a thrill just thinking about the two of us, still nervous and exploring each other's bodies and minds so long ago. He looked wonderful, the way the light from below danced across his cheeks and the breeze pushed his hair just enough out of place, making him so sexy.

I leaned across and placed a soft kiss on his lips, letting my fingers run along the nape of his neck. I couldn't help but slide my tongue into his mouth and then heard someone clapping from the car behind us. I laughed and waved and Randall raised his hand in a triumphant fist.

I spotted Nicky and Jamie, looking small as they ran for the line to the Round Up. They passed from view and for a few seconds the car hung above the crashing black water and it felt as if I was flying. This was always my favorite part, but it scared me. The pier was no longer below us and the car still moved into the black night. The moon was low and threw glowing edges onto the skin of the ocean and to the right I could see the spire on Central Pier called The Sky Needle (the locals just called it the Needle). I smiled and closed my eyes, clinging tighter to Randall. The car swung around the last support and I let out a tiny chirp and we were now heading back towards the pier. I opened my eyes and saw the city again, the boardwalk and the grand old hotels, the march of people moving back and forth as if in a parade. To either side were the beaches, now looking thick and gray in the moonlight. Gulls crowded into the glow of lights on the piers and screeched to each other.

"She's still got some style, doesn't she?" I asked, nodding towards the glowing buildings and sounding like a proud parent.

"Yep, she's still beautiful," Randall agreed, smiling and looking into my eyes and I loved that I wasn't sure who he was talking about.

Jamie

Liz and Crystal were getting onto the Roundup and Nicky and I ran over, Nicky of course making sure that he ended up next to my sister. Crystal shook her head and groaned as they locked themselves in with a loose chain across their bellies. The gulls swooped and dipped overhead, vanishing and then reappearing in the pier lights like phantoms.

"Hey, remember that one time," Nicky said loudly, obviously so the girls could hear him, "that guy last year? They couldn't stop the ride and he went around so many times that he puked and because it was going so fast, when he hit the bottom his own puke landed in his face?"

"Oh, *Christ*, you are gross," Crystal snapped.

I laughed and roared, "Yup, and then he ate it!"

"You're *both* disgusting morons," Lizard added while Crystal put her hand over her mouth and gagged. "And that story is total bullshit."

The ride hummed and began to slowly spin. Soon our bodies pressed against the cracked vinyl padding and as the ride unlocked and tilted I kept my eyes set straight ahead and watched the world blend together. Nicky was laughing and hooting and to me it sounded like the best song I'd ever heard. The motor ground on, pushing us faster and Liz squealed. I fought the centrifugal force (Nicky would have called me "Poindexter" if he heard me actually say that) and pulled my head away from the padding and looked at Nicky. He was swinging his head back and forth and yelling, his hair blowing over his face. It was beautiful.

I cheered and then craned my neck to see Lizard and Crystal laughing with us. The one thing in the world that leveled the playing field and made things smooth again was a good ride. Everybody forgot what they were arguing about or what things had been said and just enjoyed the moment together. They should force leaders of countries at war to get on a ride together, that would settle things I bet. The world spun around me crazily. I laughed out loud. The Roundup could be the greatest undiscovered instrument of peace.

You never know.

Hope

Everyone gathered and walked back out onto the boards. People milled under the large, green-striped awnings of Haddon Hall, entering and exiting the shops with windows filled with expensive jewelry and cameras, new suits or antique furniture.

I looked up at the observation deck of the old hotel. A few faces looked back but not long ago it was filled with people who would hold glasses in their hands and wave down, shoulder to shoulder, at the passing people. They might be relaxing on lounge chairs, telling stories to each other while ordering fancy drinks from crisply dressed waiters who roamed the building with trays in hand.

The crowds grew and men deftly steered motorized chairs back and forth along the boardwalk. Bright yellow trams beeped to warn pedestrians as they made their way from Garden Pier to Convention Hall, a distance of about two miles.

In front of Woolworth's an old man pranced and shuffled his feet while humming into a green kazoo tucked into his lightly fleshed hand. He played "When the Saints Go Marching In" and tipped his small hat to passing ladies. Some joined him, clapping and laughing while he blinked and smiled. His brown eyes sparkled in the yellow light as he slid back and forth.

We passed the yawning concrete archway that led to Central Pier. Topping the entrance were small parapets with thin, slit-like windows and behind them the white tower of the Sky Needle ride, so tall it looked as if it reached up into the stars. The laughter of families echoed in the tunnel and the light from inside threw insanely long shadows up to the ceiling. At the end of the pier was a miniature golf course and the Lost Mine, a lonely haunted house with a menacing, huge skull of a steer with glowing red eyes over the entrance.

The boardwalk gradually curved and the grand hotels appeared: the Blenheim and the Marlborough (Max used to call it the Taj Mahal because of its domed spires and towering minarets), the Brighton was next, followed by the Claridge, the Dennis and the Shelburne. Hundreds of windows were dark where once they glowed every night. Now the buildings looked like ancient, sleeping giants. A Japanese family clicked their cameras, pointing and smiling to each other as they talked and snapped pictures of the buildings. They're smart. They know they probably won't be here much longer. I looked over my shoulder, forgetting for a moment that we had just passed the place where one of my favorite hotels used to be.

Before it was demolished, the Traymore stood like a stone goliath along the boards for almost seventy years. City officials had deemed it another decaying piece of property that had worn out its use. Jamie was only about seven when we took Liz and him to see it go. I asked mom and dad if they wanted to go but they both declined, holding hands and shaking their heads.

It took only seconds once the flashes started and the small explosions echoed off the sides of its sister hotels. Tiny white lights erupted in some of the windows and then she collapsed straight down as planned. After the rumblings died you could still hear the roar of the crowd and at that moment I wanted more than anything to believe that the applause was for appreciation to the building for a job well done rather than a cheer for so-called progress.

Jamie got scared because Randall and I cried a little afterward, when the dust had finally settled onto the streets and there was nothing left but sky. It felt like watching a friend get executed.

* * *

1944

We walk from the boardwalk into the lobby of the enormous hotel. This one was so big that it looks like a castle. I'm still not sure why we're here - mom and dad had said earlier that we were all going to eat at Carragio's. We always had Easter lunch there and I love it because it always seemed like people are having fun there.

My jaw drops open at the cathedral-sized room with its delicately carved stonework and arched ceilings. A huge green and black marble desk is in front of us and young men dressed in crisp red jackets and shiny black pants crowd it, holding tickets in their hands. They smile brightly as they move back and forth in an endless procession to the elevators, their heels clicking on the polished floor until they reached the enormous patterned carpet.

The lobby is crowded with people in colorful dresses and smart-looking suits. A bell rings out clearly and every time young men magically appear to carry large suitcases to the elevators.

Max leaps around the lobby and calls out his name so he could hear it echo until mom finally hushes him. I look down at my fuzzy reflection in the polished gray stone of the floor and make faces. Mom and dad lead us to a bunch of elevators and as the doors close two soldiers get on with us. One is taller than the other. Mommy coos to baby Abigail in her arms and nods to me and I politely ask the operator to take us to the second floor. Just like mom had showed me. Max mopes about this, always wanting to be the one to ask so he folds his arms and presses his lips together. What's the big deal?

Once the doors close daddy talks to the soldiers and they are very friendly. One was really handsome with a round face and a moustache and he smiled down at me.

I've seen hundreds of soldiers in the city: running on the beaches near the piers making pretend that they were attacking, some marching in tight formations along the boardwalk and some lounging along the railings and (for some reason) whistling at the pretty women passing by. Why don't the women turn around when someone is trying to get their attention? It seems sort of rude. Still other soldiers – some even without arms or legs - sat in wheelchairs outside Haddon Hall, the hotel that mommy says is now a hospital. Big guns have been put on top of some of the buildings and there are even cannons pointed out to the ocean!

Max told me that there might be German submarines in the ocean and that some of the men were here because they got hurt and some were getting ready to go fight in the war. They might go to Africa or Japan or Germany.

"Why are they going if they can get hurt?" I asked and scratched my chin.

"That's where the fighting is," he answered.

"Why are they fighting?"

He thought a moment. "Well, remember when you and Shirley Brigham got into that fight last week and you said she wasn't your friend anymore?" he asked and I nodded. "Well, countries can get into fights also and when they do, they send soldiers to fight for them."

"But why are they fighting?" I asked again and Max stared a moment before shrugging his shoulders. He told me that soldiers even sometimes die but I just couldn't get it into my head.

"We were in the Belgian Congo," the smaller of the two soldiers says to daddy's question. The men say that they are engineers and mentioned a number after that - thirty-eighth something. "Glad to be back here, I can tell you." I wonder which one drives the train.

The round-faced man adds, looking down at me and Max, "The Belgian Congo is in Africa."

Max says he knows that but I can tell he doesn't. I picture bright green jungles with swaying trees filled with screeching monkeys and leaves as big as cars. Men wearing tan helmets like the explorers in the movies travel carefully behind dark-skinned guides and are followed by silent beasts that carry all their supplies.

Mommy asks them a few more questions that I don't understand and the elevator doors open.

A huge dining room is before us and I gasp. Waiters and waitresses glide from one crowded table to another, balancing trays and looking like they're dancing around each other. We walk onto the plush carpet and I look at the thick columns and framed painting on the walls. So fancy!

Daddy waits near a tall table that has a thick book on it. Brenda is giggling and spinning in a slow circle with her arms out. I take her hand to stop her because I can tell she's going to fall down soon. She loves getting dizzy. One time she did it so much she threw up.

A thin, mustached man dressed in a shiny black jacket approaches and pushes his blonde hair back with his hand. He smiles but it looks sort of fake. His cheeks are pinkish and his nose twitches a lot. His jacket seems too small for him and his Adam's apple bobs up and down while he talks.

"How many, sir?" he asks in a funny voice that sounds snooty and I bunch up my face because it sounds silly and mommy has said it's rude to laugh at people unless they are trying to be funny.

Max says, "But I thought we were- "

Mommy quiets him politely and takes his hand. I keep hold of Brenda's hand because she's teetering. I hope she doesn't get sick.

"Reservation for six, Weathers is the name," daddy answers. I watch while the man traces his finger down the page of the large leather book. I glance and can see that there are already a few people waiting and that every table is filled. Maybe there is an even bigger room somewhere?

The man asks again for daddy's name and writes it down with a fancy black pen. A white-jacketed waiter with curly brown hair quickly comes up and whispers into his ear and the man nods, looking sort of angry before smiling again.

"Is the wait long?" daddy asks and puts his hand on Max's shoulder.

The man looks at his watch and to the book. "It should be about twenty, maybe thirty minutes, sir. I'm very sorry about the confusion."

Daddy shakes his head. "Well, we did call ahead and in my line of work, time is important. We'll go find another place that's not quite so busy. Thank you." Mommy nods politely to the man and we walk back to the elevator. When the doors close both mommy and daddy chuckle.

"But I thought we're going to Caraggio's," Max finally asks in a whiny voice.

"We are sweetie," mommy answers. She hands Abigail to daddy and picks up Brenda, kissing her, "but sometimes it's fun to pretend." I look over to Max, but he just shakes his head and shrugs.

Carragio's is on Massachusetts Avenue. It's always loud and always smells great. Looking out the large glass window I can see the cars moving down Atlantic Avenue. A heavy man dressed in a white shirt with some stains on it takes our order. He tells jokes, laughs a lot and tells one *of the young boys to bring us extra bread. The man knows daddy from driving his jitney.*

I try flounder for the first time and love it. With my fork I pull apart the flaky, white flesh and savor every bite. Mommy orders a plate of shrimp and Daddy orders mussels. He also asks for oysters and shares them with Max. Max swallows two in a row and smiles smugly when he sees me scrunch up my nose.

"Betcha can't eat one," he whispers across the table. I close my eyes, turn away and let my tongue hang out of my mouth.

"C'mon, it's no big deal," he says, sounding friendlier and picking up another. He holds it to his lips, his blue eyes shining and his wicked grin softening to a real smile. I look at him and then at Brenda who was trying to find out if a french fry would fit in her nose.

"Same time?" I ask, still not sure but slowly picking one up. It looked like something that wasn't even finished, just blobby and yucky. Something that might come out of Brenda's nose.

"Here, wait, wait," he says and squeezes some lemon juice on my oyster. He then puts a drop of cocktail sauce on top of that! I look at him like he's nuts. "It helps a bit for your first time," he smiles.

"Really?" I think maybe Max is playing a joke on me but daddy would never let him do that. I look up from the wet, gray thing in the shell to Max's face and know right then that he is telling the truth.

"Ready?" he asks and I look into his eyes and immediately nod. "One, two, three!"

It slides down my throat and is gone before I know it. I lower my head and mommy claps.

Max gushes. "See? It's never as bad as you think it's gonna be, right?"

"Nope," I say, smiling back but suddenly I feel a deep, watery flavor climbing out of my stomach and into my throat. I let out a loud burp and my eyes start tearing up. The people at the table next to us start to laugh and daddy hands me a glass of water and chuckles, "You two, I tell you…"

* * *

Hope

After an hour of rides on Million Dollar Pier we walked to the end and was surrounded by the aroma of the Italian Village: sweet peppers, sausage, and pizza. We ordered lemon ices and as we sat together I admired the spin art I had done in one of the booths and decided to hang it in my classroom next year.

Nicky sucked from the paper cone and I saw him watching Liz out of the corner of his eye. She was ignoring him, busy pulling her hair back while she clasped a ponytail holder between her teeth. He leaned over to Jamie. "So how much you got left?" he asked. Jamie dug into his pocket and pulled out a few wadded bills and some coins. "About four dollars," he answered.

"So, why do you call yourself Nicky?" Crystal asked suddenly. She leaned forward, resting her elbows on the table and flipped her hair over her shoulder with a flick of her head. I recognized bait in her tone.

Nicky's eyes narrowed and he looked unsure. "What do you mean? It's my name."

"Well, your name is really, what, Nicholas, right?

"Yeah, so?"

"So then why do you call yourself Nicky? I mean that sounds like it could be a girl's name to me." She looked over at Liz, who had finished tying her hair back. "Nicky could be a girl's name, right?"

Liz nodded and smirked. "Oh, sure, there's a Nicky - I mean, Nicole - in my class." She put on a sorrowful look, biting her bottom lip and then shaking her head. "Poor, poor, ugly girl."

"It's not a girl's name," Nicky said and crumpled his cone. "And so what, you call yourself Crystal, right?"

"That's because it's my *name*, idiot." Crystal answered and cocked her head to the side.

Liz nodded and put her arm around Crystal's shoulder. "She's right, you know. Your name is one of those where you don't know if you're talking to a boy or a girl."

"Shut up," Jamie snapped. "Nicky is a boy's name."

Liz ignored him. "You know, names like Nicky, Dana…Fran, Pat…Sandy." She leaned into Crystal and grinned, "Oh, and *Jamie*." Crystal broke out laughing and gave Liz a high-five.

I let out a tired sigh. I should have known that a whole evening together would be too much for Liz and Jamie without them firing some shots at each other. "C'mon guys, we've had a good time. Let's not end the night with a fight, okay?"

Nicky pressed his lips together, the skin around his mouth going pale as he looked to Crystal. "His name is *James*, got it?" He wouldn't aim an attack at Liz - I knew that he liked her too much for that.

Crystal's eyes went wide in mock confusion and then she popped her gum. "Then why does he call himself Jamie?"

"James *is* a boy's name," Liz said, nodding, "but *Jamie* sounds like a girl if you ask me. Isn't that the Bionic Woman's name or something?"

"Shut up," Jamie said.

"It's like that guy, the one who lives around the corner," Crystal said. "What's his name, Robin?"

I knew whom they were talking about: Robin LaRocca. He lived in a small house on New Hampshire Avenue with his mother. We got to know each other one morning as I passed his place while he was busy working on his wonderful, if small, garden. I had been admiring his tiny plot of begonias and lilies for quite some time and stopped to compliment his obvious devotion and he jumped at the chance to talk flowers. I loved his enthusiasm and before I knew it I was asking his advice on our yard and he was more than happy to oblige. What started as a casual conversation turned into a warm friendship and a weekly coffee and pastry morning. We would take turns providing the baked goods and as good as he was at gardening, I think I was a bit better at the baking. I hadn't had a chance to stop by yet and was silently praying that he and his mother hadn't moved away like half the neighborhood.

Nicky curled his lip in disgust, "Aw, that guy? He's a queer!"

They all erupted into laughter.

Before I could stop myself I slammed my hand down on the table.

"Alright, enough!" I barked. "Go find something to do, all of you. And Nicky," I said sharply, more sharply than I had intended. "Next time, keep your mouth closed unless you know what you're talking about." He looked at me the same way he did long ago, uncertain, like when I held a secret out to him in the palm of my hand and my heart broke a little seeing that.

"Um, okay," he said slowly.

I kept my eyes on them as they filed away quietly. Nicky took a last quick look over his shoulder before he and Jamie mixed with the crowd and vanished. I pulled a cigarette and lit it with a trembling hand. I don't think I had never talked to Nicky that way before and it looked like it caught all of them off guard. Randall wrapped his arm around me, "They're so young they don't know any better."

"Goddamn," I muttered and blew into the air.

Jamie

Nicky and I carried blankets out on the deck and a cool salty breeze was coming off the ocean. We pushed two old plastic lounge chairs together and covered ourselves. It might have been summer but the nights still got chilly. I looked toward Benita's building and thought I saw a silhouette pass by her window and felt my stomach jump.

Nicky reached down to the radio and turned the dial until he found a station. Jackie Blue was playing and he made a face but kept it on. The distant squeal of tires told us that there was a race on a nearby street, probably Oriental Avenue. As quickly as the sound came it was gone and I wondered if it was the orange car with the stripes from the other day.

"There," Nicky said and pointed up. A short-tailed white streak crossed the sky above us. He smiled.

"One for you," I agreed and followed it until it fell from sight. The sound of crickets hummed in the air. The pink yellow glow from the streetlamps threw light over us and I could see the tiny hairs on Nicky's upper lip, chin and throat.

"Are you shaving yet?"

He hesitated. "Uh, huh."

"You're so full of shit," I said and looked back up.

"How would you know?"

"'Cause you waited before you answered."

"Who are you? Fuckin' Baretta?"

That cracked us up but then I had to shush him, pointing to my folk's window above us. "I'm right, though, ain't I?"

"Well, Gary says that he'll show me how when I'm ready, you know? It'll be soon, man."

"Cool."

He quickly aimed a finger to the sky again. "There, another one."

I peered and only saw a tiny, blinking light moving from east to west. "That's a plane, man."

"No way, that's a shootin' star, brother, just like me," Nicky said, smiling and folding his hands on his chest. "Sure it is. That's two for me, Jackson."

I didn't really care and couldn't help but grin. I was just happy to be here, sitting next to Nicky with the black night air blowing around us and the sounds of the neighborhood bouncing off the walls of the dirty old buildings. I know it was a strange friendship. We hardly ever called each other during the school year, after I went home to Philly and Nicky's family rarely came up to visit. Some friends would have to get to know each other all over again every summer but it wasn't like that at all with us; we always picked up right where we left off. It was like there wasn't a place other than where we were right then. We hardly ever talked about what went on during the other three seasons of the year and when I thought about it I was really glad that Nicky didn't live in Philly. It wouldn't have been so special to see him.

Nicky *was* summer to me.

The DJ came on. "WJJD! The sound for the shore! The sound FOR sure! We have the screeches that reaches the beaches!" A thick, man's voice with a Spanish accent interrupted and spoke, "Oh, yeah...I love the beaches, man!"

We chuckled, high-fived. I went inside to salvage what remained of the peanuts we had bought earlier that night and we started cracking shells and pinching off the red, papery skin.

"Adrienne Barbeau," Nicky said.

"Absolutely," I answered. "Suzanne Somers?"

"Oh, yeah." He chewed a peanut as he thought. "Um... Valerie Bertinelli?"

"Are you kidding?" I said and sighed. "Farrah Fawcett."

"Oh my God, do you even have to ask?"

I could hear Liz' stereo through her window and felt my eyes glazing over as Nicky continued naming girls.

"I really missed you, man," I mumbled and turned on my side. The radio was playing Hotel California and my voice sounded distant as I felt myself slipping away. I was nowhere near school and its popularity contests. I was safe now, in the town where I was born and next to my best friend who would never judge or tease me. Nicky and I were Starsky and Hutch, Bandit and Snowman and Butch Cassidy and the Sundance Kid all wrapped into one. *Or was that wrapped into two? And we have another whole summer in front of us again.*

"Aw, shit, don't get all girly on me," Nicky said. "So what do you want to do tomorrow?"

But I was leaving and Nicky's words mixed with the sound of the crickets, the soft, distant crash of the waves on the beach and the voices of the streets at night.

Before it all ended, though, I'm pretty sure I heard Nicky say quietly, "I missed you too, man."

CHAPTER
6

Hope

I leaned over and kissed Randall on the forehead before turning on my side and enjoying how the pillow cooled my cheek. Beyond the bedroom window the sky was a deep, rich blue painted with light purple clouds - still figuring out what kind of day it wanted to be.

I already knew what Seaside Avenue looked like; a light mist, recently rolled in from the beach, would be filling the alleys and hugging the street, blowing slowly past quiet doorways. The metal and wood everywhere would be sweating with dew. It would burn off by seven, the street would clear and you would be able to see across the bay to Brigantine.

I rolled onto my back and listened. The boys were already awake and heading out to the beach. The front door closed with a clump and their voices dwindled until they blended with the waking sounds of the street: a dog barking angrily, probably tethered in some nearby backyard, a car starting.

I pushed the sheets aside and placed my feet down, letting the cooler air near the bare floor snake up my legs. Randall was lying with his arm out toward me and when I woke up it was already draped over my waist. He's always made me feel safe and loved, thank God. He always managed to touch me in some soft way whenever we slept together, every night, ever since we were still curious newlyweds. It might be his hand in mine or just a few fingers resting on the small of my back, but it was always there - his skin on mine.

"Did you ever notice that?" I asked him one morning just before Liz was born. He grinned drowsily and rolled to face me. He looked into my eyes and moved closer. At the time he was growing a short beard and I thought it was very sexy, especially the way it added color to his light brown eyes. He put his hand gently on my belly and kissed my nose.

"That way I know I'll never drift off into some dream without you two."

I walked to the bathroom, closed the door and turned to the full-length mirror. Not bad: hair tousled but looking almost as if it was part of a plan. Randy said once that he loved the "early morning look": sleepy-eyed and messed up hair and I tried to play shocked but smirked and admitted that I did too.

I brushed my teeth, grinning back at myself and then turned to the mirror again. My breasts, though not as pert as they were twenty years ago, didn't look bad for a forty-year-old woman who had nursed two children. I raised my hands up and was glad to see that my waist was trim except for a little roundness that had crept up when I wasn't looking.

Pretty damn sure Randy wouldn't mind.

I moved to the bedroom feeling bold. The window was now showing a small, gray blue square of light. It was comforting, almost a shroud and I pulled off my panties, shivering slightly before sliding under the covers and pulling close to Randy. I put my nose to his back and inhaled. He smelled like sleep and the scent ran through me quickly. With one hand I played with the hair that crept down the nape of his neck and then traced my finger down the gentle valley of his spine. I placed the other around his waist and gently stroked the skin of his belly and chest. He stirred and moved his shoulders, still in a half sleep. My hand created small circles across his stomach, moving steadily lower.

As much as I loved summers at the house with the quietness after months of children and the freedom that each day brought, I missed Randy terribly during this time of year. The bed felt too big and I was so thankful that he happily slogged through weekend traffic every Friday night to get here.

I slid my fingers under his waistband and reached him and his body reacted quickly, the muscles in his stomach tensing. He rolled over and blinked the remaining sleep away. I raised myself up and climbed on top of him with my hand still on him, moving slowly. He smiled and opened his eyes fully to take me in. I slid him inside and he opened his mouth to speak but I put a finger to his lips.

"Shhh…"

I let Randy fall back to sleep and took a shower before putting on a pair of baggy shorts and Randy's old U of Delaware sweatshirt (forever spattered with flecks of white and red paint) before going downstairs for coffee and a smoke.

The walls of the porch were built five years ago after dad found a drunk sleeping next to the morning paper. I still hated them - they cut the view of the boardwalk and narrowed the rays of light in the morning. Still, it was dad's decision and he was the one living where the crime rate had become a factor in neighborhoods where it really wasn't before.

I sat and pulled my feet up, stretching the sweater over my bare knees and gazing out the window. A young woman walked down the street and I imagined she was on her way to work because of the way she was dressed. I didn't recognize her, but that was nothing new – there were so many people coming and going from summer to summer it was hard to keep track. There were only a few regulars left - neighbors who had become familiar over the years and some who had become friends like Charlotte and Evalisse. It was nice seeing them yesterday even if it was only for a few moments - it added a sense of continuity which felt so needed these days. In the back of it all there was always the chance someone might pull up stakes and get out of dodge.

The right offer…the right time…

I went into the kitchen and poured another cup. The window above the sink was open and letting in a cool breeze. I reached in my pocket and felt for the piece of folded paper. Still unopened and may just stay that way. Still, it felt important to keep it near me and I seem to be shoving it in my pocket almost unconsciously. I pulled it out to read the name again, as if it would have changed magically over the last few days. I stuck it back deep in my pocket and climbed the steps to the upstairs deck.

Right now Jamie and Nicky were tramping across the cool sand in the gray blue day and it seemed so truly unfair that they won't be able to do that every morning for the rest of their lives. Life isn't like that, but it really should be because that's how important those moments are. You're with your best friend and nothing else in the world matters. Still, those moments come to an end and you never know when in your life that will happen. Sometimes it's gradual and an almost painless slipping away like the grade school friends we had that were so important to us at that time but we barely think of anymore. Others are sudden and terrifying like when you lose your best friend, your brother, because he was killed.

* * *

1947

I love the early mornings with Max while the sun is still below the horizon like it's hiding, maybe ready to surprise us. We walk by the striped awnings and open porches of our neighbors, both of us carrying small tin pails, and I am eagerly wondering what we might find on the fresh, wet sand as the ocean offered gifts for us to discover like it does every morning.

As we pass the Schuler's house Max whistles at the new bright yellow car in their driveway. He's just learned how to do that and it seems like he's whistling about everything. I tried to do it but nothing comes out but air. I'm glad he didn't hear me try or that if he did hear me he didn't say anything.

We cross the boardwalk and I can see a group of men in the water, whipping long poles over their shoulders and letting small waves splash against their legs.

I'm thinking of something smart to say when Max races ahead and throws himself off the steps that go down to the sand. He shouts loudly and then vanishes from sight. I follow at a slow walk and stop at the top.

Max picks himself up and turns to me. He brushes the sand from his knees and then puts his hands on his hips, waiting.

"Aww, don't be such a drip!" he says as he stands at the bottom of the wooden steps, both of his feet sunk in sand up to his ankles. He crosses his arms and tries to look bossy but I just stand there staring back at him.

"I am not *a drip," I answer, slowly saying each word.*

"Yeah, you are," he says, his head bouncing with each word, "'cause you're scared."

I know he's trying to get me to do what he wants but still...this isn't like trying an oyster.

The boys from the neighborhood had all been daring each other to jump from the top step down to the beach like it was some sort of dumb test and Max had been at me for days to do it. It seemed much too high - eight whole steps. That seemed like a cliff to me.

"Look, I jumped from the fifth one, right?" I yell, hating the way my voice sounds - like I was asking for a free pass. I'd hoped it would make him clam up if I made the jump from the fifth step last time, but all I got was a sour look from him and a mouthful of sand for my trouble.

"Yeah?" he answers and scrunches up his lips as if thoroughly unimpressed.

"Well, that's pretty high!"

"Aww, I jumped from there way long ago!"

"So? You're older!" I finally snap and stamp my foot. Max is already ten and even though I'm nine, the gap between us seems to be stretching with each year. Sometimes he acts so much older than me and, apparently, ten is an important year, or so I hear many times from friends.

Max sighs, unfolds his arms and looks out to the ocean. The sun is just beginning to show itself. It brightens his blonde, short-cropped hair and sets it alight.

"Look," he says and turns back to me. "You gotta do it, okay? Trust me."

"Why?" I ask, putting my hands out in front of me. "Why is it so darned important?"

"Because if you don't you'll be scared of it all your life."

I look at his face and can tell that he's being serious, but eight steps were still eight whole steps. "Jumping off a stupid step doesn't mean anything," I say as grown up as I can and walk down, pushing past him on my way to the water. He follows and moves alongside of me.

"And I'm not a drip," I add loudly, looking at him with the most serious face I can to let him know that I mean business.

He smiles. "Okay, I know," he says and puts his arm on my shoulder, "You'll probably do it someday."

"Probably not because it's really dumb. What if you twist your ankle?" I brush hair from my eyes and squint at the long black rocks at the end of the beach. "Think they're catchin' much off the jitney?"

"You mean jetty," Max answers, bending down to look at a dried orange crab shell. "You always get those mixed up."

"What?"

He looks up. "That," he says, pointing to the rocks, "is a jetty."

"That's what I said."

"Nope. You said jitney."

"Oh," I smile. "Well, which one does daddy drive?"

"A jitney," he says and drops the tiny shell into his bucket.

"That's stupid that they sound the same, huh?"

Max shrugs. "I guess so. What would you call it?"

"Which one?"

He points to the rocks

"I don't know," I say. "Maybe a rock pier or something, I guess." I scratch my chin. "Anything but a jetty."

Thinking about piers, I turn to the boxy tip of Steel Pier, which is visible now that Heinz Pier is gone. It was mostly washed away in the hurricane a few years back and it makes me wonder where my pickle pin was. I was always losing those but now I can't get another.

Dozens of clear jellyfish litter the sand, looking like the bottoms of soda pop bottles. I remember the thunder from last night and figure they must have all been washed up by the storm. It makes me sad to think they had no choice but lay on the sand and die.

Max picks up a piece of clam shell and pokes at one of the jellyfish.

"Ewww..." I say and lean in to look closer - I feel bad for them but they're still disgusting. "What does dad say? If it's red then leave it alone, right?"

"Yup. If it's red then it ain't dead."

"He never say 'ain't'," I correct him and jog ahead. I pick up a large black scallop shell with deep ridges and place it in my pail. "And don't bring it back."

"I know."

A family of gulls facing the ocean start squawking and Max runs at them, flapping his arms and I follow, laughing and doing the same. The feel of wet sand on my bare feet is wonderful and I watch the birds take off and escape over the ocean.

We fill our buckets and head to Walt's to pick up the morning newspaper for dad. Stephen, the oldest of the Bloom boys, ring us up.

"So, what did you find today?" he asks us, leaning forward on the counter as Max digs into his pocket. I can't help but let a wide lazy smile cross my face as I proudly hold out my bucket. Stephen Bloom makes me feel happy and silly. With his dark, short cut hair and big brown eyes, he is very, very handsome and I love his excited expression as he peers in. So adorable! Max, meanwhile, tries to act casual and big brother-like as he slaps down the coins for the paper on the counter. He likes that Stephen calls him "sir."

Daddy is on the porch with his pipe in hand and I race up the steps. Mommy is next to him with Abby on her lap and a sloppy bowl of cereal in front of them. Brenda is sitting on the floor with her favorite stuffed bear in her arms and I try to remember the last time I had seen her actually let go of it.

"Dad, dad! Look at all the things we found!" I yell as I hop up the steps.

He puts his long arms around me and laughs, pulling me close. The familiar scent of pipe smoke surrounds us and makes me feel safe for some reason. Why would smoke do that? The sunlight hits the lenses of his thick glasses and hides his eyes for a second. "Got some real treasures, this time, eh?"

"You bet!" Max exclaims and places the newspaper on the table.

"Let's find out what we have!" Daddy says and goes into the house, emerging a moment later with a large book with a thick black cover. He sits down and I climb onto his lap. He kisses me on the cheek and takes a small pouch of cloth and his pipe and hands it to me. I open up the pouch and hold the brown leaves to my nose and sniff before filling the pipe.

Mommy looks over and says, "Oh, I wish you wouldn't let her do that," but daddy just smiles innocently.

When I finish he strikes a match and takes a small pull on the pipe. He releases a curl of white smoke. "I'm ready, explorers."

I pull out a shell and handed it to him.

"Oh my, that, my dear, is quite special," he says as he flips through the pages and adjusts his glasses, "it is...Aequipecten Irradians." He hands me the shell and I put it on the table, looking at it with a bit more respect. It must be very important with a beautiful name like that.

"Aequipecten Irr...Irradians," I repeat.

Max holds up a long, bent oyster shell with a chip on the edge. He brushes off some of the grains of sand while daddy looks through the pages. He picks up the shell and then looks to the book again. "This must be very rare. I'm having a hard time finding it."

Max smiles brightly at me and I clap and grin.

"Ah, here it is! Crassostrea virginica! Wherever did you find that?"

"Right near the water!" Max gushes. He quickly reaches inside his pail for another.

"My turn!" I say and hold up a small, gray and white clamshell.

"Oh, wow! That one is very valuable, it is, I can tell," daddy says and flips through the book again.

"How is that one so special?" Max complains, "It's just a clam shell. We see them all over the beach."

"Are you sure?" daddy asks. Why does Max have to say my shell isn't that great after daddy made a big deal about his? Sometimes he can be such a know-it-all.

Max thinks and then nods. "Sure, there are hundreds and hundreds of them. I could bring back whole buckets of those kinds of shells and they would be just like that!"

"I'm not so sure," daddy answers and gives me a quick wink. "But let's take a look because we're scientists, right? Max, do you have one?"

"Yeah, but only 'cause I couldn't find any more special ones," he says and gives me a smug look before digging into his bucket. The shells scrape roughly together. He sticks his tongue on the side of his lip until he lifts a large shell and hands it over.

Daddy takes both and looks them over.

"See," Max says, "they're exactly the same."

"Well, let's be sure. What color is your shell?" He holds up the one Max had found.

"Um, gray with a little white."

"Hope, what color is your shell?"

"Mostly blue and some white," I say.

"Are they the same size?" he asks both of us.

"No, hers is smaller!" Max chirps before I can answer. He winces like he had just sucked on a lemon drop, realizing what he's just said.

"Right," says daddy. "So they're not exactly alike, right?"

"Nope," I squeal. "They're not!"

"I guess not," Max mutters and rolls his eyes at me.

"Now, you're right about one thing, Max. These are both clam shells, um," he turns another page in his book, "from the Mactridae family to be exact. They may even be the same species, of that I'm not sure, but just because things look the same doesn't mean they're exactly the same.

There are very, very few things in this whole world that are exactly the same. God doesn't duplicate anything and He doesn't make mistakes."

"Just like snowflakes!" Max says, brightening a bit.

"Yep, no two are alike, no matter how much they look the same."

I'm already back into my bucket to retrieve another shell. I pull out a long, fragile-looking rectangular shell that gleams in the light.

"Ah, ha!" daddy says, his eyes growing wide and his big hand slapping his knee. "I haven't seen one of these in years, look dear," he says and shows it to mommy. "Ensis Arcuatus!"

A wonderful smile comes to mommy's lips as she nods. "Astonishing!" Her blue eyes are beautiful and have a curious look that makes me giggle.

* * *

I covered my mouth with the back of my hand as the feeling passed through. I wiped at my eyes with the soft sleeve of Randy's sweatshirt and a wet streak ran to the corner of my lip, tasting like the saltwater so near. It was so easy to pull the memories from the darkness sitting alone on the porch where all those wonderful mornings ended: dad continuing to leaf through his book as Max and I each presented our treasures to him. That book looked so large, the largest I had ever seen and it was beautiful with big gold letters on the cover, "A Field Guide to the Shore." Max would stand on his toes each time dad announced the Latin name of their discoveries and I loved to see Max so happy, his grin unfolding like a sunrise across his lips.

The week of dad's funeral Brenda and her family came and she ordered Steve to bring the cots from the basement for their twin boys

Tim and Sean. They stayed in her old room – Orange. Abby showed up with a young man who she said was a sculptor. She met him in New York and she was pleasant enough but, of course, got into an argument with Brenda when she asked about where her "life plan." She laughed at her and I even thought it was an empty phrase (especially for Abby), but Brenda always had the idea in her head that because she was older than Abby it was her job to give her direction. I never heard what the answer was, but Abby said something that closed the door on further conversation. She stayed with the sculptor in her old room as well.

And I tried to hold it all together. Thankfully, Randy kept Jamie and Liz busy so I could be there for mom, who instinctively went to me for advice and just to cry. We'd hold each other and wait until the sobbing ended and of course we would eventually start laughing over some silly story: the time dad painted the railing of the front steps and in the time it took to make a sign to warn about the fresh paint, all four children had leaned against it and were unaware that they each had a bright white stripe across their rear ends. He decided to let us go to school and discover it for ourselves. That story never failed to bring a smile to her face.

The funeral brought folks from all over the Inlet. Dad being a jitney man and former trolley man, had lots of work associates who adored him. We drove out to Pleasantville and buried him next to his mother, father and son. And that was it. Just like Max except that we put Max's death in a locked closet and for twenty years no one seemed to have the key. I think that even if we had the key it as was too dark for any of us to look into, maybe it was because he was taken too soon or too violently.

And now Stuart had a letter from Max that I knew was going to pull me back to that breezy evening when I had a chance to be there for him but couldn't. No, that's not quite right - wouldn't. I tried to force the thought aside, but it hung in my mind like ugly curtains. I had been cruel – and selfish – about the whole thing but, Jesus, I was only seventeen at the time! How much could he have expected from me? I only wished that I'd had time to tell him I was sorry before that night.

By nine o'clock the party preparations were in full swing and Randy was trying to unearth the grill from the basement. Nicky and Jamie were setting up a large round table in the backyard and placing folding chairs around it. I smirked as Jamie smiled and waved awkwardly to Benita and her mother when they showed up.

Benita was given the job of stringing the lights across the yard while Evalisse immediately set about helping me in the kitchen. "Girl, if you're gonna put me to work, we need some music and I am not talkin' about any Osmonds shit!" She found a station playing Chicago and the two of us danced around the kitchen, thoroughly embarrassing the kids.

Charlotte came over at eleven o'clock and she positioned herself at the sink, shucking ears of corn. She ripped the squeaky husks off with her powerful hands. Evalisse sat at the table with mom making skewers of beef, slivers of onion, whole mushrooms and cuts of green pepper and set them on a long plate.

"I tell you what, girls," Charlotte said roughly, speaking past the cigarette hanging out of the corner of her mouth and holding up a large ear of yellow, ripe corn. Her eyes had become lecherous-looking slivers. "This is reminding me of somethin', know what I mean?" She stroked the ear from tip to end and put it into the pot before breaking into a bristly laugh. I couldn't help but giggle while Evie rolled her eyes and grinned. Mom let out a slight gasp that only made the three of us chuckle more.

I went out to the backyard. Liz and Crystal were placing covered bowls filled with chips and pretzels on the tables. The grilled sweet potato salad and pasta salad with olives, pepperoni and chunks of mozzarella would come out soon. Nicky and Jamie were filling pitchers of Hi-C and setting them next to bins filled with ice and cans of beer and soda. Benita had finished hanging the last string of colored lights. Evie called from the kitchen window.

"C'mon Benny, we gotta go home and get ready."

"Are you coming back soon?" Jamie asked her, a little hopefully I noticed.

"Sure," she said and captured her hair with one hand and rested it across her shoulder. "Mom just wants us to get dressed."

"You *are* dressed," Nicky said, sounding annoyed. He walked up beside Jamie, dressed in cut-off denim shorts and shirtless.

Benita's looked him over and then turned to Jamie, "Oh, I'm sorry, I meant she wants us to get dressed *nicely*." She turned, her long black hair whipping around her neck. "See ya."

Nicky made a face.

Well done, girl.

By noon guests were finding their way to the backyard through the house or the side alley. Randy first grilled the kabobs and then followed it with plates of burgers, chicken and hot dogs.

Pete Doran arrived. He was a heavy man, round in almost every respect and he wore crisp, sky blue shorts and old sandals with black socks. His fleshy, pinked cheeks were decorated with bushy, copper-colored sideburns and sweat had already begun to stain his white t-shirt. The red hair on his freckled shoulders glistened in the sun.

He had never been married and said that the longest relationship he ever had was back in '64 and that ended when she told him that she detested seafood.

"It would have never worked out after that," he would say with a somewhat proud look on his face. He had moved to the inlet in the fifties and bragged that he once received a twenty-dollar bill from Sammy Davis Jr. while working at the Shelburne Hotel. "He was a great tipper," he would say with a smile.

I sat cradling my glass of Cold Duck while Randall poked at the chicken on the grill. Shortly after Pete arrived, Danny Larmour approached with a burger in hand and launched into their continuing debate. It was their usual square-off.

"It's only a matter of time, now. You know it's true," Pete said and paused to take a deep pull from his can of Schlitz. He had brought a six pack for himself, "and a lot of people could make out real nice when this all happens, y'know?" He quickly took another long sip and nodded as if agreeing with his own argument.

"Oh, absolutely. But, by the way, a lot of people are going to get screwed," Danny replied bitterly. Danny had lived in Atlantic City all his life, born and bred like me. He and his wife, Roberta, inherited their house on Vermont Avenue from his mother who had worked at the Claridge Hotel for twenty-three years and died a few years back.

I remembered Danny when he was younger; pale and rail thin, being chased home every day by the other kids after school. He was incapable of keeping himself from being a target, but if there's one thing I hate more than anything it's a group of bullies. One day I picked up a rock and chased the kids away but I was pretty sure that he didn't remember. At least we never talked about it.

He never tanned. In fact, he may have been the palest person I had ever known. How could you live at the shore all your life and still be that pale? His silver round glasses often slid down the bridge of his sharp nose as he spoke and kept his right hand busy. He had long, sandy-blonde hair parted in the middle, combed behind his ears.

Roberta came over and gently touched her wine glass to mine before sitting down. Roberta was pretty in a very natural way: curly brown hair, nice figure, a smile that showed off dimples. She was wearing faded army shorts, a banana colored t-shirt (with no bra underneath - I couldn't help but notice and I'm sure the men at the party did as well), and large cocoa-colored sunglasses over her blue eyes.

"Sure, maybe, but more people will benefit than will get screwed." Pete went to sit, looked behind him and saw that someone had moved his chair away, and he straightened up with a sigh. "That's what I think."

"You don't really think that these casinos are going to put anything back into this town, do you, Pete?" Danny pulled the tab on his beer and smiled bitterly. "Tell me you don't believe that."

Pete shrugged. "Why wouldn't they? It would be in their best interest to invest."

Danny shook his head and a lock of hair came from behind one of his ears. He slid it back with one finger, "Even if they do, it'll be years, shit, *decades* before we see anything. And by then we'll all be gone, adios."

Pete continued, "Look, if you want the people to come and spend their hard-earned money in the casinos, then they're going to have to make it a nice place to visit, right?"

"I doubt it. They'll be more worried about getting the people into the casinos than whether they want to take a stroll through town," Danny said. "In fact, they'll all have their *own* entertainment. People won't have to leave the casinos for anything." Danny looked over at me and Roberta. "I mean, man, what if folks - God forbid - are tempted to go swimming in the ocean, right? I mean the casinos can't make money off it."

"Yet," I added and instantly regretted getting involved. Must be the Cold Duck. I looked around at the backyard: it was nearly filled with people, familiar faces who were broken off into groups of four or five, gathered around tables or sitting under the overhang and chatting, laughing. Gilbert Sullivan was on the radio whining about being alone again, naturally. Jesus, what a depressing song!

"And I wouldn't exactly call Vegas nice, you know?" Roberta added. "It's a desert."

Danny nodded enthusiastically. "Oh, and they're all going to make their money, obscene amounts either way. They always do. There will always be people who are willing to sacrifice their welfare checks or social security checks for a thrill but it's going to be a long damned time before we see anything from it," Danny answered. "Mark my words. Right now, the city just wants to forget about us back here, man." His pale skin glowed under the sun and his blue eyes looked paler for moment. He slid his glasses up the bridge of his nose again.

"Back where?" Pete asked, twisting his lips and shaking his head.

"The Inlet," Danny answered. "You know, the place with all the cheap purple and pale blue squares on the Monopoly board? The place we're standing on right now, man. Right, Randy?"

Randy smiled tightly but shook his head and focused on the grill. I don't blame him for not wanting to get involved.

"The same damned spaces they put up all the cheap housing and watch it rot like old fruit," Danny continued.

Pete shook his head. "Man, you are one bitter person," he said and looked at me with a slightly amused look on his face. "Isn't he a bitter person?"

Randy looked up, "Look, Seaside isn't even *on* the Monopoly board, but Danny's got a point. We have no say so where does that leave us? I heard newspaper delivery might be stopping. Is that right?" He began placing the burgers on a large plate.

"Yep, but not officially," Pete answered and blew a breath of beer from the side of his mouth. "So you go to the corner store, right?"

"That's if they can stay open, man," Danny said. "Chick's is already gone. You know there's gonna be more leaving."

"That's true," Roberta added. "And in some areas they aren't even picking up trash on a regular basis."

"Really?" I asked.

"Yeah," Danny said, "it's just another way to get everyone to leave. I'm telling you, they're gradually going to force everyone here out. I guess the idea is if they keep taking away services you eventually get tired and sell."

"To who?" I asked and took a sip of wine.

"Who knows?" Danny shrugged, "The city? I heard that some folks are buying up cheap properties and cutting them into six or seven one-room units and renting them. It's illegal of course, but who's going to say anything, right?" The sun fell behind some clouds and shadowed his face, making him look tired. "I tell you, the gold rush of '49 has got nothing on this place, man. All sorts of people are swooping in and throwing bread at people who know they can't do any better. If they say no, well, then the city will just wait them out. I mean, it's not going to get any better around here. Just wait until the property taxes go up."

"Well, what have you done about it?" asked Pete.

"What?"

"I asked you what *you've* done about it," he said, laying his eyes on Danny and then to the rest of us. "You know, everyone complains about the shitty-looking empty hotels and the piers that are falling apart, but when was the last time you ever *stayed* in any of the hotels?"

Danny looked at him, his nose pinched. He held his hands out, palms up as if offering. "Why would I? I live here."

"Maybe so, but it's that sort of attitude that brought all this on," he said and reached for a handful of pretzels from a nearby bowl. "Look, Atlantic City is unique. Always has been. It's not like any other place on the shore – it's not Cape May, it's not Ocean City, it's not even Wildwood. If these towns were a family, Atlantic City would be the loud sister who always shows up late at the party wearing too much makeup, flirts with all the boys, but *still* goes home with the best looking guy. That's what she does."

I loved that.

"She's always lived dangerously and over the top," he continued. "Name me another place that ever had a diving horse, a dog that water skis or a typewriter as big as a tank? How about boxing cats and dancing tigers? Everything *always* had to be bigger and crazier here. The problem with this town is that it always lives in the right now or the past, never looking into the future. A lot of these old, magnificent hotels are going to be gone in ten years…and they'll never build them again. And then a lot of people are going to wring their hands and start all their sentences with, 'remember when?'

Danny sat quietly, looking slightly like the boy I protected with a rock years ago.

"But people also came here because it was convenient," Pete continued. "That's why the tracks for the trains were originally put down. An hour from Philly to the beach was a miracle at the time. These days you can fly to Disney World, Miami or Vegas, for Christ's sake. People don't need Atlantic City like they did before. We all outgrew it."

"I haven't," I said.

Pete nodded and walked a few steps to an aluminum chair, pulled it close and sat down. The frame and webbed seat strained under his weight. Freddy Fender came on the radio, singing about wasted days and wasted nights.

"Everyone used to come down from Philly, you know, to escape the heat and all but now they have air-conditioning in their homes so, why bother? People have their own pools in their backyard so why bother with the ocean, right?"

Danny looked confused and irritated. "You think the reason the town is falling apart is because people are buying air-conditioners?" His smooth brow had become creased, "Or swimming pools? That's ridiculous."

"All I'm saying is that it's a factor. This place has been going down for the last fifteen years. It's just-"

"Ridiculous." Danny said and shook his head but I could tell that Pete was getting to him. Pete might be an ass at times, but he was certainly no dummy.

"Let me finish," Pete said and put his hand up. "I'm saying that it was a factor, just like the convention in '64. Everyone remember that? We had the national stage and we, the city, the officials, whoever, dropped the ball and we ended up looking like total assholes. Who the hell would want to come visit a city with old hotels, rude staff and even ruder cockroaches? If there was ever a chance to salvage something for ourselves, it was then, but once the word got out and everyone saw how much of the town was actually falling apart, well, we were done. I think that was the final nail in the coffin."

I remembered and Pete was right: The town was filled with reporters and their photographers with not much to do because the convention and the nomination itself was pretty much a given. Lyndon Johnson would be nominated and everyone knew it so all those intrepid and bored newshounds had to seek out fluff pieces, anything that could be of interest. It didn't take long for the story to become how far "America's Playground" had fallen.

"Hell, if you really want to add it all up," Pete said, glancing around and continuing in a hushed voice, "you would even have to throw in desegregation."

Even when I was young I knew that the city existed in two worlds: black and white. I had no black friends and you never saw black families on the boards or in the theaters or restaurants. They washed dishes. They pushed rolling chairs. They cleared tables after you ate. The Northside neighborhood, above Atlantic Avenue, is where the blacks lived, unseen by white people's eyes but close enough to be able to work the jobs that the whites didn't want to do. They even had their own Easter Day parade.

"Remember Chicken Bone Beach?" Pete asked and was met with silent nods. The beach at Missouri Avenue had become the beach for blacks. The only beach for blacks. I used to look out on it under the sun and was fascinated by the prism of brown: beautiful families that moved, ran, played and laughed just like we did. I wasn't sure how they claimed it as theirs but was glad they did.

Pete continued. "Back then, it was comforting to the whites that they knew where the blacks were. They swam on Chicken Bone Beach and that was it. We weren't going to have to swim with them, sit next to them when you went to the movies or when you ate dinner," he said. I felt a stab of anger at being included in that group but there it was and it was true. "Unless you chose to," he added. "If you went Northside then that was different, but if you stayed near the boards you were pretty much assured that you would only see happy white faces and tired black ones. It was like this place was built on matchsticks."

He took a breath and thought. "Believe me, I'm all for equality, but a sad fact is that the civil rights movement scared the shit out of a lot of whites around here and a lot of them left."

A moment passed and Pete added, softly, as if dreaming, "A long time ago people came here because they believed that the sea air was healthy. They thought it cured everything from rheumatism to diphtheria. Now it's not the air or the diving horses or the hotels with hot and cold running salt water or the piers because people don't care about that shit anymore. The casinos are going to bring them back. Face it, this city has always, always survived on the fine art of deception."

Danny just looked at him. His lips moved slightly but the words never came. Randall placed the last few burgers on their buns and whisked off towards the center table where people were gathering.

"I'm just saying that it was a series of events, not just one thing," Pete finished, looking at Danny and shrugging in an almost apologetic way.

I slid closer to Roberta who had turned away and was bobbing her head to the music.

"Escaping?"

"Yeah, a bit." She bent and reached into the cooler, pulled the Cold Duck out and filled our glasses. "Same damned argument, just a different year, you know?" She had a rough sort of voice that I imagined a lot of men would find sexy. "Sometimes I just don't want to talk about it anymore, you know. I can't do anything to stop it and when I think about leaving, it, it just makes me so sad."

I nodded. It did feel inevitable most of the time when you really thought about it.

"But Danny," she said, gesturing toward him with her glass, "well, you know him. He takes it as some sort of personal crusade. I guess I can't complain. I mean his passion is one of the things about him that I fell in love with." She crossed her legs lazily. "I just don't want to think about it if I don't have to."

"That's almost impossible these days," I said and sipped her drink, "but I hear you."

I couldn't fault Danny for complaining about something that was going to hit us all eventually. Opinions would be voiced, questions would be asked and answers would be argued, but the fact was that very few people would be able to hold out much longer.

The casinos were coming next year for sure. The citizens of Atlantic City had spoken and the city officials got what they wanted the old-fashioned way: they kept putting it up for a vote until it won.

Haddon Hall, which had been around for seventy years, would become something called Resorts and it would only be the beginning.

The exodus from the city's neighborhoods - Ducktown, The Northside and the Inlet among others - would continue. It had been happening for years and this just made it, well, official.

I looked up and saw Robin LaRocca coming down the alley, a warm smile on his face and a bottle of wine in each hand. He was wearing a beautiful white linen shirt that had a large colorful hummingbird above the right breast. He had a thing for hummingbirds. He wore sky blue shorts with a subtle pattern of crossing lines and open-toed sandals on his feet. He was handsome, with a face of tanned skin and gray green eyes under a head of brown hair that showed a touch of gray. He came right up and hugged me.

"Oh, you're a sight for my sore eyes," he said and looked around the yard. "Full house, huh?"

"Good thing all our friends are drinkers," I said and laughed, squeezing him again.

"Or alcoholics."

I started to apologize for not coming by his house yet but he dismissed my words with a wave of his hand. "Not to worry, sweetie. We'll catch up."

He handed me a bottle and I looked at the label. "Nice."

"Here's what will happen, darling," he leaned in and added in a whisper, "you and I will steal the first drink from it and we'll toast the summer and kiss passionately and make everyone talk, okay?" He had a mischievous look in his eye that I instantly adored and chuckled at.

"People will say that we're having a fling," I said. "Scandalous, no?"

"Not likely, darling," he said and chuckled. "I'm just hoping to make that husband of yours jealous."

"Don't you steal him."

"Wouldn't dream of it, honey," he said, waving to Randy and looking over to the table of guests. "I believe he is still head over heels about you."

"Let me get something to open this up and we'll have that toast."

"Now you're talking," he answered and took a quick glance around. "Where are those kids?"

"Well, Elizabeth is fifteen and that's all I have to say about that, right?"

"Absolutely," he answered, "and Jamie?"

"Where any self-respecting 12-year-old would be," I said and pointed up to the small roof below Jamie's bedroom window where he and Nicky sat dangling their legs over the side, watching the party below. I probably should have been more concerned but wasn't. He hadn't fallen off yet.

Jamie

I watched Mr. Doran and Mr. Larmour talking and was nearly hypnotized by the thick belt with a red, white and blue eagle buckle cinched around Mr. Doran's waist, forcing his belly to billow out above. Seems like everything was coming out in red, white and blue last year: hats, jackets, cars, books, everything. There was even a commercial where they were selling red, white and blue tires.

"Man, if that buckle goes," Nicky said, elbowing me and pointing, "someone might get killed."

I laughed and clapped my hands. "Yeah, good thing we're out of range, huh?"

Teddy Falso showed up with his parents and I pointed him out to Nicky. We started tossing peanuts down on him. The first few missed and he looked around cautiously as each nut hit the cement with a mysterious clack. I finally landed one on top of his head and he looked up and grinned and, making sure no one was looking, threw me the finger. He grabbed two hamburgers and a soda before disappearing into the house. A few seconds later he was opening the screen behind us and pulling his skinny body through the window.

"Make room, ladies," he said and pushed his way between us.

Teddy was a year younger than me but he had the kind of face that you could tell wasn't going to change much as he got older; wide-spaced eyes above a bent nose and a long chin on a flat face. I could easily picture him as an old man already. His upper lip never fully met the bottom one when at rest and it always gave him a look of confusion. He wasn't what any girl would consider good-looking but that was what I liked about him; as far as Teddy was concerned, he was a gift to girls everywhere.

"Shit," he said and looked down. "I wish I had one of these roofs outside my window."

"Why, so you could spy on girls, you pervert?" Nicky laughed.

"Well, that would be kinda nice, you know?" He took a bite from his hamburger, then handed it to me without asking and pulled off his shirt, revealing his bony, pale chest. He leaned into Nicky. "Did ya check out Mrs. Larmour's tits?"

"Of course," Nicky said and nodded, smiling. "No bra, either."

"No shit, really?" I whispered hoarsely and tried to get another look.

"So where's Liz and Cystal?" Teddy asked, grabbing back his burger.

"Oh, Jesus, not you, too," I sighed while Nicky chuckled and put his head down. "How the hell should I know, I'm not spending my - "

Loud and angry music erupted from the Natone yard. The suddenness startled everyone and a few people hunched their shoulders as if trying to duck out of something's way. I jumped slightly and Nicky laughed harder. The sound fell quickly to sharp static, then fell silent.

A few shouts could be heard, echoing across the yard on the other side of the house.

The gravelly voice of Bruce Springsteen came next, growing louder from multiple speakers. He was growling about the night, rat traps, and soul crusaders.

"Bet they're gonna have a kick ass party over there today," Teddy said. He stood up and balanced himself by putting his hand on top of Nicky's head. "Shit, I can't see anything."

Nicky punched his leg. "Why don't you go over there if it's so god-damned great?" he snorted. "Oh, right, I forgot. They'd kick your ass."

Teddy sat down. He placed the last bite of his burger into his mouth and worked his lips and tongue around the bread and meat as he spoke. "No, I didn't mean…well, you know what I mean. They always have chicks over there, right?"

Nicky shrugged.

I looked down and, goddammit, the skin on my neck got suddenly really warm.

Benita came in with her mother. She was wearing a flowered skirt and a buttoned white top with frilly short sleeves. Her hair was pulled back, held in place by a bright blue comb. She wore white sandals that glowed against her almond skin and her small toenails were painted bright red.

She looked up, somehow knowing exactly where we were, and waved. I waved back, but Nicky just nodded, unsmiling. Teddy waved, still chewing.

Teddy made a sound with his lips. "Boy, Benita looks good, huh?"

My stomach felt like it flipped over and now I was angry at Teddy. *What the hell?*

"She's fourteen, dude," Nicky said.

"In case you hadn't noticed, that's as old as you," Teddy answered.

"I prefer older girls."

"Oh, like who?"

Nicky turned to him and glared. He opened his mouth.

"And don't say my mom," Teddy quickly said, pointing at him before Nicky could say anything. He got up. "If the girls are going to be down there then that's where I'm at." He gave me five and headed to the window. "I sure don't see any up here, at least not pretty ones."

I watched Benita as she walked with her mother to a table. "What's your problem with her, man? You used to get along with her, you know."

"She just thinks she's so goddamn smart," he said and rested his elbows on his knees before flicking a tiny chip of paint off the roof. "People who think they're better than everyone else piss me off."

"Well, she is," I said.

Nicky sneered at me.

"I mean, *smart*, you know," I added and put my hands out, "You know what I mean."

The sun was beating down on my bare shoulders and watching Benita was making my belly roll. "C'mon, man, I'm bored up here." Nicky sat still and stared down at the party before slowly getting to his feet.

Downstairs, Julie and Debbie, two girls that lived near the Vermont apartments, had come over but their parents didn't. Julie and Debbie had been Benita's closest friends for the last couple of years. They magically showed up one summer and on any given day after that the three of them could be found huddling and whispering, usually with one or all three smiling and pointing to boys that they saw.

Debbie had lots of freckles and pencil straight chestnut hair that always reminded me of Peppermint Patty. Julie was smaller, had bright blonde hair that stopped at her shoulders, and was a know-it-all. She was always flirting with one boy or another. Benita never seemed to be as interested in flirting with boys as much as the other two. Maybe she didn't need to be. She would watch and join in the conversation but I never saw her try to draw a boy's attention that way. It was as if she knew all the boys were already watching.

Most of the kids had grouped on the stairs. Lamont Gray showed up with his father. Lamont was a smaller version of his father, with the same round head, brown skin and dark eyes. Both had full, black hair, teased out with a pick to a perfect circle which added a few inches to their height. Lamont was only twelve years old but I always thought of him as older.

Lamont turned and smiled, winking and pointing to Teddy, who raised his hand in reply. When his father sat down with the Larmours he grabbed a couple of hot dogs and squeezed past everyone to the top and sat one step below Teddy.

Benita stayed close to her mother, but I watched as her eyes wandered over to us. She would smile and then look away and each time it sent a warm rush from my feet to my scalp. Her mother rested her hand on her shoulder and included her in conversations and Benita would smile and listen. She seemed so much more grown up than the rest of us.

I tried to concentrate on everything going on around us, but always found my eyes moving back to her to see if she was laughing at something because I always thought that was when she was the most beautiful. Lamont was telling everyone about going to see "Star Wars" and I tried to listen but, like two pendulums, my eyes kept aiming at her.

She finally managed to drift away from her mother. "Hey, did you guys head down the boards last night?" she asked.

"Yeah," I answered. "They got a new ride on Million Dollar called "The Scrambler." I pushed the hair from my forehead, "Real nice."

"Eh, it was pretty chicken shit if you ask me," Nicky added. "Just about your speed." He took a sip of his soda. He threw his head back and gargled it.

All the kids laughed and Teddy erupted so hard that a piece of food flew from his mouth.

Benita wrinkled her small nose, "Charming."

"You should have gone with us last night," I said.

She shrugged, making it look simple and effortless. "We had to borrow my uncle's car to get to the A&P."

"She's about as much fun on the piers as a dead cat," Nicky said, looking at her. "You don't even do the rides. How can you go on the piers and not hit the rides?"

My eyes trailed down to her awkwardly beautiful legs and her painted toenails. When I looked at her face I saw something new sitting behind the dark eyes and for a moment I swear it looked like she was going to cry. The muscles in her cheek clenched and her lip trembled just for second. Her mother was keeping her in the corner of her eye and she finally held up her empty glass.

"You're mommy wants you," Nicky said. "Look."

She was about to say something but instead shot Nicky a withering look before walking away. I elbowed him and I know he felt it

119

because he elbowed me back quietly. Her mother's eyes fell like lead weights on Nicky as she handed the glass to Benita. He was now singing along to the radio, gargling his soda and Teddy and Lamont were grabbing their sides and howling. I couldn't help it and started chuckling.

Benita's mom's eyes traveled back to me and her smile returned, big and bright. I smiled back, but it left me feeling like a traitor for some reason.

When the sun began throwing longer shadows all of the kids decided to head to the beach. Nicky and I raced up the boardwalk ramp and jumped off the stairs down to the sand. Debbie and Julie charged a flock of scavenging gulls and sent them scattering into the air. Lamont and Teddy found a stranded horseshoe crab and picked it up by the helmet-like shell and carried it back to the water. I hollered about green head flies and all of us ran screaming and laughing into the chilly water.

Benita grabbed a clump of seaweed, flung it high into the air and it landed on Nicky's head. He couldn't resist laughing and fixed it so it looked like a wig and letting it droop over his eyes.

A huge wave was cresting behind us. Benita turned and screamed, quickly grabbing my hand. I reached for Nicky and we faced the wall of water heading for us. My hand felt so warm in Benita's that I almost lost my breath. I loved that there was still a place that the three of us could have fun and Nicky and Benita could leave their bickering behind. I saw her beautiful smile and excited eyes as she turned to me just before she was swallowed up in the white foam. She disappeared with a squeal. Nicky shouted and puffed out his chest, challenging the wave and was then gone. I was pushed to the bottom and felt Nicky's hand grip tightly, refusing to slip away.

As I struggled to stay standing, my feet digging deep into the sand and still feeling Benita's hand in mine a thought hit me harder than the wave: I was in love. I was in love with Benita. It was crazy but it was that simple. I held my breath and closed my eyes, surrounded by cool water and the distant rumble of the wave as it moved to the beach to die. The three of us had been pushed back by the water but didn't let go. They slowly pulled me up, the salty taste of the ocean spilling from my smiling lips. Nicky and Benita laughed and shook their heads and the water flew everywhere. They were both beautiful. The three of us let out a cheer and I looked at the clouds to the west as they climbed high in the sky and looked like purple cathedrals. The sun shot out rays from behind them and shadows fell across the roofs of the low buildings. I looked at Benita and she was in that special light, pulling her hair back and laughing as the ocean water spilled over her body like I had never seen before. Like silver.

Nothing was ever going to be the same again.

Goddamn it.

Thank God.

Hope

"I'm telling you, it's bad," Danny said to everyone and took Roberta's hand. He leaned across the table, his eyes slightly reddened and wearing a careless smile, but he shook his head slowly as he spoke.

Paper plates and cups were scattered around the tables and Liz's radio, now long abandoned, was murmuring. Stephen Bishop was singing about Jamaica and how the pretty women steal money and break hearts. As I pictured the singer (nice beard, glasses, cute) I sighed and looked up at the string of colored lights and they looked a bit fuzzy.

The song was suddenly depressing so I turned my attention back to the conversation.

"I mean nobody is coming here anymore, you know?" Danny said. His voice was weak and sounded a bit defeated.

Randy said, "Well, we are, right?" He smiled and defiantly crossed his arms, sitting back in his folding chair. I loved his optimism.

"It's been happening for years, Danny," I agreed. "No one is coming and everyone is leaving." I finished my last mouthful and got up from my seat, scooping up Evalisse's glass. I wasn't relishing another long discussion of how the city was falling apart. I just didn't want a bad taste in my mouth after a good time.

"So where does that leave us?" asked Robin to no one in particular. He sat back and draped his leg over his knee and rocked his foot back and forth. Lamont Gray sat next to him, his chin resting on his fists and staring into his drink.

I shrugged and poured, feeling a bit guilty but not answering. Robin was sweet and was just saying what everyone in the neighborhood was wondering. Still, it seemed pointless. I sat down and Evalisse rested her head on my shoulder and it felt sort of wonderful, the sort of unspoken comfort that can only exist between truly close friends. I put my arm around her.

I knew that we, the Shepherds, would be fine. It sounded insensitive but it was true. Randy and I had jobs and this wasn't our only home. Mom had at least one child that she could stay with, but I wasn't sure what some of the older folks around here were going to do. I had heard that The Golden Years Rest Home might even close by next year.

What the hell were those people going to do?

I was worried about people like Evalisse and Benita, the ones that always seemed to slip between the cracks when these things happen. Evalisse had always been very open with me and said that they had no savings to speak of; her paycheck always went to the next month's rent or groceries and it was always eaten up with nothing left over to put away. The odd jobs Evie picked up doing nails or hair in that moving salon that she and her girlfriends had wasn't going to help much, either.

What about Charlotte and the boys? I guess she was in better shape because she had a least some property.

Some others would be able to escape and move on if they chose to, like Danny and Roberta. Their lives would go on, but they certainly would feel the pain that comes from losing friends and trying to not let memories fade but they would be able to stay afloat.

Floating is very important right now. Maybe it's the best most of us can do for the moment.

"You know what I saw a few days ago?" Lamont asked. He looked up as if the words were written in the sky. "Someone had painted on the side of a house, 'Will the last person leaving Atlantic City *please* turn off the lights?'"

There were scattered chuckles.

I heard gentle breathing near my ear and smiled, realizing that Evalisse had nodded off on my shoulder. I thought of Pete's words earlier - how the whites began the stampede from the city and looked at the faces gathered around me. They belonged to people who had been friends for years, some very close friends, but it wasn't that long ago that this mixture of colors would have been unthinkable in most parts of the city.

But nobody thought much of it. Most of the time.

* * *

1949

I'm riding in the rolling chair between Brenda and momma. I would rather have Max ride with us instead, but dad said that we could only afford one chair and Max offered it to Brenda. He's such a good brother, much nicer than me. There was no way I was giving up my seat.

I'm very excited: we had been promised a trip to Steel Pier today, dad's only day off from driving the jitney. A Ma and Pa Kettle movie is playing and I'm hoping to see it.

Our chair is particularly pretty; bright, freshly painted white wicker with dark red cushioned seats and a curved roof. The seat rumbles beneath my bottom as it rolls along the boards. I wave to people as they pass and pretend I'm Miss New Jersey and that people envy me. Some folks wave back and smile. Momma, looking lovely in her long gray coat, gloves and dark hair pulled back, waves too, a bit elegantly, saying hello to everyone.

Max and papa walk ahead. Max is pushing Abigail in her carriage and he steals a look back at me and crosses his eyes. I want to laugh but stick my tongue at him and he smiles. I'm humming a tune and looking out at the ocean. It looks dark and cold today, the waves spilling in large rolls and I can't wait for the weather to warm up so I can swim in it.

I turn and kneel on the seat to see if there's anyone I know following us. I would love it if some of my friends from school spotted me in a fancy rolling chair! I'm startled, however, to find a face looking right back at me. Somehow I forgot that we were being pushed by someone.

He is wearing a light brown coat and a scuffed black hat with a wide brim that shades his eyes. He tipped the hat politely and his brown face smiled widely when dad paid him but after that he had vanished from my thoughts. Maybe I was too busy being Miss New Jersey.

I look at the chairs moving in the other direction. They're all being pushed by black men, both young and old. The man seems surprised to see my face as well. His eyebrows go up and his head jerks a bit which I find sort of funny. He smiles, showing beautiful, large teeth. His eyelids droop a bit and there are soft brown bags under his eyes, making them look forgiving. His cheeks are creased deeply around his mouth and a patch of black, wiry hair hangs from his chin and looks uneven. He waves one hand and I see knobby calluses on his fingers. His knuckles are large and the skin between his fingers looks dry, like it's powdered with sugar. I blink, smiling back and then turn around to sit again.

I pull my coat tight. It's getting pretty chilly.

"Momma," I start, looking at the other chairs lined up along the silver railing, waiting for riders. Most are paired with roughly dressed men of different shades of brown. Gulls chase each other away from scraps on the boards nearby. I scrunch my nose up in thought before speaking, "Is the man behind us a slave?"

Momma coughs so hard that her cigarette flies from her mouth and Brenda laughs at that, clapping her hands. Momma covers her mouth with the back of her gloved hand and papa turns around, "Okay, honey?"

Momma closes her eyes and nods before clearing her throat a couple times while I watch and wait.

"Of course not," she says in a low, froggy-sounding voice, "Where did you hear that?"

"Cynthia Hagel."

"School?"

"Uh, huh." *I pull a Necco wafer from my coat pocket, but Brenda quickly reaches over and snatches it.*

"Hey! Momma, she-"

"Never mind that. She's younger than you and doesn't know any better."

"But-"

"You've had plenty of candy. Now, what exactly did Cynthia tell you?"

I throw a mean look at Brenda, who had already popped the candy in her mouth and is chewing and smiling. "Um, she told me that all black people were once slaves."

"Well..."

"And that they used to be whipped and had to pull carts and all," *I ask, looking at her.* "Is that true?"

Momma closes her eyes. "Well, a long time ago, yes, there were slaves and, yes, they were black folks. It was wrong and it took a very bad war to stop it."

Boy, when don't we have wars? I think. "So...black people aren't slaves anymore?"

"No," *momma says and pulls a new cigarette,* "No, of course they're not."

"But what about the man pushing us?"

"Well daddy gave him money to push us, remember? He's earning money and this is what he does to make a living."

"He likes to do this?"

Momma puts the cigarette to her lips and speaks out of the side of her mouth. "We all have to do something, honey."

I nod but still don't understand. The men, almost every one of them black, are pushing heavy rolling chairs up and down the boardwalk like a parade and, though they're pleasant and they smile nicely, I still see something sad behind some of their eyes.

How can they like doing this?

We roll past candy stores, coffee shops, hotels, restaurants and theaters. The sky is cloudless so the boards are full of people; strolling couples, small, smiling families with running children all dressed in their finest, but very few, if any, are black.

"Why aren't there black people on the boardwalk?"

"Well," momma says, hesitating and taking a puff, "maybe they don't think it would be much fun for them."

"Um, hmm," I mumble, but something unpleasant rolls around in my belly, something that says to me black folks might actually like to walk on the boardwalk.

I mean, what wasn't there to like?

* * *

Jamie

Me and Nicky sat on my front steps. The street was empty except for the few old folks who sat outside enjoying the cool air. The feel of Benita's hand was still in my palm and I kept picturing her coming out of the ocean water and how it shined across her body. It sent a tingle through my body and I had to shift the way I was sitting or Nicky would notice and then I'd never hear the end of it. Still, the memory was distracting me enough that all I could do was nod at Nicky's words and gaze out at the black sky over the neighborhood.

"Ah, shit," Nicky muttered. It got my attention.

I turned and saw it too: Tony Tellori's white El Camino rolling casually down the street toward us like a ghost. As it neared, it edged to our side and I could hear the engine thudding under the hood and the tires crunching the sand on the street.

Seaside Avenue suddenly seemed very empty and the excitement in my body vanished. "C'mon," I said, tapping Nicky's shoulder. "Let's go in, man."

"Nope."

I looked to the car again and moved up a few more steps toward the porch.

"They won't do anything," Nicky said, eyes locked on the approaching car.

"Why take the chance?" I was more frightened than I wanted to admit. Some people did things at night with no one around that they wouldn't dare do in broad daylight.

"Get down here," Nicky snapped. "I can sit here if I want to. Fuck them, they don't own the street."

I took a deep breath and sat down.

The car stopped in front of us and rumbled by the curb as if waiting for us to run but Nicky stared straight ahead. The passenger window rolled down, pouring smoke and music into the air. Seth looked out at us, smiling like a cat while Tony stared quietly from the driver seat with that goddamned gorgeous hair of his. Mark Sespro sat in the back, watching with his hollow green eyes and Brian and Fat

Ass Chuck were tucked on either side. I could hear Fat Ass Chuck's squeaky laugh even over the music.

"Hey fags," Seth said in an overly friendly voice and someone in the car coughed. "Aren't you supposed to be off the street by now?"

I tried to concentrate on the song on the radio, some guy was singing about being back in the saddle while thumping guitars played behind him. Maybe it would give me the strength to keep from running up the steps. I tried to put Benita in the front of my mind but she was nowhere to be found. My feet were ready to go so I imagined I was in another place, far away.

"Curfew isn't for another twenty minutes," Nicky said, keeping his voice steady but low. "If any of you monkeys knew how to tell time you'd know that."

I sighed helplessly and focused on the song. My arms were shaking so bad I was afraid to move them.

"What'd you say?" Seth shot back and turned the music down. "Say it again, shithead."

Nicky looked at him. "I *said* curfew isn't for another twenty minutes."

Fat Ass Chuck chirped, "That ain't what he said, man."

Seth glared and moved to open the door but someone in the backseat grabbed his shirt. He waited a few moments and then his face softened like a mask and he smirked again.

"Well, curfew for fags is *now*. You bitches have to get your sore asses in," he laughed, "so you can be up bright and early to give dollar hand jobs under the boards."

Tony pulled himself out of the window on the other side of the car. He sat on the door and rested his arms on the roof. "Get the fuck inside, douche bags." Seth opened his car door slowly.

Nicky sat still and folded his arms on his knees. I wanted to vanish, to be anywhere than on the steps right now and was about to get up when I spotted Nicky's brother walking down Seaside toward us. Gary must have been coming from work because he was still wearing his blue coveralls. The sleeves were cut off and all I could see was salvation in his muscular arms.

"Nicky!" he shouted. "It's time to come home!" He stopped, put his hands in his pockets and waited.

Nicky didn't take his eyes off Seth. "I'll be there," he called back. "Tell mom I'm coming soon. I'm gonna hang with Jamie for a while, okay?"

Gary nodded and slowly turned back toward the house.

I wanted to scream and run after him but my legs were shaking.

"You know, you're not always going to have your brother to help you," Seth said, his teeth clamped together and his voice straining. "You better watch your ass."

"I thought watching my ass was *your* job," Nicky answered. I closed my eyes and started to pray quietly. Fat Ass Chuck let out a howl of laughter from the back seat and Seth turned on him and yelled at him to shut up.

Tony threw his half empty can of beer at us but missed by a mile before disappearing back into the car. As they pulled away Seth watched us and nodded.

"Pussies," Nicky mumbled. He looked over at me and smirked. "Man, you okay? You look like you just saw a ghost."

"Why the hell didn't you go in like I asked?" I got up and took a deep breath. "And why did you tell Gary to leave?"

Nicky watched the El Camino turn into Seth's driveway, then got up and looked straight into my eyes.

"Why the hell should I go in? I can stay out here until nine o'clock, right? Besides," he said and looked over as Seth and his friends got out. "Gary was going to leave anyway, trust me. He always said he'd make me fight my way out of shit like that. If I get my ass kicked then that might be something different, but until then he's not going jump in, okay? He said that's the rules of the streets, Jackson."

I was still trying to keep my knees from shaking.

"You can't let people tell you what to do," Nicky chuckled as he headed in with me, "especially a car full of assholes."

CHAPTER

7

Hope

Where the boardwalk curves deeper into the inlet, the waves roar directly beneath your feet and you can look across the gray-blue water of the bay and see the town of Brigantine. Locals line the railing and fish or drop their crab cages right off the edge of the wood. The slivers of sand are regularly interrupted by jetties and could only barely be called beaches. There are no lifeguards on duty on any of them from that point to the end of the boardwalk, about a half-mile north. Signs are posted to warn swimmers away but children still dive and splash among the rocks below. Moss-covered pilings stick up from the water and sand at odd angles like alien thumbs.

"I tell you, that girl is getting to be one serious day-dreamer," Evie said, breathing out a wispy, tired sound. Benita had wandered up ahead and was walking in lazy patterns; venturing from one side of the boardwalk to the other, lingering by the railing and gazing down at the splashing waves and then moving on and shading her eyes against the sun. I watched her casually shorten the distance between her and the boys and couldn't help but notice how it made the skin on Evie's face pinch with concern.

Jamie and Nicky sprinted ahead and peered into the buckets of the fisherman. Benita jogged to join them by the railing.

I went back to drifting quietly, hypnotized by the vision of the clear blue sky and the dark water and the line in the distance that separated them. "Who, Benita?" I asked, looking again to the young girl and I thought she looked like a fawn on new legs, slightly awkward but gaining confidence. She's really going to break some hearts. Probably already has and has no idea.

"Oh, Evie, she's wonderful and you know it," I said. "You've done a hell of a job with her; A plus student, polite, beautiful…you should be damned proud."

"Oh, I am," Evie said. She shaded her eyes and smiled. "I am. She's at that age, though, you know? Sometimes she's like four different girls in one day. Head in the clouds one day, practically a monster the next and everything in between."

The three of them had gathered around a battered ice chest and Benita let out a squeal when a white-haired man pulled out a large brown fish that bucked and struggled in his oily-looking hands.

"You know me," I smiled, "I'm a big fan of daydreamers. We need more of them. Jamie's a dreamer and his sister was a champ at it, but they almost always grow out of it. You remember what it was like."

Evie's smile vanished. "Don't take this the wrong way, baby, you know I love Jamie and Liz like my own, but…" she paused and looked at the cracked, boarded up buildings that lined Maine Avenue. "They can *afford* to be daydreamers. I mean more than she can."

"How so?"

"Oh, come on. You're one of the smartest people I know," she said. "You have to see what's happening around you. Around here, it's like everything is sick from cancer or something." Her face looked as if something foul had crossed her path and she put out her hand in the direction of a gray building on the corner. The old stucco had crumbled off the side and lay in a heap along the sidewalk. "You and the kids only see this place in the summer, when everything is just a little bit brighter and shinier." We walked past a handful of pigeons battling with small, hopping brown birds over scraps. Two children ran and scared them all into the air. "Trust me when I say it looks a lot different if you live here."

I looked around us, at the graying people who lived here and would probably die here, the neighborhood children dressed in ratty-looking clothes, some smiling beautifully and others with simple, confused expressions, the young black and brown men and women with worn, straight looks to their faces that seemed to mask a desperation.

"These people might look like they're just fishing," Evie continued, now pointing to the railing, "and it might make for a nice picture on a postcard if you didn't know any better, but most of them are trying to actually feed their families. It's not a casual hobby or something - a lot of them can't get decent work around here."

We walked a few moments in the kind of silence that was still natural between good friends who didn't feel the need to fill every quiet space with words. I knew she was right - the casinos weren't going to do anything for the people who lived here. Some might get low-paying jobs and maybe it would be enough for them to stay afloat, but for others it would just turn them into the birds I was looking at who fight for whatever scraps are thrown their way.

Evie took my hand and squeezed it. "I'm sorry, it's just that I have to be so careful with her, you know?" Her eyes went back to the kids and her face softened into sadness. "Do you even want to guess how many of my friends have teenage daughters who are already pregnant?"

I had never considered the question before. It was true I didn't know what happened in the neighborhood after the summer was over, at least not anymore. While the Shepherds were gone the ocean became bitter cold and the night fell earlier. The streets became barren and the boardwalk went into hibernation. I hadn't seen snow on these streets since I was a young woman. Whenever I thought of Atlantic City these days the picture always came trapped in perpetual summer like a reverse snow-globe.

But people's lives still went on. Things didn't stop because I wasn't here to see it.

"Four," Evie finished. "Four friends of mine have daughters who are pregnant. How's that for a future? The youngest one is only fourteen and the oldest just turned sixteen. Their mothers are going crazy and who can blame them? I can't let that happen to Benita," she said flatly. "It might as well be a death sentence around here."

I watched the skin on her face tighten, the cheeks becoming like glass and her eyes bright and alert as she watched Nicky horse around with Jamie. They ran down the ramp to the street and then raced under the boardwalk. Benita ran after them.

"Not under the boards, Benny!" Benita stopped immediately and, after looking at her mother, turned and walked back.

"You don't like Nicky, do you?" I asked. She looked disarmed at the question. She waited, thinking, and a sound came from her mouth that might have been a chuckle.

"Oh come on, Evie," I pushed on, "I've *seen* the way you look at him - Gary, too, for that matter. It's obvious."

Her mouth made a straight line. "Look, don't get me wrong, I think Charlotte has done the best job she could with those boys," she said and then nodded, looking down at her nails. "Gary was no treat even though he's settled a bit, but Nicky?" she said and shook her head and continued looking down the bridge of her nose to the boards, "he has a look in his eye that I've seen before and it never ended up being something good."

"Are you worried that Nicky might get her in trouble?" I asked, leaning close.

"Oh, *hell* no," Evalisse said, looking at me as if I had just said something in a language she didn't understand. "She wouldn't have anything to do with him, but I'll make sure he never gets close enough to find out, either. That's my job."

"He's only fourteen, Evie. He's just a kid."

"They *all* start out as kids, girl."

"Yeah, but..." I began, trying to find the right words. *Not all men are like Benita's father, you know. Not all men pull up stakes and leave without a word.*

I met Evie right after Benita's father - whose white skin had given their girl her caramel complexion instead of the mysterious dark beauty of her mother - left both of them. Evie had never talked about it much until one night while we sat on the deck and shared a bottle of wine.

"I looked out of the bedroom window one morning and there he was," she said in a voice that wavered, "climbing into his goddamned Monte Carlo. He even *waved*, the little prick. I never once thought he wasn't coming back."

She and Billy had worked at the same restaurant. She waited tables and he was hired as a short order cook. She said she liked his little boy smile and his long blonde hair. He made her laugh easily and the attraction was immediate - soon they were spending most of their days together. At night they ate cheap Chinese food and she braided his hair. When she became pregnant she expected him to skip out but he didn't.

"It would have been better if he did," she added.

They came up with fascinating, exotic names that they would never really pick but said out loud because it was fun. They got used furniture and hand-me-down clothes, but they were "crazy happy" as Evie put it. They painted their small apartment and they still laughed as much as they ever did.

As she got rounder, Billy would rub her belly as they walked along the beach. He would kneel before her and gently put his ear to her stomach.

"What's the weather like in there?" He nodded as if listening. "Ah, warm front coming in, partial clouds…and then sunshine for the rest of our lives."

He kissed her belly and then her lips.

When Benita was born, things were tough. Billy was working doubles and Evie earned what she could cutting neighbors' hair and doing their nails from the apartment while Benita cooed in her cradle.

Benita adored her father, chasing him on the beach and giggling hysterically when he let her catch him. He would laugh and lift her high into the air, spinning her until they both fell down into the soft sand, dizzy and laughing. It was Benita's favorite game in the world.

"Then came that goddamned Wednesday morning," Evie continued. "I knew Billy liked to gamble a little and it had never been much of a problem between us because he kept it small, at least as far as I knew. When he left I asked around but either no one knew where he went or was willing to tell me. It was only later that I was able to piece together enough of a story that he had lost too much to stay around in one piece."

She poured another glass and held it up, looking into it like a crystal ball.

"Benny was only three at the time and for a while I was scared that someone might come knocking on our door for the money but it never happened."

And although she had been dealt a near lethal blow when Billy left, she was not going to let him hurt her daughter. Benita was *her* girl, not his anymore.

"He gave up that right when his car turned the damned corner," she said and added with a weak bubble of a laugh, "and that was one beautiful car."

She and Benita moved quickly, wanting to erase any trace of him, and settled into a cheap, tiny apartment on Seaside Avenue and that was when I had met her nine years ago this summer. I loved her dry sense of the absurd and admired her bravery. It was obvious that she wanted nothing but the best for her daughter.

Evie cried a lot that first year and she would sometimes call me in the middle of the night and ask for company, her voice warbling and faint. We'd sit at the kitchen table, both in slippers and nightgowns and hold hands. Evalisse would melt against me and breathe deeply as the sobs would advance then retreat and I felt honored to be allowed to see her in this rare, defenseless way.

Over time Evie hardened and her soft features took on a smooth tightness that spoke silently against the tenderness that I had come to know.

"Look, Charlotte had her hands full," she continued, "I know that as well as anybody, but you just can't use that as an excuse around here," she said, shaking her head. "We all have it tough out here. I'm not trying to come down on her, you know? I like her."

We walked past more shabby houses sandwiched together in rows with ancient, stained stonework acting as crowns over their smudged windows. Up ahead was Hackney's, a one-time tourist destination that had been closed for a few years and now looked lonely and sad. There was a time when the parking lot was always packed with brightly colored sedans.

I glanced at the sand-colored brick apartment buildings with weary awnings that had shredded in places. A hollow-eyed old Hispanic woman was sitting by the window, looking out. The dull blue light of a television was behind her in the dark room. The houses and apartments all looked the same, occasionally broken by the appearance of a bar where men sat in the dark and drank cheap, warm beer. Two dogs were mating near an alley while children looked and laughed.

God, it's like they're all living in the corner of a room that no one remembers to sweep anymore because no one cares.

Starns was ahead and the years had been rough on the low, blue and white buildings and the docks. The boardwalk ended here – or started here depending on your perspective. Near the entrance was a large curved bone that, according to the faded sign in front, once belonged to a whale.

We were seated in a nearly empty dining room and Evie and I pushed together two tables near the windows that overlooked the water. A short, strong-looking woman with a small but sweet smile and dark straight hair took our order. I ordered a dozen oysters and Evie ordered her usual fried seafood platter. The boys ate ravenously when the food arrived, sharing a plate of shrimp and a large bowl of mussels while Benita absently picked at her crab cake.

"You're gonna be just bones like that whale out front if you don't eat more," Evie said in her deep, earthy tone. She took a bite of her shrimp and tossed the tail in a bowl. Benita rolled her eyes a bit.

A family glided by in a small, cream-colored Boston Whaler. A small girl with her long blonde hair blowing behind her was dressed in a colorful life jacket and stood proudly on the bow. A boy who was probably her older brother, with the same shade of gold in his hair, sat on the end of the boat and wore a black captain's hat.

I remembered that Max had a hat like that and grinned. I put my hand up as the girl looked my way to see if she could see me through the smudged glass but the boat plowed further along and then faded from sight.

Benita moved her food around the plate for a few more minutes and asked to be excused. Evalisse gave her a sidelong glance. "Where are you going?"

"I don't know," Benita said. "Maybe go feed the sea lions."

She looked down to the plate and then to her. She then reached into her pocketbook slowly and put a dollar bill in her hand. "Sea lions," she said, shaking her head. "You pay attention when you're feeding them, girl, you could learn something about eating."

Benita grinned and got up and I watched Jamie's eyes following her as she walked outside to the docks. He picked up another mussel, caught Nicky staring at him and quickly looked down as if concentrating on pulling apart the shiny black shells. When they finished they ran to the back door of the dining room.

Jamie

The scent of raw fish filled the air as we raced each other along the wooden piers. I grabbed the corner of the railing and whipped around, trying to hold Nicky back with one arm. He laughed and pulled at my shirt. We dodged folks, passing the quiet souvenir stands and the bait shop.

Benita was ahead, staring down into the water and dangling her legs over the edge of the dock. We slowed to a walk but Nicky pushed me playfully toward her and then stomped on the boards, scaring a nearby gull into the air.

"They're gone," she said quietly. She straightened her tan legs over the green and black water. Clumps of trash floated on the surface and collected near the pilings.

"What?" Nicky asked.

"They're gone," she said as she turned to us. The sunlight hit her face, brightening her skin a little but her expression was like stone. She looked tired and, for a moment, bitter like her mother could sometimes get.

I looked down into the empty pen.

Benita got up slowly and brushed the rear of her shorts. "The old guy in the gift shop said they got rid of them after the winter. They couldn't afford to keep them anymore."

"Got rid of them?" Nicky asked sharply. "All three? Are you sure?"

"Do you *see* any sea lions in there?" Benita snapped and pointed to the water, her eyes narrowing. Nicky opened his mouth but didn't say anything.

I put my hands out. "Well, maybe he meant they just sent them somewhere and they'll be back, you know?"

"They're not coming back," she answered flatly and leaned against the railing. I had a sudden urge to give her a hug but something, probably the thought of what Nicky would say, stopped me.

"Well," Nicky said after a moment, folding his arms and looking at me, "big deal, right? I mean, who wants to throw around smelly pieces of dead fish anyway? I've outgrown that shit."

"Oh, shut the hell up," Benita muttered and turned to the empty pen.

Nicky hissed through his teeth and looked at me. He checked over his shoulder and pointed to his chest and mouthed the words "tits" and walked in the direction of the bait shop. I waited until he was out of sight, which seemed to take forever and was worried for a moment that Benita would follow but she didn't.

"Sorry," I said, sliding next to her.

She nodded.

The silence became uncomfortable. "So," I asked and looked around, "can you let me in on the secret?"

She glanced at me, and seeing my smile, slowly let her lips spread into a tiny smirk. Of the three of us she was the only one who could tell which sea lion was which. Nicky tried every time to guess, but was never right. Sometimes I was never sure if he was just being nice and letting her get something over on him.

She kept silent and shook her head playfully. She looked beautiful and somehow lost at that moment. I was happy that I could make her smile.

"Look," I said, "if I *promise* not to tell Nicky, will you tell me?"

I waited with wide eyes, watching her. Her expression changed the next second, her lips falling back into a straight line. "Dimah had a small black mark on her right flipper, just big enough to see. You had to look real good, you know?"

I nodded.

"Bonnie's whiskers were shorter on one side than the other and Clyde had a small piece of his tail missing, just the tip."

"Really, that was it?" I asked and brushed my hair back from his face. "Man, you drove Nicky crazy with that. Me, too," I said taking a step closer to her and putting my hand on her arm. "I'll keep your secret though, a promise is a promise."

"Thanks."

Maybe I dreamed it but I swore that there was just a fraction of movement from her towards me. I forgot that my hand was still on her arm, it felt so right, and could feel the warmth of her skin. I had this crazy idea to pull her to me, just like in the movies.

Nicky reappeared, walking slowly around the corner. "Yeah, they're gone for good," he said and let out his breath. I took my hand away quickly and was sure that Nicky saw nothing because he kept talking. I could still feel the smoothness of her skin on my fingers.

"The guy over at the fish market said they've been gone for weeks," Nicky finished. He chewed his lip and kicked a tiny shell into the empty pen.

We all leaned against the railing again.

"Where do you think they went?" Nicky asked and his voice sounded small just then, like when we were little kids.

"They probably sent them to a zoo or something like that, "Benita answered. "I read that once an animal lives in captivity they can never live in the wild again because they don't know how. They don't have the skills to survive, they forget how to hunt and-"

"Yeah, okay, I get it," Nicky said sourly as he stared at the trash floating in the empty water.

Over the next couple of weeks Nicky and I fell into a comfortable, familiar rhythm. I would see mom on the deck, sketching on her pad early in the morning while grandma Ruth worked her puzzles in the afternoon and watched the soaps. Liz and Crystal biked on the boardwalk early so they could be back in time to hit the beach by ten. Fortunately, I didn't have to see her much.

The days raced by too quickly. Me and Nicky would hit the beach early and come home for lunch. On rainy days we went to Steel Pier and watched old movies (free with admission) or simply wandered around.

Every now and then I would see Benita in her apartment window, but she was usually busy with chores - folding laundry, cleaning or cooking. She would smile and wave. If Nicky wasn't around (which was rare) she might come down and we'd would talk. There were days that it felt like I had never met her before. While she was talking about school, I was awkwardly answering with a story about Nicky setting off a stink bomb at Steel Pier. She would laugh and she made it sound musical somehow. Still, it felt like she was suddenly growing into who she was going to be while me and Nicky were still little kids who thought farts were funny.

Sometimes it seemed like we were from different planets.

And in a way that was okay, too.

Hope

I placed the pad of paper on my knees. The color of the world right now was good - melting grays and blues in the sky and a low sun that pushed shadows across the buildings. Occasionally, broken clouds would float across and allow a shaft of light to spill down that gave the whole scene a spiritual vibe.

That was what I wanted. The Nevada and the Vermont apartments, with their dusty bricks and haunted-looking windows, would frame the right side of the picture. On the left would be Evalisse's building: still living, but barely, and starting its inevitable decline. When someone looked at the painting it would be impossible not to see that this building was somehow infected like everything around it. Sad as it was, I wanted people to see it withering right before their eyes.

The center would show the slice of the boardwalk in between, the part that I had always been able to see from home, that small window to the sand, ocean and beyond. Done right, that would be the only redeemable vision anyone would get from this.

And that was okay.

Artists chronicled death all the time, even if it was a painting of a lovely flower - that lovely flower would shrivel and disappear eventually. It's impossible to observe the world and escape death or decay. For some it was almost a mission.

I reached in my pocket and pulled out the letter from Max. I had grown used to keeping it with me, absently sliding it into my pocket though I had no real intention of opening it. But eventually I would have to, right? It was a message for me he had written just after that night...the night everything went wrong. I liked to think that I could be honest enough with myself to admit that in the end I would have to – I don't think I could live not knowing his feelings after that night when the answer was sitting in my pocket all this time.

I pulled Max out of the envelope. Even after that horrible night he and I had, his blue eyes were looking back at me with life, humor and promise...and no thought that he would soon be dead.

I leaned the photo against the railing and put the envelope back in my pocket. I picked up my pencil. This painting would be different from anything I had done before. Up to now, whether it was clay or paint or watercolor (not my best medium), everything showed some sort of assurance that things would not change. Things were locked in time and upbeat.

But things are changing and it's time to face it.

How many times have I walked down this street, a thousand? Ten thousand? I can still feel the warm, rough asphalt under my feet after all these years. Max and I might hit the beach four times in one day. We'd walk everywhere, no shoes, and mom would bark at us to wear something and she'd get about as far as I do with Jamie.

And every time we reached the top of the boardwalk ramp I half expected the ocean not to be there anymore as if whoever was in charge forgot to turn a dial or something and it would be nothing but a desert, but it was never gone. The ocean was there each and every time we reached the top of that ramp and the night watchman was never asleep at the switch.

Maybe not everything dies.

* * *

1956

I adjust the hem of my new powder blue dress and admire myself in the closet mirror. I turn to the side, check again and tuck a lock of hair behind my ear before twirling around once to see it from all angles. It billows gracefully, making it look as if I'm gliding when I move.

Outside the gulls call to each other and spring afternoon light streams through the windows. I shouldn't have put the dress on so early but simply can't wait. Mom, of course, would tell me to take it off before it got all wrinkled but for now I just want to see how darned good I look in it. I peek out of my bedroom and hear her downstairs talking with dad so I scamper across the hallway and, without knocking, burst to Max's room.

"Jeez, what are you doing?" he snaps as I quickly close the door. He's propped up on his bed with a book in his hand and his elbow is resting on a pillow. "You ever hear of knocking? What if I was getting dressed?"

"Oh, please, like I haven't seen that before," I giggle.

"Yeah, well, look, it doesn't matter. You should at least knock..." His words fall off and his eyes follow me from top to bottom.

I'm smiling at him, waiting for the compliment I so richly deserve, but when none come right away I put up my hands in defense. "I know. I know I didn't do my hair yet because it's still four hours until the dance but this is pretty close to how I want it to look," I say, talking fast and spinning once more, "but if I do my hair now, it'll be a mess by the time Mike comes to pick me up, right?"

"Right," he says, nodding, and his eyes soften. "Wow, you look great."

"Thank you," I answer politely and twirl once more. "And I know."

"Still," he says, looking serious once again and blocking his face with his book, "if she catches you, mom is going to tell you to take off the dress."

"Yeah, yeah, but I wanted to see how it looked."

"Well, you look great," he says, lowering the book so I can see his crystal blue eyes. "Really."

I do a couple of royal waves to my surrounding fans and look around his room. There was a time, not very long ago, when we would spend all our time after school in here, hanging pictures of our favorite movie stars on the walls or dancing to records until mom and dad complained. I remembered how Max stayed by my side on my first nerve-wracking day of high school; walking with me and introducing me to some of his friends. He made those first few days less horrific. Of course, it didn't hurt at all to have such a popular guy as your older brother; teachers loved him, girls loved him.

I wander over to the record player and, catching myself before I sat down and wrinkled the dress, bend to flip through his albums.

Max knew more about real music than anyone I knew. While my girlfriends were listening to Rosemary Clooney, Al Martino and Frankie Lane, he was telling me about musicians I had never heard of like Son House, Charlie Parker and Bobby Blue Bland. I became curious in the way his eyes lit up when he talked about music, especially jazz and blues. He had money from his job at the theater on the boardwalk and would bring home a new record every week. The two of us would sit on the *floor of his room and listen for hours, sharing licorice whips and doing our homework.*

"So, what about you?" I ask, pulling Dinah Washington from his collection. "You know that a girl like Beth Desmond is going to expect her date to be dressed to the nines." Max takes his book in one hand and points absently to the closet. Hanging on the door is a steel blue tuxedo.

"Very nice," I say and turn the record jacket over to look at the back. "God, I wish I could sing like her."

"I wish you could, too," he says.

"Why?"

"Then we'd be rich."

I put the record back and walk over to the closet. Just out the window there is a seagull perched on the little roof, totally oblivious to us. "Yeah, but then we'd probably move away and go someplace where everyone had as much money as we did. I'd hate that." The gull spreads its wings and lifts into the air. "Besides, I like it here just the way things are, don't you?"

He doesn't answer so I walk over and take the tuxedo by the hanger and look it over, nodding. "She won't know what hit her," I say. "One of the perks of being on the basketball team is getting a girl like Beth to go to the dance with you I guess, huh?"

He smiles but it fails gently at the corners. He's become much moodier in the last year and as much as I adore him there are times, especially lately, when I want to scream at him. Beth Desmond is one of the most popular girls in school! Boys follow her down the hall like a string of ducks! She has the blonde hair that any girl would dream of: smooth and wavy and so brilliant it's almost platinum. All her other parts were in the right place as well, or so I'd heard several boys say.

"Excited?" I venture.

He shrugs and sticks his nose back in his book. "I guess."

"Um, is Stuart going to the dance?" Stuart is a classmate of Max's and they had become close friends and, truth be told, I had a crazy crush on him. Black wavy hair, piercing green eyes...

"What do you care? You have a date already," he practically snarls without moving the book from in front of his face. I'm glad he can't see my face. It's warm and I'm sure I'm blushing a bit at the statement. True, I would love to go to the dance with Stuart but he's practically Max's best friend and, well, maybe it's not that crazy.

"Geez, I'm just asking. I'm very happy to be going with Michael, you know."

"Stuart is taking Tabitha Bryce," Max mumbles and I sigh to myself.

Any boy would be thrilled to have Beth on his arm at the prom and here was my brother, calmly sitting on his bed finishing a book with his legs crossed over each other and quietly moping. I wanted to kick his butt on behalf of all the boys who wouldn't be taking a Beth Desmond to the dance tonight.

What the heck did he have to feel bad about? He was popular, good looking and smart while I considered myself only the last one of those. He might not have been the star of the basketball team but he was a good player and he had that certain quality that drew people to him.

I miss some of the things we used to share - a weird sense of humor, which was definitely wildly to the left or right of what most people found funny. What would send Max and me into fits of laughter usually made other kids our age just stare with a concerned look on their face.

Which is fine with me. I love having that secret signal that only we know about when something strikes us silly. Even Brenda and Abby think we're both nuts.

But it's been a long time since we've dissolved into a really good laugh together. Maybe it's our age or maybe things only seem that funny when you're a child which, according to all my friends, none of us are anymore.

Max is reading again. I want to say something to cheer him up, but am beginning to detest his attitude right now. Tonight, I am going to be picked up by Michael Lesch, who is widely known around school for constantly having his nose in a book and dressing horribly.

Max, on the other hand, is going with the glorious Beth Desmond.

What the heck is there to be down about?

* * *

I had stopped sketching. I blinked and tried to focus on the steps that led from the boardwalk to the beach but they were hard to see, the vision swam in and out. The photo of Max's flashing smile was right in front of me and I saw his raw, wet eyes in the shadows of his dark room that night. Maybe he only wanted me to just hold him, but that sudden feeling of disgust that was so unfair to him grew again like a weed in my stomach. He had always been there to look after me and suddenly he was the one who looked so helpless and was asking me to be the strong one.

He made me promise him something that I never wanted any part of.

Don't tell anyone, please.

It didn't seem fair that you had to get older before you realized that most of the things that were so important to you in high school wouldn't matter for anything later in life.

I let go. I dropped my head and cried like I hadn't in years.

CHAPTER
8

Jamie

I was glad I wasn't in Philly when the heat wave hit. The temperatures had climbed steadily from the low nineties every day, re-melting the black spots of gum on the pavements and making it impossible to walk barefoot on the sidewalk or the boards. From New York to Washington, everyone was trapped under a giant magnifying glass. The few clouds that did appear were fluffy and hazy, ruling from high in the sky and looking mountainous, teasing everyone with the prospect of rain but never delivering. The news channels had been reporting a break in the weather for days and when it came they promised it would be one *heck* of a storm.

We sat on the front steps of Nicky's house and passed a tomato back and forth, each taking sloppy bites from it. The heat was coming off the sidewalk in waves and it made me feel slightly dizzy. Across the street Mr. Doran's black lab, Scotch, was lying on the porch panting and rolling his eyes. I felt sorry for him to have all that fur. Just looking at the poor creature made me wish I could take him to the beach and let him jump in the ocean.

Gary opened the front door and trotted down between us. He stole the remainder of the tomato from Nicky's hand and plopped it into his mouth before crossing the street to his car, the purple Gremlin with patches of primer and no hubcaps.

Nicky's eyes quickly widened and he slapped my arm with his hand. "Hey, Gary!" he yelled and turned to me. "I'm bored, man," he said, "You wanna go for a ride?"

"What?" Gary shouted back. He sounded irritated as he hung his muscular, tanned arm out the window.

"Sure," I answered after checking down the street to see if mom or Lizard was in sight. Mom liked Gary enough but she wasn't too cool about joyriding, especially in his broken down old Gremlin.

"Can we go with you?" Nicky asked.

Gary's face dropped and he waved his hand at him. "Man, you don't even know where it is I'm going," he said.

"Don't care," Nicky answered and looked around, raising his hands. "Nothin' goin' on here," he looked to me, "right?"

I smiled and nodded.

Gary thought for a moment. "Yeah, alright, but I got things to do. Quick, climb in."

Nicky ran calling shotgun. He pulled open the passenger door and pulled his seat forward. The heat from inside the car was smothering, but I jumped in anyway and saw too late that there was no back seat, just a nest of discarded bottles, crumpled cigarette packs and wadded up food wrappers littering the floor. Nicky leaped in and shut the door just as Gary hit the gas, hard enough to make me fall backwards. The tires squealed as the little car raced down Seaside.

"Hey!" I yelled as I rolled to the back. Gary cackled and Nicky hopped up on his knees in the front seat and turned around. I was trying to get myself straightened out when I saw that Nicky was looking at me with a shit-eating grin.

"Guess I shoulda told ya…uh, no back seat!" he laughed.

"Right 'bout that little brother," Gary chuckled. "You know how it is, Jame, I had to make room for the laaaadies!" He quickly turned the corner of Oriental Avenue and I had to grab the back of his seat to keep from being thrown to the side.

We sped down Oriental and the houses and buildings flashed by. The rush of air felt good on my skin, cooling the sweat. Turning onto Rhode Island, we rolled away from the ocean towards Pacific Avenue. A group of children were kicking a deflated and dusty basketball ball back and forth to each other in an empty lot. A heavy black woman in a flowered house dress shouted to them to come inside from the top step of her dull, yellow and red brick house. She held an umbrella in one hand while nursing a newborn on her large, round breast.

There were hardly any trees anymore. I had a faint memory of when trees lined the streets. All that was left now were tiny squares of dry weeds in the sidewalk where they once stood.

Corner bars with dark interiors and faded signs were plentiful. Old and young men sat on folding chairs in front, some nodding to sleep while others talked to each other or themselves. More houses went by in a blur, more empty windows, more warped staircases and untended yards.

Gary slowed and stuck his hand out, waving to a couple of dark-haired girls walking down the street. He honked and they turned and waved.

Nicky stuck his head out of the window. "Man, I would love some of that. Man, oh, man!" He blew kisses to the girls.

"You wouldn't even know what to do with it, little brother," Gary replied and tapped the back of Nicky's head, laughing. Nicky punched him in the arm and grinned.

"You gotta be like my man behind us, dig?" Gary continued, pointing his thumb back at me. "The quiet ones like Jamie here? They're the ones you gotta watch out for. They're the real killers, right?" He looked in the rear view mirror at me and smiled. "How many girls you got lined up, little man?"

I didn't exactly like being called "little man" but it was kind of cool when Gary said it. I would trade a hundred Lizards for one Gary. I laughed and was about to answer when Gary suddenly reached for the radio.

"Awww, here is the song!" Gary cried. The Eagles were singing "Already Gone" and Gary turned the knob until the song blasted out of the windows and into the neighborhood. Nicky smiled and bobbed his head, his brown and copper hair bouncing into his eyes and hiding his face.

Gary sang off key and sounded horrible. Nicky joined along, missing every other word, and I hammered the back of Nicky's headrest with my hands and shook my head.

"Man, these dudes know everything, you know?" Gary yelled to us. "It's what you gotta do. If the lady don't understand you, then you gotta skate, am I right?"

Nicky nodded, then turned and winked at me. I thought he looked suddenly older.

The buildings flew past, but I hardly noticed anymore. We all screamed the song out and laughed every time we messed up the words. We began making up our own words and cracking up.

Gary slowed down the car, letting it slink between the sun-blasted buildings like a warm cat, going down small streets and hugging corners. Every now and then Gary would shout to someone he recognized. The heat began to rise in the car.

Gary turned down the radio. I could tell he was watching something on the street. The smile left his face. He looked into the rear view mirror, but not at me...he was watching a small crowd that was hanging near a corner store called The Arctic Market.

We rounded the block twice.

Nicky noticed and said, "Man, what are you -", but Gary cut him off by putting his hand up and pulling over to the curb. He got out and leaned in the window, looking both ways before saying anything. "You two stay here for now. I mean it, don't move, got it?" He looked directly at Nicky. "If you have to, I mean if I'm not back in five minutes, you drive home and tell mom where I am, okay?"

Nicky looked confused at first but then his eyes focused and he nodded.

Gary casually walked towards the group. A young black man dressed in tight tan pants and a denim vest was talking and clapping his hands together. His full afro had a red, black and green pick stuck in it. Gary reached into his back pocket and when the man turned he saw him and bolted down the street, pushing everyone out of his way. Gary ran after him, rushing through the group and chasing for a half a block before vanishing around the corner.

Nicky leaned over and turned the radio back up.

"What's going on?" I asked and suddenly felt trapped in the car.

He shrugged. "I don't know." He began bobbing his head again. The song ended and he grimaced at the next one: KC and the Sunshine Band were rolling into *Shake Your Booty*. "Oh, man I fucking *hate* these guys."

The women and the men had scattered from in front of the store like no one had ever been there. The air was still and a trickle of sweat ran down my neck. "Turn on the AC, man."

"Nice try," Nicky answered, sliding over into the driver's seat, "it's broke." He chuckled, "Did ya ever notice that, how AC can mean Air conditioning or Atlantic City? Pretty funny, huh?" He began fiddling with the keys in the ignition. The key chain was a green metal pot leaf.

"Can you really drive this thing?" I asked, trying not to sound nervous. The neighborhood suddenly looked menacing and I imagined the heat as the breath of some huge beast, something with teeth and waiting to bite.

"I think so." Nicky flipped the visor down and a pair of sunglasses dropped into his lap. He smiled as he put them on and gripped the wheel.

"You *think* so?"

"Yeah, what, you don't believe me?" Nicky snorted before checking his face in the rear view mirror.

I started to speak, my voice raising, "Well, no, it's not that, but have you -"

Gary reappeared, walking slowly around the corner and looking over his shoulder. Nicky slid quickly back into his seat while Gary opened the door and lowered himself in, brushing the hair back from his sweaty brow. He reached down between his legs and tucked some-thing out of sight.

"Jesus, those blacks are *fast*, man," he said as he started up the car. We pulled away and the air washing over my face from the window felt wonderful. So did the distance we were putting between us and the corner. I looked out the back and saw that the people were slowly gathering again in front of the store.

"What was that all about?" Nicky asked.

Gary hesitated for just a second. Nicky didn't see it but I saw something in Gary's eyes in the mirror. "I whipped his sorry ass last week at pool and he owed me money, man," he answered. The after-noon sun streamed through the windows, making everything hazy and suddenly I felt sad and tired.

The next week Nicky, Gary and their mom went to visit his cousins in Virginia and they were going to be gone for a few days. I was insanely bored and had to keep coming up with creative ways to deal with Lizard and Crystal, who took over the television and silently threatened me every time I tried to change the channel to something I liked. I started rereading *The Hobbit*. I headed to the beach alone.

High above a jet traced a white line across the sky. I watched it and walked slowly, wandering into the street and then back to the side-walk. Two black girls were playing a radio loudly and dancing on the sidewalk in front of Benita's apartment building. I slowed as I passed under her window, hoping that she would poke her head out and call my name, but nothing happened,

Only a few people were in the ocean and the lifeguards were lazily twirling their whistles. I walked down the stairs and tramped across the beach, which thankfully, was not as hot as it was last week.

I sat down by the water and picked up a handful of wet sand and let it pour through my fingers.

A boat from Starn's, one that they used for day fishing trips, was chugging along. I watched it until it slipped from view. I walked along the water and stopped to watch a small girl with dark hair pour water from a plastic bucket onto a sand castle. She used small mussel shells for the windows and a clam shell for the door. I had this weird urge to sit down with her - just rest on my knees on the dark sand and dig into the softness with my fingers, but I didn't think kids my age did that anymore.

I looked up and, like a mirage, saw Benita alone and laying out on a bright green towel. I walked over, drawn by just the sight of her. When I reached her I tried not to let my shadow fall across her closed eyes. I just wanted to watch her for a moment, but in the back of his mind I was worried that she might catch me staring. How would that look?

"Hey," I said. It was all I could manage.

She opened her eyes and tried to shade them with her slim fingers, that beautiful dark ocean blue came back to them as the light touched her face.

"Oh, hey, Jame." She grinned crookedly and sat up, her hands moving to untie the thick braid behind her head. With her arms back I noticed the beautiful shape of her breasts and tried to not stare. I think I said something stupid about the nice weather while I watched her let the loose, still damp hair fall over her shoulders.

"Where's Nicky?" she asked and pulled herself up to her knees. She shook the sand from her towel.

I tried to seem casual. "Don't know, visiting family or something, I think. He might be back tomorrow."

"Oh."

I felt like there was too much of a pause. Did I even think about things like that before?

"Um, haven't seen you around lately."

"Yeah, Mom's got me working a lot at the shop."

"Busy?"

"Yeah."

"Where is it now?"

"Over on Rhode Island." She waved a small fly from her face, adorably crinkling up her nose. "The cops chased them from Miss Alvaredo's on Maine a week ago so they moved. I shouldn't even be here - I still got chores to do but," she said and looked out at the water, "I should have some time for myself. I mean, summer only comes once a year, right?"

The thought depressed me because it was already the middle of July. I looked at her in her suit and the thought vanished faster than I would have believed. "Been in yet?"

"Mmm-hmm."

"How is it?"

"Good waves. Not too chilly," she answered.

The sun came out from behind the clouds and filled the beach with color. The ocean sparkled and I could see that the waves were crashing from one side of the beach to the other and far out.

I looked down to the boardwalk, thinking I might ask if she wanted to go to Steel Pier later, but without saying anything she began walking to the water. I hadn't planned on swimming and was only in my shorts but that didn't matter right now. I followed.

We swam out past the small breakers and floated near each other. We laughed and caught good waves. The swells lifted us off our feet and made me feel like I was flying. I realized how happy I was that Nicky was nowhere around and it felt wrong somehow, but was erased anytime I looked at Benita.

After she dried herself off she handed her towel to me and I inhaled softly through my nose as I rubbed my hair and face. We walked to the lifeguard station which was really just a wooden building on thick stilts. Underneath was a fresh water spigot you could use to wash off. Nicky and I never rinsed off after swimming, but if she was going to, well, I was definitely following.

The sand was cool and gray and I felt a slight chill in the shade. Benita rinsed her hair and then walked to a spot where the sun reached and brightened the sand. As I bent and let the water pour on my hair I turned and saw the yellow light catch the curve of her lower back as she sat and squeezed water from her long black hair.

I walked over to sit next to her. An ice cream man was calling out and the waves were loud, plunging over themselves as if playing. There was a time when the call of the ice cream man would have sent both of us running, but right now that seemed like another life. All the sounds were alive and moving. I glanced over and saw tiny goose bumps on her skin.

I swallowed and said, "So I'm thinking of going to Steel Pier later, do you -"

The next thing I knew her lips were on mine! My eyes went wide and I clumsily put my hands on her warm, smooth shoulders so I wouldn't fall onto my back. Her hands were on my face, her eyes were closed and I could feel her tongue in my mouth, seeking and conquering everything inside of me. I started shaking, whether she noticed or not I'll never know. The soft hiss of her breath through her nose, so warm and close to my ear that it seemed to push away every other noise in the world, sounded like wave after wave crashing onto the beach.

I curled my tongue around hers and was suddenly aware of the rest of my body. I was feeling myself getting hard and uncomfortable. I tried to move, but couldn't breathe and only made some sort of strange sound out of my nose. She darted her tongue in and out of my mouth and I moved my hands to her stomach, then toward her chest. She pushed against me and I became dizzy, ready to fall backwards or forwards, I couldn't tell which direction. Suddenly she pulled away and I fell onto my belly.

She sprung to her feet with a small smile on her lips. Her eyes were wide and curious-looking and she was breathing quickly. I was on my hands and knees at her feet and breathing again. Her taste still on my lips, I opened my mouth, but before I could say anything she grinned and ducked below the rafter of the station and ran over the rise of sand.

"Wait!" I called after her and jumped up. A spike of pain like an electrical shock ran from the top of my head to my feet and I dropped back down to the sand, rolling onto my back. Bright white streaks spun in front of my eyes and I rubbed at the top of my head. I looked up and saw a thick, rusted bolt sticking out from the wood.

I slowly lifted myself up on one arm and crawled up the slope to look for Benita, but she was gone. I wanted to run after her: maybe catch her in the water and kiss her until we both fell under the waves, we would share our breath so we would never have to come up for air. She kissed me! And not just any kiss! She put her tongue on my mouth! I could feel a smile washing across my face and was helpless to stop it.

A wet trickle slid from my forehead toward my cheek and I wiped it away, only then looking down and seeing my hand smeared with bright blood and sand and suddenly I felt like I was going to throw up.

"How many?" mom asked the doctor.

"Only a few," he said, looking at her and smiling. "The cut isn't deep, but head wounds have a tendency to bleed quite a bit. It'll be over before you know it."

"Will it hurt?" I never had stitches before and even though it was kind of cool, I was a little nervous.

"Well, a pinch, but that's all," he said and put his hand on my shoulder and it felt heavy and large. "My patients aren't usually so happy about it." He smiled again at mom and could tell he was flirting with her a bit.

I saw the puzzled look on mom's face and quickly wiped the grin from my lips. I nodded and tried looking worried. As the doctor was working I thought of Benita and how her lips felt pressed against mine.

Everything was fine.

For the rest of the day I was back under the lifeguard station and kissing Benita. I tried to recall everything about it: how her skin felt when I touched her, the goose bumps on the flesh of her shoulders and the softness of her lips. I remembered some wisps of her hair tickled my face and quickly got hard again.

Did she feel the same way? Was she thinking of that kiss right now and wondering when we would kiss again? I ended up on my knees, looking up at her like she was some wonderful statue that I had just discovered. I wanted more. I wanted to kiss her all the time.

164

She smiled at me and her eyes widened, looking beautiful, and her hair sparkled. She felt the same as me, I was sure of it.

But then she was gone and running away over the dunes and I thought about the way the sunlight caught her and showed off the curves of her body. I would have followed, raced into the waves after her, if that's where she was, and kissed her again. I would like to chase her, capture her and maybe she would laugh and throw her arms around me. She would kiss me over and over and say -

"…potatoes?"

I opened my eyes. Mom was looking at me from across the table with gentle concern in her eyes.

"Huh?"

"I asked if you wanted potatoes, sweetie." She tilted her head and pursed her lips, the same look she might give a crab that was stranded on its back in the sun.

Lizard was chewing her food and looking at me with bored, half-lidded eyes. "I would have said that you knocked yourself stupid, but that happened a long time ago."

"You know," mom said after throwing a quick look at my dear sister (who just grinned innocently back at her), "you had that look the whole time you were getting the stitches. Are you sure you feel okay?"

"Yeah. Still stings a bit, though," I said, feeling the rough surface of the stitches, four stitches to be exact. Nicky would be so jealous because I was the first one to get stitches.

"Honey, don't touch," she said and walked around and patted my shoulder before removing my plate. "If you aren't hungry that's fine, but keep up your fluids. You don't feel sleepy or anything, right? The doctor said he was sure there was no concussion."

"No, I'm fine, mom, really." *I don't think I'll ever sleep again.*

I excused myself and went upstairs to the deck and looked down the street toward Benita's apartment. The sky was deep blue, the kind that made the outlines of the buildings look sharp and beautiful. The lights in her apartment were on but the shades were drawn. Maybe she was thinking of me in there.

That night I lay in bed and tossed, unable to think of anything but Benita. I pictured her above me, floating somewhere near the ceiling of my bedroom, clasping her hands together. *Like my sand idol,* I thought and remembered looking up at her. She smiled but there was a question on her face and I wondered why she ran.

Why did she kiss me then and how long had she wanted to?

Why had she disappeared for the rest of the day? Would I see her tomorrow?

I had to.

And just when I thought I wouldn't be able to fall asleep with the picture of her flying in my mind, I did.

* * *

"Shit man, there ain't nothin' down there," Nicky complained as he pulled his crab cage up again. He was lying on his belly, his head and shoulders hanging over the edge of the warm boards and looking disgustedly at the empty wire cube on the end of his rope. It swung lazily in wide arcs and the piece of chicken tied to the center, now looking soft and formless, remained untouched.

"Maybe you don't know what you're doing," I laughed. I was glad that Nicky was back. It was almost unbearable for a couple of reasons.

One: I missed Nicky

Two: I needed a distraction to stop thinking about Benita.

I hadn't seen her much since our kiss and the few times that I *did* she just waved and acted like nothing happened, which was really messing with my head. I was never able to talk to her because she was either in her apartment or with her girlfriends.

I brought my cage up with the same result. "Besides, you have to use the necks, isn't that what you always say?"

"Yeah, I wish we had some." Nicky had managed to steal a couple of uncooked pieces of chicken from his freezer, but we had been crabbing for over an hour and didn't have much to show for it. I could hear the desperate scraping and scuttling of the three we had caught in the bucket and wanted to throw them back.

"I'm gonna catch hell when mom sees that I took some of our dinner," Nicky continued and then his eyes brightened with a new idea. "Hey, can I come over for dinner? Sure beats getting yelled at by my mom."

"Yeah, guess so."

"We're not going to catch nothing, probably because the waters all churned up. The crabs and fish know when a storm is coming," he said. The sky over Brigantine was slate gray and angry with coffee-colored clouds blowing in off the water. Most of the people had left the boards for home to avoid the storm.

Nicky dropped his cage and lowered himself by his arms off the edge of the boardwalk. The water foamed over the green and black rocks fifteen feet below.

"So, do you think your sister likes me?" he asked and swung his feet out over the water. I tried not to show how much I hated it when he hung from the boards. I pictured him slipping and crashing onto the mossy rocks below and doubted seriously I would know what the hell to do if that happened.

"Are you serious?" I answered.

"Yeah."

"No."

"Really?" he asked looking genuinely confused.

I shook my head and pulled up the cages. Two small calicos scrambled around inside and they looked suspiciously like the two I threw back ten minutes ago. They were useless. You needed to catch pointers. I dumped them, watching them flip end over end before making two small splashes.

Nicky pulled himself up and climbed over the railing. He picked up the bucket and looked into it, "It's your lucky day, boys." His voice sounded louder in the plastic container. We only caught three small pointers so he let them slide back into the ocean. "Not even worth bringing them back, right?"

"Let's head back."

Nicky looked at the end of the jetty. No one was out there right now and the water was coughing up small breakers far out. Boats were making their way back to the marinas, trying to beat the storm. Brigantine was now barely visible across the bay.

"Cool," Nicky said and whistled. The heavier waves met the end of the jetty and erupted in foam. He turned to me and flashed a smile before skipping down the steps to the rocks.

"What are you doing?" I asked, following. He didn't answer and kept walking along the jetty. The waves were cutting across the bay as well, hitting the sides of the rocks steadily and throwing soapy-looking foam into the air. What sun had remained vanished and the beach and ocean were swallowed in shadow.

"Hey, what are we doing?" I looked out at the distant end of the rocks. They looked like they were swimming only a few feet above the surface of the ocean. On the news it had said that a hurricane had just touched the Carolinas and went back out to sea, though, the blonde sexy newscaster said that we might get some after effects, so, "Watch out, New Jersey."

"C'mon, have you ever seen a storm up close?" He turned and swung his cage casually, "Besides, we won't go out far...just halfway." I jogged up next to him. Halfway was fine with me. This was the long jetty, the one that marked the end of the inlet and it was twice the length of any of the others, stretching about one hundred yards into the water.

"Hey," Nicky said, gazing out at the water, "when I marry Liz, then you and I will be related, right? What will we be?"

"Do you ever listen to anything I say?" I snickered. "But, for the record, you'd be my brother-in-law and I would never visit and would thank you for taking my sister away."

A large wave broke onto the rocks and we ducked, chuckling as warm ocean water rained on us. A small, blue-hulled boat was pushing its way around the tip of the jetty. It rocked heavily in the swells.

"She wouldn't give you the time of day, anyway, and you know it."

"You must've hit your head *real* good, Jackson," Nicky said. "What chick wouldn't want me?"

A gull floated on the wind, flying sideways and fighting the wind. Waves ran the length of the jetty, splashing up over some of the rocks ahead. "And speaking of hitting your head," Nicky said and smiled, "tell me again how you got that cut."

"Uh, I told you already. What, you got amnesia? *I* hit my head, not you." I was kicking myself for not coming up with a solid story and didn't expect him to ask about it again.

"Uh, huh. I know," Nicky nodded. "Tell me again."

I stared at him, looking annoyed. "I hit it on one of the bolts under the lifeguard station, okay?"

The breeze was blowing his long hair across his face but I could see a smile growing as his eyes watched me.

"You're a shitty liar," he said, shaking his head. "You're worse than me, man."

"What do you mean?"

"Why were you under there?"

I hesitated. I couldn't help it. "I was washing off the sand before I got home."

Nicky folded his arms across his chest and curled his lips.

"Mom doesn't want me dragging sand through the house anymore," I added, and put my hands out. "You know that." I was scrambling.

"Man, you're full of it." Nicky said, finally laughing.

"Well, what the hell do you know?" I didn't like being cornered like this. I'd always been a bad liar (all those genes must have gone to the Lizard) and when I thought about it I couldn't remember ever lying to Nicky before.

"More than you know, Jackson. I heard you were under there with Benita."

"Who said that?" I asked quickly.

Nicky ignored the question. "Man, only chicks wash themselves off after the beach. When was the last time you washed off your goddamn feet before heading home?" Nicky looked at me, waiting for an answer.

"*Okay*, so she was under there," I said helplessly, "We were talking about stuff, that's all."

"So how did you really hit your head? Or did you try something and she hit it for you?"

I tried to come up with an answer, but forgot the original question and now I was confused. This was why I was so bad at lying, I could never keep my stories straight. Nicky nodded his head and smiled as the pause grew longer.

"You guys were doing it under there, weren't you?" he asked loudly and laughed.

Benita's face swam in front of me, I don't know how else to describe it. She was in the crashing waves and the white foam. I could taste her lips again, even the hint of salt that was on her tongue...like she was part of the ocean...the feel of her bathing suit under my fingers. I couldn't stop myself from smiling.

Nicky began hopping up and down from one foot to the other. He shook his head. "You and Spot, doing it under the station!" he yelled again.

"Shut up, will you?" Nicky looked as if he was about to leap out of his skin. "Look, we didn't do it, okay?"

"Well, what happened?"

I wondered why I was so embarrassed all this time. I know I was worried about what Nicky would say, but wasn't this what I'd been wondering about? Haven't I wanted to shout it out since it happened?

"I don't know, I guess we kinda made out."

Nicky nodded, still smiling, but his expression was blank. His eyes moved about. "What's the difference?"

My mouth dropped open and I tried to think of an answer. "Well, 'making out' is just kissing, right? 'Doing it' is something else," I said. "I think."

Nicky looked confused. "So…which did you guys do?"

I smiled proudly. "We made out. She even stuck her tongue in my mouth."

"No way!" Nicky was hanging on every word. "What did you do?"

"Same."

"Did you touch her titties?"

"Yup. I'm pretty sure I did." I was tired of keeping it to myself. If Benita was going to walk around and make believe that nothing happened then I was going to do the exact opposite. Tell everyone.

And everyone thinking that we might have done it was even better.

Nicky let out a whoop and turned back toward the boardwalk. He started singing *Love Machine* and stomped his feet. I laughed and began strutting behind him. Moving from side to side, Nicky turned and walked backward, singing and then clapping his hands on either side of my head.

It felt great to get it out in the open and have Nicky celebrating with me.

Then I looked down the jetty and saw five gray figures coming down the steps from the boards. It was Seth followed by Mark, Fat Ass Chuck, Brian and Tony.

I grabbed Nicky by the shoulders and turned him to see. The beach was empty and I could only see an old man leaning on the railing of the boardwalk. The fishermen had all gone home and we were alone.

Nicky dropped his cage and looked at either side of the jetty. Water. Nothing but rough water.

"Back this way," he said and tried pulling me in the direction of the end of the jetty but I was frozen, watching Seth and his friends make their way toward us. They planted their feet solidly on the rocks as they moved but they were becoming more uncertain the further they got.

"C'mon!" Nicky snapped.

I dropped my cage and bucket and raced after him.

We sprinted along the wet rocks and I tried to focus on the old steel tower at the end while the wind whistled in my ears. I could hear shouts behind us, but couldn't make out the words as we leaped over gaps between the huge black rocks. The tide had risen higher than I had ever seen and the waves were pushing the water almost to the surface of the jetty.

As we reached the end Nicky stopped and turned. He put his hands on his hips and breathed deeply. Another wave hit and water rained down. I leaned on him to steady myself as a wave rolled across and came up to our ankles. Through the drizzle I could see Tony holding onto Brian's shirt as they navigated far behind Seth and Mark. Fat Ass Chuck had given up and was heading back and I was praying that the rest would follow him. Seth slipped, but quickly got up and kept moving toward us.

Nicky, his hair soaked and falling in front of his face, slapped me on the shoulder and pointed to the tower.

"Up," he shouted, trying to shield his eyes from the rain. I thought about us diving from the rocks and swimming for the beach but we'd never make it. The ocean had turned a color that I had never seen and could only describe as bitter. It looked pissed.

Nicky grabbed onto the rusted ladder and was pulling himself up. I followed, desperate not to be alone. I looked over my shoulder and only Seth remained, soaked and yelling taunts that I couldn't make out over the crash of the waves. I got the general idea. Mark, Brian and Tony had turned back and were holding each other up as the water tried to push them off the rocks.

I turned and gripped the ladder tightly. My breath left as I looked out to the ocean. The water had swelled and then just as quickly receded, almost draining down to the sand at the end of the jetty. I reached up and frantically swatted at Nicky's leg.

I screamed, my voice cracking, "Hold on!" The water kept rolling back from the tip of the rocks and for a few seconds it rested there, as if it was thinking.

Then it rushed forward.

I swear I felt the jetty shudder when that wave hit. I had wrapped my arms around the rough ladder and locked my hands as tightly as I could, ignoring the scraping of the old metal against my skin. Nicky yelled something but it was drowned out by the roar of the wave. An explosion of water and white foam flew into the air and just before I closed my eyes I thought of Nicky and prayed that he was able to hold on.

The force of the wave tried to push me off the ladder and I felt something slimy hit me in the chest. When the shower of warm water finally ended I looked up and saw Nicky hanging onto the side of the ladder, his eyes still closed, frozen in place.

"Quick!" I screamed at him and climbed down to the rocks, slipping and scraping my shin. I didn't want to wait for another hit. I scanned the rocks back to the boards and couldn't see Seth anywhere and had a sudden deep fear. The rain was coming down in sheets now, making me squint and forcing me to wipe my eyes every few seconds. I spotted Seth. He had given up and went back, dropping to the beach and I was surprised at how relieved I was to see him.

Nicky slowly got down, shivering, and then helped me limp along the surface. We moved carefully toward the beach and shouted if we saw a wave coming. We'd wedge ourselves between the rocks and hold our breath until the ocean finished washing over us.

After fifteen minutes we had made it close enough to leap down onto the beach. Nicky fell to his knees, then onto his belly and his face hit the wet sand. I staggered a few steps and then sat down, still trying to catch my breath. Then I fell on my back and sucked in air. The sky was swirling gray and white like marble, the clouds moving fast high above. I heard the low sound of thunder roll across the sky and to me it sounded like laughter.

I eventually rolled over to look at Nicky who was still face down in the sand.

"You," I started, catching breaths, "are a...goddamned...idiot." I rolled back, put my head down and closed my eyes.

Nicky was drawing in air and it mixed with the blowing wind. The pounding of the waves sounded rhythmic and I thought of the sound in my ears when I kissed Benita. It sounded so much the same. I opened one eye and saw Nicky's face above me. He was looking down at me and that small grin formed again, the black and silver clouds high above him.

"So you really touched Spot's titties, huh?"

CHAPTER
9

Hope

I wrapped the still warm muffins in a large napkin and placed them in the basket, adding a few pieces of fruit for good measure. I poured the coffee into a thermos and left the house, walking down to Oriental Avenue. Robin's house was only a five minute walk and we both agreed that, since he baked his famous (to the two of us) banana bread last week, it was my turn to impress him with my cranberry orange muffins. The coffee was nothing special, just Folgers, but I had spent the winter perfecting my muffin recipe and knew I'd knock his colorful socks off.

He answered the door on the first knock, smiling broadly and looking like he had been ready and waiting for hours. We walked through his tiny living room where his mother, Joan, had positioned herself right in front of the TV. I made sure to give her one of my muffins and she smiled, giving me a small hug before returning her attention back to the set. His two parrots, Girlfriend and Mr. Robinson, squawked from their cage and the TV chirped words that faded as we moved through the kitchen to the yard on the side of the house.

I loved Robin's yard. It was a bit smaller than ours and was surrounded by vine-covered walls that made it seem even smaller, but he used it so smartly, placing day lilies, begonias, hydrangea and lupines. Boastful sunflowers rose high above a hosta bush on the corner, their heads big enough to double as umbrellas if necessary. A small table with two chairs sat in the middle, looking as if as if it had been made especially for us.

I made a bit of a show about my muffins, pulling off the napkin cover like a magician and thoroughly enjoyed his reaction. I poured out two cups and we caught up with each other since last week.

Robin worked as a designer which usually took him out of the city. His specialty was store windows and usually the local big names like Wanamaker's or Strawbridge and Clothier would contract him out for his unique talent of dressing a display window perfectly. I've seen some of his work in Philly and was always impressed. Still, like many of the folks around here, he was never able to (or never wanted to) fold his tent and move away. Atlantic City meant too much to him and he had his mother Joan, now in her eighties, to take care of.

He secured a promise from me to share the recipe and we finished our coffee but seconds were always in order.

As he poured my cup (which had "Best Son in The World" printed on it in bold, black letters), I could hear the faint, tinny sound of the TV just inside the house. I held the cup in both hands and asked, "Robin, when did you know?"

He looked at me quizzically and offered me sugar.

I realized I was being cryptic. "That you were gay."

"Oh," he said and began pouring his cup. "Wow, I guess since I was just a kid. It's always been that way with me...ever since I can remember."

I nodded. "But when did you, you know, realize it?"

"You mean accept it?" I didn't think there was anything defensive or bitter in his reply, but sort of felt like I was standing on ice that was breaking up under my feet.

"I'm sorry, I..."

He waved at me and sat back, thinking, and I could see that it was genuine. He wasn't just amusing me and I was relieved to see that I hadn't crossed a line in our friendship. I've always known he was gay and he always seemed to be comfortable around me but he never spoke of any lovers or boyfriends to me and I never asked. I certainly never saw any other men in his house. We had an unspoken understanding of each other.

He suddenly looked at me and smiled, showing his beautiful white teeth. "Are you coming to our side?"

"No," I said, smiling, "but I'm sure the water is warm, crystal clear and the sun is always shining over there."

"And the men are gorgeous," he added with a laugh. I loved his laugh.

I thought of his mother in the small house that the two of them have lived in all their lives. Robin had no brothers or sisters and I knew next to nothing about his extended family.

"Does your mom know?"

"Oh, sure," he said and plucked another muffin from the basket and split it with a knife, giving me the other half. "I mean I don't bring any guys around here or anything but I told her before anyone else."

"How old were you?"

"I think about twenty or so," he said, taking a bite from the muffin.

"What did she say?"

"Well, I think she knew already because she didn't seem that surprised to be honest. She's always just accepted it." he said.

* * *

1957

The day has been a full one, God knows, and I should be more tired than I am.

Max, looking so ready for the world, waved to us from the stage, smiling, the rolled paper in his fist high above his head. Abby and Brenda looked bored. The whole ceremony took about two hours and I didn't mind; I was happy to see Max enjoying the day.

The party was wonderful: a backyard full of family and friends. I couldn't help but glide near Stuart a bit, just to hear his voice and his laugh – he has such a wonderful laugh! Max, meanwhile, was congratulated over and over and asked what his plans were for the future, to which he had no answer but a shrug and a smile. Dad, of course, told everyone that he was going to Rutgers on a basketball scholarship.

When no one was looking I made faces at him while he glad-handed the guests. He mugged back and I could tell that he was beginning to tire of the whole party.

After the party the guests filtered back to their cars and Max and Stuart decided to take in a movie. By the time they're about to leave they still hadn't chosen between The Caine Mutiny *or* Dial M for Murder. *In the back of my mind I had hoped they would invite me along.*

"Great party, huh?" Max said. "Tell mom I said so, okay?"

"No way, she'll want to hear that from you herself," I took him by the shoulders and pointed him toward the kitchen where mom was cleaning up.

Stuart drifted over to the fireplace and gently picked up one of the small clay sculptures I did last summer. a dog's head, a collie, and I have to admit that the details were pretty good. I'm getting better. Dad liked it so much that he placed it in the center of the mantle. Over the past year the collection had grown to include a starfish, a child holding a teddy bear and an angelfish. I enjoyed making them but am done with sculpture for now. I'm more interested in painting.

Stuart is so handsome in his suit and the way it brings out the color in his light blue eyes took my breath away. My crush on him has only gotten worse over the past two years. I think I might be in love with him! I adore his loopy smile and the way a few strands of his dark brown hair always seemed to fall perfectly across his forehead - untamed and defiant. He was also really funny which is absolutely a must for any man that I'm going to be with.

I would love for Stuart to be that man.

"I did that," I said and then felt stupid because I had nothing to follow it up with. I just smiled and put my hands together.

"Yeah, I know. Max said you're growing into quite an artist," he said and brushed back a couple of those rebellious strands from his face. "You did all of these?"

I tried to act casual, glancing at the tiny pieces on the dark wooden mantle and then quickly away. "Oh, yeah, a while ago," I said. "He told you I was an artist?"

"Among many other things," he answered, grinning and I was beginning to think that he had a wonderful secret living behind those beautifully sculpted lips. Maybe he'd been feeling the same way about me and just wasn't able to admit it.

I took a few steps closer, looked back at the kitchen doorway and said quietly. "Like what?"

By now I could tell that he knows I like him. It's something in his face and eyes, but that didn't matter. He moved the dog head nearer to the little boy and flashed his perfect-teeth smile again. "Oh," he said, looking at the ceiling as if thinking, "uh, let's see...scholar, music expert -"

"That's him, not me," I smirked.

"Great swimmer, wonderful dancer-"

"Well, that's true," I laughed.

Max came out of the kitchen and Stuart quickly leaned in, "He goes on a lot about you, you know. He says the guy who gets you will be the second luckiest man in the world."

I turned away, suddenly feeling shy and exposed, but then stopped. "Wait, second luckiest? Who's the luckiest?"

But Stuart backed away, shaking his head gently and smiling. Max looked at the two of us curiously. "What are you two going on about?"

Stuart closed his eyes and shrugged innocently.

"C'mon, man, let's go," Max said, patting Stuart on the shoulder. On the way out the front door he called back, "See ya, Drip!"

I followed quickly, trying to think of a way to stall them and corner Stuart for a few more seconds, but nothing came and all I managed was to tell them to have a good time. I really wanted to punch Max in the arm for calling me Drip in front of Stuart. I would do that later for sure.

I folded my arms and watched as they walked down Seaside toward the boards. The sky over the ocean had turned sapphire in the fading light from the west and they became black shapes before disappearing.

Right now I'm enjoying the quiet of the house, laying in bed and watching the dull light from the street lamps seep through my open window and play in the corner of the room. Occasionally a car passes down the street and I track the reflected lights as they move across the ceiling. Stuart's smile materializes as I close my eyes and imagine him asking me with his beautiful lips to go for a walk alone on the beach. I hope that it is my last thought before sleep. That would be so nice.

I take a deep breath. There will be time for Stuart later because, if what I heard was true he wasn't going away to college just yet. Max said that he had been trying to convince him to apply to Rutgers next year so they could room together but it looked like Stuart was staying put in the city at least for the time being.

I wonder why? Maybe a certain sister of his best friend is always on his mind and he just can't imagine a life without her. It would be understandable. It's never easy telling your best friend that you're in love with his sister. I try to imagine how awkward that conversation would be for him. I hear him saying...

"...Max, the fact is I'm crazy about Hope and always have been and I'm gonna be with her, got it?"

Okay, best not to start hearing wedding bells just yet. It will be nice, though, having Stuart around without Max always swooping him away to another movie or party.

The front door opens and I listen, waiting. I picture Max closing and locking the door gently, aware and a little cautious that he's late getting in. I rest my cheek in my palm and follow the sound of his climb up the stairs. He manages to skip over the squeaky step that dad never fixed, third from the top and I smile before feeling sleep finally tug at me. The clock on my bedside table reads 12:57.

When I wake up I'm staring at the clock again.

2:13

The gauzy haze of a dream lingers and an uneasy feeling fills my belly like cold water pouring into a steel pail. I sit up and look at the corners where the dark blended out the light from the street. Then I hear a muffled sound from out in the hallway.

I wait a moment and push my covers aside. The sound comes again: a hushed, distorted moan. I open my door quietly. A dim slice of light is coming from under Max's door and I slink over, cupping my hand to my ear and listening.

A cough, slight and fragile. Max clearing his throat? Quiet.

Maybe he and Stuart celebrated a bit too much. I take a step toward his door and then stop when I hear a familiar, rough force of breath and then another, gentler.

"Max?" I whisper.

There's only silence on the other side so I slowly open the door.

He's sitting on the end of the bed and quickly wipes his eyes before looking at me. He's still dressed in his slacks and shirt, though they looked a bit rumpled. His eyes are puffy and pink, the skin under them looking tired and the color drained from his cheeks. His blonde hair, a bit longer than he usually kept it, is combed with a messy and uneven part. He smooths it down with both hands and attempts a smile.

"Hey, Drip."

"What's going on?" I stay in the half open doorway with my hand on the knob, keeping an ear out for mom or dad. "Are you okay?"

"Yeah, sure, everything is…great," he says, talking slowly and slurring a little. He's looking at me but past me, his bloodshot eyes fixing on the hallway beyond the door. He puts up one hand and waves slowly. "Close the door, okay?"

I nod and pull the door quietly. When I walk over and catch a sharp smell, I wince. "Are you drunk?"

"I don't know, am I? Is that what this is all about, being drunk?" He blinks and shrugs, "If so then I'm not drunk enough."

I sit next to him and watch as he swayed to the left and uses his hand to steady himself.

"Well, look, I don't care, you know that, but if dad or mom catches you, you're in big trouble, so here," I try to lean him back but he stops me.

"I don't wanna go to sleep," he waves his hands.

"Well, fine, but try to keep it down, okay?"

He looks up, his lids drawn heavily over his eyes, but focused. "Okay."

I get up but he quickly grabs my wrist. "Wait, don't go."

"What?" A tear spills down his cheek and he wipes it away with the back of his hand. I sit down again and take his hand. "What's wrong?"

He chews his bottom lip. "Tonight Stuart told me that after the summer…that he was going to Florida…to work for his uncle." His voice breaks slightly, fluttering, and he looks over at his dresser. He presses his fingers against his eyes, "or something like that. Apparently, he has a company that distributes appliances and his dad thinks it would be a good experience if he's going to business school. He's going to apply to a school down there."

Visions of Stuart leading me by the elbow, introducing me to his parents evaporate and I close my eyes. "He only told you just now?" I ask a bit louder than planned.

Max nods. "After the movie. We got into a fight about it." His bottom lip is trembling and he puts his hand to his mouth, swallowing.

"Are you gonna be sick?" I ask cautiously, putting my hand on his shoulder and trying to reach for his wastebasket. Max shakes his head but I'm not so sure. He doesn't look too good.

"I...I don't think so," he manages.

That's all I need now - cleaning up after him the same night I find out Stuart was soon going to be out of my reach. That would make it not just a great night, but a splendid one.

"I'm really going to miss him," Max says and puts his head into his hands.

"Tell me about it," I agree and when he looks at me with a curious look in his glazed eyes I shake my head dismissively and rub his back. "I'm sorry, really. I am."

"Thanks." His voice is warbling. His shoulders shake and more tears come.

"Hey." I lean in closer and try to sound encouraging, "it's not like he's going around the world or anything, right? I mean, I'm sure you can call each other and he'll have to make a trip up every now and then, I guess, for family."

And then he'll reveal his true feelings for me? Maybe. That dream is getting a little fuzzy at the edges right now.

Max pulls his hands away and looks to me. I've never seen him so desperate looking - the skin around his eyes is pinched tightly and looks so white. His mouth draws back. Tears have traced their way to his chin and it scares me. He's drunk but that isn't all that I'm seeing.

"I love him," he says quietly and looks down as if ashamed. His chin is touching his chest.

"Well...yeah, of course you do." I know that on the rare occasion when dad has a few too many he suddenly loves everyone. "We all love Stuart."

Some of us more than others...

He shakes his head silently.

"Hey, I love my friends, too, you know," I add, "and a lot of them are going away when they graduate: Gina Tedesco...Margaret's going to University of Alabama for some reason or another and Sheila Spieler - "

"I'm tired of lying," he whispers, not looking at me anymore, but at the floor and then out to the window. "I'm just so goddamn tired."

"What are you lying about?"

"I've been lying to you, too," he says, his head still turned away. "I'm sorry."

I wait. My mouth is open but nothing comes out.

"Stu and I aren't just friends." The words dribble out and he finally looks at me.

I feel a bit warm and dreamlike as if I never really placed my foot on the floor and opened his door. Somewhere maybe it was still ten o'clock and I was enjoying the end of a good day, a good party. Maybe somewhere Max was still out of the house and when he came back, he would be whistling and smiling. We would laugh over breakfast about the day before and –

"What do you mean?" I ask, the words coming fast and without thought. I don't want to sound angry, but the question comes out sharp and a look of guilt flashes through his eyes. I regret it immediately and realize that I truly don't want to know anything more.

"For a while now we've been," he says and drops his eyes to the floor again, "closer than friends. Neither of knew what was happening but then..."

I look around the room, as if my answer might be hanging on one of the walls, maybe framed into a neat wooden square. The small red flowers on the wallpaper looked orange in the dull light from his bedside table. I shake my head, still unsure of what to say.

Max keeps his head down, slow breathing.

If what I thought Max was saying was right, then I'd heard the word before. Kids joked about it in school but of course no one would ever admit to actually being one. The boys are called fags and the girls are dykes. There are other words...

Is my brother telling me he's a fag? A queer? A homo? The words bounce around in my head in the voices of my friends and other faceless students, unwelcome, but still screaming loud. Whenever anyone had said the words we all laughed every time, not knowing what else to do. The boys would usually single out someone each year and it was that poor boy's fate to be a verbal and even physical punching bag for the year. It wasn't any better for the girls and it didn't matter if it was true or not, once that rumor got legs it was social death for you and anyone who was a friend.

Or a sister.

Jesus, leprosy would be better.

Max suddenly looks pathetic to me, small and strange and I want to leave, leave him and his problems on this side of the door. Leave, shut it, and go back to bed. My brother's not a queer. How could he even think that Stuart is a queer?

"You're drunk," I say flatly and shake my head, "and it's been a really long day, okay?" This night will end and by morning he'll feel different and then I'll give him real hell for scaring me so badly.

I get up.

"Wait!" he hisses desperately and reaches for my arm. "Please, don't go!"

I turn and pull away from his hand. I don't even want to be sitting next to him but I'm not sure why. "What do you want me to say to that? That I think you've been drinking too much and you don't know what the hell you're saying? Because that's what I think about this." I fold my arms, "I'd rather talk to you in the morning when you're sober, okay?"

"I'm not that *drunk!" he snaps. "The reason that I drank at all tonight was because of what Stuart told me. Do you think I would make something like this up?" He looks at me. "Why the hell would I do that?"*

"I don't know!" I stab back at him through my teeth. He's betraying me...and now Mr. Popular brother is wrecking anything that could have ever been with Stuart and me.

"You have no idea what it's like to live with like this, okay?" he continues, now firing back. "Every day I try to fix it, fix me, but nothing changes. Nothing. I used to think that I would wake up one day and be better, but it never happened. So I walked around with my friends and talked about girls and dating and making out and all of it's a lie. Do you know how hard that is?"

He sits quietly, slowing his breathing. "The prom was the worst. The whole time I was with Beth I wanted to be with Stuart but he was with his own date - miserable like me but unable to do a damn thing about it!"

He bunches the sheets into his fists and everything inside me says go to him but the distance between us, even in his small room, is growing larger with each word and every silent pause. He lied to me, had in fact, been lying for a very long time and now my feet won't move - they refuse to carry me closer to him. If he's looking for sympathy it's going to have to come from someone else. He's draining everything from me and now he's telling me that he's been with the boy that I...

"Jesus, I'm so scared, Hope." He watches me for a moment and then his body gives out, collapsing in a small way as he sees that I'm not moving to him. "I don't know what to do," he moans. "I've tried to make it easier, but it's not." He begins crying. "I'm sorry."

After a few moments his sobs slow and he manages to sit up straight, but as I watched him, seeing his red eyes and his sallow-looking skin, I felt the anger bloom again. "But you did *lie," I say plainly, "and even if this were* true, *which I don't think it is, then you've been lying to everyone in this house, to all of us…to your whole family." The words seem as if they're coming from another person's mouth. "Both of you are liars."*

"We never really did anything," Max says in a whisper. "We were both too damned scared, but I still love -"

"I don't even want to think *about what the hell you might have been doing!" I snap. I'm worried we might be heard, but he flinches from me and I can't help but relish that each word from me now is a tiny slice into him, a thorn that stings. I can hurt him back.*

"Where have you been going? Down to New York Avenue?" Everyone in town, at least the locals, knows that New York Ave is where the queers all hang out. The cops would make an arrest now and again

to keep things looking proper, but for the most part it was a fairly well-kept secret.

I feel heat creeping up through my chest and lodging in my throat. It's controlling my words. I'm afraid. That's what it is. I'm afraid. I watch him nod guiltily.

"Jesus, Max!" I turn away and look out the window, out to the street where things still make sense.

"It was the only safe place," he mutters.

"There are no safe places! Someone could have seen you! What would you have done if someone saw you two at one of those places?" I point a finger at him and don't know why. It feels strange. I try to remember if I've ever pointed my finger at him before. Does it matter? "Did you ever stop to think what it would do to mom and dad? What would it do to his job?"

I put my hands on my hips because I don't know what else to do with them. I don't want to look like mom, but my body is making movements and saying words on its own now. I'm not in control anymore. "How could you be so goddamn selfish?"

"Is it really them you're worried about?" he spits out. "Or is it that you don't want anyone to know that you've got a fag for a brother. Is that what this is all about?" There's the hard edge of anger under the fear now and I welcome it. Easier to deal with that emotion right now than the simpering, sagging older brother pleading for forgiveness.

"Shut up. I don't have a fag for a brother. I don't know who or what you are, but you have a hell of a nerve asking me about honesty after this." I face him squarely, "and, if you have to know then, yeah, the last thing I need right now in my life is for the whole school knowing that my brother's a queer."

He swallows and puts his hands up. *"You have to promise not to tell anyone, okay?"*

He's right. He doesn't even have to ask. Something like this could wreck his chances of getting into college, getting a job and God knows what else. It would all vanish if this got out. I would be singled out as well. I'd have to put up with the questions, the smirks and the finger pointing. No way, that can't happen. Max can choose to destroy his own future, but he's not pulling me under with him.

"Believe me, I won't," I say, "but what about mom and dad?" I ask the question with mock honesty and the sharpness of a dart. I mean to make it hurt and uncomfortable.

"Jesus, no, especially them!" he hisses, looking as if the walls were about to fall and crush him. "What do you think they would say? Do you think that dad's going to give me a great big hug if he finds out? Think mom will invite the neighbors over?" He rests his hands on his knees and his shoulders sag. "I can't take that chance. You have to promise me that you won't say a word, okay? I mean it, not a word."

I realize, growing angrier, that he had it all and he acted through it all. He put on a show and took the popularity and the cheers when he needed them, but now, now that he was asking for help he comes to me and asks me to keep his secret, to keep both of their secrets. There's this nagging desire to burst that bubble with what I know. I could tell everyone except that it was a double-edged knife and would cut both of us to shreds.

I nod and take a step toward him. "I told you that I wouldn't say anything and I won't. But since we're both being so open with each other," I say and glare at him. "I wish to hell you hadn't told me," I mutter and leave.

I pray that Max tells me the next morning that he was so drunk that he didn't know what he was saying but it never happens. For a week the two of us make counterfeit, polite conversation at the dinner table. It's painful, but I can't find forgiveness no matter how deep I dig, it just isn't there. Stuart is out of my reach now, for the most unfair of reasons and Max has no clue how much I'm hurting because it's all about him.

There are no more visits to each other's rooms and the doors stay closed.

CHAPTER
10

Jamie

For three days the sky remained cloudy and rain poured both morning and night. Probably the last of the storm moving away. I was starting to feel like a bug under a glass, maybe under a big gray bowl. Nicky and I practically camped out in the living room watching reruns or escaping the boredom by going to Steel Pier. I still hadn't seen Benita much and it pissed me off that my early morning patrols - going out onto the deck and trying to act casual as I watched her building hoping to see her - hadn't paid off.

One of the worst days of the summer always came in the last week of July – can't say I cared enough to remember when – Seth's birthday. It was never hard to see it coming; the week before an army of cleaning crews and cooks would arrive at the house, vans would pull up in the driveway and out would spill dozens of workers. They would sweep, dust, wipe and polish everything in sight, crawling up to windows and cleaning out gutters while deftly slipping past each other with their sponges and buckets. They spoke very little, and what few words they did say were in Spanish.

Streamers and balloons would decorate the front of the house. The family cars would be cleaned until they sparkled and large circular tables, not yet draped with colorful tablecloths, would roll out of the back of a small truck and into the yard.

The rest of the neighborhood was treated to this closed affair every summer and could easily see the goings on through the gates but were certainly not invited. The guests arrived in shiny cars and wore expensive jewelry and deep tans. The guests would wear shirts with emblems on them and laugh too loud at their own jokes while they balanced mixed drinks. The women would smile, wearing bright lipstick and shapeless dresses.

This year, Seth's party was on a Friday and started around noon. A large banner reached across the yard with "Happy 16th Birthday Seth!" on it.

The weather broke that Friday morning which only further pissed off Nicky. He had been pulling for a downpour on that day for a week. We stood on the deck and watched the Natone yard fill with guests and I tried suggesting other things to do to get away from it all, but Nicky would shake his head and stare, hypnotized. It was like he enjoyed torturing himself. An olive-colored VW van bumped down the street leaving a trail of gray smoke behind it and the two of us watched it empty out.

"He even got a band this year?" Nicky moaned and raised his hands in the air as half a dozen men began unloading instruments. He slapped the railing and his eyes darted about as he watched Seth greet them with hugs.

"Are we going to have to hear crap all night?" Nicky bitched.

Liz and Crystal came out and leaned on the railing.

It didn't take them very long to set up and the first song they played was Misty Mountain Hop. I think their name was Sugar Train or something like that. They followed with some Segar, Badfinger and then some Boston. The music echoed off the house fronts and down the street.

They were pretty damn good, too. No way I was going to say that to Nicky, though. The whiskered-faced singer leaned into his microphone as the girls shook against the stage and my eyes fell on their tan legs that disappeared into their tight shorts. The street was filling with neighborhood kids and I spotted Benita out on her steps, dancing with Debbie and Julie.

Are you kidding me?

The band finished their first set with Mississippi Queen and the crowd cheered. The singer asked politely for their attention. "Excuse me," he said, looking around. "Excuse me, can anyone find Mr. Natone?" He looked to the band in a badly acted display of confusion and asked again. The musicians began looking around, shading their eyes and scanning the yard.

"Oh, please," Liz said, folding her arms.

"Maybe, but he's a total fox," Crystal added and both girls nodded.

"Well, I'm sure that Mr. Natone will be here any minute," the singer continued, "but in the meantime let's hit it one more time. This song goes out especially to Seth. We love ya, man!"

They launched into "Yer Birthday" and everyone began to jump and clap. At the end of the song an angry sound erupted from the other end of the block, near Oriental Avenue. From around the corner came a Corvette, growling, yellow and bright as a sunrise. Mr. Natone was driving and he was smiling, waving his hairy, tanned arm as he neared the house.

"Oh, no," Nicky said and his mouth dropped open. We all stood in silent respect as the Corvette slithered into the driveway.

"Whoa, kick-ass ride," Crystal said and Nicky glared at her.

Seth raced out and hugged his father. They said a few words that I couldn't make out, but I knew what it was about and watched as Mr. Natone handed the keys over to his son.

Nicky's face went dark and he let out a slow breath.

Seth climbed in. Friends and guests cheered and he gunned the engine.

Nicky made a clicking sound with his tongue, turned, and went inside without saying anything. I followed, leaving Liz and Crystal to admire the yellow monster roaring in the yard.

Nicky and I saw Seth and the Corvette frequently over the next few days – way too frequently for Nicky's taste. It roamed the streets like a hunter, slow and menacing and if Seth spotted us he would make a point of pulling up near us, hang his arm out the window, smile brightly, and toss us the finger. He'd rev the engine a few times before peeling out and disappearing.

"Ain't fuckin' fair, man," Nicky said one afternoon while we walked along the beach. He spat into the sand and angrily whipped a gray shell over the waves.

"Nope, it's not," I agreed. Maybe Nicky was expecting more of a response, but I didn't know what else to say and quietly watched the shell disappear.

"Here I am…got to borrow my brother's shitty bike just to get around and *that* asshole gets handed a rod like that?" he cried and bent to pick up another shell. "How is that fair?"

"It's not," I repeated tiredly. Nicky had been bitching about this since the party and that was three days ago. When we talked, no matter what it was about, it always came back to Seth's new toy. It wasn't helping that every time I managed to get Nicky's mind off the subject, Seth and the corvette would appear like a phantom and get him started again.

Nicky flicked his wrist and the clam shell flew out. "I mean, the guy does nothing but treat us like shit, insults my family and he…*he* gets a new car. Is that fair?"

"No," I snapped. "Why do you think it's supposed to be fair?"

"I don't know," Nicky answered and sat in the shallow water, crossing his legs and facing the waves. "Still, it pisses me off, ya know?"

I nodded.

After walking the jetties to see if anyone was catching anything Nicky and I headed home. I could feel my skin baking and was looking forward to the coolness of the living room. We passed the locked gate of Seth's yard and there he was with his usual pack of mutants and a couple of girls. They were all hovering around the new 'vette, talking and laughing loudly but quieted when they spotted us.

"Whoa! Hey fags, wanna ride?" Tony Tellori shouted, followed by that annoying, screechy laugh of Fat Ass Chuck. I glanced over and saw Seth waving a can of beer. Mark and Brian were behind him, chuckling and cradling cans in their paws.

"I know you guys are dying to take a ride and I'll let you, no problem, but on one condition," Seth said loudly and then chuckled. "Ya gotta blow me first, ok? Martre, with that beautiful mouth you gotta give good blow jobs, am I right?"

I put my head down and kept walking, already thinking about what shows might be on (anything to distract me) and how I was going to convince Lizard to let us watch what we wanted instead of reruns of that Hardy Boys shit.

One of the girls laughed and as I turned to say something to Nicky I saw that I was alone - Nicky was walking back to the black iron fence that surrounded the Natone yard. I could feel the muscles in my cheeks tighten and trotted back after him.

"What are you doing?" I asked in a hoarse, low voice. I reached for his shoulder to slow him but he shrugged me off.

"Shut up," Nicky muttered and walked along the side of the fence until he was facing Seth, his friends and the gleaming Corvette. They quietly watched him and smiled as he wrapped his fingers around the warm bars and stood still. Chuck was still giggling but Seth focused his bright blue eyes on Nicky and a smirk hung on his wide lips. He took another swig and dropped his can onto the driveway.

"What the fuck are you lookin' at?" he spat and started walking over. He was wearing white cut-off shorts and I could see the muscles in his tan legs as he got closer. The rest of the group watched but didn't move. Seth stopped when he saw Nicky reach for the zipper of his shorts. His eyes went wide and he laughed, showing every tooth.

"Oh, shit! He *is* a fag, look! Him and his blonde girlfriend! Both fuckin' homos!" He shouted and looked back. The gang hooted and clapped their hands as Nicky unzipped his shorts.

Tony yelled, "Holy shit, Seth, hold on, *he's* the one who wants the blowjob! Why don't you get it from your bitch there?" He pointed to me and cackled, holding his sides.

"What are you *doing*, man?" I asked desperately but Nicky was silent and watching Seth. The next thing I saw was Nicky's holding his dick and sticking it between the iron bars. The gang howled and the two girls went wide-eyed and giggled, covering their mouths.

Seth turned back, his lips still pulled into a crooked smile. "No fuckin' chance of that." His eyes became sharp as needles, aimed at us. When he saw a wide grin spreading across Nicky's face, Seth's lips dropped to a straight line and, except for Chuck's cackle, the laughter behind him faded. The moment seemed to slow in time. Chuck's squeaky laughter sounded hollow and was the last sound in the air before Seth turned to his corvette, shining in the bright daylight and looking like the sun had landed on earth.

Nicky released a stream of piss into the air that arced before dropping perfectly into the open window of the car. It splashed loudly inside, thrumming off the leather seats and sounding like rain.

"You fucker!" Seth screamed, his face suddenly flushed red. He charged the gate while everyone else let out a confused gasp as if the air had just been sucked out of their lungs. Nicky turned and aimed in his direction and Seth hopped back, avoiding the splash as it hit the hot blacktop. Seth rolled his tongue around in his mouth and I couldn't help but let out a nervous sounding laugh. I couldn't believe what was happening right before my eyes.

Nicky aimed his stream back into the car window and smiled, speaking out of the side of his mouth. "Get ready to move your ass, Jackson." Seth picked up his empty can and threw it at Nicky but it bounced off the fence and Nicky didn't even blink.

Nicky's arc slowly died and Seth raced for the fence, his eyes wild. He tried to grab him through the bars but Nicky backed up out of reach just in time. He laughed, shook himself off and zipped back up. Tony and Brian reached the front gate while Chuck just shared the girls shocked expression.

"Seth, the keys!" Tony screamed. Seth fumbled through his pockets, his lips going white and quivering. Brian started climbing the fence.

"Go!" Nicky yelled, grabbing me by the shirt. He pulled me with him back toward the boardwalk. He ran a few steps backwards, shouted, "Fuck you!" and then turned and kept running. He didn't have to pull me along anymore - I was booking by now, faster than I've ever run in my life.

We didn't stop until we reached Garden Pier. I kept looking behind us until we were sure that no one was following and we slowed to a trot. We ducked into the men's room to catch our breath.

"*Man*, that felt good," Nicky said, the words coming out in spurts between the hitching in his chest.

"You dumb ass," I said and shook my head, but smiled when I played the whole thing over in my head: Fat Ass Chuck with his eyes wide and mouth a perfect O, not believing what he was seeing. Nicky smiling like a lottery winner, his pee flying through the air, looking like liquid gold as it caught the sun and falling into the open window like it was always meant to happen that way.

"He shouldn't have said that to me when I had to take a bad leak..." he smiled and shrugged his shoulders. "I was holdin' that in all day."

"If you're that good of a shot why not play the games on the piers, man?" I chuckled. "You'd probably take them for everything they got."

Nicky laughed. "I need a reason to, I guess, and stuffed animals and the cheap crap they have isn't enough, you know? But that," he said and smiled widely, putting his hand on my shoulder, "that was the best reason ever."

We stayed in the bathroom for a while longer, waiting and making sure that the coast was clear, but Nicky seemed less worried than me. Neither of us had any money so we wandered the pier for a while.

As the sun fell in the west we made our way back home, keeping our eyes out on for the yellow Corvette or any sign of Seth and his gang. "Let's go along the beach, it's safer," I suggested and after Nicky rolled his eyes we leaped down to the sand and walked along the boardwalk.

"Whatcha wanna do tonight?" Nicky asked as we walked along the water.

"I don't know, maybe we can still catch something on TV." I tried to sound calm as possible, but I was busy scanning ahead for any sign of Seth and his apes. Nicky seemed to almost have forgotten what happened and it was making me angry and short. The closer we got to home the more nervous I was getting. As the sky grew darker I was feeling vulnerable again and as much as I couldn't blame Nicky, I knew he had just crossed a line. Seth wouldn't let this go or forget about it - he would take it out on both of us even though I wasn't the one who turned his car into a toilet. Because of Nicky I might end up getting my ass kicked as well.

I felt a bit nauseous, like the fear was poking around on the inside of my stomach and trying to find a way out. I listened for any sounds that might signal danger but the waves seemed louder as they crashed over each other. I don't think I've ever been angry at the ocean but right now it was pissing me off because it might be masking the sound of danger coming at us.

Nicky was walking casually, looking as if the world was care-free. He grinned and gazed out at the water, occasionally reaching down to scoop up a shell and cast it out over the water. I kept watch on the city side, over at the shadowed buildings of the neighborhood. "What do you think Seth's gonna do?"

Nicky looked as if the thought had never occurred to him. "Who knows and who gives a shit, right? I mean, you got my back and I got yours."

I nodded. *Right, we're like Starsky and Hutch, Butch Cassidy and Sundance, the Bandit and the Snowman…they would always be there for each other.* Still, I tried to spot any trouble ahead without looking like it. When we reached Vermont Avenue we took our regular route and cut under the boardwalk, at the point where it rested on concrete columns and loomed ten feet above the sand. The jetty met the boards here but there was an opening in the huge black rocks that we always used to climb through to reach the street side. Nicky headed for the deep blue light that showed the way.

I stopped, suddenly feeling cold and isolated. The whole place looked like a large black mouth we were walking into. "Why don't we just play it safe and –"

Nicky stopped and turned, his mouth open and about to argue with me, but he suddenly stopped, looking past my shoulder.

I turned around to look behind us.

Don't know why I didn't see it coming.

The shadows had grown long and reached into the darkness of the underside of the boardwalk, but I saw what Nicky was staring at: Seth, Tony and Mark had been using the concrete pillars as cover and now they moved into plain view.

CHAPTER
11

Hope

Max's room was remarkably the same after all these years, though now it was considered Jamie's room. The pretty little red flowers on the wallpaper seemed so bright back then and I can't tell if it's time that's faded them or my bitterness. It's been twenty years and the feeling is like a kettle that's been left boiling. It's always there, simmering under the skin but coming here, back home, makes it feel closer to the surface.

I had broken down in front of Robin, a first for the two of us. Talking to him about Max and that night was like confession and he couldn't have been more sympathetic.

That Max was gay was not news to him. I had told him years ago and had even told him what happened to Max and Stuart and why. What I could never get the courage up to tell him was how I pushed him away the night he told me. I didn't tell him that the wound was still open in the days between that night and the day he died. That I was ashamed that I never talked to him again or that we were both in love with the same man. So I brought the letter and let Robin read it.

"You're not the only one hurting here, sweetie," he said after he had handed it back to me. "It sounds like you both need closure." He took my hand. "Twenty years is a long time to be in pain."

I wandered down the steps and halted half way, where the turn of the stairs overlooks the living room. The furniture had changed a bit since that night when we all learned that Max would never come home again and even though it's empty, it seems smaller than it used to.

* * *

1957

Since I was a little girl I had pictured myself working in a shop on the boardwalk and Mr. Katz, who owned a small candy store near Tennessee Avenue and had pretty much known me my whole life, hired me right away. Now I was selling salt water taffy and macaroons to "shoobies," which is what everyone calls folks who came to the beach for just the day. I asked Max once what it meant and he told me that it was because they usually packed their lunches in a shoebox.

*"You know," he said and held out his hands, "'shoebox'…'shoobie."
We laughed and promised to never, ever become shoobies.*

At night I walk home along the boards, enjoying my first few days at the store and imagining how many stars I could see if the glow from the city weren't hiding them.

Millions and millions, I think.

The waves crash off the beach and I can make out the white lines of foam that roll in toward the sand. The buoys, flashing red and green, wink at me near the black horizon of the water and I spot the white lights and hulking shape of a large ship far away.

Things could be a lot worse, I decide, and walk over to the stairs that lead down to the beach. I remove my shoes and dangle them by the fingers of one hand.

The sand, still drying from the recent rain, feels cool and rough under my feet. I wander to the water and step along the edge, splashing one foot in the ocean and one on the wet sand. A wave charges, washing over my ankles and I jog away, smiling as if playing with an old friend.

I realize how much I miss talking to Max, laughing with him. I'm still angry but it has softened over the past couple of weeks. We barely exchange words anymore and it seems like he's given up trying altogether. Still, there are moments (maybe simply out of habit) when I think of something funny and he's the first person I think to tell because only he'll get it. I can tell when he wants to say something but is still giving me a wide path and I have to admit that I've enjoyed the little power handed me just by watching him look uncomfortable.

Maybe I'm being a bit unfair. Our conversations, when I allow them to happen at all, are stiff and uncomfortable. Something was lost that night between us and it may never come back if it isn't fixed soon. I have a hard time picturing myself laughing with him about anything anymore...

I enjoy the bite of the cool water on my sore feet before climbing up to the boards and then down the ramp to Seaside Avenue. The lights make hazy yellow and white orbs on the sidewalk and I hear the familiar woof of the Clarke's dog, Mollie. She has a loud, rough bark that can be heard from one end of the block to the other. maybe I'll find a treat for her from the fridge and take it to her.

Maybe surprise Max and ask him if he wants to go with me.

The houses on the street are quiet. I can see the white, electric glow of the occasional television set through some of the windows. Nights have become much quieter since televisions started becoming furniture. Is that a good thing?

Cars line the street and the glint of colored glass on top of one in front of my house catches my eye and as I get closer I see it's a police car so I move a bit quicker.

The living room light is on and two officers are standing by the unlit fireplace. One is speaking in low tones so I can't make out any words as I cross the porch. Both have their caps in their hands and the picture of that sends a drop of fear into my belly where it begins to warm slowly like a piece of coal catching heat. I try to ignore it as I open up the front door.

Abby and Brenda are sitting safely on the sofa but clinging to each other. Abby's head hangs down and Brenda has her arm wrapped around her, her cheeks flushed red and wet.

The officer who had been speaking is tall and has a long face. His hair is black, looks oily and is combed forward on his large forehead. His face is not a face that smiles easily, I can tell - it doesn't have the right structure to naturally invite grins or laughter. Nothing wrong with that, I've met people like that before, people whose faces are more suited to grave statements and somber expressions. No, when he looks at me, the part of his face that ignites the fear, the part that blows on the coals in my belly and makes them burn hotter and become ash-colored on the tips, are his eyes.

I've sketched, painted and modeled from clay hundreds of faces and they come in every flavor: cheery, perplexed, sly, polite and proper. I'm good at reading faces. This man's eyes, and for that matter, the eyes of the skinny, young officer next to him, with their crisp blue caps in their hands in a solemn gesture, flared the coal to a full burn, making it go white hot. It is a face that I'm not used to, had never seen before.

Something's happened. They don't want to be here right now. They would rather be almost anywhere in the world than right here. I open my mouth but nothing comes out. It seems like weeks since I was think-ing about getting Mollie a treat. Brenda raises her head and her lips are trembling. Her face has gone gray.

"Miss?" *the tall officer says. His name tag next to his badge said Marone. I guess that his first name is Paul. For some reason he looks like a Paul to me.*

"Excuse me, Miss, are you Hope, the other sister?"

My legs feel weak with those words, the other sister. *It brings every-thing into a murky light. Max is somehow outside that group right now. I can tell it's difficult for this man to speak, but I'm not going to hide from his sad eyes. Time slows and I feel like somehow I am controlling it in a distant way. Right now I can slow the world, but this man is going to say something, something that I know that I don't want to hear. I think for a moment that I might be dreaming and almost giggle.*

"I'm sorry, but there's been a very bad...incident in town." *He stands directly in front of me and I try to focus on him, maybe bring myself back from the place I've been floating to: Max swimming past the breakers and the lifeguards keep calling us back. He would always pretend he didn't hear the whistle the first time and swim further and it always scared me. But he always came back, always. Why is he not in this room right now? Where is mom and dad?*

The skinny, shorter officer clears his throat. I don't look at his name tag, someone is moaning upstairs.

"Oh, God, Hope," Brenda sputters. "No, no, not..."

I nod to the officer slowly, as if it might delay his words. Something is rising and clawing its way up from my belly and I try to force it back. It might be a scream or bile, I'm not sure, but it burns. My stomach suddenly rolls.

"I'm afraid your brother was involved in an accident," he says slowly and hesitates. "Well, 'accident' is not the right word, I'm sorry. There apparently was an altercation between your brother, a friend of his and a group of young men," his voice catches. "We are still trying to find out what happened, but it seems that during the fight your brother was badly injured. He was taken to Atlantic City Memorial," the officer keeps his eyes on me and suddenly his voice is the only sound in my ears. "He was unconscious when he arrived and I'm afraid that he never regained consciousness."

I stare at him and feel my head still nodding.

"His friend, a Mr. Stuart Patchick, was taken to the hospital as well and he's in bad shape, but it looks like he'll..." the officer's voice trails off or maybe I just can't hear any more words. I'm suddenly aware of my weight and how hard the world pulls it down, how strong gravity can actually be when you think about it. The officer put his hands on my shoulders to steady me, did I sway? I look at the floor and it looks so far away.

He glances anxiously to his partner before speaking again. "I'm very, very sorry."

I see my figurines on the fireplace mantle. Distantly, I think I would like to sculpt the tall officer's face. It's a nice face, even if it's not used to smiling.

I step away, toward the stairs. "No...no," I mutter, shaking my head and the next thing I know I'm bolting up the steps two at a time. "Mommy! Daddy!"

My shoes make strange hollow sounds as I race to the third floor. I think the officer is calling to me, but it isn't a real voice anymore – just a clump of words thrown together that hold no meaning. Maybe everything he said to me tonight was nonsense, it had to be.

The house looks different, as if the rooms have been rearranged or the lights put in new places since I left for work this morning. Shadows appear where I hadn't seen them before. The muscles in my legs threaten to give out as I turn onto the second landing.

There is no light coming from under the closed door, but I hear voices – deep, sad and painful. Dad is moaning on the other side like a wounded animal while mom is trying to speak to him. She's pleading with him and her voice sounds frail, as if it might shatter any moment. I knock so hard on the door that my knuckles hum. "Mommy! Daddy!"

Something is spinning crazily inside me like thread spooling out and falling from my belly to the floor. I'll never be able to wind it up again. Some vital glue that had protected me through the years, one I never knew I needed is becoming dried and cracked and can't hold my pieces together anymore.

Max and me are in his room. We're spreading white glue on our hands and drying it with our breath, then giggling as we peel off the opaque skin from our fingers. I cough and panic blossoms in my chest, first tight and then contracting.

"Mommy! Please!" *I slap on the door with my palm.*

My face is hot and wet. Abby is crying louder downstairs. I put my hand to my mouth and hit the door again, this time softly. My energy drains from my head to my feet.

"Please, mommy...please."

A choking sound is filling the room beyond the door and it puts a picture in my head: dad, sitting on their bed with his fists pounding on the sides of his head, tears racing to the corners of his mouth and the salty taste as they reached his lips.

Everything sounds hushed and distant but the door unlocks and mom's face appears. Her eyes are focused. Her hair, normally impressively brushed back and uniform is untidily combed, if it's combed at all. Her cheeks quiver.

I break into fresh sobs, "Mommy, no, not him, mommy." I look past her, into the dark column of the half-opened door. I can't see anything and try to move into the room, into the warm darkness where I hear dad, his sobs lost in there. For some reason it seems so safe except for the soft whimpering. I want to be inside, safely warm and untouched like I imagine when I was still in her mom's belly, hearing nothing but the soft beat of her heart. That was when Max was still in the world. My breath leaves and I'm afraid it won't come back.

Mom leans against the door, keeping it half closed. "Hope," she whispers urgently, her head tilted back as if trying to push the words out. "Hope, I can't let you in here right now. Honey, listen," she urged, her eyes wide and fixed on me. "Right now I need you to be downstairs with the girls, okay? I need you downstairs and taking care of things, okay?" It sounds like she is speaking through someone else's voice. "I want you to call Saint Catherine's right away. The number for the church is near the phone and I need you to call and tell them we need someone right away, okay? Right away!"

"Mommy, please I'm scared-"

"Right now, Hope!" she snaps, "I'm not sure how long I can keep this under control. I've never seen your father like this before. He's saying all sorts of crazy things. Listen," she says and her eyes narrow, "do not let

those policemen leave until Father arrives, okay? We might need them. In fact, ask them to come up here."

Before I can answer she touches my cheek in a sweeping caress and then disappears behind the door again. The voices rise again and I hear mom say something. Dad had been reduced to something sounding not quite human anymore.

I catch my hot breath off the door and the smell makes me feel ill. I walk down to the living room, my legs still hinting at giving up and I lean heavily on the banister. When I reach the bottom I ask weakly if the sad-faced officers would go upstairs.

"Of course," Officer Marone answers and he climbs past me.

I numbly tell the other officer that I'm going to call the family priest. What was his name again? "I'm calling him now," I say, still trying to slow my breathing and hoping that the nauseous ocean in my belly will go away. Panic has settled in and I'm afraid that it may never leave. "I'm calling him now, okay?" I repeat (I think?) and he nods as he heads upstairs.

And then I go blank. I can't remember where the number of the church is and mom had only just told me. Max would make fun of me for that. I think I can still hear the sad sounds of the dark room upstairs. I shake my head as if the thought is captured in a web and I can loosen it, maybe have it tumble down into my conscious mind.

Nothing comes, just mom's drawn and weak face. It looked ready to split and fall on the floor like a thin mask. She's just lost her only son, a voice says to me. He's just been killed. Your brother has been killed. He's dead. Max is dead.

Brenda is leaning against the mantle, wiping her eyes with the back of her hand and I go to her, shaking my head to get the voice out, make it go away. You never said sorry. It's too late now...

I wrap my arms around Brenda. "Where is the number for the church?" I ask.

"What?"

"The number for Saint Catherine's. I need to call them."

Brenda looks thoroughly lost. Fresh tears spill out. Her face contorts again, with her lips trembling and her skin flushing pink.

"Where does mom keep the phone numbers? I need the phone-" I reach out and hold her shoulders, not sure if it's in frustration or to help me stay standing.

She pulls away and points to the phone. "Near the phone, where do you think?" she cries out.

My heart is racing too fast to breath. I put my hands down and grab my skirt in fists. I feel stupid and helpless.

I close my eyes and I'm back in the last minutes of a life that was still not shattered: the wonderful, cool barefoot walk along the sand and the soothing sound the water made as it ran up the beach, the sound of the wind whispering in my ear and the barely perceptible call of a boat out at sea, the crashing sound of the waves as they rolled along the black jetties, losing a little bit of themselves with every splash.

What was on my mind when I was on the beach tonight? What was I thinking and will I ever be able to get back there?

I'm back in the house. It's quiet and all I can hear is my own breathing and the clock ticking in the kitchen. Not tonight...no, not ever again. My breath is slower and I walk over to the phone. I find the book where mom had said it was and pick up the receiver. It rings three times before being answered.

"Hello," I begin, trying to keep my words from warbling. "This is Hope, Hope Weathers from Seaside Avenue..."

Neighbors come to offer their regrets for the next few days and as the story spreads across the Inlet more and more strange faces arrive: friends from school, teachers, neighborhood kids. One unusually bright morning I come out onto the porch and find a beautiful bouquet of flowers sitting on the steps with a note that simply said: "I miss him." It's probably from a girl who had a crush on him.

The newspapers give few details: five men had been arrested and were being held. They were from out of town and visiting for the weekend. They were out for some "fun" on the night it happened. Max and Stuart were walking up New York Avenue when they crossed paths. Words passed between them and, according to a witness, the men surrounded Max and Stuart and began beating them.

Stuart is in the hospital for a week and on the day he is released, he and his family come to Max's funeral. His parents offer their condolences and Stuart tries to hug me, but I can only play the part so much and pat his back weakly in return. It takes everything inside me to not scream at him, to let him know that if he had never been with Max he might still be alive. Whatever this thing was that they thought they had together managed to kill one of them. I don't want both of them dead but I don't understand why it had to be my brother.

The numbness of Max's death settles in my bones and radiates out to my skin, an unwanted and constant guest. The door to Max's room is closed during this and everyone avoids opening it as if it was a tomb. I often find Brenda or Abby staring out windows quietly as if waiting for someone to round the corner of Seaside and Oriental.

Superlatives vanished into the woodwork of the house and nothing is anything more than "fine" or "okay." Dad begins drinking again, something that he hasn't done in years. Mom is silent about it and we follow her lead. I begin taking walks along the beach in the morning and sometimes I sit on the jetty and listen to the waves crashing until I cry. Every sound that was beautiful to me has somehow become muted since that night.

Did he ever forgive me?

Dad rarely comes down from his room during this time and I bring him his meal or a pack of fresh cigarettes upstairs. He only smokes cigarettes when he's nervous or upset mom tells me. I usually find him sitting in his low chair with the colorful cushions, staring silently out the window and can't see how the room, which was meticulously swept and dusted, could have looked like it aged so quickly. It looks like an old painting to me.

One night I come up quietly behind him and put my arm around his neck and rest my chin on the top of his head. The only sign of life he offers is to gently stroke my arm. He then begins to cry again; a muffled and deep sound from his body. I join him.

By the end of that first week mom gently orders him to dinner downstairs and he reluctantly agrees. She gets him back to taking regular showers and shaving. Soon it looks like Gerome Weathers has rejoined the human race, though for the time being he is a thin and papery member.

The trial results in multiple convictions with the one who is considered the instigator and who delivered the kick to Max's head getting ten years for second degree murder. Knowing that they all have lost a bit of their lives gives me little consolation. I keep my gaze away from Stuart for the whole trial. He sits across from the defendants at a table with his attorney and I feel him looking over occasionally, but never give him the satisfaction.

* * *

Jamie

The sand near the concrete supports was cluttered with cans of their favorite brand of beer - Piel's - so they must have been waiting here for a while. I only counted three of them right now: Seth, Tony and Mark. Where is -

We both took a step backward but I bumped into something and Nicky was shoved forward and landed on his belly. Someone grabbed both of my arms and pulled them behind me. I tried to break away but one of my wrists was twisted and I cried out and went down on one knee.

Nicky picked himself up quickly and his eyes darted from one approaching form to the next. He backed up but wherever he stepped, he was cut off.

I could smell beer on the breath of Fat Ass Chuck who had my arms locked up. He whispered into my ear, "Stay the fuck down, faggot." He kicked the back of my other leg and I dropped to both knees. Brian moved ahead to join the other boys surrounding Nicky.

Nicky tried to keep all the boys in front but they circled until Seth squared up in front of him. "Not so fuckin' smart now, huh?" he said, slurring his words. Nicky swallowed quickly and his eyes went wide, his pupils looking like pinholes in paper. "That car is worth more than your whole shitty house," he continued. "And now you're gonna pay for it, you prick."

They closed the circle around Nicky.

"Faggot."

"Piece of shit."

"Fuckin' homo."

"You're dead, motherfucker."

"Hey!" I screamed before I was slammed face first into the cool sand. My breath shot out and a few stars sparkled in the corners of my eyes.

I had only seen a couple of real fights in my life. They were always quick schoolyard things and never like the movies; some chest banging then words and then fists. They were sloppy, but no one ever really got hurt except maybe a bloody lip or nose. It usually ended either by someone giving up or a teacher running over.

This was no school fight and there was definitely no teacher coming. Nicky was pushed from one to the other until they had enough and together descended on him. He threw a couple of fists, but they were only awkward and he was quickly grabbed and knocked to the ground.

They brought their fists and feet down hard on him. Mark and Brian were laughing while they kicked and I could hear Nicky crying out. My face was pushed back into the sand again and I could taste the wet grains. I spat out and tried to yell for help.

Seth filled the air with cusses and his voice grunted under the effort of each kick. He dropped to his knees and hammered into Nicky with his fists.

I was able to turn my head and saw Nicky curled into a ball under the beating. Grains of sand stung my eyes and blinking only made it hurt more. Nicky could only let out a dull moan as the blows rained down on him. He wasn't moving or trying to cover up anymore, but he still winced at each hit. I was sure they were going to kill him and then they were going to kill me.

As I felt my eyes turning wet and warm I realized that the pressure on my back and arms was gone. Fat Ass Chuck had gotten up, walked over and added a few hard kicks into Nicky's back.

They finally stopped, admiring their work. Mark was still hopping from one foot to the other and landing a punch every now and then. Seth's voice came out in puffs. "Try pissing now…asshole…you'll be pissing blood." He spat on him and Brian picked up a half full beer can and emptied it on Nicky's head. Tony kicked sand into his face, some of it going into his open mouth. A weak grunt came out of Nicky's mouth as he tried to spit out the sand.

"Oh, and this is for my ride," Seth snorted and unzipped his shorts. Nicky was motionless as soon the other boys joined in a circle, chuckling. Seth shook himself off and finished with a kick to the side of Nicky's face. It made a wet sound.

I managed to get on my knees. Brian shook himself dry and calmly moved over and shoved me onto my back and I covered my face. I couldn't stop crying and they laughed, pointing, and stepping over me before they ran out into the last of the daylight, their shadows thrown across street in long, distorted shapes.

I waited to be sure they were gone before crawling to Nicky, who had managed to roll onto his belly and push himself up on his elbows. He sucked air in but it was coming in deep rattles. The cheek below his left eye had already begun to swell and his t-shirt was torn and flecked with blood.

"Holy shit," he said in a muffled voice that sounded like he had food in his mouth that he couldn't swallow. Blood ran from his lower lip to his chin and I could see a clean split right in the middle. He spat and wiped gently with the back of his hand and I tried to help him stand. Nicky got to his feet and steadied himself and then pulled his arm away.

"C'mon, we gotta get you home, man," I said and leaned in to inspect his face. "Can you make it?" His eyes looked unfocused until they were aimed at me. He stared at me sharply for a moment and slowly nodded.

The air felt cool and smelled like rotten clams. I put my arm around him and guided him as best I could. Out from under the shadows, I could make out dozens of cuts and scrapes along Nicky's face and arms. His nose had a deep gash across the bridge.

"Jesus," I breathed. "We can't let them get away with this." We walked slowly through the alley and the deserted parking lot of the Vermont Apartments to Seaside. "We'll think of something to get them back."

"What's all this 'we' shit?" Nicky hissed through his teeth. He spit some more blood onto the ground. Another moan came and he slowed, his legs bending.

"What do you mean?" I said, stopping with him.

"You keep saying 'we', man," he said, trying to clear his throat. "I didn't see you doing a fuckin' thing back there." He took a few steps away from me. "Not a thing."

"What?"

"You, man!" Nicky growled and pointed at me. "Why the fuck didn't you do anything? Where were you?"

I wanted to say something, but nothing came to mind that sounded right.

"Some fuckin' friend, man," he added bitterly. "I thought you had my back!"

"What was I supposed to do?" I snapped back. "How could I help you with that fat bastard sitting on top of me?"

Nicky thought for a second and then his face grew darker. "You know what I heard? I heard fucking crying, man...you were crying!"

He winced and put his hand to the side of his belly. "They didn't touch you at all, did they?" he said and looked me up and down before his lips curled into a sneer. "I guess they don't kick the shit out of their *own* kind, huh?"

"What the hell does that mean?"

"You know what it means." Nicky's left eye was swelling closed and tearing. His voice sounded wet. "You're just like them. Nice house, two cars," he said, "I guess it was easier for you to just lie there and cry like a fuckin' baby instead of helping me."

"What?" I yelled. "Who was the asshole who thought it would be funny to take a piss in Seth's car in the first place? Me?"

I waited but Nicky just looked at me and wiped his mouth.

"No, that was you!" I shouted before he could answer. I turned away and could hear a thumping in my ears.

"Where the hell are *you* going?"

My face felt warm as if the blood had all rushed up and I realized I was crying again. I quickly wiped my face. I didn't want Nicky to see that.

"That's right, go ahead and run away! You didn't do a goddamn thing back there, you pussy!" Nicky screamed, "You rich, fuckin' pussy!"

I walked quickly back. "It never seemed to bother you before, did it? That's because you never have any of your own goddamn money, do you? No, I'm always paying for shit because you're broke!" My hands were trembling so I kept them at my sides and balled up into fists. "You're always ready for a handout, right? And when the hell did you ever invite me to do anything except eat the shitty dinners your mom cooks at your shitty house? I guess that's why you're always hangin' around at my house, going places with us, right? Because you know you live in a shit hole!"

"My mom is always working!" Nicky screamed and took a step forward, "and Gary-"

"Fuck you!" It felt like my stomach was about to fall out of my body and land on the sidewalk in a messy, wet heap. Nicky looked at me and then slowly nodded.

"Fuck you, too," he said quietly and turned.

I stood, breathing hard and watched as he took another three steps before stumbling and falling face first onto the pavement.

Hope

I've seen Jamie cry many times over the years - too many to count, probably, but when he threw the porch door open I could see in his eyes that there was something really wrong. He and Nicky were jumped by a gang (he said he didn't know who they were) and Nicky got hurt bad. "He started walking and then fell and couldn't get up," Jamie blurted through gasps for breath. I tried my best to calm him down, but his words all came out in a flurry. Someone must have seen it happen and called an ambulance. Jamie stayed with Nicky, but he couldn't wake him up.

"He wasn't moving," he said, starting to cry. "The ambulance came, but they wouldn't let me go with them."

I grabbed the car keys. Charlotte was probably just getting ready for work so I called and thankfully Gary picked up. He said they would meet us there. Liz even let her guard down and helped by cleaning the few cuts on Jamie's cheeks and chin while I was on the phone.

She would stay with mom and wait by the phone for us to call. I saw a young woman now, someone who I could rely on and I was grateful for that. She nodded and listened, never once rolling those beautiful brown eyes of hers. I gave her a kiss on her forehead as I followed Jamie out to the car. The only hospital they would have taken Nicky to was Atlantic City Memorial.

Hell, it was the only hospital in the city.

We checked with the nurse at the emergency room desk as Jamie scanned the place, probably hoping to see Nicky somewhere, sitting up and waving. He kept wiping his eyes and looked like he was about to jump out of his skin. The nurse found Nicky's name just as Charlotte and Gary came in. There wasn't much information the nurse could give us as we held on to each other, but she said that Nicky was taken right into surgery. Jamie looked lost for a moment and Gary took him away gently, putting his arm around him and speaking softly into his ear. Jamie sobbed, but managed to nod and hugged him.

We waited three hours before a doctor was able to come out and talk to us. He looked like someone's grumpy but still lovable uncle. He wore a pair of small spectacles that rested on the end of his nose and had thoughtful-looking green eyes. His hair was pure white and he wore it combed back. I liked that he sat down with us and smiled at Jamie right away.

We learned that Nicky had regained consciousness by the time he was brought into the emergency room, but was having labored breathing probably caused by an excess of blood surrounding his lungs. The term he used was *intubated* and I hated the way it sounded. I explained to Jamie that it meant they sedated him and put a tube down his throat to help Nicky breathe.

"The blow to the head that your son received is now our main concern," he said to Charlotte and a sound escaped me. It was between a gasp and a small chirp that a bird might make and I instinctively put my hand to my mouth. He looked at me for a second before continuing: "He is still sedated and hopefully the picture will be much clearer by morning."

"Meaning what exactly?" I managed with a fluttery sound in my throat. *Please no, not again.*

"Well, to be honest," he said and hesitated, looking at Charlotte and Gary, "to see if there was any damage to the brain. We were ready to remove a piece of the skull if we had to relieve any pressure due to swelling, but that doesn't seem to be necessary. Still, whenever you're dealing with head injuries like this my strategy is to be cautious. I'd like to keep him sedated until tomorrow morning."

I felt Jamie move closer to me and I put my arm around him. After another few more minutes of answering our questions, he excused himself and said he would check with the nurses to see when we could see him.

Charlotte signed what seemed to be an endless stack of release forms. Gary's face was fixed into a determined stare as Jamie asked me if Nicky was going to be alright. He sounded so young.

"I'm sure he will be, honey. They have great doctors here. Don't forget, this is where you were born, right?" That didn't seem to convince him, but I was so shaken myself that I didn't know what to really say. I honestly didn't know if Nicky was going to be alright.

"We were yelling at each other just before this," Jamie said quietly and stared ahead. "We said some pretty shitty things to each other just before he fell."

Normally Jamie would have caught himself using a swear word in front of me but he didn't bother and I was fine with that. There are times when other words aren't enough. I put my hand on his shoulder. "Friends sometimes do that."

He shook his head gently and his lips trembled. "I don't think we've ever gotten into a fight before," he said. "At least not one this bad."

"What was it about?"

He looked at me as if he had just woken up, blinked his eyes a few times and shrugged. "Stupid stuff."

"It usually is, right?" I thought about the last words between Max and me. How I wished that I could have used the days between then and his death better. Seventeen years of words every day and then nothing for a week and then nothing ever again.

"What if something's wrong with him when he wakes up?" Jamie asked, making sure to whisper so that Charlotte and Gary didn't hear.

"Like what?"

"What if he wakes up, but his brain isn't working like it used to, what if..." His voice warbled before he could finish and he leaned into me.

I pulled him closer and kissed him on top of his head. "You only have to let him know that you're still with him and you need him to come back. If you have anything that you need to say like you're sorry or whatever, you just say it now. He'll hear you."

A young pretty nurse with short blonde hair came and told us that we could see Nicky. It would have to be short and only immediate family was allowed. Without a glance to me Charlotte nodded and told her that Jamie was her son. I kept quiet and sent a thank you through the air to her. The nurse, if she wondered why Jamie had such bright blonde hair compared to the rest of his "family," didn't show it and led them away. I watched them disappear through the doors and prayed that he would find the words that I was unable to twenty years ago.

Jamie

Half of his face was covered in gauze and white tape and there were wires taped to his chest that snaked under his sheet. A bag of clear liquid hung from a pole near his bed and another damn tube ran from that into his arm. Of course they had to have that machine you saw in every hospital TV show - the one that beeped and made you worry just when it would make a long steady beep. Nicky looked like he could have been asleep at home except that he almost always slept on his side or stomach.

When I realized I knew that little detail about him I could feel my neck getting warm, but I didn't want to cry in front of Gary. His mom stroked his head and face and it looked like the bruises he had earlier had spread like some disease or something. His cheek was puffed out and the cuts that he had around his face and head were wrapped now. One eye was swollen shut. I couldn't see his legs, but his arms were covered in scratches. Gary leaned in close to his ear and whispered something that I couldn't hear and his mom moved her lips quietly and looked to the ceiling as she crossed herself several times.

After a bit a nurse came in with a pillow and blanket and a young black guy carried in a folding cot. Nicky's mom would stay the night with Nicky. I asked if I could have a moment alone before I left and they both nodded, giving him a kiss before leaving the room. I moved closer and put my hand on his shoulder and was glad that it felt warm and alive.

"I'm sorry I didn't have your back," I croaked. "If I could have gotten over to help I would have but…" The words seemed useless and I replayed the vision of Nicky surrounded, a look of fear in his eyes that I had never seen before. "Please be better, Nick."

I heard the door open and the nurse smiled at me in a way that let me know I needed to go.

"And I never meant those things I said, man. You have to get out of here and be okay because…well, there's too many chicks that would be heartbroken." I took another look at the nurse and she was holding the door for me.

"So come back to us, man."

I tried to smile back at the nurse as I walked out of the room.

CHAPTER
12

Hope

I hated to leave while Nicky was still in the hospital and Jamie was needing me most but seeing his eyes as he came out of the room told me everything I had to know. I think I knew all the time.

When I told Randall that I was going to Brigantine to see Stuart he thankfully asked very few questions. We sat on the deck and he read the letter with his arm around me and kissed me on the forehead, asking if I wanted him to go and knowing the answer would be no. He needed to be here for Jamie in case there was any news.

I truly wasn't even sure if I was going to find Stuart. I never called the number, but still remembered the address. Maybe he never even came home or maybe he's already gone but if it was always supposed to happen this way, then in less than an hour I would be face to face with him. Randall walked me down to the car and gave me another kiss. I drove with the windows down and watched him wave to me in the rear view mirror as I pulled away.

* * *

1959

I see him out of the corner of my eye, nodding gently as he passes by the spotless glass cases filled with colorful, thumb-sized taffies wrapped in wax paper.

Eleanor, a woman with soft gray hair pulled into a bun is on the phone placing an order for delivery and she smiles as he stops in front of her to inspect each flavor in the case. He moves on, humming a tune and I can tell right away that he doesn't know what he's doing and is probably too nervous to ask for help.

I finish ringing up my customer, a man with glasses who smiles widely and has bad teeth. The last thing in the world he needs is taffy I think as I place his order in a crisp powder blue bag.

"I hope you have a nice weekend," I say.

The young guy looks over, hesitating and blinking. A child-ish-sounding bell rings as the man walks out the door and onto the crowded boardwalk. I duck below the phone cord and put the receipt into a drawer behind me.

When I turn around the humming guy is closer than before, but still eyeing the display counters curiously. He looks in my direction once or twice.

"Can I help you?" I venture. I like his looks though he's a bit slick for my taste. He has a curious glimmer in his eyes, something that says

he finds things interesting and I like that. He's all angles, however, with long, spindly legs that poke out from his shorts and pale arms that stick out from his short-sleeved shirt. The glasses don't help either. Still, he seems comfortable in his body and that speaks for something.

He looks like he's thinking for a moment before walking closer.

"Uh, yeah," he says and scratches his chin, awkwardly trying to remain casual. I've seen this behavior from quite a few men lately and have decided to take it as a compliment. Apparently, it took all four years of high school for me to finally bloom.

He looks at the black and white photos on the wall behind me. A few show the store from years ago: the workers are unsmiling and posing in front. "So what's the real story behind the taffy?" he asks. "My aunt asked me to get her some and, well, I don't want to hand a box of this to her and not have the whole story, know what I mean?" He bends down and peers through the glass. "She will ask. Is there real salt in these?"

I bend and look at him through the other side of the case. "Well, my favorite story is the one my dad told me when I was just a kid."

The tiny bell tinkles again as the door opens. Eleanor welcomes the customers; a young boy and his very elegantly dressed mother.

"How long have you lived here?" he asks, still bending to inspect the rows of colored candy. His eyes look large and fish-like behind the two slices of glass and I want to giggle.

"All my life. I was born here."

"Really?"

I laugh and straighten up. "Yeah, why, does that sound so strange?"

He holds his hands up. "No, no. I just...I guess I never heard of anyone ever being born here, you know?"

"Well, believe it or not, we have a hospital and everything. Babies are born here every day."

"Yeah, I'm sure. I just...uh, I just... I think I just talked myself into a corner." He nods and grins. "So," he says, shaking his head helplessly, "what's the story?"

I place my hands on the glass top of the counter, imitating the motions of Madame Cassia, the gypsy who has a shop a few blocks down on the boards. I visited once to have my fortune told and Madame said that great things were in my future. She probably tells that to everyone. I was hoping for something a bit more specific.

"Well, a long time ago this guy ran a small taffy stand right here on the boardwalk, on this very spot, back before they even had the rolling chairs. He wasn't selling much, though, and he had nothing to draw in the customers, uh, no 'hook' so to speak, right?"

"Right," he answers.

"So, after a whole summer of nothing and more nothing, he closed up one night, deciding that he was done. 'This will be my last summer!' he cried," and I hold up a finger to emphasize. "But that night a storm came in off the ocean; the waves were crashing against the boardwalk and the wind blew everything all over the place. It even tore up a section of the boards down near Virginia Avenue. People say they found the whole piece way over near Brigantine."

"Wow," he says and it's clear that he has no idea where Brigantine is. He's too busy watching me and I notice that his eyes are a different shade of brown than I first saw. The color is deeper and warmer.

"Well, the next morning this poor guy," I continue and put a finger to my chin. "I think his name began with a G or something, he thought, 'Well, I'm done for sure now, I don't even have a shop!' The door was blown off and half the roof was gone, all the windows were missing and *when he got inside the shop was flooded with ocean water. His whole stock of taffy was completely ruined." I nod to make my point.*

"Hope, honey, can you run in the back and get me some more of them smaller boxes, please?" Eleanor asks and I excuse myself after getting a promise from him to not leave until the end of the story.

"Are you kidding?" he asks, laughing. "Wouldn't miss it."

I twirl and disappear into the back room quickly. Bringing out a small stack of cardboard boxes, I check the door to see that no one was coming in. I can't help but smile when I see him in the same exact spot he was standing in when I left.

"So, where was I?"

"The man whose name started with a G," he says and puts his finger to his chin just like I did, "went to his store and all the taffy was ruined."

"Right! So a little later, while the poor guy was adding up his losses and ready to retire from the whole shebang, this little girl comes up and asks him if he has any taffy left and, again, according to legend now, he said, 'You mean saltwater taffy' and gave her some. Next thing he knows, kids are coming from all over Atlantic City and asking for it. He sold out that very day when word spread around. And that, sir," I finish with a satisfied smile, "was how saltwater taffy was born."

He claps his hands together and leans on the counter. "So, is that true or are you just a good story teller?"

"Bit of both," I say. "And do you know what happened to that little girl?"

"Let me guess," he says, looking around the store. He points to one of the photos. In it, there was a young woman with dark hair and a stern expression. "Her?" he asks hopefully.

I shake my head and point to Eleanor, who is waiting on the newly arrived customers. "Shhh...she's very modest."

He pulls his head back a bit, "Really?"

"You don't believe me?" I ask, arching my eyebrows. "Hey, Eleanor," I continue and keep my eyes locked on him playfully, "you were the little girl who discovered saltwater taffy, right?"

Eleanor doesn't turn, but smiles while boxing up her customer's order. "That's right, sweetie," she says, "tell your boyfriend there that I built the boardwalk, too."

He grins. "My name is Randall."

"I'm Hope," I say a bit too quickly and hold out my hand. He takes it and I swear I feel a warm wave run up my arm.

"I am, too," he says, still holding my hand.

"Too...what?"

"I'm hoping."

"Oh, God," I chuckle. "That's really bad."

He asks my advice on what to buy for his aunt and I guide him around the store, so thankful that there is no one else coming in. For some reason I know Eleanor will handle any new customers and I catch her smirk as she watches the two of us. I rattle off the flavors, which ones I like ("molasses, chocolate and lime"), which ones to stay away from ("peanut and black licorice...ewww") and what each size box costs. He asks me to repeat the flavors and we kept getting into other subjects, but we glide into them so effortlessly I don't mind a bit.

"So, you're obviously not from around here," I say.

"Nope. Wilmington," he points into the case. "Uh, three molasses, please."

"Wilmington?" I place the pieces into a box. "People are born there?"

"Every day."

"Hospital and everything?" I grin. "So what's it like there?"

"Boring, pretty much, you know? Nothing like around here."

"No seventy-foot tall elephant houses?"

"No."

"Any diving horses?"

"Uh, no."

I look at him disbelievingly. "Rolling chairs?"

He shakes his head in mock disappointment.

"Wow, that is weird," I say.

He settles on two small boxes, but continues to drift around the counter. The words between us seem so clear and natural. His laugh is wonderful and easy. When he cracks about something I sometimes have to cover my mouth to keep from laughing too loud. I've never felt so comfortable with anyone before except maybe Max.

"So," he says, looking out the window to the parade of people out on the boards, "where is the famous Steel Pier?" he asks. "I figure I have to see that diving horse, right?"

"Oh, absolutely," I answer, straightening my lips in mock serious-ness and nodding. "A must see."

"My aunt would never forgive me if I didn't bring back some sort of souvenir or something from there, right?"

"I know I wouldn't," I agree.

"Exactly, so can you show me where it is?"

"Sure," I point out the window. "It's that way, about seven blocks or so. You can't miss it. Virginia Avenue."

"Well, I was hoping that you might be able to walk me there...I'm near-sighted, you see," he says.

"Mm, hmm, but you're wearing glasses."

"Oh, these?" he says and pulls them from his nose, "Old prescription." He squints at me. "I've been meaning to get new ones. I could sure use someone like you to show me around to make sure I'm safe and don't wander off into the ocean."

"Well, that's easy, just don't make any right turns, but," I look to the ceiling, "if you are asking me to actually show you where it is, then you'll have to wait until five o'clock."

"Five o'clock?"

I smile. "That's when I'm done here."

"Great," he says, gathering his bag from the counter and putting his glasses back on. He walks to the door and keeps his one arm out in front of him, feeling through the air.

"See? I'm almost helpless," he says and shrugs innocently as he works his way cautiously out the door and into the crowd, still waving his hand in front.

"You better make sure that you stay in the shade!" I giggle and call after him, "You look like a burner!" I take a long last look and think that, yes, he wears himself very well.

Randall arrives at the store before five o'clock and I wave to him through the window and point to my watch. It seems like I've known him so long already...strange. He waits patiently outside, sitting on one of the benches that overlook the beach.

Later we walk along, taking a peaceful pace and peering into the windows and I unveil the tiny secrets that make up my town. It's nice that we have no real plans and Randall isn't someone who had to know everything that was ahead of him. He asks me to give him a real local tour, not the carnival stuff. I decide to give a bit of both.

"Well, jeez, you're in the wrong place if you don't want a carnival," I say and toss a few pieces of popcorn into the air. Two gulls swiftly dive and I giggle at how he ducks nervously. I hand the bag to him. "This whole town is a carnival, always has been. We've had pole sitters and guys jumping out of hot air balloons. At one time they had live babies in incubators on the pier and the world's largest dead whale on display. This was the starting line for cross country car races and, of course, where we crown Miss America every year." I can't help but spin and put my hands into the air. "And this was the only city in the country that was actually converted into a military base during the war. They called it 'Camp Boardwalk' and had training maneuvers right on the beach. I still remember seeing the soldiers sitting on the rails and whistling at the girls that walked past."

"I can see what they saw," he says, looking at me and I feel blood rushing into my cheeks. "So what's it like living here? I mean can you ever get bored living in, what is it, "America's Playground," right?"

"God, no, I've always loved it," I gush and walk over to a store that sells large oriental rugs. "I mean the smell of the air, the sounds, the sea gulls. What's not to love?"

"Well, I could do without the gulls, you know," he says squinting into the sky. "Don't they ever keep quiet?"

"Oh," I push at him playfully, "how could you even say something like that? To me, the sound of seagulls is the sound of the ocean, the sound of home. If I were a seagull I'd be calling out to everyone all the *time, singing my own song, you know? It's like a song if you listen close enough. Try it."*

Randall stops and listens to the endless banter back and forth; the squawking that climbs in pitch and then fades; the stuttered laugh that stretches as it's picked up by another gull and carried through the sky. "I hear a lot of arguing, but not a song. Not yet." He steps aside as a young boy runs in between us.

"Well, if you keep listening, eventually you'll hear a song, too. You have to promise me you'll keep trying."

"Promise." He looks ahead to the enormous sign on Steel Pier. Del Shannon is appearing, his name in letters twenty feet high. "You can see why I might miss it."

"Mmm, hmmm," I agree and grin.

Randall pays the admission and I immediately begin leading him around, pointing to the games of chance and taking him upstairs to the movie theater. Moby Dick with Gregory Peck was playing, but I wasn't in the mood for a movie. I pull close to him and cover my eyes as we ride through the darkness of the haunted house. I admit to him that I'm a bit of a chicken.

On one side of the pier, a diving bell drops down into the water and we listen to the passenger's voices from a nearby speaker. We hear giggling and nervous laughter. I had gone on it a few times and tell him, "You don't see anything, really, just sand and water, but it's still kind of fun."

We walk through the enormous Marine's Ballroom where every week hundreds of kids gather to listen to the current hits and boys try to romance girls. At the end of the pier is the water circus and the Diving Horse.

People fill the bleachers. To the left and right, white-crested waves roll to the beach where people stroll along the waterline. The show begins when a half dozen clowns wearing striped bathing suits charge out. They never stop moving, shouting to the audience and challenging each other to duels. They play tricks on each other, ask the crowd for cheers and pick up water-soaked weapons to slap each other. Some fall down to the water far below.

Children cheer for their favorite clown and sounds are piped from loudspeakers that make the whole show seem like one big cartoon. After some salutes and waves, they trot off, making big watery splashes with each step.

The next act was Rex the Wonder Dog, and he speeds through the water on a tiny board pulled by a motorboat as the crowd roars its approval.

Each act is more outrageous; a husband and wife tightrope-walking team, performing seals, a pair of dancing bears that twirl around the stage with their trainers and a group of poodles that ride tiny bicycles.

Finally, the announcer's voice comes over the speakers asking for quiet as Dimah was introduced, a magnificent brown stallion. He shimmers brilliantly as the fading rays of daylight strike him. The rider is introduced. Her name is Margaret. I lean in to Randall to tell him I had met her once and she was really nice. Randall nods, transfixed by the sight of the horse climbing the steep ramp to the top of the platform.

The crowd hushes as the rider climbs onto the horse's back and they approached the ramp above the pool of water. Forty feet above the pier Dimah stands poised with his hooves placed firmly on the ramp at the end. He seems to be basking in the attention, waving his head left and right and then watching a passing gull glide above. Margaret is patient, stroking his neck and leaning into his shoulders, her long blonde hair draping down his side. Her lips are moving and a few seconds later Dimah's muscles trigger and his body moves forward, sliding his forelegs down the ramp so that he's pointed at the waiting pool. A second later they are falling and the surface explodes as they both vanish into the water and the crowd erupts.

For a moment it looks like Randall isn't sure that Dimah was going to surface, but he does and with Margaret still firmly straddling his back. Dimah climbs out of the pool along a ramp and Margaret smiles and waves to the audience. She then pats and kisses the horse's neck. I cheer and whistle.

"Wow," Randall says, nodding and clapping.

"Yeah, the funniest thing is that each horse has its own personality. Some are show-offs and might take minutes to jump and then you have others that go right in. There's even one that doesn't stop at the ramp and the rider has to hop on his back as he charges off the end."

"But that's crazy," Randall says as we join the crowd that is leaving.

I take his hand. "That's why I love this place!"

We dodge rolling chairs and pedestrians and manage to find two stools together at the counter of Woolworth's near the Hotel Belmont. It's noisy, tight with kids and we order two cheeseburgers, fries with gravy and two cherry cokes. Andy Williams is singing "Butterfly" on the radio.

"So, I've seen what you do," Randall says, picking up a fry and dipping it into the gravy, "what about the rest of your family?"

"Well, my dad used to run a trolley, the line that started at Starn's," I say and then realize that he probably doesn't know what I'm even talking about. "Um, that's a place near where I live. A lot of tour boats and fishing boats go out of there. Anyway, now he drives a jitney. It's like a bus but different."

"So far everything I've seen here is different than everywhere else."

"Yeah, I guess so. Well, he complained a lot at first, you know, 'why do things have to change' and all, typical old folk stuff, but pretty soon he got used to it." I take a sip of coke. "And my mom, well, she's just my mom, but she's terrific, too."

"Brothers or sisters?" Randall asks and waves to the waitress. "I'm actually more interested if you have a brother, to see if there is anything that I should worry about. You know how brothers are."

"Uh huh." I place another fry in my mouth and slowly wipe my lips with a napkin. It's weird hearing about Max...we still don't mention him much at home anymore and it's already been a couple years.

"Me, I'm an only child," Randall continues, "but I always wished I had someone, you know, like an older brother or something. Someone to show me the ropes and all." He looks into my eyes and gives me a slick grin, "Or, even better, a younger brother that I could boss around, you know?"

I nod, but the smile that I have worn for the last couple of hours suddenly feels like it weighs too much. The muscles are acting as if they had been asked to do an enormous task. I don't try to make it return.

"You say that a lot."

"Say what?" he smiles, either not catching my tone or deciding to ignore it.

"'You know'," I say flatly. "You say it a lot."

He looks at me and the corners of his mouth droop slightly. His eyes tell me that he's considering my words, but isn't sure how to proceed. He taps his finger on the counter and the waitress comes by.

"Anything else, Hon?" she asks in a gravelly voice. She has pale skin and a pleasant smile. I stir the ice in my coke with the straw.

"Uh, no," Randall says. "Just the check, I guess." He scratches the side of his head and waits a few moments before asking, "Are you okay?"

"I have a brother," I say and my voice rattles a bit and it sounds like the words are being forced through an old can. "An older brother, but he's dead."

Randall opens his mouth but then closes it. I sit and turn to the crowd on the boardwalk. Finally, he says, "Hey, you wanna go for a walk?" and we leave the noise of the shop for the cool of the deepening night. The newborn light from the streetlamps throw our shadows together.

After a few minutes I manage to force some muted words out. "I don't talk about him much."

He takes my hand softly. "What's his name?"

"Max." I like that he didn't ask what his name was. We're quiet again as we pass by Child's Restaurant. "He was killed a couple years ago. I'm sure you wanted to know that, right?"

"Hey, I'm real sorry I-"

I shake my head and squeeze his hand. Our fingers are laced together and it feels natural. "Please don't be, you couldn't know. I'm sorry I acted that way...I guess I'm still not sure how to act when I think of him. Summer is especially tough but..."

A family walks past and I feel a small smile creep back. The mother and father are following as their children pull tiny wisps of cotton candy from a pink cloud that they share. I was glad that Randall was just letting me talk.

"I also have two younger sisters who are, in my opinion, little brats," I say. "But I guess they'll outgrow it, right?"

He shrugs good-naturedly and adjusts his glasses. "Can I buy you an ice cream?"

"Boy, you do like to eat don't you?" I smile.

"It's something about the air. Everything smells so good."

"Ah, you're being seduced by the allure of the shore, I see," I say and hook my arm into his and pull him along. "I know just what you mean."

We order two vanilla cones. "I'm sorry I snapped at you back there, that wasn't fair at all." I lick around the side of my cone. "Like I said, we don't talk about Max much – but sometimes it feels like he never existed. I know it's still painful for everyone, especially dad..." I realize I've trailed off and don't know where the next words are coming from, like looking down at your feet and realizing you've just reached a dead end street. I shake my head gently. "Anyway, don't stop saying 'you know'," I say and look at him. His face helps to clear my mind. "I think it's sweet."

"So now tell me about your bratty sisters," he says, "you know."

We stop to gaze into store windows and point out things to each other. It seems that we never run out of things to talk about. We laugh at a lot of the same things and I love his curiosity about nearly everything.

"Wanna see something cool?" I ask as we finish our cones. I guide him to the beach-side railing before he can answer. In front of us the sand disappears into the darkness before it reaches the water, but I can hear the waves crashing over each other beyond. I take his hand and place it on the railing, resting my hand on top. The skin of his hand feels smooth and warm, and a slight tingle runs through me.

"What am I feeling here?" he asks.

"Wait." I press his hand gently down. "Feel it?"

He slowly shakes his head and then stops, his eyes widening slightly. "It's vibrating, just a bit."

"Now look around."

He looks to his left and right. No one is near us. I lift his hand off and then smile before putting it back and feeling the subtle vibration.

He grins. "That's pretty amazing."

"You want to know what's even more amazing? My house is in the inlet," I say and point over my shoulder in the direction of the glowing Steel Pier. "It's way down past Steel Pier where there isn't all of this going on; no piers and no crazy shows, you know. It's quieter and there are lots of houses and families and such but sometimes at night I'll go out on the boards near my beach and put my hand on the railing and I," and my voice catches for a moment. "I can still feel it humming even there, even when there is no one in sight."

"It's like a pulse," Randall says and takes both of my hands. "Like a living thing, right?" he places both of my hands on the railing and rests his hands on them, standing behind me. I close my eyes and feel the vibration running through my skin, into my bones, up my arms and into my chest. I want him to wrap his arms around me and hold me. It would just feel right somehow. I think of Max but don't cry this time and it doesn't feel like my chest is about to collapse in on itself. An image grows in my mind that I haven't been able to retrieve in a very long time: Max with a smile on his face.

We go to Reese's Records on the boards and flip through rows of 45's while Frankie Laine plays.

"Did you know that Frankie Laine once won a dance marathon contest here?" I ask as I come up behind him and look over his shoulder.

"Really, when?"

"Oh, before I was even born. My dad told me about it." He has a collection of records in his hands. "Whatcha got?"

Holding the discs like a card hand he reads them off to me. "Jo Stafford, Pat Boone, Buddy Knox, and uh," he looks at the last one, "The Everly Brothers."

I nod.

"What about you?" he asks, turning and looking at my empty hands. "Couldn't find anything?"

"Not down here." I playfully take the records from him and look them over.

"What do you mean, 'not down here'?

I lean in close and whisper, "Do you want to hear some real music?" and before he can answer I quickly place the stack of 45's down and pull him out the door.

* * *

Hope

I still remembered the address after all these years. 305 Sandy Lane, right off Harbor Beach Boulevard on the southern end of town. I remember because one time I told Stuart that his street sounded like a Hollywood actress's name and when he laughed it felt as if it was just for me.

The sun was beating hot through the windshield so I rolled the windows down as I neared his street. Brigantine was like another world from Atlantic City: small, separate colorful shore homes and only one large hotel to speak of. Much more of your picturesque seaside town, it was quieter than Atlantic City as well; there was no boardwalk and the only pier was at the other end of the island.

Max was gone, but the only real living connection I had to the Max that lived those weeks after our fight was Stuart. He was the key and he had sent Max's last words to me in a small envelope with my name on it. Just for me. It seemed right that I fill in those gaps with the man that Max loved as much as I did.

I found 305 and pulled up to the brightly painted green fence. A "For Sale" sign seemed to hover right above it and beyond was the lemon-colored, one story house surrounded by a small yard. The sign depressed me more than anything. Who knew how long it would be before one of them was planted in front of our house?

Outside, the cars looked long and dream-like in the heat that rose from the asphalt. If I didn't know any better I might very well be asleep and not really sitting in my car in Brigantine outside Stuart's house.

I pictured how he looked the last time I saw him; still handsome as a devil despite the bruises and glancing my way sadly from his church pew, pleading with his eyes to not tell anyone. Keep the secret. I simply turned away.

What will he look like now? Will I even be able to recognize him when he opens the door? Of course his skin would now be looser on his bones rather than smooth and tight, maybe his eyes will be a little hollower because of all the years without Max. Has he moved on? I hope so but should I be mad if he did? It seems like we all tried to move on after that summer.

Maybe he still relives that night or maybe he visited those memories only when he dared, like me. Is it only when a life ends that we realize how much of our own lives they occupied? Maybe our lives mean nothing without other lives in it? That seems right...

"Hope?"

I turned and was staring into the face of Stuart Patchick. Of that there could be no doubt. He was peering into the passenger side window and I hadn't even seen him approach. Even from here I could see that his eyes were still a lush green. Some gray strands haunted his hair at the temples, but for the most part it held the rich black that I remembered. It was combed behind each ear and had retreated from the crown of his head slightly. Thick, clear plastic frames rested on the bridge of his thin nose.

He smiled genuinely when he had silently determined that he was right and I was, in fact, Hope. I smiled back and nodded, feeling a bit trapped now that I had been seen. I rolled up the window on my side and quickly got out, wanting to be out of the car that suddenly felt too small.

He gave me a small hug as I reached him and invited me inside. "I wasn't expecting you, obviously, but I'm so glad that you came. It's good to see you, Hope," he said in a soft voice that I instantly recalled adoring in high school. He led me into the kitchen and gestured to a pair of chairs. A very handsome young man with a short, dark beard and long blonde hair was collecting dishes and placing them in a cardboard box. He was wearing khaki shorts and a loose blue tank top that showed off his muscular arms and chest. "Hope, this is Michael," he said and Michael came over and shook my hand and offered a bright smile. "Michael and I have been together for, oh, going on - "

"Ten years, sweetie," Michael said and asked if I wanted anything to drink.

"Just water, please," I said and thanked him.

"I don't remember you ever being here before, is that right?" Stuart asked.

"I don't think so," I answered, looking around the room.

He offered me a chair at the small kitchen table and sat opposite me. His smile was reassuring. The cocksure look that I used to dream about at night was still hidden somewhere in there, but now - with the feathery lines at the corners of his eyes, the slightly stretched look of his upper lip and the smooth brow - he seemed more of a fellow weary traveler than an ancient crush.

"I'm so glad that you decided to come. I truly hope I wasn't being too forward," he said and took a small sip from his glass of water. The ice clinked. "It's been, what?"

"Twenty years," I answered and wasn't sure what more to offer. "Um, it was very nice of you to write me."

"What made you decide to accept my invitation? I must admit, I had sort of resigned myself to the fact that you weren't interested."

"I'm not sure, really. Curiosity, I guess."

"Well, I can say that I'm certainly glad you did," he offered. "At the funeral I didn't know what to say, especially to you. That was a tough day for everyone. I'm sorry that I didn't keep in touch after that."

I shrugged, but the reality was that if he had tried, I would have made it very unpleasant. That day was a bad hangover to be forgotten as quickly as possible. I myself only had clips of memories left and it was better that way. My family had managed to shut out the stream of recollection of that day or at least we never spoke of it.

"At the time, I was hurting, hurting too much and, well, I didn't really want to keep in touch." I said and realized I had been staring at the floor and forced myself to meet his gaze.

He nodded slowly before getting up and holding the door for Michael, who was carrying a box outside.

"Stuart?"

"Yes?"

"Why did you send that letter?" With that I pulled my cigarettes from my purse and reached for the ashtray. I felt myself becoming defensive and was conscious of my tone, which I wanted to keep cordial. "I mean," I lit the end, inhaled and slowly let it out, "why now? It's been so long."

"Well," he chuckled and sat again, "if you hadn't guessed already, we've finally decided to sell the place. Mom died a few years back and the place has been just empty."

"I'm sorry. I didn't know."

He nodded. "And there are things going on in my life right now that, well, just make it harder to come back anymore. My brother and his family aren't interested in keeping the house so we just decided it best to sell and split the money."

The more Stuart talked the more I felt isolated and disconnected. I never even knew his mother and completely forgot that he had a brother. So much happens in other people's lives that you don't realize when you're wrapped up in your own drama.

"How is Dennis?' I asked, dredging up the name from the murk and hopefully not letting on that he didn't exist in my world until five seconds ago.

He placed his hands together, lacing the thin fingers. "Not as close as we used to be." The sentence had a period on it and I left it there.

He told me how had visited the house about twice a year since his mom passed, just to make sure that all was safe. While going through boxes in the attic, the tiny envelope descended from the pages of the senior yearbook. He turned it over, saw my name and remembered the day Max spent half a day writing a letter to me.

"He wouldn't let me read it," Stuart said, smiling. "He was going to sneak it into your room, maybe place it under your pillow or in the sleeve of one of your favorite albums. I don't think he had a real plan." He ran his fingers absently across the table between us. "He wanted so much to say he was sorry. He just didn't know where to start. That's all he ever told me."

I could feel the expression on my face - the tightness on the forehead and cheeks, the slight parting of the lips – all of it must have showed how heavy the weight was. I managed to smile, but it felt like there was a vice squeezing my belly and I shifted in my seat.

"Max loved you so much, you know. More than I've ever seen a brother love a sister."

"We were so close," I murmured but felt my defenses lurking, waiting.

Stuart excused himself, assuring me that he'd be right back and returned quickly with a box in hand. He sat, placing it on his lap. "This is all Max's stuff…a few photos and books. I gathered everything I could find. I think you'll like the photos particularly. I had quite the eye with the camera and it helped that he was so photogenic."

I pulled the envelope from my pocket and placed it on the table.

The light of the room reflected in his eyes. "You still haven't opened it yet?"

I took my hand off the envelope. "I'm curious. I guess I want to know more about the man that my brother died for. I think I need to know what you were to each other."

"Well," he said, "He was my very first love. I'm sure you know that already." I nodded. His sentences were clipped and quick, as if simply bringing the words into daylight was difficult. Maybe he, like me, had been holding these words in some dark cave that he was afraid to enter after all these years. "Since then I've had other relationships, some mad crushes on movie stars, other loves as everyone will have, but Max... he still holds my heart like no one else has ever been able to."

I remembered Max's eyelids pressed together and how the light from the window, the off-blue that only occurs at certain evenings, slid across his features and showed every painful crease in his face as I closed the door. The bruise of guilt was growing inside again like a tumor.

"Of course, we were both scared out of our mind," he continued. "Being gay now is tough enough, but back then...and the only son of a proud father...well, you can imagine."

"Did your family ever find out?"

"No," he said, "but eventually I got up the nerve to tell Dennis."

Dennis: small and wiry with glasses and always a handful of books under his arm. He was one grade below me and I'm pretty sure he had a crush on me back then. He waved to me whenever he spotted me in school or the neighborhood.

"How did that go?" I felt like I was reaching for some redemption, something that might take the sour taste out of my mouth. Maybe I wasn't so alone in my fearful condemnation.

"Well, I told him about my...situation...one morning while we were alone in the kitchen. I still can see it. I was visiting and it was just the two of us. It was after breakfast and Maggie, his wife, had taken the children out for a walk in town and, I don't know why, but for some reason I had to tell him then. I didn't plan it, it just came to me that moment. I mean he was my brother, right? It was the biggest mistake I've ever made. I still regret it."

"He didn't take it well."

Stuart got a funny look to his face then, as if he was trying to pull the memory from a deep hole that had been dug long ago and was covered with heavy soil. The polluted soil infused his expression with a bitterness that was not there a moment ago.

"If not allowing me in his house or near his children ever since then is 'not taking it well,' then, no, he didn't take it very well at all." He picked up the envelope and looked at the writing. He traced it with his finger. "Maggie, who I had always considered a close friend, tried to calm things down and to hear me out, but Dennis wouldn't have any of it. He kept going on about me being a liar and how I might influence the kids and all…I felt like I didn't have anything to say to defend myself. Maggie eventually just stood there wordless."

Stuart removed his glasses and gently wiped his eyes before placing them on the table. "I don't blame her, though," he said. "They moved to Chicago a few years after that and I guess we'll end up as two old brothers who never got over this thing. Well, *he* never got over it." I hoped that the bitterness in his tone wasn't directed at me for taking the same route as his brother. "We still talk, but it's different now."

"Max didn't want you to find out from someone else and he knew a secret like us would be impossible to keep. He trusted you more than anyone and, well, when you reacted the way you did, he made me swear to never tell anyone. It scared the hell out of him."

"When Max told me," I said softly, "he made me promise pretty much the same thing. He practically begged me." My voice was a far off sound, like a child speaking into a shell on the beach.

"I know," Stuart said.

"I…didn't take it very well, either." My face quickly felt warm. "There were a few reasons why I treated him the way I did that night. None of them good." I sounded like I was testing each word before it hit the air. "You were important to me back then, much more than you knew." I was suddenly seventeen again. He was as handsome as ever but there was no reason to fear him, to fear his rejection now. "I was determined I was going to marry you."

I actually enjoyed his reaction; his eyes went a bit wide and then focused on me. The same beautiful green that I always remembered. No wonder Max loved him. You had to. He smiled widely and showed his straight white teeth and then awkwardly looked out the window, to the world outside. He tapped a finger on the tabletop, rested his chin in one hand before looking back to me.

"I had no idea," he smiled.

"I know." I felt a grin crawl across my lips. It felt good, like finishing a long book, to put those words outside of my body. "You were too busy being in love with my brother and, let's face it, who could blame you." I smiled but the sour taste came back like high tide. "But it was sort of a double punch when I found out. Max had no idea how I felt either."

Stuart nodded quietly. He finished his water and put the glass in the sink. "He told me that he was sure that you'd come around eventually. In fact, the day before he died he said he was going to find a place in your room to hide this letter."

"But he didn't just die," I said a bit more harshly than I intended. "He was *killed*. Saying he died makes it sound like some sort of accident. It was no accident."

"I'm sorry," he said, turning and leaning against the sink.

"I don't blame you. I think…I *know* I did for a long time. In my mind none of it would have happened if you two weren't together. I'm sorry."

Stuart looked helplessly glad and slowly shook his head. "You also came here for a reason. Because you want to know, because you want to finally forgive yourself, and I, for one, think that you should do that. You're not like my brother. He'll keep running from something that he doesn't understand. He's been like that since he was born. I'm not going to say that it makes it right, but that's the way it is. You've been carrying this around with you for too long, I can see it in your face. Whatever words were said that night between the two of you can stay here and you can walk away from them and out that door." He looked at the envelope and then to me. "I think it's time for you to listen to what your brother has to say."

Stuart's house was like most houses down the shore - a short walk from the beach. We gathered up our things and within ten minutes we were at the water's edge. Children raced back and forth into the splashing water.

Stuart handed me the envelope. The corners were yellowed and weak-looking. My faded name was printed on the outside and I immediately recognized the handwriting. I stared at the soft letters that had been carefully laid down on the paper. I looked to the honest green of Stuart's eyes and knew then that he was always meant to be here with me for this.

I think it's time to hear what your brother has to say.

I tried not to tear the paper. One last look into Stuart's face, with the light adding a sparkle to his glasses and his lips curved into a small, knowing smile, told me that he was almost as excited as I was.

Opening a twenty-year-old letter from Max, in front of a man I swore one day was going to be my husband ...

I let out a nervous giggle and Stuart smiled wide enough to show his teeth again and he rubbed his hands together, chuckling as if we were opening a present on Christmas morning.

Dear Hope,

I want to start by saying that I'm sorry for the way things turned out between us. I never meant to upset you but I guess in a way I knew that it would be hard for you to understand right away. We haven't talked much lately and I miss that. I know you still feel that I lied to you about everything but you need to know that I was also lying to myself for most of my life. I knew that deep inside I was putting on a show for everyone but I didn't know what else to do. I think you can see that. I wanted to tell you so many times what was going on with me but there was never the right time and although I'm glad that I finally did tell you I wish that it would have turned out differently.

Things with me are not going to change, that's a fact. I wished for too many years to think otherwise so you now need to try to accept me for who I am, whether you like it or not. I don't expect miracles overnight, it might take years but that's how special you are to me and if that's how long I have to wait then so be it.

I thought about how I managed to push everything under (the feelings, fears) while I was in high school because I knew that it was the only way I could survive. When I finally got the courage to tell you I realize that it was unfair for me to expect you to suddenly accept it. I know that if others found out, your final year would have been hell. That was unfair of me. I think about us a lot and though it may never be exactly like it was, maybe we can start fresh. I won't say much more but I will say that I'm happy right now.

Love ya Drip,

Max

I looked at the words for a while, listening to Max's voice speak them as clear as if he were sitting next to me and they began to move absently through tears.

A little girl was looking at us with a quizzical look and Stuart wiped his eyes, smiled tightly and nodded to her that everything was okay and she ran off running and laughing. He took my hand and we walked slowly. "Are you able to stop beating yourself up now? Has Max finally convinced you?"

"I've felt so hateful about myself after he died. I was so scared then, so selfish - "

"So *young,*" he said.

"Yeah. Jesus, all I was worried about back then was what it was going to do to me if anyone ever found out. God, it was so important back then, what everyone thought of you, especially in school," I said and pulled a tissue from my bag to wipe my nose. "Everything small seemed so damned important back then."

"Sure, the most important things in the world," he agreed.

"What's funny and sad is that I don't even know anyone from high school anymore, I never really kept any of them as friends. They moved away, started families, jobs...went on with their lives and I carried all this, this anger at myself. I was angry about being the only one to know and angry about being unable to say I was sorry for the way I acted that night when he needed me."

"You can always say you're sorry, even if Max isn't right here. He talked about you so much when we were together. We both knew that you were very special," he said and a pleasant gleam caught in the corner of his eye. "I remember one time he said to me that the guy who got you was going to be the second luckiest guy in the world."

I looked up. "I remember that!" Suddenly I felt elated, a rush of memories calling to me, inviting me into their secret places. "And you," I laughed, "You were supposed to tell me more about that but you never did!"

We watched each other quietly, smiling, and for that moment we were back in the living room near the mantle and the clay figures and the sky was blue and Stuart's eyes were green and beautiful. No one else was with us.

"What did he say after that?" I asked eagerly and in a slightly hushed tone.

" Well," he said, obviously relishing this new level of our conversation, "he said the *luckiest* guy would be the one - "

" - that got him." I finished, laughing through more tears now that piece of the puzzle had found its place. That definitely sounded like Max. "And that was you."

"And I'll always be thankful for that," he said and hugged me. It felt wonderful.

We sat in the sand and looked across the bay to Atlantic City. My home. I told Stuart about becoming a teacher, meeting Randy, about Elizabeth and Jamie and he seemed to take real joy in hearing about all of it. He was still crazy about Michael even after ten years together. Michael owned a small book shop and that was where they met. They traveled as much as they could and were making plans to go to Europe. He said had only been back to Atlantic City a few times in the twenty years since Max.

"Too painful," he added. "The memories..."

I nodded. "They weren't all bad, though, right?"

"No. No, they weren't."

"Well, as someone who has become an expert on putting herself through pain over the years," I said and held my hand out, "I've discovered that the best thing to do with painful memories is to not forget them but just keep adding good memories." I looked over to the city. "There are still a lot of good memories waiting there for both of us."

He looked at me, handsome as ever, with that scandalous smile back on his lips.

"Care to join me?" I asked and led him toward my car.

"I would be honored," he said. Michael waved as we pulled away but not before getting a promise from Stuart to finish packing when he got back.

So we drove through town, past old haunts on Pacific Avenue and pointed out places that were either no longer there or defiantly remained. We shared stories and laughed as we circled the old high school and then rolled along Atlantic Avenue. Stuart put his hand out and caught the air while we coasted from Albany Avenue to Maine Avenue and then back again.

We held hands. We put on music. It was our first date.

* * *

1959

We walk to Kentucky Avenue and from there we turn and leave the boardwalk. The streets are alive, moving in a colorful parade of cars and people. We pass Atlantic Avenue and Randall follows me up a narrow wooden staircase on the outside of a worn brick house and into an open doorway with orange-yellow light coming out from it. A young black boy comes running down as we reach the top and he skips down the stairs two at a time, an old voice shouting after him to get home. Randall hesitates but I grin and put my hand on his shoulder, looking down at him from one step above.

"Trust me?"

He nods.

There are only a few lights on in the room and along one wall there are a few cabinet-style racks filled with records, some in simple brown paper sleeves with handwriting on them. Three black men sit in the back playing cards at a small table with a weak lamp on it. One is thin and has a loose-fitting, colorful short-sleeved shirt while another is roundish and has a hairless head. The third one looks pleased with his hand and a smile graces the shiny skin around his mouth. He places his fingers to the wide brimmed hat on his head and tilts it back gently. The smell of stale cigarette smoke mixes with incense.

Randall walks quietly over and glances at the records. He hesitates before touching any, checking the table of men to see if it was okay, but they aren't paying any attention to him so he pulls a few up and takes a look. He looks over to one of the men playing cards and smiles. The man nods and then looks back to his cards.

"They don't talk much, but boy oh boy, do they know their music," I say and stroll away, letting my fingers lightly brush the tops of the sleeves and sort of enjoying how unsure Randall is right now. I love that he is here and is exploring. I wave to the owner, the man I know only as Cecil, and he greets me with a warm voice saying, "Miss."

Randall pulls more records and I can tell he still doesn't recognize the names or faces on the covers: all black musicians and singers and most hardly ever heard of. They smile on the covers, some with brilliant brass instruments behind them. Some are women elegantly dressed in gowns that sparkle under colorful stage lights.

I read over the back of one of the jackets and then hold it up, looking over to the card players. The man with a saggy-skinned face looks over, moves his lips and then slowly shakes his head before going back to his game. I place the record back. A moment later I find another; the cover has a black and white photograph on it and the jacket is scuffed a bit, with one of the corners bent. The man in the picture has rich, black skin and carries a wide, gap-toothed smile. He is cradling a saxophone that shines like a comet and there is a group of musicians around him, mostly black, but some were white. It looked as if they were still in the middle of enjoying a joke someone had told. I hold it up silently to the table and the man in the colorful shirt nodded appreciatively. I thank him with a polite nod and walk over with the record still in my hands.

"What do you think?" I ask, handing it over to Randall. "Isn't it so funny that I still only know one of their names? They're very nice but very quiet."

Randall looks at the album. "Bull Moose Jackson and the Buffalo Bearcats?" he reads with a puzzled expression on his face. "Never heard of him."

"Yeah, you don't really hear these on the radio much," I say and point to the collection surrounding us.

"So how did you hear about them?"

"My brother."

"Max sounds like quite a guy."

I like the way Randall says his name, as if they had been old friends, as if Max had never gone away. "You know if you want to hear the real *thing we only have to walk a block or two. That's where you can find some real music."*

I pay for the record and we walk further down Kentucky Avenue passing the small restaurants and stores. The scent of cooking meat perfumes the air. We turn onto Arctic Avenue and there are fewer white faces now. Bright signs line the streets and hold names of performers that, for the most part, I am sure that Randall had never heard of. Music blends with laughter and rings from each corner club.

The street is like a little city of its own and Randall looks around, maybe deciding that you could get just about anything you'd ever need right here. There are food joints, clothing and record shops, places to buy your groceries, musical instruments or tobacco. Even a place to have your shoes repaired.

I point out a bright sign to him, the color so strong that it shades our skin orange.

"This is Golden's Cocktail Lounge, *but I never was able to get in there. That one is the* Timbuktu *and that one across the street," I say proudly, "is* Grace's Little Belmont. *That's a place for sure. All kinds play it: Moms Mabley, Wild Bill Davis, even Laverne Baker."*

"What's going on over there?" People were already lined up, eagerly waiting to get in. There is a large neon sign of a woman in a grass skirt beating on a drum glaring from above.

"That's Club Harlem!*" I squeal and squeeze his arm gently. "You've never heard of* Club Harlem?*"*

"Well, don't make it sound like a crime, now," he jokes. "I'm not from here, you know."

"Okay," I say and help massage his arm. "I'm sorry. But, really, almost everyone has heard of it. Anyone who is anyone plays Harlem.

In one summer alone you could hear Dizzy, Count, Duke, or Sarah. Sometimes they just show up unannounced and start playing when they hit the floor. I've never actually been inside, you see, but, still, it's like a legend."

We walk to the end of the block and turn into a narrow alley. We finally stop at a plain and faded green door.

"Where are we going?" he asks, unable to keep the lilt of concern from his voice.

"Scared?" I ask playfully.

He says nothing so I giggle and lean in close to his face. "I thought you trusted me?"

He thinks on it and smiles. "I do."

"Good. Come on." I rap shave and a haircut on the door. The door opens and dim light pours into the alley which is quickly overwhelmed by the shadow of a large man.

"Hi, James," I say sweetly and motion for Randall to go in. He takes a deep breath and proceeds, smiling nervously.

James closes the door behind us and as usual he lets no emotion glide across his face. It is an unopened book right now and I think that's wonderful. James stands well over six foot three and has a bald head that sits on his shoulders like a boulder on a mountaintop. He is wearing a bright blue long sleeved shirt and gray slacks that look just a bit small on his large frame but I can't imagine what wouldn't look small on him.

"Hello, Miss Weathers," James says in his deep voice.

"Oh, James, stop it. Call me Hope, okay?"

"Sure thing, Miss Hope," he replies and cracks a small, child-like smile.

I lean in and elbow Randall softly in the ribs. "That's kind of our joke, get it?" I then take a step back and smile at James. "I like the new clothes!"

He looks embarrassed for a second and rolls his eyes. "I hate it, but Miss Alice wants me to wear it on account of it makes the place looks classy," he says before looking at his shoes. "At least that's what she says. I just feel funny in them."

"Well, you look absolutely handsome," I gush.

Randall looks around at the small room we're in: painted off-yellow, complete with a desk, stacks of boxes, a small table and some chairs. One wall has shelves that hold dozens of notebooks.

"Who's on tonight?" I ask James, clapping my hands together.

"Michael Duvale."

"Great!" I notice James looking past me, his eyes resting like dead-bolts on Randall. "Oh, I'm sorry, James. This is Randall, I'm showing him around town. He's from Delaware."

James makes a sound with his lips, but Randall puts his hand out and James takes it in his meaty fingers and squeezes. Randall's hand nearly disappears and I can see he is trying not to wince.

"Pleased," Randall says and James grunts.

"So, where is Alice?"

James releases Randall and turns to me, a move that requires the shuffling of his large feet in the small room. "She out front, making sure everybody behaves. You know her, always gotta be in the middle," he shakes his head. "I think she might even be helpin' pour drinks 'cause Carl had got sick and didn't show up today."

I turn to Randall and say, "Carl is the bartender," and he nods as if in the know. It's cute .

"I'll go get Miss Alice for you, Miss Hope," James says, moving to the doorway.

"James, you can call me -"

"I know, I know," he says and puts his hand up as he walks down the hall, "Miss Hope." I hear him chuckle deeply as he leaves, his body filling the corridor.

I pull two chairs up to the doorway for Randall and me and motion him to join me. As we sit, Randall leans his head out the door and, looking like a thief, sees that the empty hall leads to an open door where the noise of a crowd is heard. The scent of cigarettes, old beer and detergent mix together in the hall.

"So," he starts to say and then stops, maybe not able to think of a delicate way to ask his question. "Where the heck are we?"

"One of my favorite places in the whole world."

He looks up and then to the left and right, "A small, empty office?"

"No," I shake my head, "not the office, silly, but what the office is near."

He attempts a knowing smile, but it's quickly pushed aside by another perplexed look which makes me laugh.

I take his hand. "You should show a little respect, Mr. Shepherd, you are right now in the famous Cadillac Lounge. It is owned and operated by my very dear friend, Ms. Alice K. Cletcher."

He continues to look at me with a blank but casually amused and warm expression. "Miss Alice?"

"Exactly. The Cadillac might not be as famous as, say, the Wonder Garden or even the Top Hat," I say, "but for my money it's the best thing going on at Kentucky and the curb." I nod to confirm the statement.

"And what exactly are we here for, my dear?"

I look both ways down the hall like a sneaky school girl before pointing to the open door at the end. "That."

A clear voice, speaking into a microphone rises above the coughing and laughter. "Good evening, ladies and gentlemen and welcome to the Cadillac Lounge, I'm your host Freddie Vase but I promise I won't be doing much talking tonight, no sir! We got a full house it seems and I think that everyone here is ready for a good time, am I right?"

The crowd responds and I picture a room of faces and smiles, smoke draping the air from smoldering ashtrays. I hear the stomping of feet on the floor. Someone shouts something that I can't quite make out and the crowd erupts into laughter and the host chuckles.

"Okay, okay, well, we'll make sure that happens, my friend. We never want to disappoint here at the Cadillac and I'm here to make sure that we keep on moving. So, without further delay, let me tell you how pleased we are to be able to announce the return of a fabulous act that has gotten attention not only across the United States, but across the oceans as well. This is their second time here, and let me tell you they knocked them tables back a few feet when they were really hitting it, you never seen nothing like it."

People are now calling back at him, clapping and laughing and sounding like one, long, multi-layered conversation. Randall looks over to me just sitting there with my elbows on my knees and my chin cradled in my hands like I do every Friday night.

The crowd quiets after the band is introduced. The drummer starts out softly on the cymbals and teases until it begins to sound like a snake hissing madly and maybe slithering down the pale corridor toward us. A soft, suffering trumpet joins and it builds up with the steady climb of the cymbals until they peak and then fall away to allow the rest of the band to join. I make out a sax and a clarinet but the speed and how they weave together throws off any pure definition as to what they were or how they were supposed to sound. They are one.

They change tempo and two instruments go off together and banter back and forth as if in a heady conversation. The sax, sounding dusty and wise, eventually hands off to the drummer, who spits out a beat that sounds like soft rain as words of encouragement come from the audience.

"Go on!"

"Uh, huh!"

"Naw, naw you're gettin' loose!"

Then the fellow playing the clarinet picks up as if a ball had been thrown his way and people clap to let the drummer know they were there for his magic. The clarinet leads off on a wondrous adventure of highs and lows, alternating almost as if to keep the other instruments a bit off balance but also inviting them along as friends. After each player has their turn the band comes together again as one, combining to please the senses, ring the ears and call out to anyone willing to listen. They finish with a staccato rap on the drums to time them and then stop. The crowd shows their appreciation with whistles and cheers as the band immediately drives into another tune, this time with the vocalist preaching out.

Randall and I sit there, neither of us saying anything but holding hands when a large black woman dressed in a flowing gown comes down the hallway: Alice Cletcher.

She has large, knowing eyes and honey-colored skin with a few tiny freckles near her cheeks. Her hair is pulled back tightly against her scalp and it glistens under the lights as she nears, her large arms swinging freely from her body.

"Hey, Sweets," she says in a confident, earthy voice as she wraps me in her arms. I give her a big kiss on the cheek and excitedly introduce Randall and Alice smiles after looking him up and down. "Boy, you're all elbows and knees, ain't ya?"

Randall smiles and scratches his chin, unsure what to do with his hands. Alice chuckles deeply at the motion. The band starts again. The singer has a smooth tone that sounds perfect and cuts through the crowd.

"They sound great tonight," I say.

Alice makes a sound though her nose. "As long as we can keep the drummer away from the booze, they'll be able to play."

"Are you going to sing tonight?"

She shakes her head and walks over to the shelves. "Too busy, baby. I'd love to but then who would look after everything, right? I mean, somebody's gotta keep these dumb men in order," she glances at Randall, "No offense, Sugar." She pulls a notebook and opens it. After looking over a page, she swears quietly and closes the book before planting a kiss on my forehead. "I gotta go. Listen, we'll have a real celebration on your birthday, okay? Remember, it's a date."

"Okay," I answer, wishing she could stay for a bit and talk, and hug her again. "Love you."

"You too, Honey. And you," she says to Randall, pointing a thick finger at him. "You never ever hurt my baby, you hear?"

"Yes, ma'am."

She gives him another tight look up and down and, after a quick smile, is out the door again, her sandals slapping on the hallway floor until it mixes with the soft beat from the drums and disappears.

After the set ends I lead him back into the alley. I pull a cigarette from my purse and light it, then lean against the wall.

"So, I'm sure there's a great story back there, huh?"

"Oh, yeah,"

"So why were we sitting in the office? Wouldn't you rather sit and watch them?"

"Of course, but I'm not old enough. Not yet."

He nodded. "So Alice wouldn't let you-"

"Oh, no, I'm lucky she even lets me sit and listen from the office. That was our deal." I inhaled and in the warm glow of the cigarette I saw Randall raising one eyebrow and grinning.

"Okay, to be honest," I offer, "I had been trying to sneak into the Cadillac for over a year and sometimes I would even get in...but most times they would catch me right at the door and I'd be sunk for the night. The night Alice caught me I got in because they had this new short little guy at the door and he wasn't warned about me."

"Warned about you? How many times were you caught?"

"Uh," I look up and pretend to count, "eventually, every time. Probably over a dozen times. I tried anything: once I even wore my mom's shoes to make me look taller and borrowed a wig from a friend of mine. It was this real ugly red thing and I thought it would work but they spotted me right away and I never even got close. Sometimes I would try to blend in with the crowd, you know, act as if I was with a group or something and that worked once or twice." I stub out my cigarette and can't seem to put away the smile on my lips. "But I always ended up getting spotted and they'd come and walk me back out the door. Still, I got to see a little Laverne Baker that way so I'd say it was pretty worth it."

He smiles at me. "Were you always such a risk taker?"

"Oh, gosh, no," I say and lean against the wall. "I guess when we lost Max I kinda went a little nuts for a while. I missed him like crazy *but in his own way he showed me that you have to walk your own road, right? He was listening to all this kinda music way before it got hot with any of the other kids. He was willing to take chances in life and I guess it rubbed off on me."*

It got quiet again. Not an uncomfortable quiet like last time Max came up but more like a respectful pause. Randall softly offered, "So what tripped you up the night Alice caught you?"

"I'm not sure. She swore she'd never tell me, but I remember Joe Tex was about to go on and as soon as she saw me she came steaming at me like a train, grabbed me by the wrist and started hauling me out. I guess I just pushed it too far or maybe she was having a bad day or something but she had a grip on me like I've never felt and was pulling me across the floor," I say still smiling. "So there I am trying to stop her and my feet keep sliding no matter how hard I try."

"What did you do?"

"Well, I knew that there was no way that I was going to be able to stop her, right?"

"Heck, there's no way that I could stop her."

"Exactly," I say, "so I guess I sort of panicked and I just start rattling off the names of every black performer I could think of. Every one that me and Max had listened to together in his room until our parents told us to turn it down. There she was telling me to come back when I grew up and dragging me by the arm through the crowd while I'm trying to dig in my heels and now I'm shouting out names like," I hold my hand out and count on my fingers, "Bobby Blue Bland, T-Bone Walker, Sam Cooke, Illinois Jacquet, Sonny Stitt, and, of course, Laverne Baker. I was shouting so loud that people turned around to see this tiny white girl yelling out names of black musicians while being dragged across the floor and I guess it was quite the picture," I laugh.

"Well, I could see that I was getting somewhere because pretty soon even Alice stopped pulling me and turned around. I almost fell when she let go of my wrist, but this nice man caught me before I hit the floor."

I close my eyes and smile. "So now everyone's looking at me and not saying a word, and I decide I'd better keep going. I felt like even Joe Tex was waiting behind the curtain, letting me have this moment and smiling to himself. I just kept saying names and everyone brought a smile from all the faces around me. I mentioned Lowell Fulson and they nodded and clapped. Big Maybelle brought raised eyebrows and a few said, 'Go on, go on!' so I did. Little Richard made their feet stomp with pride and The Cookies brought whistles. With the mention of Count Basie, well, as you can imagine, all their hands were in the air. It was beautiful to watch, I'll tell you.

"So, Alice has her hands on her hips this whole time and I could tell that she couldn't believe what she was hearing. Here's this little blonde-haired kid who knew more about soul and R&B than most people in the whole place. Her eyes just kept getting smaller and smaller, like she was trying to see inside me who was 'talking that talk' as she said to me later.

"Then she takes me by the arm again and just as everyone was asking her to let me stay she just tells them to mind their drinks and drags me down the hall to her office. She closed the door and told me to sit down and I tried to say something, anything to defend myself, but she just told me to be quiet.

She sat down and put her hands on her knees and looked me straight in the eyes and said, 'I seen that look in the eyes before, little girl, and I can tell that no amount of talkin' is going to make you stop trying to do what you're doin', is that a fact?' I waited, afraid to speak and not sure what to say even if I did so I just nodded. She sat back, folded her arms and shook her head. 'I ain't got time to play around, chasing you *out of here every couple of days, you know. I'm a business woman,' she said and then asked me where I learned about all that music. I told her about Max and me listening to the records he bought, the stations out of Philly that played black music and dancing in his room and my dad telling us to stop it or the pictures were gonna fall off the walls. She finally laughed when I said that. God, I love her laugh.*

"We talked for a while longer and then she started to come around - her smile showed up more and more as we sat together. I guess she just succumbed to my infinite charms, hmmm?" I joke.

"Oh, absolutely. Who wouldn't?"

"So we came up with an agreement, and she even had me sign a paper and everything. It's still in her desk drawer and it says, oh something to the effect of, 'I, Hope Weathers, do hereby promise to quietly sit in the office of the Cadillac Lounge while said bands are playing and I furthermore,' uh, oh right, 'do hereby promise to advise Mrs. Alice K. Cletcher on financial matters having to do with the functioning of said Cadillac Lounge until said agreement has been terminated on the twenty-first birthday of Hope Weathers.' Then we each signed it."

Randall looks at me curiously. "Uh, financial advising?"

"Yeah, I've always had a pretty good head for numbers. I could see that she didn't want to have to worry about me sneaking in anymore and it was easier to bargain with me. She said she would let me stay in the office and listen to the bands, but I was not allowed any further. If she ever caught me on the club floor again, or even in the hall, before I was twenty-one that would be it for good, and I could tell that she meant it. I offered to look over her financial records in exchange for payment and she agreed.

"I always had to let her know when I was here, and if she wasn't here when I showed up, then I couldn't come in. I'd listen to whoever was *playing while I looked over inventory sheets, payroll, whatever…it was fun. I wasn't allowed to bring any friends with me, ever, but none of my friends listened to this kind of music so that didn't make much difference." I feel the need to squeeze his hand. "Plus, I got her to loosen up a little over time." I lean in and give him a kiss on his cheek. "I like talking to you, you know that? I feel like I can talk to you about near anything."*

Later we hold hands and walk down Kentucky Avenue, which is still filled with people, and it feels natural to me, his hand is warm and it fits perfectly, just like our steps feel exactly in time with each other.

"I'm glad that you got Alice-"

"Miss Alice," I correct and giggle.

"Yes, Miss Alice, to loosen up," he says. "She seems real fond of you."

"Yeah, she's a bit of a mother hen whenever I'm there, but a real sweetheart."

We make it back to the boardwalk and head toward the brilliant mass of hotels near Park Place. The buildings tower over us and Randall looks straight up to the dizzying spires and balconies.

"Incredible," he whispers. "They're even more amazing at night."

"Here's my favorite," I say, directing his attention to a building topped with dome-like lids that call back to ancient Byzantine empires.

"That is the Marlborough," I announce admiringly. "My absolute favorite in the city."

He gazes at the minarets of the cream-colored building. Two trim shafts are in front and behind them stand two cupolas columned in white stone and topped in gold. Behind that is a larger and broader dome that sings out even in the dark night, crying out in hues of gold and yellow.

I lead him through the front doors and we are welcomed by a comforting coolness. The main lobby has twenty-foot arched ceilings and he almost trips on the huge rug while looking up admiringly. We can hear the steady clack of shoes on hard marble floors echoing from other corners and halls and it adds to the sensation of being inside a castle.

Afterward we walk down to the sand and remove our shoes and watch the foamy waves, lines of white on the black glass of ocean, roll toward the beach - a beach that looked blue under the glowing moon. As we walk the stars are clear above and I think about how far away they are from us. So far away.

The sounds of the piers and the crowds are so distant to almost be nothing.

I want him to kiss me right now. He must hear my mind...does he?

I slow my steps and he turns to me. I move closer and take his face in my hand and kiss him. I feel his arms wrap around me and I yield, placing my hands on his back. "This is crazy," I whisper in his ear and he simply pulls me closer and grins.

"Yeah, it is."

"I really have to get home," I tell him after a few minutes, although I want to stay and kiss him for hours. We walk to Pacific Avenue and catch a jitney back to the inlet. At my door we kiss once more.

"So, what's happening here?" he asks as we pull apart.

I shrug and smile. "I think I might know, but I don't want to ruin it. Will you be coming back here again?"

He nods quickly. "Absolutely, without a doubt."

I watch him walk down Seaside from the top step and realize that I don't care how late it is. It feels like the world might let night go on forever.

"Oh, hey," he turns and called to me. "You know that song you said the seagulls are singing?"

"Yeah?"

"I think I'm beginning to hear it."

CHAPTER
13

Jamie

The doctors were going to wake up Nicky today. Last night I asked mom if I could stay overnight in the hospital but she said that we would come back as soon as the visiting hours started. Nicky's mom promised to call with any new information. I didn't sleep much last night. I kept seeing Nicky covering up his head and Seth and his gang laughing and kicking him. I remembered how light I felt after Fat Ass Chuck got off me and how helpless I felt when I realized I was too damn scared to jump in and save him. It seemed like my body just refused to move. Seth and his thugs laughed as they stepped over me like giants.

Mom said we would go to the hospital as soon as we got word that Nicky was awake. She tried to feed me, but I was too nervous to eat. I needed a walk so I headed to the beach. Today we would know whether he was going to be alright...whether, I guess, if he would still be the

Nicky that we all know. Would he remember things we did together? Would he have amnesia like in the movies? Would he recognize me?

Seth and his gang weren't in front of his house and that was fine with me. If I ran into them I don't know what would happen, but I think they already did what they wanted to do. For some reason, just like Nicky said, I got a pass from them. I almost wished that they would come after me so that I wouldn't feel like such a coward about the whole damn thing. If they did I wouldn't even fight back.

My face in the morning mirror looked disappointingly fine; just some healing scratches, but no deep cuts or bruises. *You are one poor excuse for Starsky... or Sundance for that matter. You're no Goddamn Bandit. Hell, you're not even fucking Snowman. Afraid to even jump into a fight to help your best friend? Jesus Christ, you were practically crying, you pussy! Nicky was right!*

"Hey!"

I had just wandered past Benita's building and looked up to her window, but it was black and lifeless. Benita had somehow vanished from my mind over the last twenty-four hours. I shaded my eyes and let them climb higher until I spotted her waving from the roof.

"Come on up!" she hollered and disappeared.

I climbed the front steps, went in and let the heavy wood and glass door close behind me with a rattly bang. The floor of the entryway was made up of small, dingy green and white tiles. There was a single blue lounge chair with a slice in the back cushion where cracked yellow stuffing was pushing out. The small lobby smelled musty and down a narrow hallway was a small, dented washing machine. There was a dryer next to it but the door was open and filled with trash.

I climbed up the stairwell and could see straight up to the fourth floor with its weak yellow lights. Behind one of the doors an audience was applauding and laughing from the tiny speaker of a cheap TV.

Benita was alone on the roof. Her long brown hair was pulled into a ponytail and it looked perfect. She turned and deposited a folded towel into a warped green plastic hamper. The wind was blowing, making the clothes hanging from the lines crisscrossing the roof look alive. The sun was behind her and showed the gentle, soft hairs on her arms.

"Hey."

"Hey," she said and pulled a pair of shorts off the line.

"Where's your mom?"

"Work."

My heart skipped a beat. *Alone.*

"So, what's going on?" I asked, trying to sound calm. She looked so beautiful in her cutoff denim shorts and tight top, but I hated the way she was busying herself with the laundry. So much for running into my arms.

"I can make a few extra dollars a week if I dry and fold the laundry for our neighbors as well as ours, so..." she shrugged and smiled. "I haven't talked to you in a while."

No kidding.

She dropped the shorts into the basket. "I haven't seen Nicky, either." She pulled more clothes off the lines, moving from one to the other.

"Oh, crap, you didn't hear."

She stopped folding and aimed her eyes at me, "What?"

I told her about Seth, Tony and getting jumped, that Nicky was in the hospital and how bad he had gotten beaten. I told her the whole story about us getting into a fight before he passed out. Well, maybe not the *whole* story.

"Jesus," she muttered.

I reached down and pulled a small stone from the warm tar of the roof. She must suspect that I chickened out if I had hardly a scratch on me.

"I wonder why they beat him so bad. I mean they've always been jerks but, you know, they never really did anything before, right?" She dropped the sheet into the basket and went to another line. I followed until she stopped me with a raised hand. "Stay here," she said. "If you think I'm going to let you watch me fold my underwear, you're crazy." She walked behind one of the sheets.

"Well," I started, now trying to not picture her in her underwear, "Uh, Seth and those guys were making fun of us, you know, being jerks like always and we were walking past his house just trying to ignore them, right? We didn't want any trouble."

"Yeah," she answered and waited motionless. I drifted back to watching her shape play on the sheet between us, looking as if she was dancing with each breath of the breeze.

"Well, Seth starts calling us fags and - "

"He's such a dickhead," she snapped and I could see her shake her head as she bent to pick up the small hamper.

"Yeah, so Nicky walks back and," I paused and felt a grin spreading across my face, "unzips his fly."

She stopped and poked her head out from behind a faded blue sheet. "He did *what*?" Her eyes were wide, brown and beautiful.

"Yup," I said and nodded. "He unzipped his pants and, um, stuck…you know, *it*…through the fence and then…well, Seth's new 'vette was right there so…he peed into it."

"Oh, Jesus!" she shrieked and took a step back, almost knocking over the hamper.

"You should've seen Nicky's face," I said and laughed. "I don't think I've ever seen him happier in my life."

"How did he get away with it?"

I shook my head, still smiling. "Well, Seth still had the gate closed and locked."

A large, beautiful smile appeared on her face.

"And every time Seth tried to get close," I continued, now laughing harder, "he aimed it at him!"

"No!" Benita screamed and let out a goofy cackle which I instantly loved. She clapped her hands and sat down on the roof. I acted out what Nicky looked like while Benita held her stomach, laughing. "Oh my god, that's so wild," she said when she finally caught her breath.

"Then we beat it the hell out of there and we didn't stop running until we reached Garden Pier."

"I bet," she said, wiping her eyes. "So why exactly did *you* two get in a fight?"

"They beat us…I mean they beat *Nicky*…up pretty bad. That fat shit Chuck grabbed me and held me down while they took turns on him." I felt foolish with her eyes on me. Maybe she could see right through my words and knew I was half lying. "I tried to get away and help him but I couldn't."

She slowly got back up and brushed her rear end with both hands. She was watching me, her eyes looking like two deep wells.

I thought she was going to say I was a goddamn liar. She didn't and moved back to the laundry.

"So when they left he got pissed off at me for not helping. He started calling me names and stuff, saying I was rich and all."

"How could you help with Chuck sitting on you, right?" She vanished behind the clothes again. "But, well, he's right. You are rich."

"Why would you say something like that?"

"Because you have more money than we have," she said flatly and came out with the plastic basket full of folded clothes in her hands.

"So? That doesn't make me *rich*."

"That's easier to say when you have more money," she answered. "You don't have to do other people's laundry to make a few extra dollars, right?"

"Look, if I was rich, I'd probably be spending my summers down in Stone Harbor or Avalon," I said. "And I'd be an asshole like Seth and his goons."

She gave a sort of shrug and then looked down to the hamper in front of her and her shoulders sank slightly. "Well, Nicky *did* ask for it when he peed in the car," she said after a moment, then smiled, "even if it *was* funny." She shaded her eyes. "How bad is he?"

"Pretty bad. They've been keeping him under sedation." I wanted to explain more but she didn't look like she needed it. It was nice to see her smile, she looked so beautiful. "Anyway, I'm going to go see him soon. I hope he's awake enough so I can talk to him and tell him I'm sorry."

She handed me the basket and walked over to the corner of the roof. "He'll get over it." She looked down to the street and watched as a long blue car rocked slowly down Seaside toward the boardwalk.

"Think so? I'm not so sure."

She sat on the concrete shelf that crowned the building and I put down the basket and sat next to her. The clouds were trimmed in purple and gold. They were broken a bit near the horizon and the sun poked through, shining like a bright penny. "He will," she said and her voice sounded a bit distant, "he needs you."

I could see his plain brick, worn out house at the corner. The house that I called shitty. Beyond that was the lighthouse on Pacific Avenue with its old white paint flaked off in large pieces and leaving scab-like patches of gray.

"No one really sees him much except during the summer," she finished.

"What do you mean?"

"Well, the only time I ever see him hanging out with other kids is on the way to school or back. I don't think he has any real friends except you. You come around and suddenly we see him all the time," she continued, "it's like he's a different person."

"No way," I said, shaking my head. "He's got lots of friends, like, Lamont."

"He doesn't hang out with Lamont," she said. Her toes were pointed in toward each other and she looked down at the roof. "He doesn't really hang out with anyone."

"Yeah, but…this is Nicky we're talking about."

"Yup." Benita looked down. "The truth is that most of our parents tell us to stay away from him. A lot of people around here think he's just trouble. Gary, too. My own mother tells me to watch myself when he's around like I haven't known him practically my whole life. She can't stand him, but I know Nicky better than she thinks I do. He can be a jerk sometimes, sure, but that's all."

At the end of the street a few children played with the inner tube of a bicycle, stretching it and screaming joyously.

"I heard my mom talking to someone on the phone yesterday," she said, looking down and her voice had a faraway sound to it again. "She said that this place is dying. She's says we have to get out."

The idea of Benita leaving left me feeling like I had a hole in my belly, but I had heard the same thing enough times - adults talking about how the city was bleeding away and that the casinos might be the only thing that could save it. I didn't know what to think anymore so I thought of Nicky and sighed. I wanted to see his eyes open and tell him that I was sorry for letting him down. It might be the only damn fixable thing left around here.

"I actually think she's right," Benita continued. "I didn't use to think so, and maybe it sounds stupid, but I didn't feel that there was anything really wrong until the sea lions went away this year. I know they're not ever coming back. Then I started thinking about everything else that's gone like Chick's store or the miniature golf place over on Vermont Avenue and how nothing is going to take their place. They'll just be empty lots. Do you know that my mom won't even let me go up to Pacific Avenue by myself anymore, 'too dangerous' she says?"

She put her hands out in front of her. "Shit, I can't even go to Walt's without someone to walk me." She hesitated, looking as if she wanted to say something more, with her mouth slightly open and her tongue playing over her lips. "It's just not fun here anymore," she added, softly shaking her head. "And I'm afraid that if we *do* go away," she said and paused, "then my dad won't have any way of finding us, ever."

I waited. We had never really talked about her dad. "Do you really think he'll ever come back?" The words came out clumsily. She didn't answer. She bent her head forward and closed her eyes. "Do you *want* him to come back?"

"Yeah," she said quickly. "I do, but if I saw him on the street tomorrow I don't think I'd know it. I can't remember what he looks like anymore and my mom got rid of all his pictures a long time ago. I went through all her drawers and boxes one day when she was at work and couldn't find one picture. Nothing," she said. "I sometimes have this weird dream that he's this color," she said and brushed her cheek with one finger, "but all over. Maybe because it's the only damn thing he left me." She walked over and picked up the plastic basket of clothes. "I know that some of the kids make fun of me because I don't go on the rides and most of the time I don't care what they think," she said.

I shrugged. I always figured she had her reasons.

"The real reason is that it reminds me of him."

"What does?"

"The spinning," she said and she closed her eyes. "It's weird, like a feeling that's still with me. Sometimes it even ends up in those dreams. I don't remember much about him, but I'm sure that he used to pick me up and spin me around and in the dream we're always on the beach. It feels like I'm flying, going in circles with everything spinning around us. I'm so happy and then I try to look at his face but I can't see anything. It's like it's blank. Just a blank red and purple face. That's when I get scared. I can't even go on the carousel without feeling like throwing up. Maybe it's because everyone else is smiling and having a great time and the whole time I want to scream. Every time I get that spinning feeling I just want to die."

I held out my hands. She put the basket down and, as she came close, I pressed her hands in mine; they felt rough, the skin soaking in too much soapy water over the years. Without thinking I leaned in to kiss her, but she pulled her head away and lowered her eyes.

"What's wrong?" I asked, trying not to sound desperate. Suddenly I felt like an idiot and a ripple of anger washed over me.

She walked back towards the basket and picked it up. "Nothin', I just don't want to," she said. She opened the steel door that led down and I took a deep breath before following.

* * *

Nicky was awake.

On the drive over with mom I watched the storefronts whiz by and listened to the soft jazz play on the radio and didn't even care that it was crappy music. What was going to happen with Nicky? I was so happy that he was finally awake but until I talked to him I didn't know how he was going to act toward me. Our last words still rang in my ears.

Gary and his mom were just leaving Nicky's room when we arrived. Mrs. Martre smiled and hugged us. "He's going to be okay, they say. It'll be a few days before he can leave, but things look good. We're going to go to the cafeteria to get something to eat and then we'll be back. Do you want us to bring you something?"

"No, thanks Charlotte," mom answered.

Gary patted me on the shoulder and walked past.

"Can I go in by myself first?" I asked mom as I watched them head down the hall.

"Of course."

Nicky's eyes were closed. He didn't look that different than he did a couple of days ago. The beeping machine was gone and I was glad for it. Outside his window the sun was creeping in between the blue curtains. I walked closer and, for some reason, held my breath.

"Hey," he said without moving or opening his eyes. His voice sounded gravelly.

"Hi," I said quietly. "How did you know it was me?"

"Heard you talking to my mom."

"Oh, yeah." I looked around the room. I couldn't read Nicky's tone and my mind stuttered as I focused on the charts on the wall and then to the pair of chairs over near the corner of the room. "So...uh, how're you doing?"

He opened his eyes and turned to me. A tight ball of guilt dropped from my chest into my stomach. The bridge of his nose had a square of gauze covering it, held by white tape. A bruise under his one eye had yellowed and his upper lip had a deep cut that was blackened on the edges.

"Shit," I said, "you look like Rocky."

"Yeah, and that's just the stuff you can see. Look here." He slowly pulled himself up into a sitting position and I imagined (maybe hoped) that I caught a bit of eagerness in his voice. He raised his shirt and I saw a line of angry scratches and welts that covered one side of his ribs.

I walked closer and bent down to get a better look. "Wow."

Nicky lowered his shirt gently. "Yeah, good thing they got me to the hospital right away," he said and then winced. "Doctors said that I was in some seriously bad shape when I got here." He looked out the window at the fading light coming in and then his face brightened a bit. "Man, you shoulda seen the nurse who took care of me, a stone cold fox." He smiled but swiftly put his hand to his upper lip. "Ow."

I pointed to stitches on the bridge of his nose. "They say chicks dig scars, right?"

"Right," Nicky said solidly, "and I now officially have cooler scars than you. I needed six stitches just on my nose."

"Six? Great," I laughed but felt like we were both doing some sort of weird dance around what happened. "Hey, about all that –"

Nicky shook his head. "I know, man, I know. Chuck had you and there was no way you were getting up from under that huge ass," he said and tried grinning again. "Besides, even if you could have jumped in they just would've turned on you and then we'd have both been headin' to the hospital, right?" He smiled. "I hear it was you who called for help. Thanks, man."

I nodded. I didn't think Nicky meant anything by it but it sort of made me sound like a chicken shit. I looked out to the hallway. "The thing is...I could've gotten over there," I mumbled. "To help, I mean."

He blinked and then looked down at the floor, rubbing the tips of his fingers gently across his bottom lip - a habit that I hadn't seen him do in years. His long curls covered his eyes and I had to fill the awkward silence. "Chuck got up off of me, see, and it happened kinda fast, and, well, when I looked up I saw him laying into you," I continued, not knowing where the words were coming from. "I...probably...coulda gotten there...maybe done something. I don't know."

I waited. Did he hear me?

"So why didn't you?"

"The truth?"

He stared at me.

"I got scared."

Nicky looked at me for a moment and then the familiar grin returned and I felt the muscles in my shoulders loosen. I didn't even realize how heavy my whole body felt until he smiled at that moment.

"Nice try, Jackson," he said and pushed me gently with his forearm. I wanted to laugh with him, but something didn't feel right, it was like a bug was crawling around inside my head.

"Nick –"

"Yeah?"

"I'm serious. I really *was* scared."

He looked up and his expression reminded me of someone who had seen a strange-looking stone along a path in the woods and didn't know exactly what to make of it. He rolled his tongue into his cheek and laid back on the bed.

"S'okay, he said. "I was scared, too. And it wasn't like you ran out on me or anything."

"I would never do that," I said. "I should've taken my chances. You know I'd go to the hospital with you any day, man."

"What, and have you going after my hot new nurse girlfriend?" he said, laughing and shaking his head.

"So," I said, "have you thought of anyway we can get back at them?"

Nicky shook his head. "No need to."

I waited for the rest of the words to come out. There was a strange satisfaction growing on his face.

"What happened?"

Nicky was relishing the silence and stared at me, now with a definite smirk on his scabbed lips.

"What?" I asked again.

"Well," Nicky started slowly, "When Gary got back from the hospital someone called him, a friend of his, and said he saw Seth and his asshole friends taking off down Vermont Ave right around the same time. So he makes a call and the next night he goes out to meet some more friends. He just told me that those guys won't be bothering us anymore."

"How bad did they hurt them?" I felt a little numb.

"Pretty damn bad, I guess. Told me that they broke one of their arms."

"What about Seth?"

"Not sure, but have you seen him lately?" he asked grimly.

It made me think of all the faces that I wouldn't be seeing if what Benita and everyone had been saying was true.

"*It's just not fun here, anymore...*"

"*Mom says this place is dying...*"

Now that I thought about it I realized I hadn't seen Seth or any of them lately - not driving around, not hanging out at his house or carrying their boards and heading for the beach. They weren't anywhere to be found on Seaside. My numbness was pushed aside softly by satisfaction. Revenge.

"Where did they get them?"

Nicky tucked his hair behind his ear and I saw an angry gash near the top. "Right down on the beach the next night. Dumb shits had some girls with them, but the chicks took off as soon as they could see that there was trouble. Gary said you should've seen how some of those assholes were crying." Nicky nodded his head with his half-smile.

"Was it the same guys? You know, Chuck and Tony and all?"

Nicky look at me with a puzzled look. "Sure, I guess so. Hell, I don't know, man, they didn't interview them. Gary told me what they looked like and one sure sounded like that fat shit Chuck. They definitely got Seth. Gary's wanted to kick his ass for a long time."

"Why?"

"Dunno. I guess just cause he's a rich - " Nicky stopped. "Anyway," he said, "He's just a prick and I guess whoever was unlucky enough to be hangin' around Seth at the time got their asses whipped."

"Rules of the Street?" I asked softly.

Nicky nodded. "Rules of the Street. You can't let anybody push you around, Jackson."

He managed to pull himself up into a sitting position. "If anyone got beaten who wasn't supposed to, well, then they were...what do they call it?" He asked, his brow lined in thought. His face lit up, "Oh, yeah, 'collateral damage,' right?"

Yep. Stands to reason that if you hang out with assholes long enough then you take the risk that those assholes are going to piss someone off bad enough. Rules of the Street.

"Hey, I'm sorry about what I said to you, man," Nicky said. "You're not rich...at least not like those guys, you know? I was just really pissed and I didn't know what to say, okay?"

"It's okay. I'm real sorry for saying those things about your house..."

"That's cool, thanks. But still...I know what kind of house it is. I'm not a retard."

"But I'm *not* sorry about saying that about your dinners." I felt like I could reach a bit and crack one.

"Oh, you asshole…" Nicky said and soft punched me in the chest, laughing and then laying back. He looked tired again. "You're lucky I'm still sore…"

Nicky got out a few days later and he and I went to the beach every day and things began to fall back into the familiar groove of trips down the boards and nights on the deck counting stars and thinking about girls. He loved showing off his scars to anyone who would look. I still felt a bit nervous about Seth and his gang, but Nicky proudly walked around almost as if he was daring Seth to do something.

And then we finally spotted him.

He was in the passenger seat of his father's car as they pulled up to the house. When he got out we saw what Gary and his friends did.

Seth's arm was wrapped in a cast from elbow to wrist and there were several nicks and scratches still visible on his tanned face. He saw us watching him, but he remained quiet, his eyes following us until he was back inside his house. I tried to read Seth's face to see if he was going to come after us but it was impossible to tell. I didn't see anger or fear or even sadness - just a blank sheet of paper waiting to be drawn on. And for the first time I could remember there were no other cars in front of the Natone house.

CHAPTER
14

Jamie

Benita came over with her mom late in the afternoon. I could hear her voice from my room and I quickly dropped my book and headed downstairs trying not to look too excited. She smiled when she saw me and everything else vanished. Mom made up some quick snacks and hung out in the kitchen to talk with Benita's mom while the two of us filled a bowl with Fritos and sat in front of the TV. I could have jumped and touched the ceiling when mom suggested that we all go down the boards for a few hours. I knew that the Lizard wouldn't want to go, but I wasn't expecting her to ask me if Nicky wanted to go. I hadn't even thought of him.

I felt kind of lousy about it, but then I looked at Benita and thought of how just having him with us would ruin everything. The memory of kissing Benita was all that was in my head. I didn't want to share her or have Nicky pull me away.

Should I say I heard he got in trouble and had to stay in? I knew it was easy enough to believe and Benita's mom sure wasn't going to complain. Everyone knew that his reputation was he either made trouble or it followed him like a hungry dog.

How bad was it to use that? About as bad as it could get. Didn't you just get over telling him that you had his back no matter what? Still, I was eventually going to have to explain it to him because he would ask what I did and then maybe mom would be there and she would say how sorry she was that he couldn't join us...

Nicky would have to understand, right? After all, we're talking about chicks, maybe getting another chance to make out. The idea that our parents would be nearby almost made it more exciting. I pictured putting my arm around her. Even though she was being so cool about the whole thing lately, what had happened between us was no accident. She kissed me first! At just the right moment, I'll turn her toward me, lean in and –

I felt myself getting hard again and quickly headed to the kitchen. Come clean with Nicky and just tell him. The phone rang twice and then he picked up.

"Hey man, whatcha doin'?" His voice annoyed me right away. It was filled with that typical Nicky excited-and-ready-for-action sound. "I was about to call ya."

"Uh, not really much."

"Cool. Whatcha wanna do?"

"Well, I think me, mom and the Lizard are going down the boards." I winced when I saw Liz come in the kitchen and I'm pretty sure she heard me because her mouth dropped open and then closed tightly. Probably pictured my skin hanging from her bedroom wall. I didn't care. I waited for Nicky's response, dreading what he'd say next and hating that I was hiding from it.

"I'll head over."

I would have done anything to patch up things between the two of us after the fight and now I was trying to ditch him in the worst way. All I could do was listen to Nicky breathe. "Uh, well, see…Benita's going too…and her mom."

"Okay."

"So…I think it's just going to be us – just this once, you know, um, because…"

I could hear Nicky chuckling over the line, way down at the end of Seaside Avenue. "Oh, I *know* why, man, no need to explain anything to me. Summer ain't over yet, got me? You better tell me everything when you get back."

"Really? I mean no hard feelings or anything?"

"Hell, no."

"You sure?"

"Enjoy the titties, Jackson," he laughed and hung up.

Benita and I walked with our parents a few steps behind. While we talked I fought the urge to take her hand, just to see what would happen, to take in her smile as she wrapped her slender fingers around mine.

We passed the shops and the lights, the piers and hundreds of other faces and I imagined that Benita was my girlfriend and that every guy was jealous of me. They should be. She's beautiful. She seemed to be just arrived from another world or something - her eyes looking at everything as if for the first time. I felt both clumsy and a little bitter that she seemed so relaxed while inside I was bubbling like a bottle of coke.

"Jesus, there she goes again," Benita muttered after we both overheard her mom begin a sermon on the value of men. She shook her head softly and said it with a sad sort of smile then looked out at the darkening ocean. I tried to walk as close to her as possible just to let my arm brush against hers every now and then. It was enough for me right then and I could see that it didn't mean much to her but each time it sent a shiver through me.

When we reached Steeplechase pier Benita asked her mom for money and then turned to me.

"Wanna go play some games?"

Her eyes - or maybe it was the way she asked - might have been saying something more, but I couldn't tell because by then I so wound up I was probably filling in the blank spaces with my own fantasies. I nodded helplessly as the two of us left our moms with the promise to not leave the pier.

Benita led me into the crowds and the colored lights of the rides came to life, making them seem magical. She walked quickly, moving towards the games of chance and then stopped in front of one. Until now I hadn't noticed how tightly she had been holding her body while we were walking. I knew her mom could be tough on her and demanded a lot more from her than either Nicky or my mom did. Now alone, her body lost some of its stiffness and her shoulders sloped a bit more gently from her beautiful neck. She was staring at a rainbow wall of stuffed animals.

I didn't waste any time putting a dollar down for three darts and actually popped two balloons on the wall which won me the choice of one of the smaller animals. I let Benita pick and she chose a sky blue frog. She gave me a quick hug and tucked it under her arm and now I was suddenly jealous of a mindless stuffed frog. I looked across the pier to a pizza stand and next to it a place to get soft ice cream. I decided I wasn't hungry yet and watched the rides nearby: the roundup, the scrambler, the bumper cars…

"You feel like doing a ride?" I asked. I was thinking about the Sky Ride or the bumper cars but her spine straightened and her shoulders raised. Her eyes fell on me and then darted back and forth a few times as she considered and she looked over my shoulder and pointed. The Paratrooper. A dozen metal chairs hung from a frame that looked like the spokes of a bicycle. The wheel spun in a tilted circle and riders screeched with delight at every dip.

"Really? I was thinking more like…I mean, that's a bit fast, uh, for someone who doesn't usually go on these –"

She took my shirt by the shoulder and pulled me to the nearest booth. She bought a small book of tickets and all I could think of was how her body would press against mine as we whirled high above the pier.

"You'll be fine, really, I ride this one all the time," I said as we approached the line. "The one you don't want to go on is the Zipper, that one is just freakin' crazy." She nodded and watched as the cars flew down past us and then back into the air with the fascinated look of a little girl. She said nothing but I could see her chest moving as she breathed in and out.

When the line moved I stepped ahead and led her by the hand. We had to race around to the cars in the back to find one that was empty. I let her get in first and then climbed in after her. A skinny guy with a bushy brown mustache, wearing a dirty t-shirt and his baseball cap backwards closed the door with a bang and then slid the lock into place. I felt her next to me, shivering slightly and looking around, making quick, bird-like movements with her head. I tried to take the stuffed frog from her but she shook her head and held it to her chest.

"Hey, you okay?" I asked. "We can still get off if –"

"No," she said quickly. "No, I can't," and the muscles in her neck tightened, moving her tan skin. She reached across and took my hand and even though I had been waiting for that to happen all day there was no jolt this time, no electricity moving up my arm to the rest of my body. Something was different now. She just needed me right then.

"Hey, remember how no wave was ever able to pull us apart?" She nodded but stayed looking straight ahead. It looked like I was talking to someone who was deaf but I could tell she could hear everything right now. Every sense was alive. She swallowed quickly.

"Right now, nothing can pull this apart, okay?" I held up our hands so she could see.

"Okay," she looked quickly at me and then let out a small mouse-like squeak as the ride came to life. For a moment she *was* a mouse, a frightened mouse that had been trapped. She licked her lips as the speed increased.

I tried a weak joke, but she just pressed her lips together and as the cars lifted off the ground she closed her eyes. I let her crush my fingers as we climbed higher into the air. Her hip slid against mine and I tried to enjoy it, but when I looked I saw her lips trembling. I would have said that she was crying but she wasn't, not really. Even though I saw a tiny silver stream make its way toward her ear and then down her throat, pushed by the wind blowing across both our bodies, I saw anger and bitterness.

I wanted to scream for someone to stop the ride. Benita peeled one hand from the safety bar and covered her eyes and I put my arm around her. The ride seemed to last too long and with each new rotation, each time we flew into the sky again I leaned into her, promising that it would be over soon. She nodded quietly and wiped her eyes. I was never more grateful than when the ride began to lower and slow down.

"You okay?"

She nodded and unlocked the safety latch. She moved quickly and I followed, catching up to her right outside the exit. A group of kids passed and someone joked that she was going to puke. I guided her over to a bench and we sat quietly for a while.

"Stay here." I trotted over to a stand and bought a 7up. "It's what my mom always got me if I felt sick or something," I said as I sat down next to her and watched her, in a sort of slow motion fantasy, sip from the straw. "Actually she would get me ginger ale but they didn't have any. This is the next best thing." She handed it to me and I took a sip. I felt a bit foolish mentioning my mom (it made me sound like a little kid) but when I looked out on the pier and the colored lights on the ocean, I knew that sitting next to Benita was enough. In fact, it was more than enough.

"Thanks," she finally gurgled out. Small beads of sweat showed on her brow and she wiped them away with the back of her hand. "That was horrible," she managed and took a deep breath before grinning tightly. "But, maybe someday I'll do it again."

"Why'd you change your mind?"

She looked around and took another long sip. "I guess I'm tired of not being in control of how I feel." She handed me the soda and put her hands in her lap. "That doesn't seem fair that he can make me feel sick on a ride, does it?"

She let out a small burp, giggled and began to look better so we walked. I kept a watchful eye out for mom but had already decided that if I saw her I'd sink back into the nearest crowd with Benita before she saw me.

Before I knew it she was pulling me toward the haunted house on the pier, Spook's Shangri-La. "You know, I heard once that you aren't cool with the haunted houses."

"Where'd you hear that?" I said, looking anxiously at the cars lined up on their greasy tracks waiting to enter the double doors of the dark ride. "Is Nicky making up stories about me?"

"Doesn't matter where I heard it." The light danced again in her dark pupils like I loved. She was smirking and looked beautiful. "Are you?"

"No. What, scared?"

"Your turn," she said and pulled me into the short line for the ride. "Time for us to get over our fears, right?" She held the frog up to my face and giggled, "Look, Jamie Jr. will keep both of us safe."

"You named it after me?"

"Of course," she said and before I could argue against going into the rickety nightmare she pushed the tickets into the attendant's hand and moved us to the next empty car. I faintly heard my name being called and turned. Mom was waving at us. I hopped into the car and Benita laughed before quickly climbing in after me. As soon as we sat the car moved toward the painted doors. I looked over my shoulder once more to see both our mothers taking a seat near the exit.

The car crashed into the doors and pushed them aside. It was now darkness with a cool breeze and a smell like fresh paint, sawdust and oil. The unsettling sensation of moving forward in blackness made me want to reach into the void and protect my face. I squinted, waiting for something to leap out. I hated that. There were a few screams ahead of us and we were bathed in a sickly blue glow. On either side of the narrow hallway dancing skeletons and ghouls were painted in bright orange and yellow paint. Their mouths were sad toothless cracks and they looked up to the ceiling with empty eyes. Benita giggled and pointed ahead.

A witch slowly stirred her brew directly in front of us while a bald man, his face full of terror, raised his head mechanically up and down from the pot. "Want to be in my stew?" the poorly painted witch asked as we quickly spun to the left and crashed through more doors. Now things were brushing against my face, it was a soft tickling that I tried to bat away and I heard Benita squeal with laughter. The car dipped quickly and more ghostly wails erupted from speakers hidden deep in the walls.

Benita's warm hand fell on mine. The ride slowed and we were under steadily flickering lights, the kind that make you look like you're moving in slow motion. Paper and cloth ghosts were suspended above us and I saw her face in between the black and white flashes.

"Hey." Her voice was quiet and secretive.

I quickly kissed her on the mouth and my arms wrapped around her. Her lips curled into a smile and her tongue touched mine. The car jerked to the left again (I think?) but all I could hear was her breath in my ear like a roaring wave. My hands moved up her body to her chest. My body was pulsing, alive and I wanted all of her. She pushed my hands down, but kissed me harder, softly biting my lower lip. I could hear the ocean, wave after crashing wave but that couldn't be possible, could it? My hands went to her hair and cheeks and then down again, tracing her neck to her shoulders. I didn't know what to do with my hands - they seemed both useless and invaluable at the same time.

Her tongue wrapped around mine and suddenly I wanted to climb onto her, to lay her down in the car. I felt my body pushing against hers, but she resisted. A dull ache was growing between my legs and I lifted her shirt. I felt her lips smile again and she didn't stop me this time. Her skin of her stomach was soft and my clumsy hands suddenly seemed too rough, like they were punishing it somehow. Still, my hand traveled up.

I reached her bra and every sound and smell came to me at that moment: the screams of the other riders, the smell of her hair, the clack of the car on the rails, the scent of the salt air coming closer, her breathing and the ocean...always the exploding ocean. I reached around her back and began pulling gently at the clasp of her bra. I wanted so much more, so much more that I didn't know or could even name.

Beneath my pulsing body I could feel the ride still moving and knew that it had to end soon and the two of us would be back in the world of lights and parents. My hands kept trying to unlock the clasp and she squirmed against me, not resisting but adjusting her position. She kept her lips pressed to mine, her tongue sliding around in my mouth.

She pushed me back, gently at first then more forcefully. In the dim light he could see that her cheeks were flushed pink. My body was humming and I could hear my own heartbeat. My groin throbbed painfully, but I quickly reached down and re-positioned myself despite the tenderness. Benita pulled down her shirt and ran her fingers through her hair just as the exit doors were pushed open and we returned to the world. As the cool air hit me a shudder ran through my body, starting at the scalp. Benita wiped her mouth with the back of her hand and put on a smile as we rolled out to a stop under the lights of the pier.

I was hoping that our moms would have wandered somewhere, anywhere to let us take another ride, but they were both there with happy faces. I slowly got out of the car, pulling my tee shirt down as low as I could and followed Benita over to them.

For the rest of the night I tried to find any way I could to get Benita alone, but it was just not happening - our mothers were always nearby. We walked as far as Central Pier before turning and heading home. All along the deserted stretch from Steel Pier, Benita walked next to her mother and neither of us spoke much, just awkward small talk. At Benita's apartment, they said their good nights and I mumbled something to Benita and she smiled and followed her mother into her building, not looking back.

Hope

It was time to finish the painting. Only a couple weeks left.

I sat up on the deck and looked at the neighborhood. The view had changed a lot since I looked out at it all those years ago. On summer nights we would sit up here and sing songs until dad got home. Max would, of course, join in and be the loudest. We always sang, "He'll be Coming 'Round the Mountain" as we waited. Every window in both the Nevada and the Vermont wore curtains as a beautiful lady might wear a new dress. I could smell the fresh paint on the railings! Mom bounced me on her knee and cars lined Seaside end to end and they sparkled under the lights like jewels.

What was it that Evalisse said? *It's like this place has cancer or something.*

Today Seaside was a weary gray and the pavement was cracked and shot through with choking weeds. The Nevada was empty and boarded up and the Vermont was not far behind. I laid down gentle strokes against the canvas and could almost hear the movement of the brush as it wove its way into the cries of the gulls and the lost voices and laughter that seemed ghost-like.

By four o'clock I was done and before me was the complete defeat of my neighborhood. Anyone who looked at it would certainly feel the desperation. They might not know it, but they would reconstruct in their minds and hearts, even if they had *never* laid eyes on Seaside Avenue before, what it might have been before all this. Looking down at the crushed tubes of paint I saw, not too surprisingly, that I had used up most of my grays and browns. That seemed appropriate.

I felt out of breath, as if the picture had somehow come from inside my body. That was good. My best work tired me out. Looking at the brown and somber lines and delicate open space I felt a slight dizziness and began to see other colors seeping in that I could use. Maybe brighten it a bit.

No. This was done.

I looked at it and yet I wanted to both smash it and hold it and cry. It was what I always knew was inside me and was inside the house, inside the street…

"It's beautiful."

Mom stood in the door with a half-smoked cigarette between her fingers and her robe tied tightly around her waist. She looked at the painting and then to the street, "Though it's not the prettiest site anymore, not like it used to be."

"Oh, I don't know," I said and looked again, tilting my head a bit, "it's kind of beautiful in its own way. Don't you think?"

"As an artist, you're supposed to find beauty in everything," she answered and offered a tiny smile. She pulled a chair up and sat down and after a moment, folded her arms and tapped her foot. "The thing is," she began, "is that I don't really see anything beautiful here anymore. What I see are people, people who have been thrown together, only to become good friends, just like you and Evalisse or Jamie and Nicky, and then they are simply pulled apart. It seems senseless and it makes me sad and angry."

"Still looking out for me, hmm? "I put my hand on her knee. "You know, I thought by the time I reached forty-"

"Your babies *never* stop being your babies." She said the words firmly and turned to look at the slice of ocean between the Nevada and Benita's wilted apartment building.

"I know, mom. I was only-"

"The only time they stop being your baby is when they die before you do." The cigarette in her hand was burning down and leaving a long, curved ash. "You have to understand something, Hope," she continued and her voice swayed, "when your baby dies…"

I touched her arm.

"When you lose a child it's like they suddenly become *older* than you. Does that make any sense at all?" She asked. "They've… experienced something that you haven't but will, eventually. And supposedly they're waiting for you but it's the parent that's supposed to be the one waiting for her children, helping them find their way and waiting with an embrace, not the other way around. It's all so goddamned backward."

The last word came out quickly and she put her hands to her mouth.

"Max has never left my thoughts, but for some reason...this summer..." She stopped and flicked the cigarette over the railing. "Why is he talking to me so much this summer?

"Oh, mom," I said and leaned into her, feeling the brittleness of her ribs and the movement of her chest as it drew breath.

"I couldn't face it. That night when we heard...how your father cried. I never in my life saw him or anyone cry like that."

I waited and mom pulled away slowly and looked at me. I had never seen her eyes that shape before, looking like they had been cut out of glass.

"I know you were angry at me for not letting you in."

"I was terrified, mom."

She nodded. "I've never been so scared in my life. I know at the time it didn't make sense to you but I needed you to be with the girls. I kept trying to remember where your father kept his gun and nothing came to me and I was terrified to leave him alone."

"Dad had a gun?"

"He had bought it years ago. Said it was for protection. But no matter how hard I tried I couldn't remember where he said he had hidden it. I just blanked."

"I know what that feels like," I said, trying to picture dad pointing a gun at anything. Mom wiped her eyes and looked at me with a strange expression. "Remember when you told me to call Saint Catherine's?"

Mom put her hand to her lips and nodded.

"Well, from the moment you told me to the time it took me to reach the bottom of the steps I had totally forgotten where you said it was. My mind just erased it, it was the strangest thing but I guess it wasn't just me. I couldn't even remember Father Hagen's name."

"Oh, no, not at all," Ruth said. "I could have easily told you where your dad kept his little water pistol if you had asked me any other time, but at that moment I guess my mind was just going too fast. I was so scared that he might hurt himself or someone else."

I waited. "What did you think he was going to do with the gun?"

"Oh, I don't know," she said, "maybe go down to the police station and do something crazy. Maybe find one of those boys that killed your brother."

We were both quiet for a while then and all the sound that was alive was the city: the distant bleating of a horn and the soft underbelly of sounds that accompany the city...an ever present hum that is the gathering of all the sounds that you can't make out individually.

"So what happened to the gun? Did you find it?"

"Yes, a few days later in the bedroom closet. I remembered him telling me that he didn't want you kids to get it so he hid it in one of the ceiling tiles. I tried a couple with no luck and then your father came in. He had that look on his face and said, 'Ruth Regina, I know what you're looking for and it's right there,' he said and pointed it out to me. Then he said, 'I hope you don't think I was going to do something stupid with it, do you?' I waited a second before nodding and he came over and put his arms around me. 'I would never do something like that. I still have you and three beautiful daughters and that's a lot, a whole hell of a lot.' Then he began crying."

She let out her breath and blinked before pulling another cigarette from her pack and swiftly lighting it. "Jesus, has it really been twenty years?" she asked and exhaled. Her hand trembled slightly and the skin rimming her eyes was pink.

"Mom," I started slowly, not sure what words were going to come out. "Why do you think we never talked much about Max for all that time? I mean, after he died it sometimes felt as if he never existed."

She waited before shaking her head. "That's bothered me for a long time and I don't know the answer. I loved him so much that it hurt to even think about him after. And to think of the way that he was taken from us, well...your father and I, I don't know, every time we started talking about him we would just start bawling and there were times when I thought I would never be able to stop. I think that we just got scared with how much it hurt, so scared that it was easier to just avoid it. I know that I was sure scared as hell."

I watched a seagull swoop down to inspect something on the street. It poked at a bit of trash and took flight.

"I still miss him. We talked about everything."

"I know. The two of you couldn't be separated sometimes."

"I never told you this, but he and I got into an argument the night he graduated."

"About what?" she asked.

"He was really upset when he got home that night. He and Stuart had gotten into a fight. He was sad Stuart was leaving for Florida."

"The Patchick boy. Very handsome as I recall."

"Yeah, yeah he was," I said. "The thing is...well, he and Stuart were more than just friends."

I caught myself looking down as if ashamed of the words so I craned my head up and looked into my mother's eyes. And was surprised to see a casual smile on her face.

My eyes went wide. "Did you know?"

She shrugged and looked out at the neighborhood. "I had thought that maybe he was with how close he and Stuart were, and, well, it didn't seem impossible." She looked at me and smiled. "They were both so beautiful."

"Boy, I wish I had been as insightful as you back then," I blurted. "I had no clue."

"Well, come on now, you're a mother. What don't you know about *your* children?"

It seemed that I knew less and less about them as they grew older. Still, I knew the important things by instinct – when they were scared, in trouble, mad, sad....I could tell that there was more to the story when Nicky and Jamie had gotten jumped. Jamie obviously had a huge crush on Benita and Liz was nuts for this boy back home named Ted on the soccer team.

"He told me that night and at first I didn't believe him, you know?" I said. "Then I saw how scared he was and I knew he wasn't lying." I looked into her blue eyes that were a shade darker than mine, more like the color of the ocean just before night. "I treated him horribly. It didn't help that I had this crazy crush on Stuart, either but, still, he made me promise never to tell anyone, ever. I was pissed and accused him of being drunk and I didn't want to talk about it. I left him alone crying in his room and...that was the last time I spoke to him."

Mom nodded and took my face in her hand. "How long did you punish yourself for that?"

"Oh, not long. Only about twenty years."

Two figures were coming down the ramp from the boardwalk to Seaside. It was Jamie and Nicky. I could tell from here from the familiar rhythm of their strides as they walk side by side. Only best friends walk like that. Like me and Max.

"When he died," I continued, "I still had this promise and I didn't know what to do with it but it turned itself into a lot of anger. I almost told you a few times and once I was about to tell dad."

"I'm glad you didn't," mom said flatly. "Your father was the sweetest man I have ever met, you know that. I adored everything about him and he loved his family more than anything." She tapped her cigarette and ash fell from the tip like snow. "But I don't know how he would have taken that. Knowing that his only son was, well - "

I nodded.

"I think it would have been like he died twice. To not know something like that about your own son and then for him to die, well, it would have been too much for him. I made the decision not to tell your father about it as well and I have to live with that. I just didn't want to add maybe anger or disappointment to his sadness. I'm not especially proud of it, either."

Her eyes had taken on a hollow look. "At least you were keeping a promise you made to him. I had to decide for myself that it was for the best." Her lip trembled, "I hope he doesn't hate me for it."

"Mom, he doesn't. I'm sure of it. He was a very forgiving person, you know. You raised a hell of a son." I pulled the envelope from my pocket. "A friend gave me this."

I described my lunch with Stuart and watched as mom took the letter, watched her lips silently move along with the words. She put her hand to her mouth and the two of us cried, but it was mixed with some sweet laughter. Mom leaned in. "Was he happy?"

"Yeah, he was, mom. Stuart promised me that he was."

She folded her hands and rested them in her lap. "Then that's a good thing." She kissed me on the cheek. "Let's go downstairs, what do you say?"

"I say great. I have a hot date tonight."

I picked up the canvas. The lines became a bit clearer and when the early evening sunlight reached it, it unleashed more color than just the muted browns and grays. Colors that I hadn't seen before. The more I looked at it the better I felt.

* * *

Randall was waiting outside, dressed in a dark brown corduroy jacket with a white shirt and no tie, tan slacks and deep brown loafers. I called it his "sexy professor" look. I opened the front door and presented myself in my favorite - a dark blue dress and heels. I put my hair up and subtle hints of makeup toned my cheeks and eyes. I admit it was a little bit of an old-fashioned look, but it was how we did this late summer date every year. Even after all this time, this one special night still sent bees humming throughout my stomach. Not bad for almost twenty years of marriage.

I reached the sidewalk and he held out his arm, adjusting his tie and saying, "Excuse me miss, can you help me find Steel Pier?"

"But what about your glasses?" I answered as he took my arm.

"Oh, these things?" He removed the glasses and squinted at me with a grin. "Old prescription."

"I just bet they are." I kissed him on the cheek.

The beaches were almost empty. I watched an old man wearing shorts and a shirt that billowed in the breeze slowly scan the furrowed sand with a metal detector and I silently wished him luck.

We walked past reedy lots and empty streets, all the places that used to be vibrant. We joked and remembered good times, determined not to let the decay surrounding us infect our thoughts. The ocean crashed, roaring in white foam and echoing madly. We passed Garden Pier and I thought of how long ago it had been since Max and I had gone to hear the military bands play there.

I pulled out a cigarette and watched the soft orbs of lights down the boards grow stronger with each step we took. We strolled through the crowds, arm in arm, sometimes hand in hand. I pulled him to some of the shop windows and we pretended that we had a million dollars and decided what they would buy. I found three lovely coats and Randall picked out an antique trumpet that he said one day would be his. He had been saying he'd like to learn to play an instrument. Not too late for anything, right?

The gulls cried overhead, some soaring near the tops of the tall hotels, looking spiritual and fragile. We wandered down to the Marlborough, now quiet and dark in the high corners of its arched entrances. You couldn't go inside anymore - the city was in a complicated fight with some residents who were trying to save her. I imagined what the worn carpet of the lobby, once so bright and crisp, must look like with all the color bled from it. Maybe all it could offer now was a muted, barely perceptible pattern. Did the great chandelier still hang high above and was it even lit like it was waiting for a friend to return? On the outside, it was as if we were watching a great, ancient actor performing Shakespeare to an empty theater.

We stopped to look out over the dark sand of what used to be Chicken Bone Beach, watching the thin white lines of waves tumble to the shore. The night was cloudless and the stars were beginning to come out, clear on the horizon and less so above, where the pink and yellow lights of the city hid them from sight.

It was wonderful despite how much everything had changed. There were still families softly padding along the gray and brown wooden walkway, still retired folks resting on benches and watching the world go by - enjoying the human parade. There was even evidence of permanence: the gulls will always be here, that's a fact. And the waves will still crash at the beach. No one will ever be asleep at the switch. Not here.

I put my hand on the cool metal of the railing and waited maybe a minute, waited for that gentle pulse. I don't think it was my imagination...it was there, faint, but still there.

I let my mind race out over the sand and the waves and then turn back to the city and watched it from a distance, watched what life it still had. Lights burned like little irises and surrounded gray buildings as big as giants. From far out over the water it would be impossible to think to there was no life here.

We walked back in the direction of home and stopped to buy two custards. The arcades cranked out their music and rolling chairs passed by, though now they were driven instead of pushed by kindly men with floppy caps and large smiles. The piers reached out to the ocean and colored the sky with bright moving lights and screams that carried far through the salty air.

"Ah, there it is," I said, pointing to Steel Pier. The sign was still there, still three stories tall.

"I'd never have found it without you," he smiled. "Should we go see our friend?"

The pier had seen much better days but it still had some sparks of magic floating around in the air. You still only paid one price to get in and music echoed down the cavernous tunnels as we walked out to sea, near the end of the pier. Not much else was left, though. The pier had been battered over the years and the exhausted-looking paint, cracked and peeling, added to the notion that she was about done. The diving bell still clung to the side of the pier like a barnacle. Apparently, it still performed its job but even I didn't think I'd trust it at this point. Movies were still shown but they were barely even second run any more. A poster for *The Phantom of the Paradise* claimed there were three shows a day in the upstairs theater.

We missed the last water circus of the day, but I still wanted to see the diving horse one more time. I had a feeling that I might not get the chance again. I pulled Randall by the hand toward the end of the pier, giggling as he tried to balance his popcorn and failed miserably. We maneuvered through the audience and found two seats. The crowd hushed as a brown and white patchwork stallion climbed the ramp to the platform above the tank of water. The sound of the hooves hitting the wood echoed and the snorting breath of the animal was rhythmic. The horse climbed higher, its strong legs pumping it farther up until it reached the top. It stopped there, its tail swishing and its head pulling to the left and right on the reins. A woman wearing a ghostly white bathing suit and a bathing cap waved before climbing onto its back. The gulls called out to each other, flying over the black ocean and disappearing into the indigo sky to the east.

The rider coaxed the horse to the edge of the platform, to the point where it dropped off sharply, to the point of no return. A shiver ran under the animal's skin and the muscles reacted, flexing instinctively.

The woman leaned forward, her body becoming one with the horse, and she patted it gently on the neck. Her lips were moving and I wondered what was being said to the magnificent beast. Then, quickly, the horse took two steps forward onto the last platform and the forelegs began to slide. The woman tucked her head down close to the brown mane as its powerful back legs kicked off.

The two plummeted toward the water below. I closed my eyes and for a brief, wonderful second the rider and horse were lost in time and frozen in air; the mouth of the horse open and eyes staring, looking almost mad with anticipation with the woman tucked onto its back like a small package.

I must keep that picture, save it in my head where it can never fold, crease or yellow.

The water splashed high and wide and a cheer broke from the crowd, some immediately standing and sounding their approval. I jumped up, too, and brought my hands together hard. Randall joined, cheering and whistling loudly. Children were yelling and hopping up and down and soon everyone was on their feet. The horse reappeared and the woman raised her hand and waved to the crowd as they continued to cheer. They climbed out of the pool, which splashed up water over its sides, and the two of them trotted down the ramp and took their place in front of the audience. The girl dismounted and placed a kiss on the neck of the snorting and tramping horse.

The woman waved her hand to the glistening steed and it lowered its head in a half bow. She then offered one more bow and the crowd whistled and clapped. A small girl with blonde hair came out and presented them with a red rose and the woman looked up, smiling. She hugged the girl and took the flower, placing it in the drooping mane of the horse. She then stroked the neck of the creature and then gave it one more kiss. The woman wiped her eyes, grasped the reins and waved, turning away and leading the horse until they both disappeared into the gray shadows.

As we walked home along the boards, Randall draped his jacket over my shoulders and wondered aloud how long the rain would hold off.

"I wouldn't care if it poured right now," I answered, looking up. "It's been such a wonderful night."

"I thought you were going to run right up to that horse and give it a kiss."

"I would have if I could have gotten down fast enough. I would have given them both a big kiss." I smiled, "But I think that little girl did a fine job, don't you?"

Randall nodded and put his arm around me. A sound, very faint, was coming from somewhere up ahead as we approached the turn near at the Vermont Apartments. It was like a voice calling out low, summoning us. As we neared I realized it was an instrument.

A saxophone.

"Someone's got a decent radio station on." Randall said.

"That's not a station," I said and grinned.

Around the corner he came into view – short and hunched, wearing a small hat and blowing into the curved instrument. At his feet was a battered case of cracked brown leather, open like a crying mouth.

He was somewhere in his sixties, maybe seventies (it was hard to tell), with rich brown skin and swaying with a dulled gold bari-sax in his rough hands. I could see the man's soft lips were perfect for caressing the mouthpiece. He wore thick glasses that exaggerated his eyes, though they were closed now. He seemed as if he was floating away somewhere in his mind. His body moved gracefully from side to side, seeking and locating the rhythm buried deeply in the tune. He wore old green plastic flip flops, an oversize jacket with pants that draped off his small frame like loose skin and had a tangled beard of dark gray and white that looked like a storm brewing under his nose. When the man was finished Randall floated a couple dollar bills into the case and the man smiled, offering a small nod.

"Thank you," I said and stepped closer. I took his hand, feeling the scratched and hard skin in mine. "You play beautifully." My lips curled into a grin and I looked around. "I don't think you're alone. I think there are a few others playing with you right here. I can feel them," I said. "Can you?"

I thought of Alice and the Cadillac, another piece of history that was no longer here. Alice sold the place ten years ago and moved to Ft. Lauderdale to take care of her mother. We spoke over the phone a couple times each year, both of us always promising a visit but never making any real plans about it. It's like we are afraid to stop saying it because then that would mean that it really will never happen. It would be giving up. Who knows, maybe someday we will see each other again.

The man's cheeks pulled into a wide smile and revealed a missing front tooth. "Yes, ma'am, all the time," he said with a slight lisp, then turned my hand in his and offered a soft kiss. He then waved as we walked away.

He put the sax back to his lips, blowing out a long, dry note.

Seaside Avenue was empty, the windows just quiet amber squares. A pair of dogs barked nearby, maybe the next street over on New Hampshire. As we climbed the front steps Randall tugged gently on my hand and coaxed me back to the pavement with a playful look. I narrowed my eyes, not sure what to make of his expression, but slowly stepped down and let him lead me to the street. Halfway across, he turned and placed his hands on my hips.

"Mister Shepherd, what are you doing?"

"I'm not really sure yet." He pulled me close and I rested my arms around his tan neck. It was silly but wonderful to be in front of all the houses here like they were watching us. His body moved from side to side and I followed.

"Can you still hear it?" he asked.

In the stillness, somewhere underneath the hum of the city, I could make out the doleful notes of the man near the Vermont. "Yeah. Yeah, I can."

"Good." He slowly turned me in his hand and I instinctively slid up against him and took his other hand.

Randall dipped me and my hair dropped toward the street and I thought for a moment that the neighborhood didn't look quite so bad this way. Randall raised me and I stepped out away from him, holding him by the hand at the length of our arms. When I came back he wrapped his arm around my waist and we stood front to back, slowly moving from side to side. I turned in his hold and our hands traced softly down each other's arms until they met and clasped. We pulled closely to each other, noses almost touching and turned to let our cheeks brush together.

We spun lazily, holding each other and I saw the street once more, with families all around us out on porches, sipping drinks and enjoying the cool night. Shiny cars lined the street and young kids leaned against some of them as they watched and admired while up on the deck of our house was Max, propped against the newly-painted railing and smiling.

CHAPTER 15

Jamie

It was a gray, windy morning and I was wandering along the water when I heard Benita shouting my name. It rained the night before and the sand still had millions of tiny divots, making it look like the surface of the moon. She was waving to me from the boardwalk and my heart skipped until I saw that she wasn't alone. Debbie was posed next to her and, for some reason, she had her arms folded and was wearing a smug grin on her face.

"Jame," Benita said, and she sounded out of breath. "Deb heard something that someone told her…wait, is that right?" she asked and turned to Debbie, who nodded quickly. "Anyway, something about Nicky that she heard. Tell him."

Deb looked smartly over to Benita and then to me like she was being introduced on a talk show or something. "Yeah, word has it that they're all moving after this summer."

"What?"

"Sure," Debbie said, and placed her hands on her hips, the position that most girls took when they were telling you something you didn't already know. With the wind off the ocean blowing her hair across her face I couldn't see Benita's face too clearly, but I could tell just from her voice that she was upset.

Debbie popped her gum and continued, "I heard about it a few days ago from this kid who lives down my street. His brother works with Gary at the garage and he said that they're selling their house and leaving after this summer. It's already a done deal. I think he said they were moving to Virginia or something like that. How far away is that?"

All I could think about was the globe in my classroom back in Philly and how it squeaked whenever I spun it. Deb's words weren't making any sense but Nicky *did* have family in Virginia.

"You didn't hear?" She seemed genuinely pleased that she was able to be the one to break the story.

On a normal day Nicky would be hanging with me already but with only a couple weeks before school he was like a bear getting ready to hibernate and always slept in later. Benita joked that he must be practicing for always being late.

I wasn't listening to Deb anymore but looked at Benita. She had an expression I had never seen on her face before, like something had broken inside of her.

"He must've forgotten to tell me," I said numbly.

Deb said. "Yeah, people are always forgetting that they're moving, right?"

"Shut up, Deb," Benita snapped and then looked back at me. "Maybe it's not true, right?" she asked, sounding suddenly younger and smaller.

"Oh, it's true," Debbie said, looking at Benita and moving her head back and forth with each word. "Can't say I'll miss him, either."

My neck felt hot. Benita opened her mouth to say something and thought better of it. I stared at them for a few seconds and then climbed the sand-covered steps to the boardwalk and started down the ramp to Seaside.

Benita called, "Jame, let me know what you find out, okay?"

I didn't answer. I had no clear thought on what I would say or ask, but I'd be able to take one look into his eyes and see if it was true. That he had been lying to me this whole time. I pounded on Nicky's door and looked through the smudged glass. Gary soon appeared holding a bowl of cereal and opened the door. "Oh, hey, little man, it's you..."

I brushed past silently and headed for the stairs. Marching down the tight, dark hallway I pushed open Nicky's door and found him in his underwear, putting on his favorite t-shirt, the one with Farrah Fawcett in the red bathing suit.

"Hey," he said with a quick smile, "I was just about to head over-"

"When were you going to say something to me?" I shouted. My voice cracked and my hands kept balling themselves into fists. "Huh?"

"What the hell are you talking about?" Nicky asked and finished pulling his shirt over his head.

"You know what I'm talking about! Selling the house! Moving? When were you going to tell me?"

Nicky looked down at the floor and then closed his eyes. He put his hands up. "Ok, look, I swear I was going to tell you, I really was, but I never got the chance." He casually scooped up a pair of shorts off the floor and put them on.

My mouth dropped open. "What do you mean you never had the chance? You had all *summer* to tell me! You had plenty of chances! I even asked you!"

"Hey man, we weren't even sure about it until a few weeks ago, okay?" he answered and his eyes darted to my hands and then back. "And what if I *did* tell you about it, then what? You woulda been moping around for the whole summer!" He headed for the door. "I did you a favor."

"I had to hear about it from Debbie!" I moved to get in front of him. "What, were you going to take the easy way out? Let me go back home and next summer then you'd just be gone?"

"No. No way! I was going to tell you!" Nicky clenched his teeth and let out a hissing sound. "Why did she have to open her fat mouth about this anyway?"

I took a step towards him. "Don't blame her. She thought Benita and I already knew! When Benita found out she made her tell me."

Nicky took a step back. "Oh, so *that's* it then, huh? Your new girlfriend had to come tell you? Tell that bitch to mind her own business."

I froze and then blinked. "Take that back."

Nicky stared at me. "Are you joking? No way, man."

"Take it back," I said slowly. "Now."

Nicky's face screwed up. "Forget it, man. What, now that you finally got a chance of getting into Spot's pants I'm supposed to do what you say? I'm not gonna let that bitch –"

I charged, but he was quick enough to hook his hands under my arms and get me off balance. I grabbed his shoulders and we stumbled back and crashed into the wall behind him. Nicky's breath shot out and he got a hold of my wrist and tried to twist my hand behind my back, but I slipped away and spun, spinning around his waist, pulling sideways and throwing us both towards the corner.

We landed on the small wooden table, breaking it and falling to the floor. I flipped on top of him and grabbed him by the hair. He was slapping up at my face, not using fists. "Get the hell off me!"

He grunted and rolled to the left and I tumbled off.

He managed to get a knee on the floor and I rolled back and grabbed the back of his shirt, ripping the collar.

"Let go!" Nicky screamed and turned around, pushing into my chest and knocking me onto my butt by the foot of the bed.

He checked the collar and gritted his teeth, "Aw, shit, man, why'd you have to-"

I shuffled over and laced both arms around his shins and Nicky pinwheeled his arms to catch himself. He thudded to the floor and I pounced on his back, wrenching his arm behind him until he stopped struggling. All I could hear for a moment was our breathing.

Nicky laid his head on the floor. "Jesus Christ, man, you know I was just out of the hospital, right? What are you a psycho?"

"Take it back," I said and swallowed. *Please take it back.*

"No way!" he shouted. I pulled up toward his shoulder blade and he let out a yelp.

"Say it, Goddamit!" I ordered but Nicky was silent except for his breathing. I pulled the arm again.

"Ow, shit man!" Nicky turned his face to the side and winced.

"I mean it!" *Please say it.*

Nicky breathed slowly. "Look, man, she's not my –"

I pulled his wrist up to his shoulder again. "Ow, ow, ow oka-ok-okay! Jesus!" Nicky's face was set, his jaw clenching and unclenching and then he said, clearly, "I take it back, I take it back."

I waited a moment before letting go. I'm not sure why. Maybe to catch my breath. I let go and fell back on the floor, pulling air into my chest as best I could while Nicky rolled onto his back and winced, resting his arm on his belly.

I took in the room quietly; the small square of a window and the gray of the sky, the wallpaper that peeled from the corners of every wall and the light in the ceiling that never seemed to work. The closet door was closed, but I knew it was a jumbled mess in there, filled with old games and toys that neither of us played with anymore and probably never would. I turned my head and looked under his bed: there was a beat-up electric guitar with no strings that Nicky had gotten two years ago by trading his old bike. He swore he was going to learn how to play someday. Someday.

Still catching my breath, I looked up at the ceiling. "You know… your room…is really…goddamn dirty, man."

Nicky snorted and then grinned. "Why do you think we're moving?"

We both erupted into laughter and it felt amazing. It was the kind of laughter that you know won't fade away quickly but grow and spread. Each wave was stronger and it kept me from even speaking for a while, though I tried. I looked at Nicky and motioned with my hands, pointing and spinning my arms and then falling back and laughing some more. He nodded and he coughed out laughter and winced.

Just when I thought I'd stop I would start again, thinking about the whole thing: his expression as I barreled into him and all the thumping that we must have made. The fact that no one in the house said anything made me laughed again, so hard it hurt my stomach. Did he hit me there? I pictured the two of us spinning across the room and then crashing onto his crappy little table and breaking it.

Nicky had his hand over his eyes, laughing like I had never seen before. He even laughed harder when I checked the stretched and torn collar of his shirt, stuttering out that I would buy him a new one because I was rich. He nodded and my eyes were feeling warm and wet but we were still laughing.

"Doesn't anyone in this house give a shit if someone is killing you?" I asked and another howl of laughter came out. Nicky was holding his stomach and shaking his head, tears racing down his temple to the floor.

"What," he managed, still chuckling, "what were you trying to do, put me back in the hospital, man?"

"Yep! I was gonna sit on you like Fat Ass Chuck!"

"No!" Nicky yelled and we both burst again.

Tears were running along my cheeks and I watched Nicky roll from side to side, his knees pulled up to his chest and his hands on his stomach.

We were both still giggling when I rolled on my side, finally feeling like I could catch my breath. "So, you really *are* leaving?"

Nicky's stopped laughing and wiped his eyes. He turned, but said nothing for awhile, just looked at me. "I'm sorry I didn't tell you. I didn't want to even think about it...ya know?"

"Yeah."

"I'm sorry I said that about Benita. I guess I'm kinda glad that she was the one who finally told you." He smiled weakly, "How is it with you guys?"

The words sounded strange, like in the movies when two old men ask about each other's families. "Good, I guess." I shook my head. "Hell, I can't figure her out."

"Of course you can't, man," Nicky said. "But do you love her?"

"I think so," I said and then let out a tired laugh. "I don't know."

Nicky nodded and said, "I think that's good enough."

I piled the luggage into the back of the Pinto and went into the house. The windows were closed and I roamed, opening each door one last time and inspecting each room. I know I was just putting off the inevitable.

I walked out to the deck and leaned over to the railing, looking down Seaside toward the ocean. It was still pretty early and the sky was bright in that direction so I peered with one eye closed. I could hear the gulls arguing over their meals on the beach but the boardwalk was empty. A few people were already moving about on Seaside; a small black boy tagging after his older brother. Two old men talked on the front porch of the first house on the corner of the next block. A dog was sniffing its way down the street. It had no collar so it was likely a neighborhood stray, but I didn't recognize it. Almost all of the summer people had already left for home.

Nothing looked that much different than it did three months ago. You could look out on the view and say, though it may be a bit depressing to see such a mess of a neighborhood, it looked like a hundred others across the country. Being within sight of the ocean might convince a stranger that this must be a decent place to be. To them it might look almost normal, like nothing was out of place but there was.

Nicky was gone.

The Martres packed up and left like so many other families. I was still angry at Nicky for a while but, seeing as there was only about a week between that day and when he was leaving it didn't make sense to keep that anger. I knew that my situation was different than his (or many others who lived in the Inlet) and my family could afford to try and hang on a little longer. Maybe things would change and we could stay. Maybe we wouldn't have to sell the house but even if we did we would have a home, a whole other life, waiting for us back in Philadelphia. Nicky was moving his whole life away.

Our last days together were already beginning to fade. It was just a jumble of emotions and everything was all mixed together: anger and sadness, joy and fear, bitterness and love.

Except for the day when Nicky climbed into his car the last time.

That day sucked.

Gary was at the wheel with Ms. Martre in the seat next to him and they rolled away down the street. Debbie had been right after all, they were going to Virginia.

"What the hell's in Virginia anyway?" I asked a little more sharply than I meant to.

"I don't know. My Aunt Talia lives there. Family, I guess," Nicky said and flicked a shell out over the water. "That's something right?" Yeah, family was something, but I even resented *that* comment because it pointed out that I *wasn't* family even though I felt like it.

We went crabbing one morning near Starn's and we actually caught a few that were worth keeping. Nicky's mom cooked them with some pasta and we all had dinner at our house; mom, dad, Gary, Benita, her mom. Even the Liz...I mean, Liz. I heard her tell mom that she wants to go by Beth from now, in honor of the Kiss song. Not sure I'll get used to that.

Even though Benita was on my mind as much as ever - I thought about her all the time - I wanted to spend these last days with Nicky. The two of us spent every night on the deck, seeing who could find the most shooting stars and floating the names of beautiful women to each other until we fell asleep. I even snuck Benita's name in there once and Nicky just chuckled and patted my shoulder as he nodded off. We tried not to think about the end of this summer.

Benita had been hanging around more lately and, though she would never admit it, I could tell it was because Nicky was leaving soon. She even joined us for a last swim in the ocean together and the three of us held hands. Nicky complained that he had just managed to get himself a rep and we looked at each other and tried not to laugh.

"What? You two think I ain't got a rep?" he said as a wave splashed around us.

"Oh, you got a rep alright," Benita said and giggled. "And here you are, holding hands with us and playing in the water."

"Yeah, but this isn't playing. This is serious stuff, right?" he said and smiled.

Benita and I agreed. Serious stuff.

The three of us held hands one last time and the biggest wave of that day, a monster that fell and crashed only a few feet in front of us, roaring. I took a last look at my best friends and wondered if I had the same look on my face, a sort of wondrous, child-like expression. The water exploded and hit me and I heard their excited screams once more. Nicky's hand ripped away, leaving my palm feeling cold and empty. I couldn't stay on my feet and was tumbling backwards and my hand twisted out of Benita's. I scraped along the bottom as the wave rolled over our heads and I reached out for either of them. I wanted to stay under until I found them again and maybe forget that summer was ending. If I could find their hands then maybe Nicky would stay and Benita would fall in love with me. Maybe the three of us could stay here forever.

I came back up, sputtering, and saw that Benita had been pushed into the shallows and Nicky was completely turned around off to my left. We laughed and Nicky loudly claimed that nobody would have been able to beat that wave. I looked into their eyes and the three of us still broke into a cheer.

The next day Nicky left. The smile he had kept placed under his nose for the past week was gone and he kept wiping at his eyes with the back of his hand. Benita just cried (I had a feeling she would) and hugged him. Nicky started mumbling something about feeling bad about the whole 'spot' thing, but she stopped him, choking out, "We still had some real fun times, didn't we?"

Our families stood in the middle of Seaside Avenue and said our goodbyes with hugs, tears and a few laughs. Mom was pretty much a mess; red-faced and sniffling constantly. I thought she'd never let go of Nicky, hugging him and telling him to take care over and over. He nodded and looked over at Liz, who looked like she couldn't be bothered, but she managed a smile and a polite goodbye. Benita's mom hugged Nicky's mom tightly and told her to hang on. Gary hopped in the driver's seat and his mom slowly followed.

Nicky came over and held me tightly. "Virginia isn't that far away, right Jackson?"

I shook my head. What to say? I was afraid of letting any words come out because they might not stop. I was aching inside and wiped at my eyes. "We'll call each other, okay?"

Would we?

He nodded and put his hand on my shoulder. "No place will ever be like this, Jackson. Ever."

"I can't watch you leave," I blurted and took a deep breath. Nicky looked at me and slowly nodded.

After another hug he silently climbed into the Lincoln and closed the door. I stood in the middle of the street and closed my eyes. Voices were saying goodbye, but all I could think about was the first time Nicky and I went fishing together and he helped me tie the hook on the end because he was always better with stuff like that.

The car starts.

I remembered the time we were flying those wooden gliders from the deck of my house and Nicky's landed in the street and a car ran over it and how mad he got.

The car pulls away.

We took turns with my glider until it ended up broken as well. Those cheap gliders never lasted long but that's what best friends do. So many trips down the boards. It would be impossible to count how many times we went to the beach together.

The sound fades.

How many rides? How many shooting stars? How many beautiful women we fell asleep dreaming about?

I couldn't hear the car anymore and opened my eyes.

The street was empty and Benita was sitting on the sidewalk with her arms folded and her head down. I walked over to my mom, my sneakers making scuffing sounds on the street, and put my arms around her and cried.

Down in the street I watched Dad bring another suitcase out and lift it into the back of the car. In an hour we would be going back to the real world. Kinda overrated in my opinion.

Liz was, as usual, a bit slower than everyone else with her packing. I walked past her room, glancing in the open door and watched her fill her suitcase with the last of her clothes. She looked up at me and blinked before giving me a small, smiling nod and turning away. It was the most pleasant she'd been all summer.

Mom was downstairs on the porch. She was holding a large white clam shell in her hand and gazing out the window.

"Um, I'm going down to the beach one last time before we go," I said. I felt awkward, pulling her away from the window like I was breaking a spell.

"I know," she said. "Going to say your goodbyes?" She looked different somehow, peaceful maybe.

"Do you wanna come?" I asked after a moment and wasn't sure why. I never had before. My end of summer ritual was always a solo trip (I never even invited Nicky when he was still here) but this had been a very different kind of summer. Different for all of us. I looked at her and something said ask her.

I saw what she must have looked like when she was a small girl living here all those years ago, with her blue eyes as deep as the sea and the whites of them the foam. A curious and wide smile spread across her face. "You don't mind?"

"No, it's okay," I said. "We can say goodbye together."

She folded her arms like she didn't know what to do with them until her eyes suddenly brightened. "Hey, I have an idea," she said and got up quickly, "a wonderful idea." She disappeared into the house and came out with a black marker in her hand. She picked up the clamshell and began writing. I leaned closer.

"What are you writing?"

"Show you later," she said playfully, blocking my view. When she was done she tucked the shell into her pocket and opened the front door. "Come on."

We both kicked off our shoes and walked down the front steps. Dad looked at us curiously as we passed him. "Hey, guys, we're not done quite yet."

"I'll be back soon," mom answered. "Carry on, MacDuff."

Randall put down his bag, "But we still have to..."

She spoke without turning around. "Promise I'll help you when I get back, okay?" I turned to dad and smiled, shrugging helplessly.

"Where are you going?" he called after us.

"To say goodbye!" she shouted and trotted along the sidewalk. I stayed by her side, watching a wide smile grow on her lips. She quickened her steps and I was matching her stride for stride as we moved faster down to the street.

Our shadows raced along with us and I was impressed with how fast mom was. The sun threw our forms across the street and now they were dancing next to us, looking long and thin. I looked taller and mom's hair was longer (was it?), like before she got it cut and it was trailing behind her and floating in the air. I laughed and ran faster, trying to get ahead.

Hope

Jamie laughed and turned to me and I saw his beautiful, toothy grin. He was pulling away from me, moving faster but that felt okay. These things happen. I laughed too and it made a sound that was both ancient and childlike.

"C'mon," I said to myself and moved to a sprint, pumping my arms like I could grab the air and pull it behind me. The salty wind whistled in my ears and I remembered Max and I handing a conch back and forth to each other and putting it up to our ears. "That's the ocean," Max said and smiled. His blonde hair was blowing in the wind and he brushed it aside with one hand. I listened to the whole world from the porch of our house and giggled.

Of course he was right.

Jamie and I neared the ramp and I charged ahead, delighting in the surprise that Jamie showed when I did. He still managed to keep ahead, but I put my arms out like wings and felt the air curl around me. He laughed and joined and we were both gulls soaring over the street. We made the small leap from the cracked, sun-bleached sidewalk to the asphalt and I heard more laughter. Waves falling onto the ocean, onto the sand. It was Max, laughing like he always did when we were together. He was next to me, running as a shadow, flying like a gull and showing me how I could hear the ocean whenever I wanted.

We raced to the top of the ramp and I saw the ocean and it was still there. No one was asleep at the switch. It was the same blue when Max and I first saw it so long ago. It would never change.

I had one last surge in me and I aimed for the break in the railing and the top of the steps. We raced across the old wood and leaped off, both of us shouting joyously. I pedaled my legs and for a second I was nothing, I was air, floating straight to the ocean. I was coming down to earth like the Great Diving Horse.

I heard Jamie crying triumphantly next to me. He sounded so like me, shouting out all the joy, fear and anger that made this place.

We both landed and I collapsed to my knees. I kept my head down, still heard the laughter rolling around and mixing with the thunder of the waves and the calling of the gulls. Max was here and any second he would spot the ice cream man and the two of us would race each other to see who got there first. We would spend the day in the water and mom and dad would call us in to go home…

I blew out a breath and tiny grains of sand flew up and tickled my nose.

Please don't go away again, Max. I don't think I could take it. Stay here with me and run along the boards and let's collect shells every morning and show dad. Let him pull that big old book from the shelf and sit me on his knee. Let's both jump off the steps together from now on, okay?

I did it. Drip did it.

The ocean faded and the birds quieted and I heard chuckling. It was only Jamie's wonderful laughter now. I slowly raised my head.

His handsome face looked at me like I was a little crazy, but then he smiled crookedly and I recognized the tilt of the lips from a beautiful face long ago. "You okay, mom?"

I nodded and smiled, blinking. "Yeah, I think I am."

"I never knew you were that fast."

"Me either." I looked back at the steps. We sat on our knees for a minute and then I followed him to the water's edge. This was Jamie's tradition and I felt honored to be invited. Still breathing hard, I put my hands on my hips and watched rolling whitecaps far off and the rich, inviting blue. The sun came from behind finger-like clouds and shot diamonds across the surface for a moment before hiding again. He asked me about the shell and I dug into my pocket and pulled it out. I handed it to him.

211 Seaside Avenue
The Shepherds
Thank you

He looked at it, then nodded and grinned.

"Anything you'd like to add?" I asked and offered him the marker.

He thought for a moment, looking out over the water and then back to our house. "No, I think that pretty much says it all."

I took a few steps into the water and watched the waves play against my ankles. Max would leap up and down in water up to his belly, and I remembering how he seemed so brave while I watched him from the safety of the sand.

The ocean seemed so endless then. Thank God it still does. I leaned back and whipped the shell sidearm. It caught a breeze and rose higher and angled to the left. It paused for a second, still spinning tightly before it fell to the water with a tiny splash.

Jamie was staring at me.

"What, you think you're the only one who ever learned how to pitch shells?" I asked, cocking my head to the side and smiling. "Of course, it's been a while."

"Coulda fooled me," he said. "Nicky would have been proud. Nice throw."

"Thanks."

Jamie looked lost for a moment in the smaller waves as he watched them slap down on the sand.

"Do you think it will ever come back again?"

"The shell?" I shrugged and moved closer to him, "Eventually. Maybe some lucky little kid will find it and take it home."

"No," Jamie said quickly, "I mean the city. Do you think it will ever come back?"

I looked at him and rested my hand on his shoulder. He was taller, stronger, a young man in his eyes. "No, not really," I said finally, "At least not the way we know it now."

"Are we selling the house?"

Jamie

Mom's expression changed, became a bit gray and she looked back toward Seaside. The buildings behind us, the Vermont, the Nevada stood looking out over the ocean but they seemed tired right now. Past that, the gold dome at the end of Steel Pier was visible through the haze but it looked like a ghost in a long-abandoned house.

"You deserve an honest answer," she said and turned to me. "It's probably only a matter of time until we sell - not *want* to sell, but have to. You're too old now to hear me say everything will be fine and rosy - besides, you're too smart to believe it anymore, anyway."

"Yep," I agreed, "especially after this summer."

"We've had some offers – not many - and nothing that even remotely interests us but it's only the beginning, you know."

"Yeah, I know." I started walking along the water and mom followed.

"The city is changing-"

"Benita's mom said it's dying."

Mom nodded. "Well, I prefer to think of it as changing, just like it always has, ever since I was a kid. When I was younger everyone told me about how great the boardwalk was way back when, before I was even a thought in my parents' heads. They said that it had changed and that it would never be the same and that I never got to see the *real* Atlantic City. They always looked on me with a sort of pity, but they never understood that they were only talking about *their* Atlantic City, not mine. This place means something different to everybody. Sure the boardwalk was great before I was born but you know what? It was great when I was a kid, too. I'm sure you think it's been great all these years, right?"

"Sure, the best."

"Well, see? Just because you didn't live here when it was supposed to be in its heyday doesn't mean that it's not important to you. Everybody always thinks that *their* Atlantic City was the best, you know? They still do that… 'When I was young' and 'You should have seen it back then' and all that other stuff. I hate that. I'm just happy to have had it at all."

She gently put her hand on the back of my neck. "But you never quite get the sand out of your shoes, do you?"

"No, you never do."

"Somehow I seem to get more strength when I'm near the ocean, you know?"

I did.

"You're like me. We're what my dad used to call 'water people.'"

"Is that like being a Pisces or something?"

"No, more like just someone who's drawn to the ocean. We would take you to the beach as a baby and you'd crawl right to the water every time. Your dad or I would pick you up and carry you back and then as soon as you hit the sand you'd be crawling back again. No matter how many times I tried to stop you, you would crawl around me and go right in. We always had to keep an extra eye on you." She folded her arms. "My dad said I was the same way."

I saw the gulls hovering over the long jetty, just above the fisherman's heads. "I'm really going to miss Nicky. It's not going to be the same around here without him." I wanted mom to say something, anything but she kept quiet. "He taught me how to pitch shells."

"My brother taught me."

"Uncle Max?"

She nodded. "I guess we've never told you much about him, huh?"

"Not really. I mean I've seen pictures of him and he looks like he was a nice guy."

"He was," she said. "He was my best friend."

I've seen mom cry plenty of times and could tell that she was holding it in. Her lip trembled and her voice caught a bit. I put my hand in hers. "Nicky was mine."

"I guess we have more in common than just being water people, huh?"

"Guess so."

"I'm sorry I never talked much about him."

"So, what was he like?" I asked and we both walked along the foamy, shallow waves.

Mom reached down and held up a shell that was tucked neatly between her thumb and first finger. "Well, he always said that the best way to spin a shell was to hold it like this," she said and slung her arm over my shoulder.

Mom went back to the house. She waved from the boardwalk before she vanished. We had walked between the jetties three or four times and talked while we threw shells. We talked about Nicky and Uncle Max, about collecting shells and piers, and unfortunately, the coming school year. Still, it was nice to just talk. Uncle Max sounded pretty cool. I can see why he was her best friend.

I faced the ocean, closed my eyes and listened...the gulls were singing just like mom used to tell me when I was a little kid. I could almost feel them dipping and swooping beyond the waves. A crisp breeze wound around my legs and into my shirt, searching like fingers. My feet had sunk into the wet sand.

The sun looked like an old bruise behind the thumbprint clouds that marched over the water. Nicky was some place where I couldn't reach him anymore. No one would answer the door at the end of the block if I knocked and we would never run the beach, the boards or the jetty anymore. I knew that and it hurt like hell.

I placed my fingers into the shallow water of the incoming tide and put it to my mouth. Salt on my lips. It was time to go. I turned and headed to the boardwalk.

We finished loading up the rest of the luggage and piled it into both cars. Mom was in the Pinto with grandma next to her and the rear filled with bags. Dad would drive the Buick with Liz next to him and me in the back. 211 Seaside was secure, the storm windows in place and the doors locked.

The car rolled and the tires crunched their way down seaside.

I looked out the rear window and caught Benita leaning out of her window.

"Dad, wait!"

Liz slid forward and had to put her hands out to stop from bumping into the dashboard. "Jesus!"

I quickly pushed opened the door and ran down the sidewalk, stopping under her window. I had to cup one hand over my eyes to see her clearly: her hair was loose and she hooked a lock with a finger and tucked it behind her ear. It might have been the most beautiful thing I had ever seen. I didn't know what to say and stood helpless below her.

"See you next year?" she asked, her lips curled into smile.

I wanted to race up and kiss her, hold her until next summer and make sure that she would never leave no matter what. I could only smile back. "Yeah, you bet. Will you be here?"

"I guess. I hope so."

I remembered her breathing in my ear, soft. I don't ever want to forget that sound.

"Good luck in school." She leaned on both elbows, her brown arms folded across her chest.

"You too."

"Ready for high school?"

"Hell, no," I said and laughed. "You?"

She shrugged effortlessly, magically. It was only a little move, a slight motion of her head and shoulders but I caught it. Her hair came alive with the breeze and it blew across her face and eyes. I remembered how she felt in my hands, her skin imprinted on my palms and the smell of her hair everywhere.

"Well, I gotta go," I said. "See ya."

"So long, Jame."

I ran back to the car. The weeds and cracks flashed past, blurry. I saw Nicky again, his tan face smiling and laughing, asking me to hang out, drop cages for crabs, run the boards, walk the railings and talk about girls. I wanted to capture it, freeze his face like a photo and keep it forever smiling and joking but his brown eyes were looking beyond me, asking a million unanswered questions while his lips were still twisted into a wry grin.

What do you want to do tomorrow, Jackson?

Isn't this the best place in the world?

No place will be like this, ever.

So long, Jame.

I slowed to a stop and turned to Benita's apartment. She was gone from the window. A blue curtain fluttered in the window of her room.

"I love you!" I shouted as loud as I could.

Her hand pushed aside the curtain and I saw her once more. I waved both arms in the air and she waved back, laughing and putting her hand over her beautiful mouth and blowing me a kiss. I took a few steps backward, nearly stumbling over a gap in the cement and then turned and jumped in the car.

Liz threw her arm over the seat to stare at me. She rolled her eyes and shook her head but the corners of her mouth pulled into a small, stubborn grin. Through the back window I could see Benita still waving from her apartment window, but now, with the gold cast of the sun behind her she was just a silhouette. I knew she was smiling though, and maybe wishing, like I was, that summers never had to end; it seemed cruel to start something so good knowing that it could never, ever be finished properly.

The car pulled away and I waved back, hoping that she could see me. We turned off Seaside and I craned my neck to keep her in view until she was gone.

Liz put on the radio. She fiddled with the dial until K.C. and the Sunshine Band began singing. She loved them and joined in, moving her body from side to side. I could only grin and laugh until she finally looked back at me with a curious look in her brown eyes. Eyes that I never noticed before were almost the same color as Nicky's.

"What's so funny?"

I shrugged, smiled to myself and laughed some more.

Man, Nicky really hated these guys.

The End